BABY-SITTERS LITTLE SISTER®

KAREN'S KITTYCAT CLUB

**DON'T MISS THE OTHER BABY-SITTERS
LITTLE SISTER GRAPHIC NOVELS!**

KAREN'S WITCH

KAREN'S ROLLER SKATES

KAREN'S WORST DAY

ANN M. MARTIN
BABY-SITTERS LITTLE SISTER®

KAREN'S KITTYCAT CLUB

A GRAPHIC NOVEL BY
KATY FARINA
WITH COLOR BY BRADEN LAMB

graphix

An Imprint of
SCHOLASTIC

Text copyright © 2021 by Ann M. Martin
Art copyright © 2021 by Katy Farina

All rights reserved. Published by Graphix, an imprint of
Scholastic Inc., *Publishers since 1920.* SCHOLASTIC, GRAPHIX,
BABY-SITTERS LITTLE SISTER, and associated logos are trademarks
and/or registered trademarks of Scholastic Inc.

The publisher does not have any control over and does not assume any
responsibility for author or third-party websites or their content.

Library of Congress Control Number: 2020943059

ISBN 978-1-338-35622-9 (hardcover)
ISBN 978-1-338-35621-2 (paperback)

10 9 8 7 6 5 4 3 2 1   21 22 23 24 25

Printed in China   62
First edition, July 2021

Edited by Cassandra Pelham Fulton and David Levithan
Book design by Shivana Sookdeo
Creative Director: Phil Falco
Publisher: David Saylor

For Jennifer Esty, a big sister
A. M. M.

For my cats, Poe and Guinness, and to
every animal that warms our hearts
K. F.

CHAPTER 1

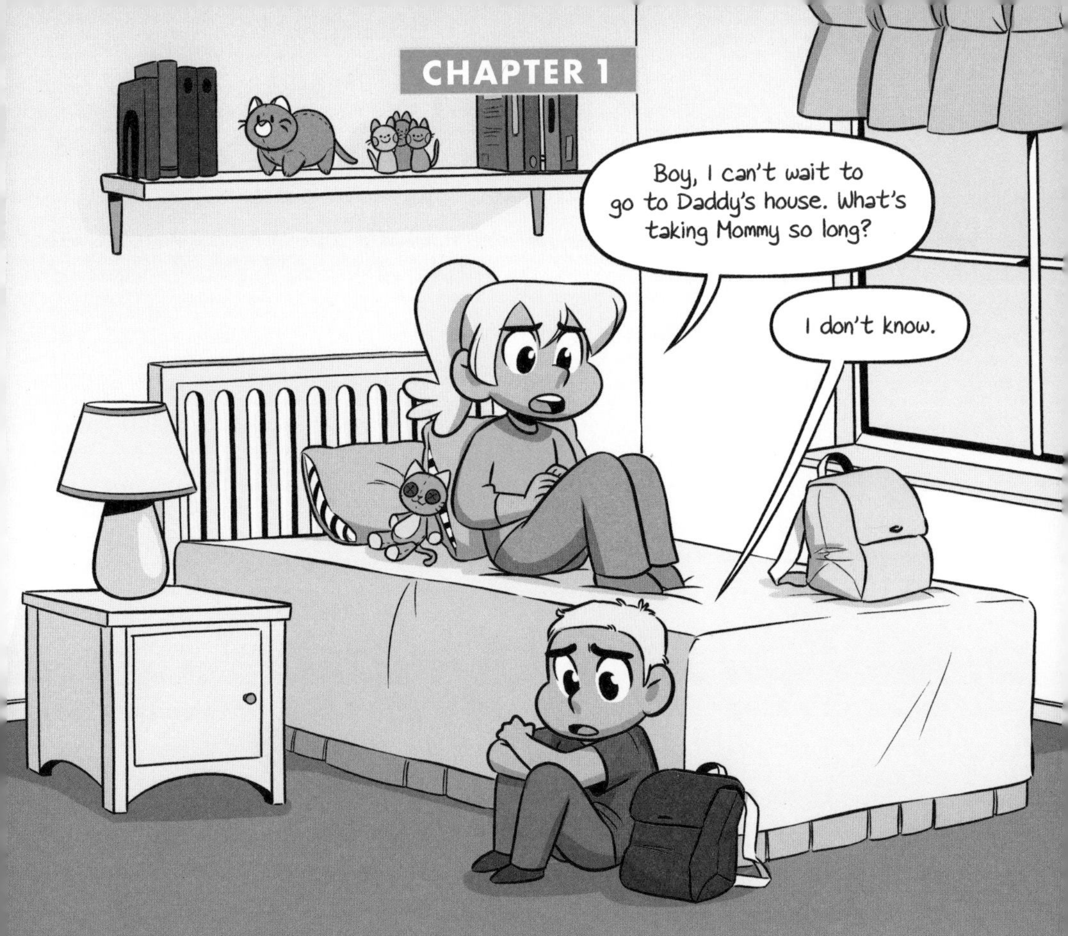
Boy, I can't wait to go to Daddy's house. What's taking Mommy so long?
I don't know.

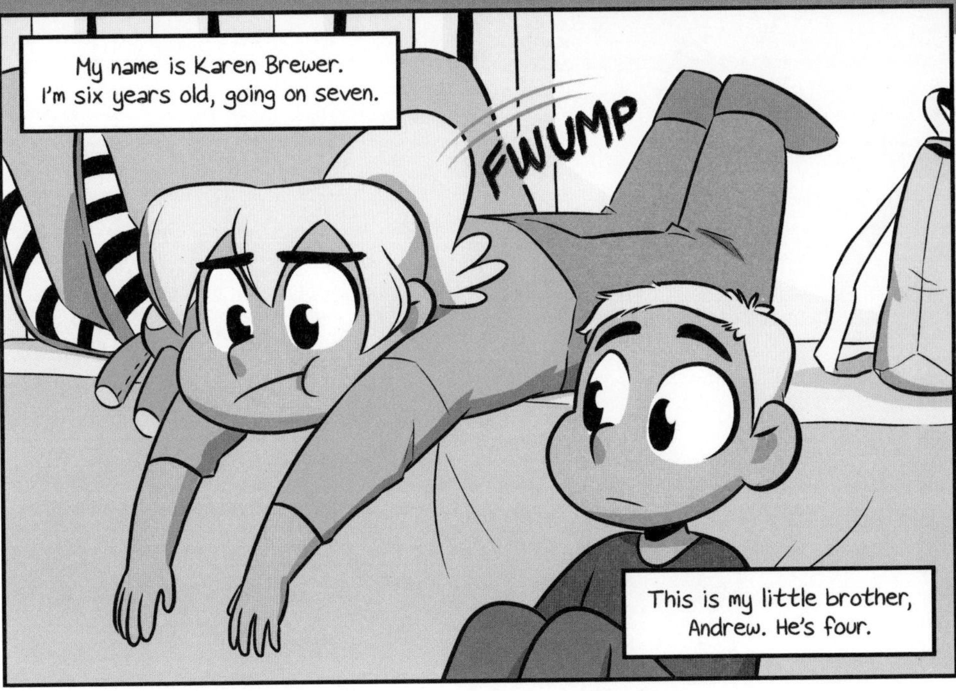
My name is Karen Brewer. I'm six years old, going on seven.
FWUMP
This is my little brother, Andrew. He's four.

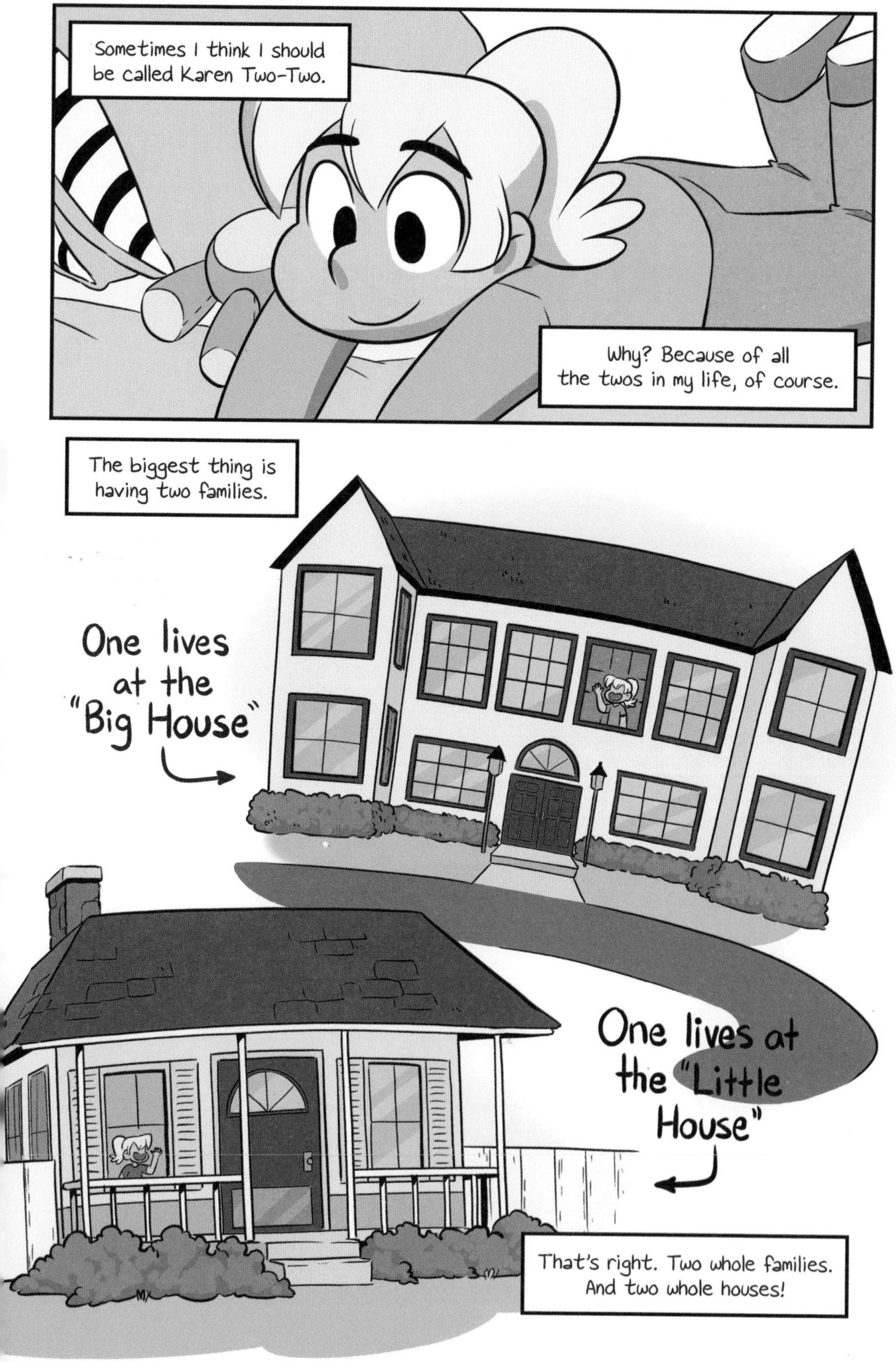
Sometimes I think I should be called Karen Two-Two.
Why? Because of all the twos in my life, of course.
The biggest thing is having two families.
One lives at the "Big House"
One lives at the "Little House"
That's right. Two whole families. And two whole houses!

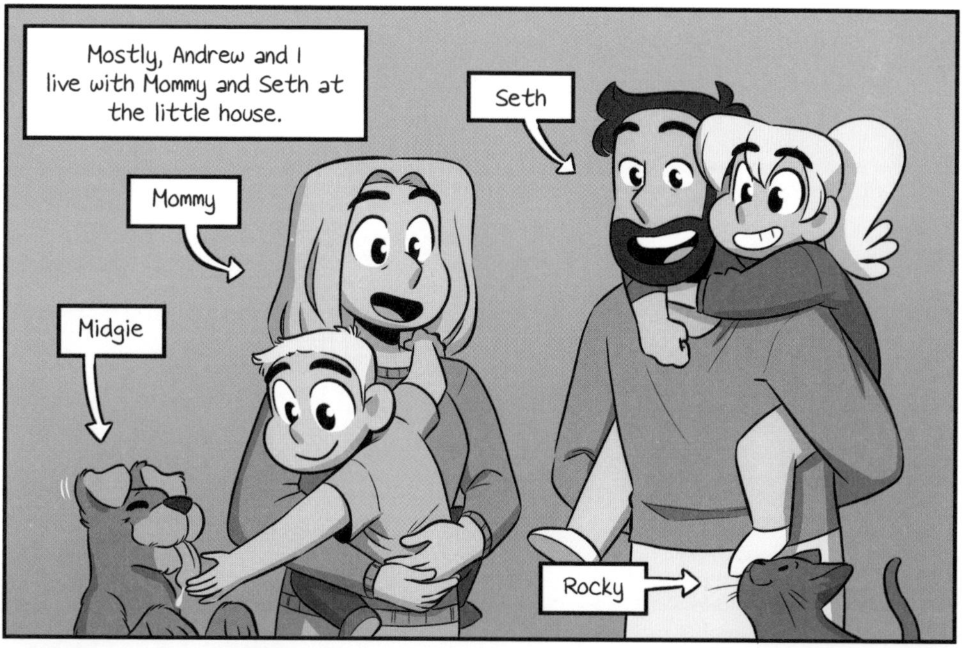
Mostly, Andrew and I live with Mommy and Seth at the little house.
Seth
Mommy
Midgie
Rocky

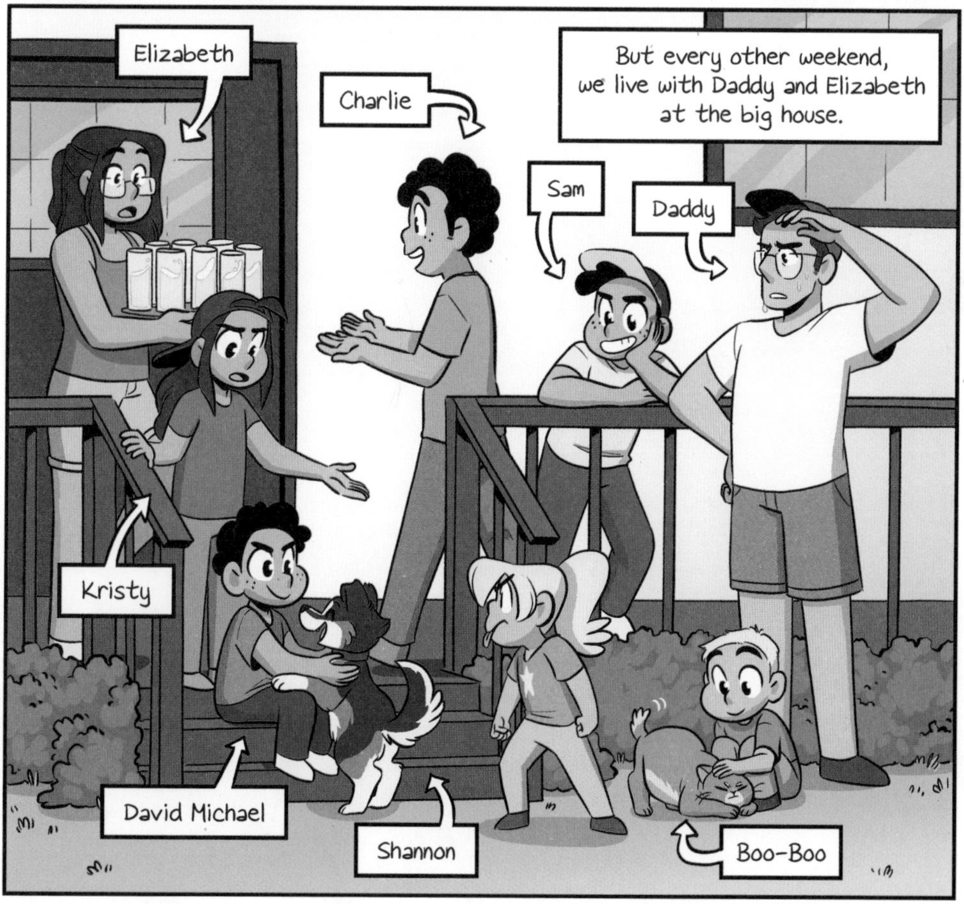
Elizabeth
Charlie
But every other weekend, we live with Daddy and Elizabeth at the big house.
Sam
Daddy
Kristy
David Michael
Shannon
Boo-Boo

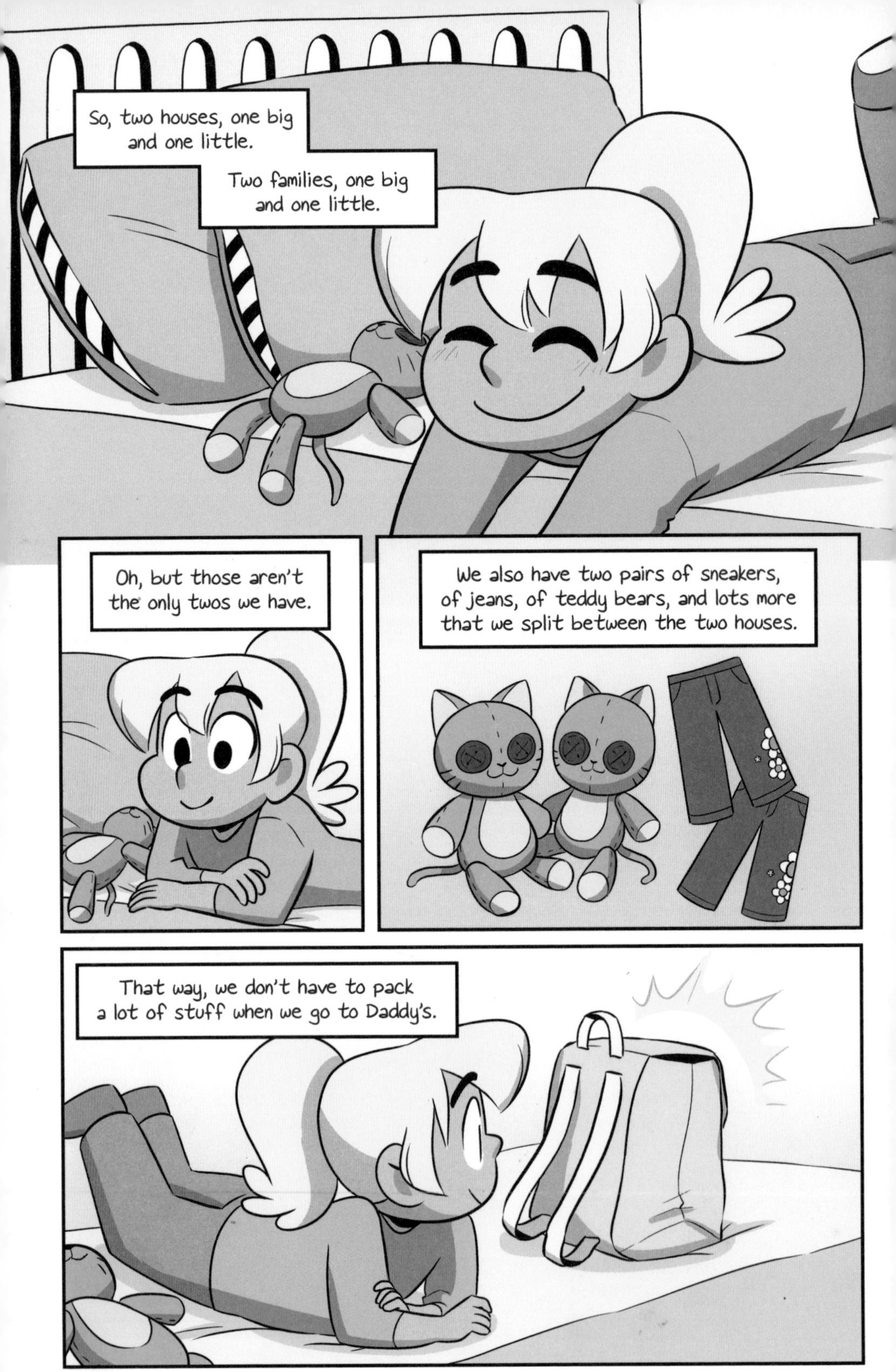
So, two houses, one big and one little.
Two families, one big and one little.
Oh, but those aren't the only twos we have.
We also have two pairs of sneakers, of jeans, of teddy bears, and lots more that we split between the two houses.
That way, we don't have to pack a lot of stuff when we go to Daddy's.

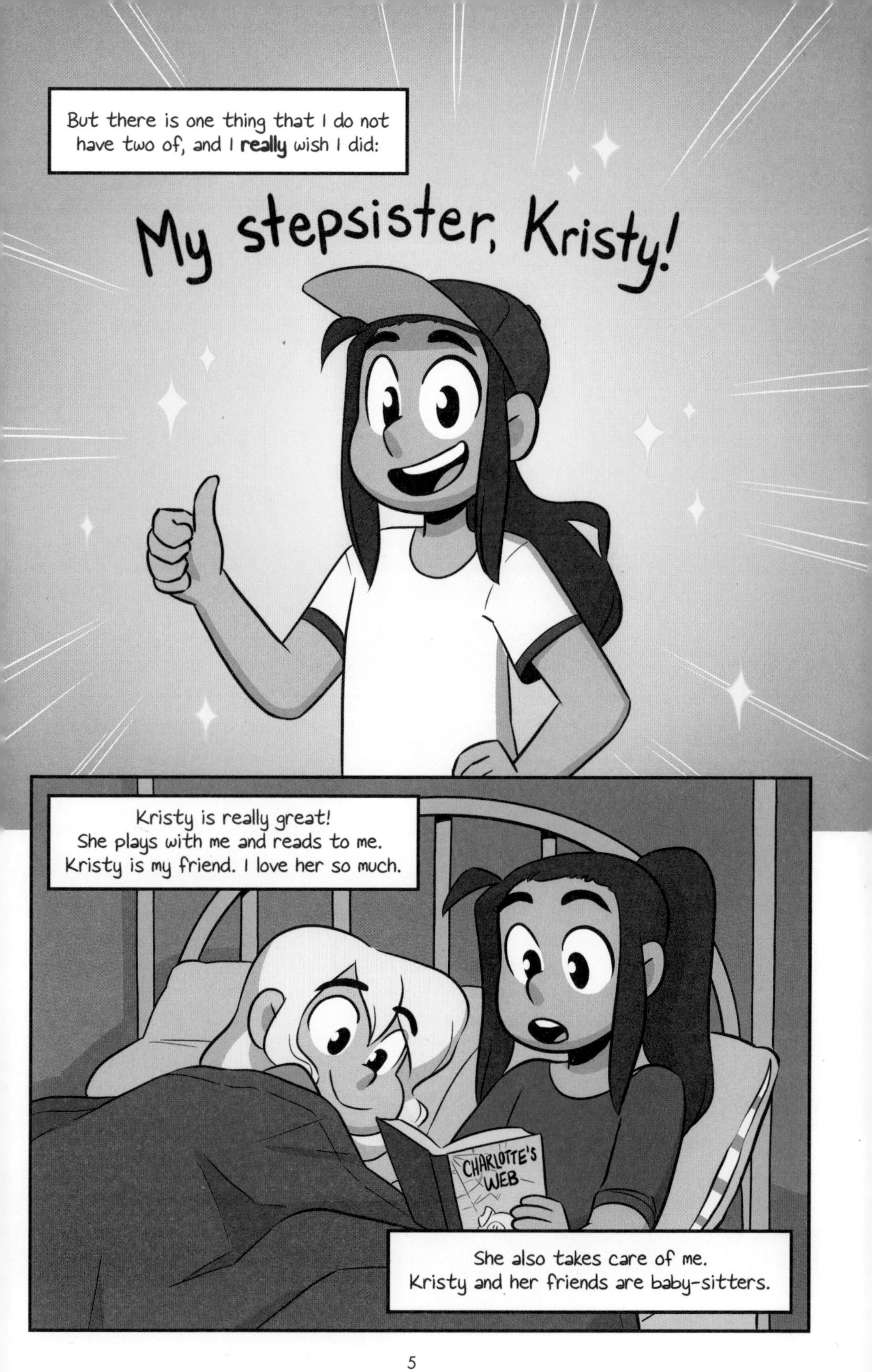
But there is one thing that I do not have two of, and I **really** wish I did:
My stepsister, Kristy!
Kristy is really great! She plays with me and reads to me. Kristy is my friend. I love her so much.
CHARLOTTE'S WEB
She also takes care of me. Kristy and her friends are baby-sitters.

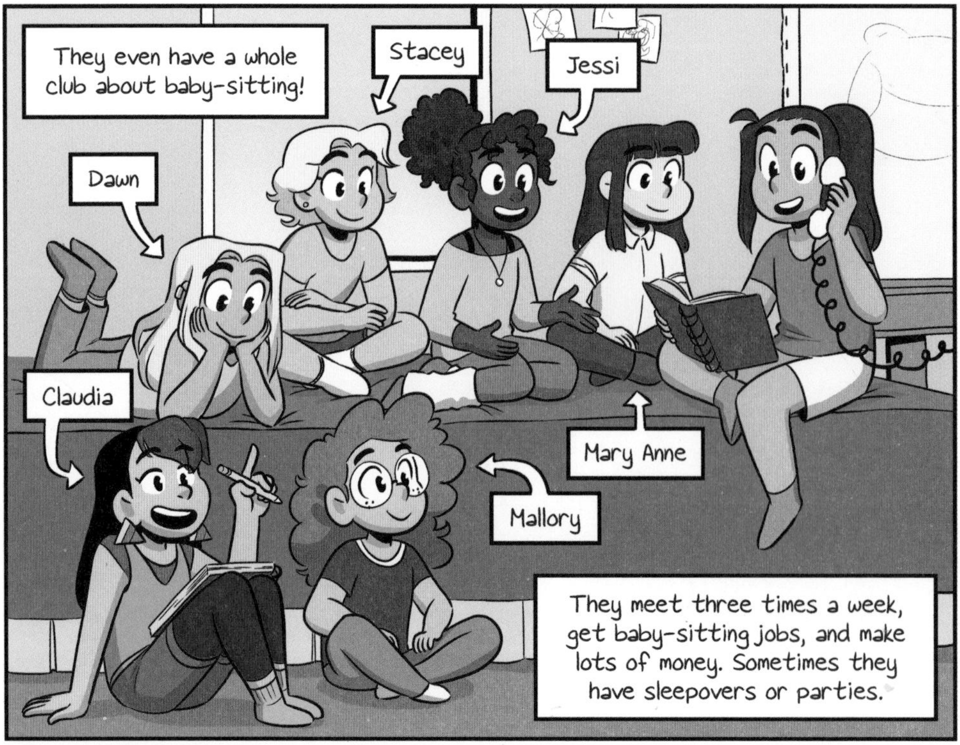
They even have a whole club about baby-sitting!
Stacey
Jessi
Dawn
Claudia
Mary Anne
Mallory
They meet three times a week, get baby-sitting jobs, and make lots of money. Sometimes they have sleepovers or parties.

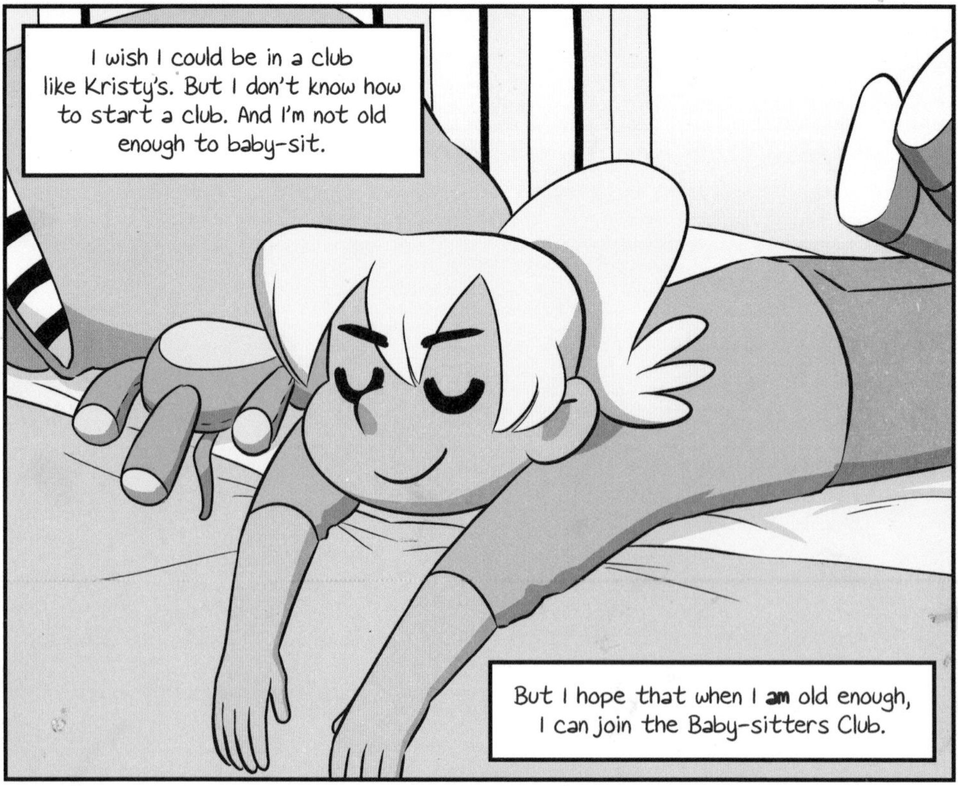
I wish I could be in a club like Kristy's. But I don't know how to start a club. And I'm not old enough to baby-sit.
But I hope that when I **am** old enough, I can join the Baby-sitters Club.

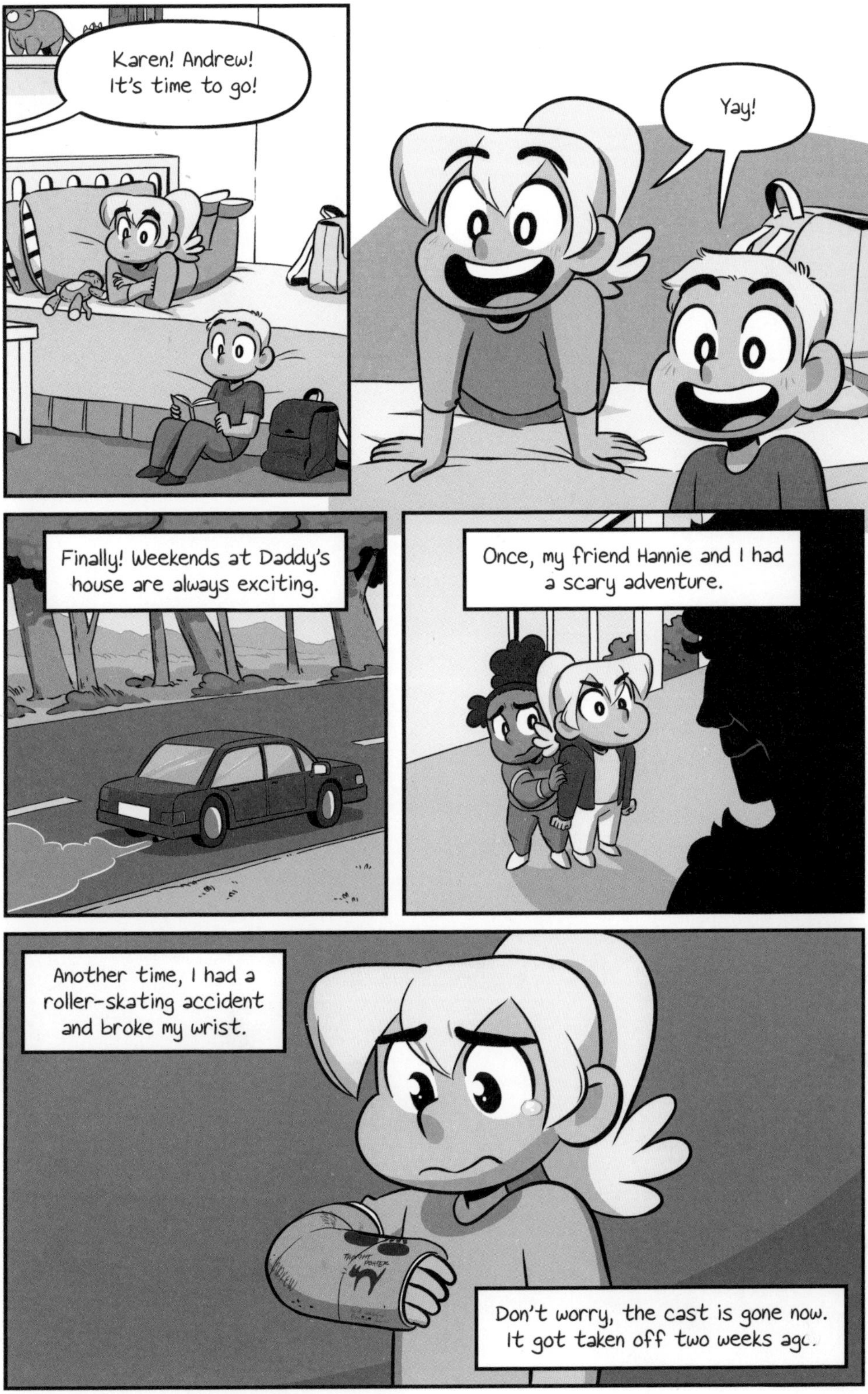
Karen! Andrew!
It's time to go!
Yay!
Finally! Weekends at Daddy's house are always exciting.
Once, my friend Hannie and I had a scary adventure.
Another time, I had a roller-skating accident and broke my wrist.
Don't worry, the cast is gone now. It got taken off two weeks ago.

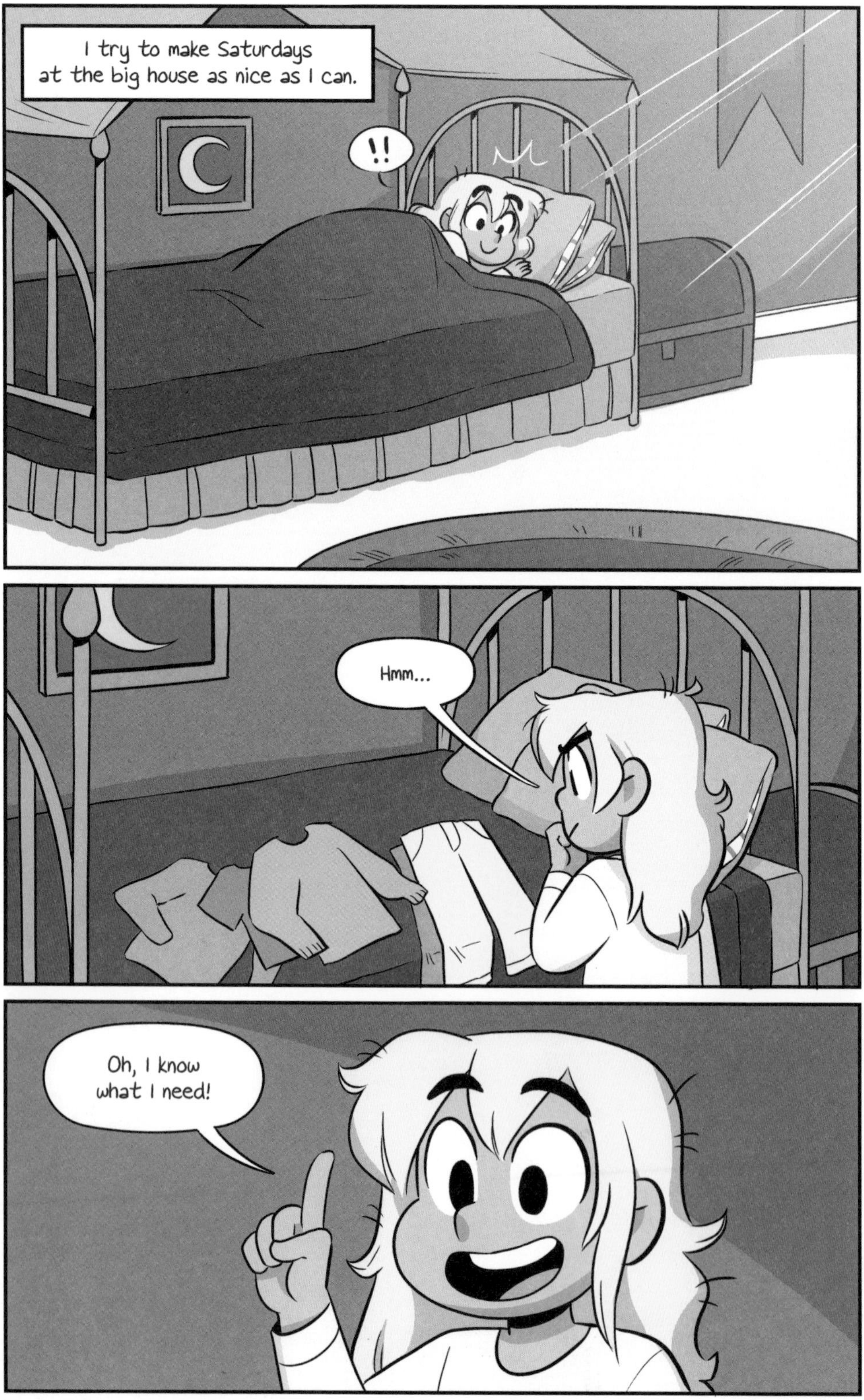
I try to make Saturdays at the big house as nice as I can.
!!
Hmm...
Oh, I know what I need!

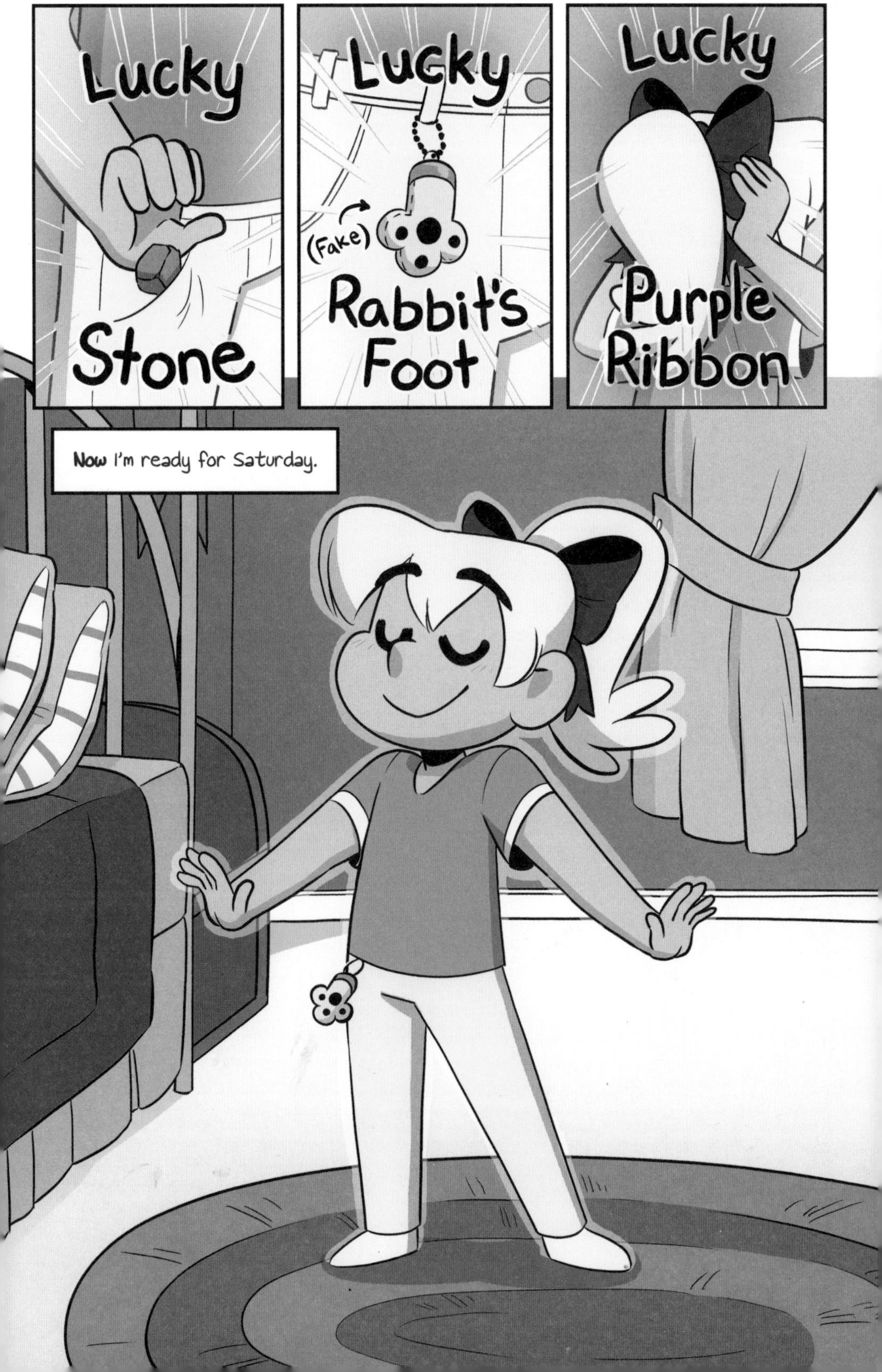

Lucky Stone
Lucky (Fake) Rabbit's Foot
Lucky Purple Ribbon
Now I'm ready for Saturday.

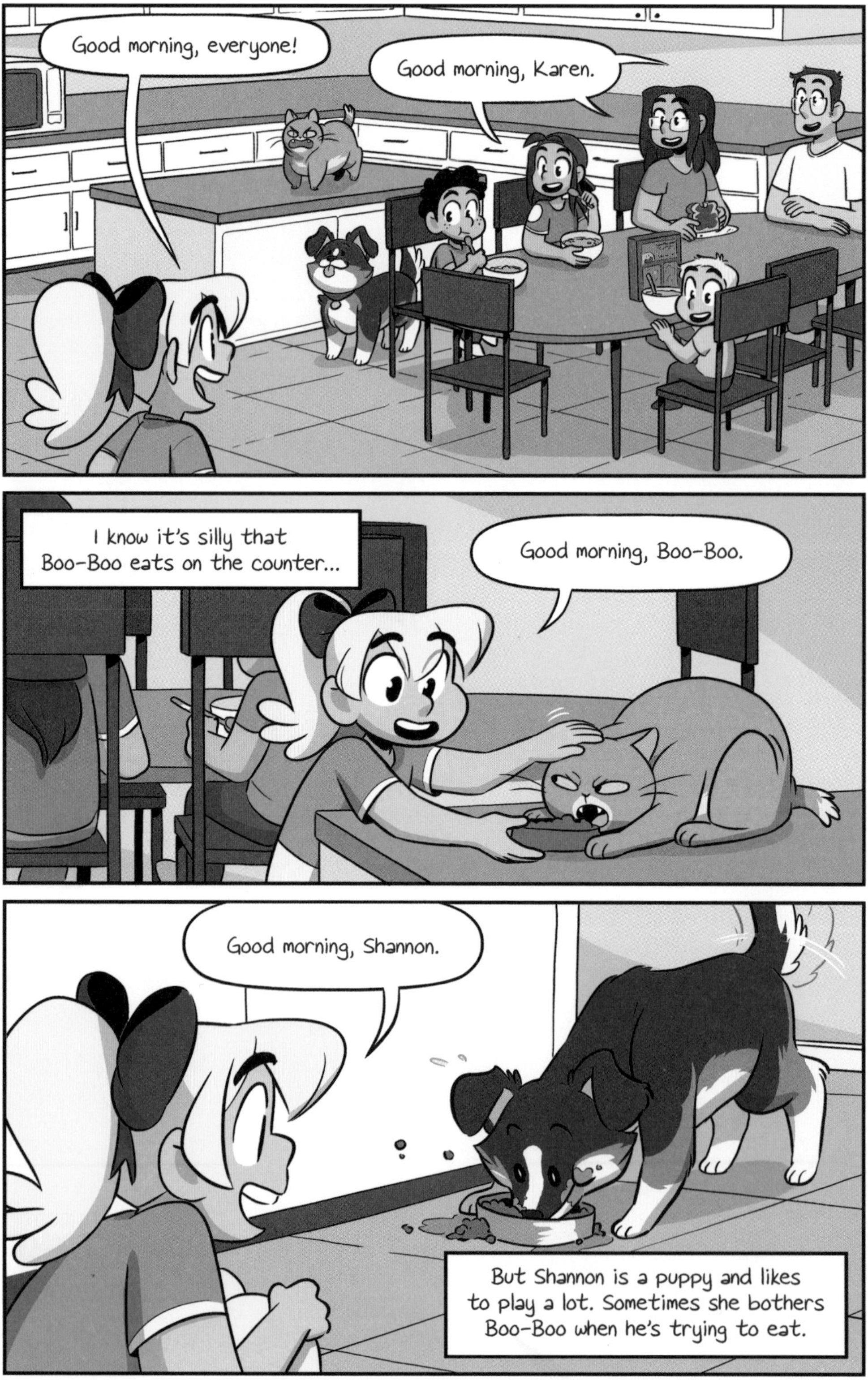
Good morning, everyone!
Good morning, Karen.
I know it's silly that Boo-Boo eats on the counter...
Good morning, Boo-Boo.
Good morning, Shannon.
But Shannon is a puppy and likes to play a lot. Sometimes she bothers Boo-Boo when he's trying to eat.

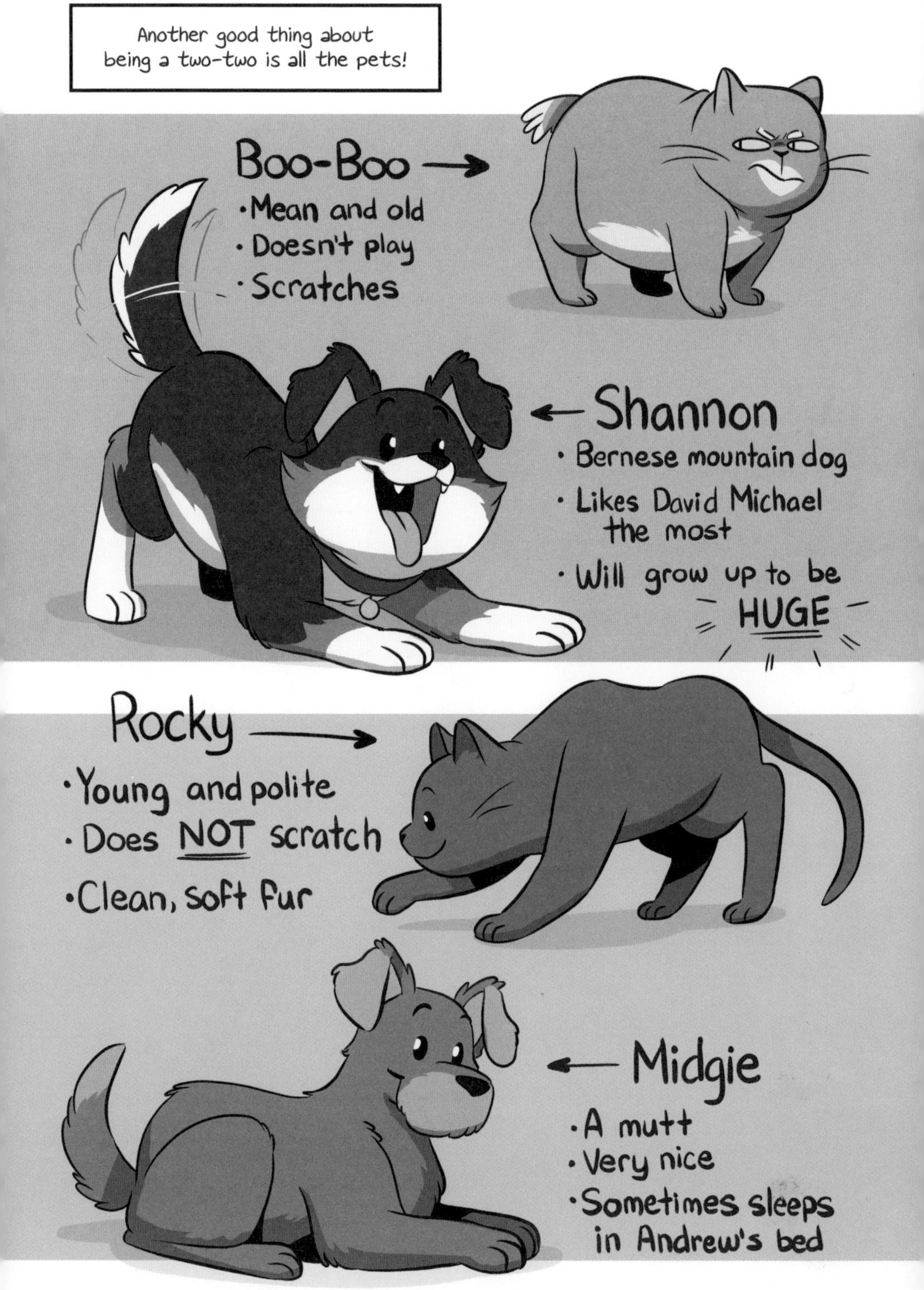
Another good thing about being a two-two is all the pets!
Boo-Boo
•Mean and old
•Doesn't play
•Scratches
Shannon
•Bernese mountain dog
•Likes David Michael the most
•Will grow up to be HUGE
Rocky
•Young and polite
•Does NOT scratch
•Clean, soft fur
Midgie
•A mutt
•Very nice
•Sometimes sleeps in Andrew's bed

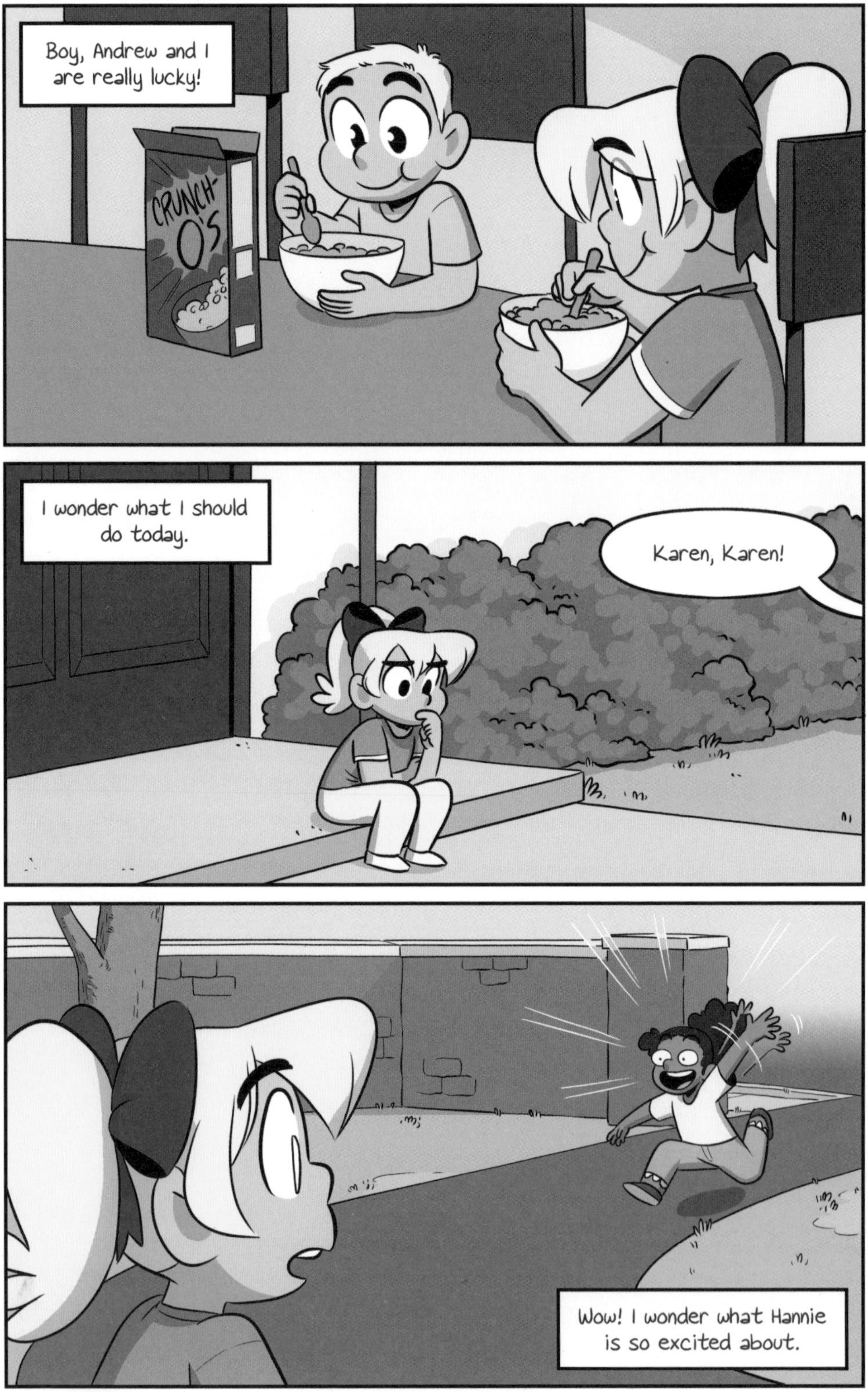
Boy, Andrew and I are really lucky!
CRUNCH-O'S
I wonder what I should do today.
Karen, Karen!
Wow! I wonder what Hannie is so excited about.

CHAPTER 2

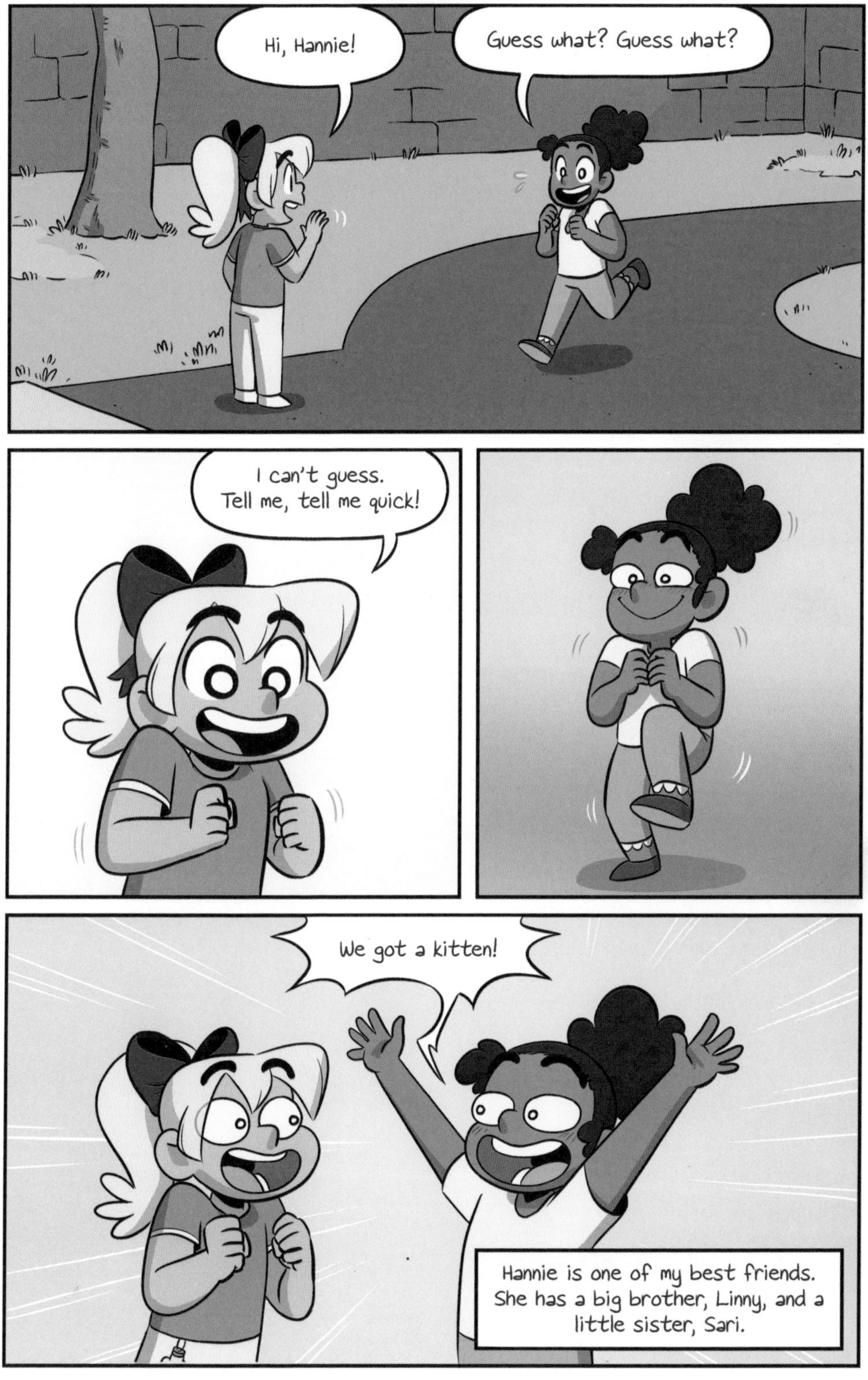
Hi, Hannie!
Guess what? Guess what?
I can't guess. Tell me, tell me quick!
We got a kitten!
Hannie is one of my best friends. She has a big brother, Linny, and a little sister, Sari.

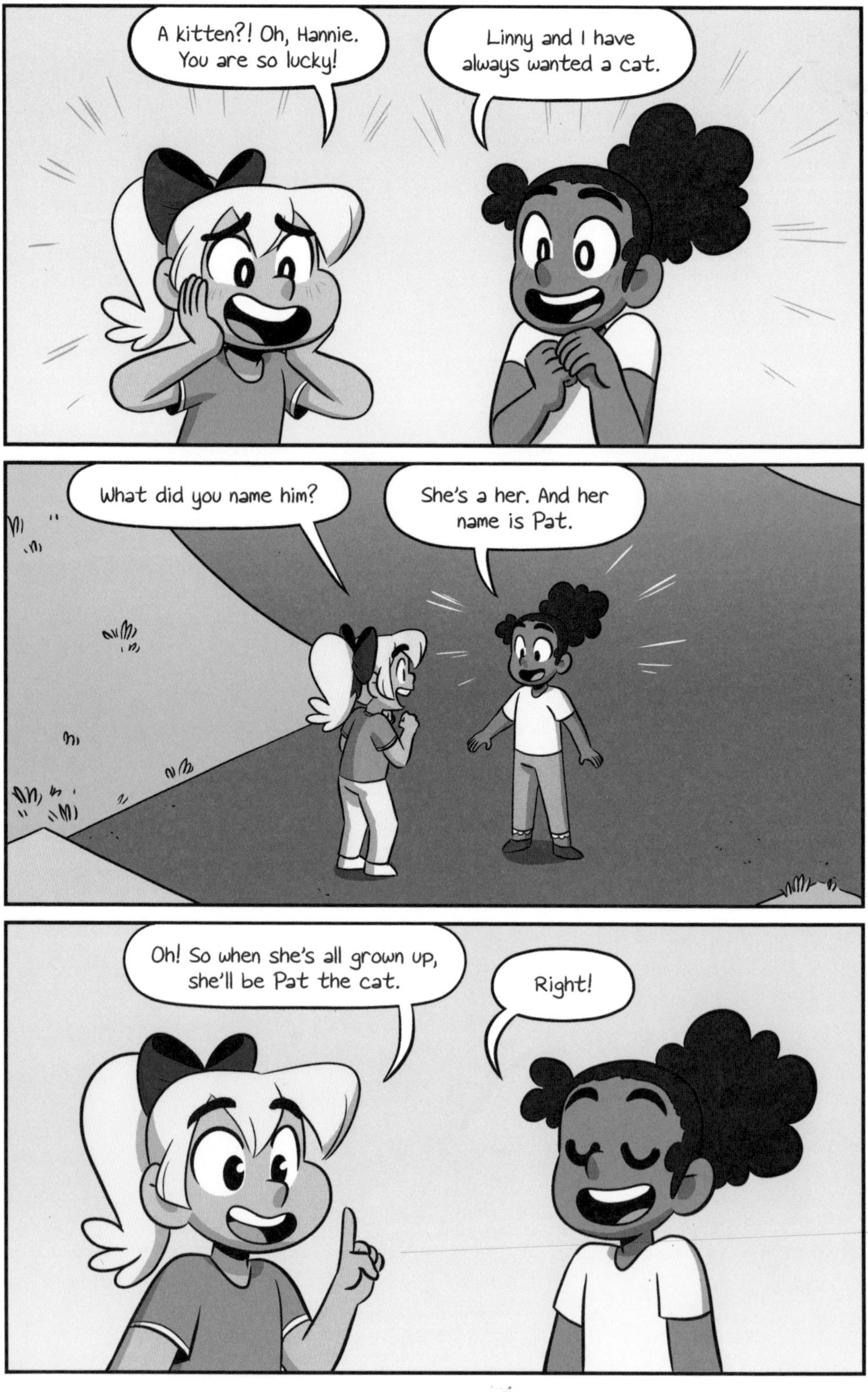
A kitten?! Oh, Hannie. You are so lucky!
Linny and I have always wanted a cat.
What did you name him?
She's a her. And her name is Pat.
Oh! So when she's all grown up, she'll be Pat the cat.
Right!

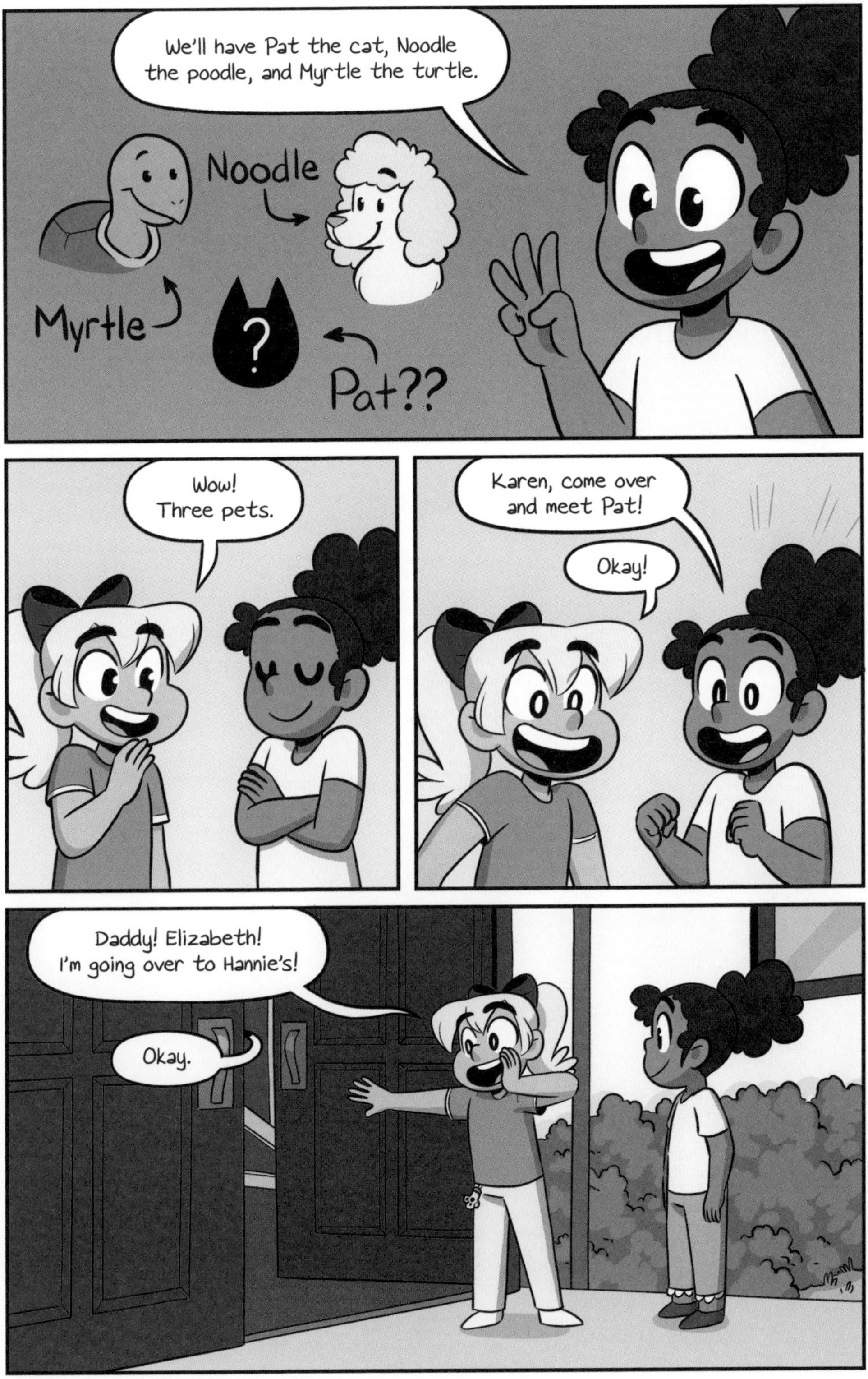
We'll have Pat the cat, Noodle the poodle, and Myrtle the turtle.
Noodle
Myrtle
?
Pat??
Wow! Three pets.
Karen, come over and meet Pat!
Okay!
Daddy! Elizabeth! I'm going over to Hannie's!
Okay.

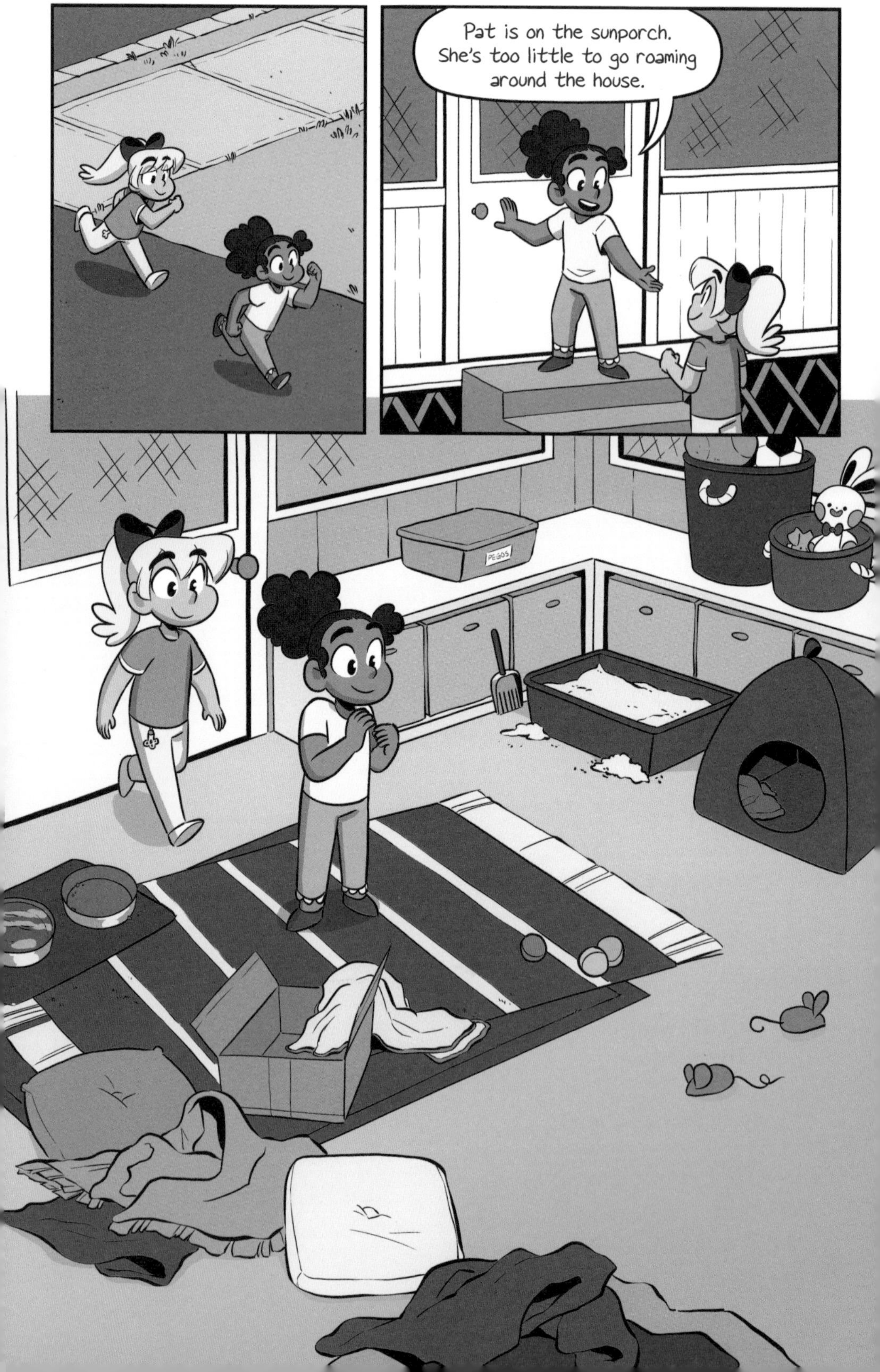
Pat is on the sunporch. She's too little to go roaming around the house.
PEGOS

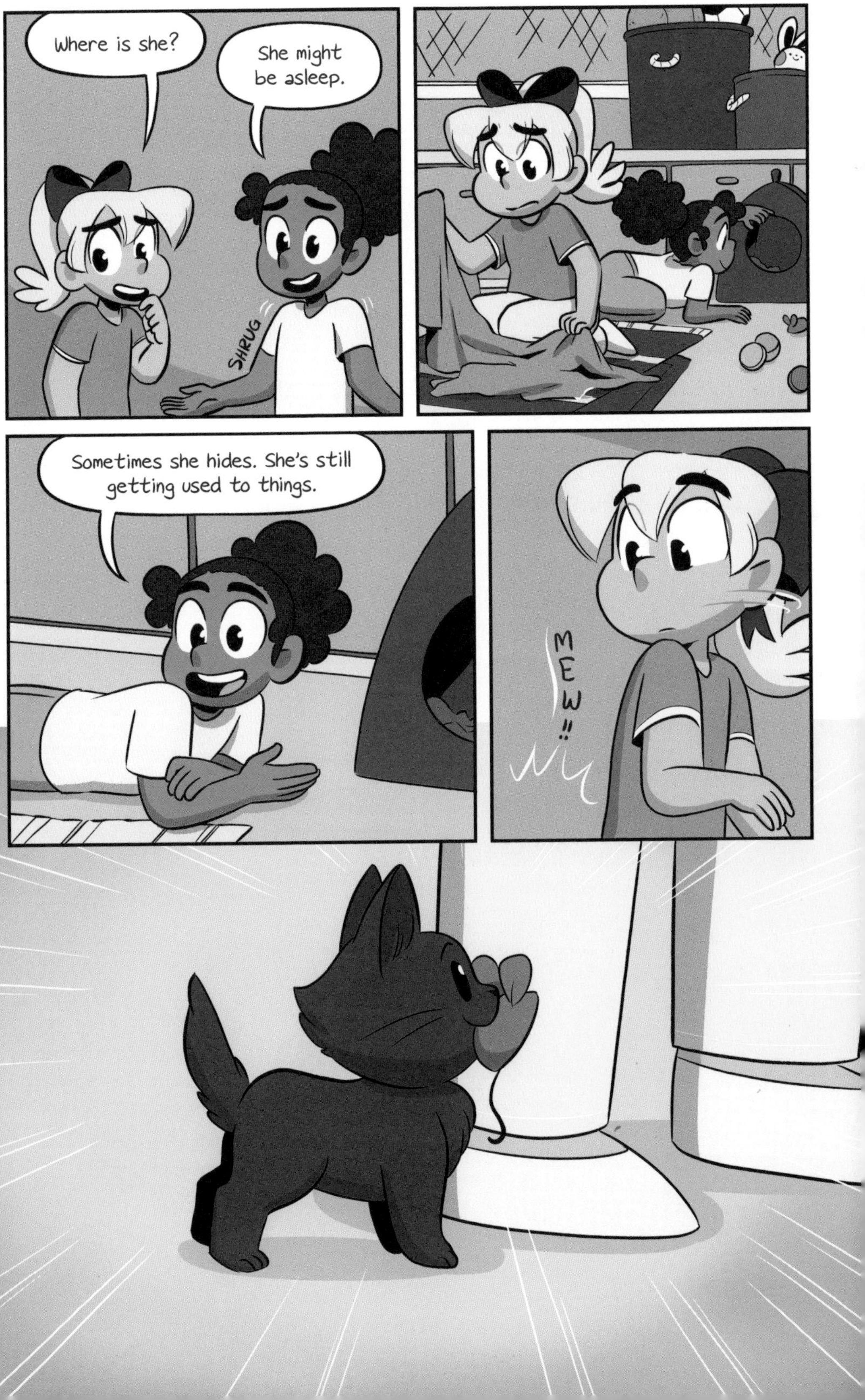
Where is she?
She might be asleep.
SHRUG
Sometimes she hides. She's still getting used to things.
MEW!!

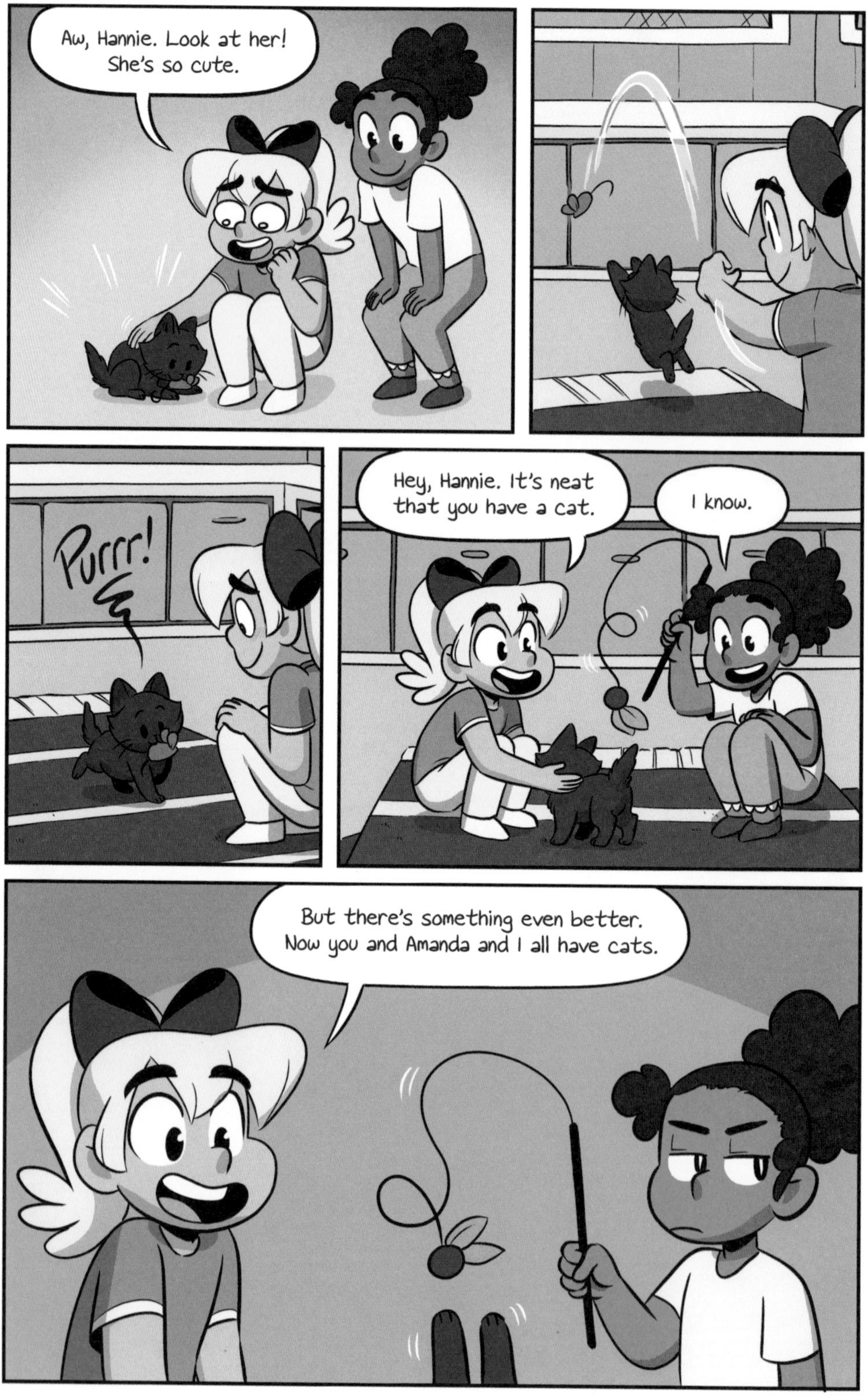
Aw, Hannie. Look at her! She's so cute.
Purrr!
Hey, Hannie. It's neat that you have a cat.
I know.
But there's something even better. Now you and Amanda and I all have cats.

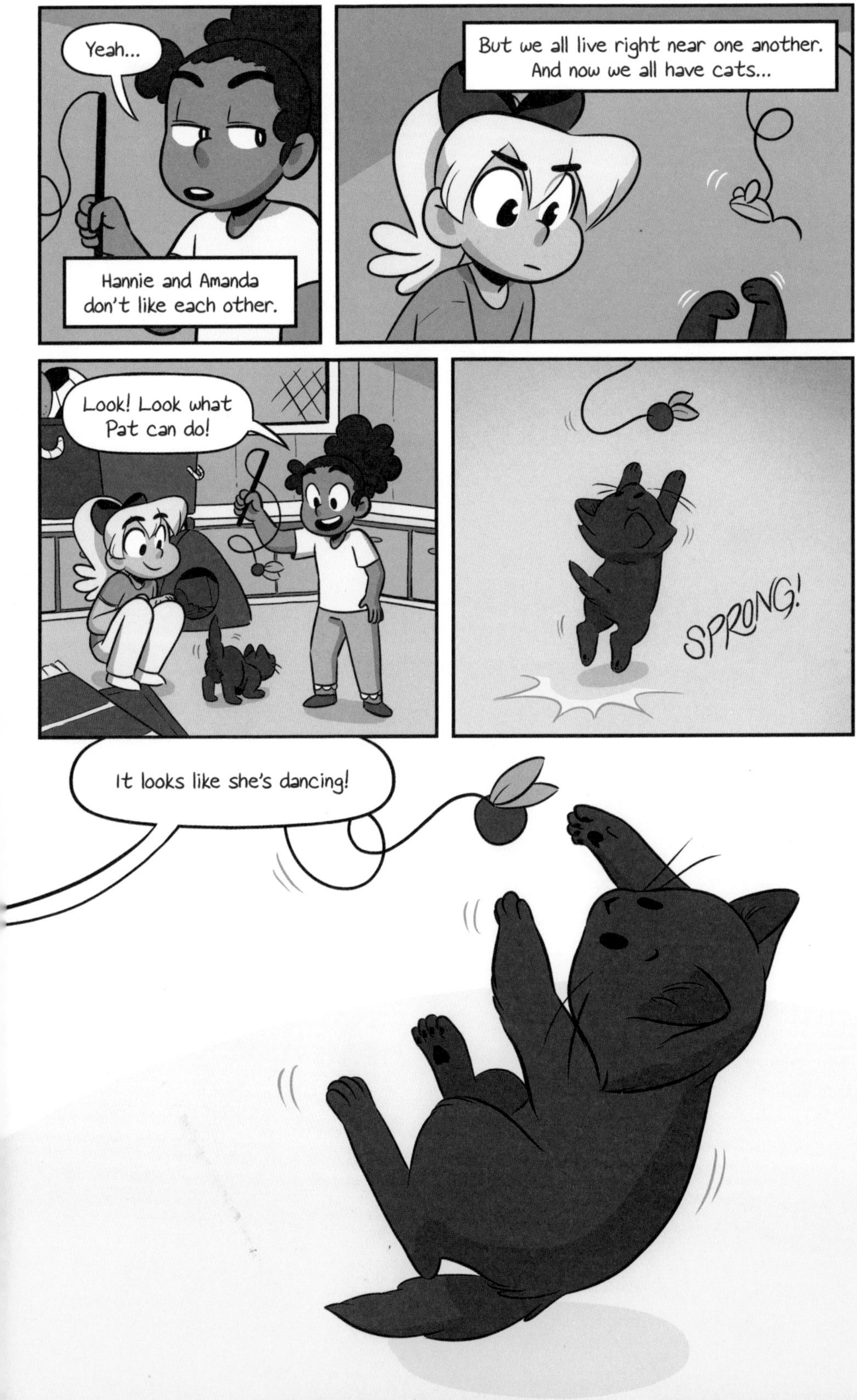
Yeah...
Hannie and Amanda don't like each other.
But we all live right near one another. And now we all have cats...
Look! Look what Pat can do!
SPRONG!
It looks like she's dancing!

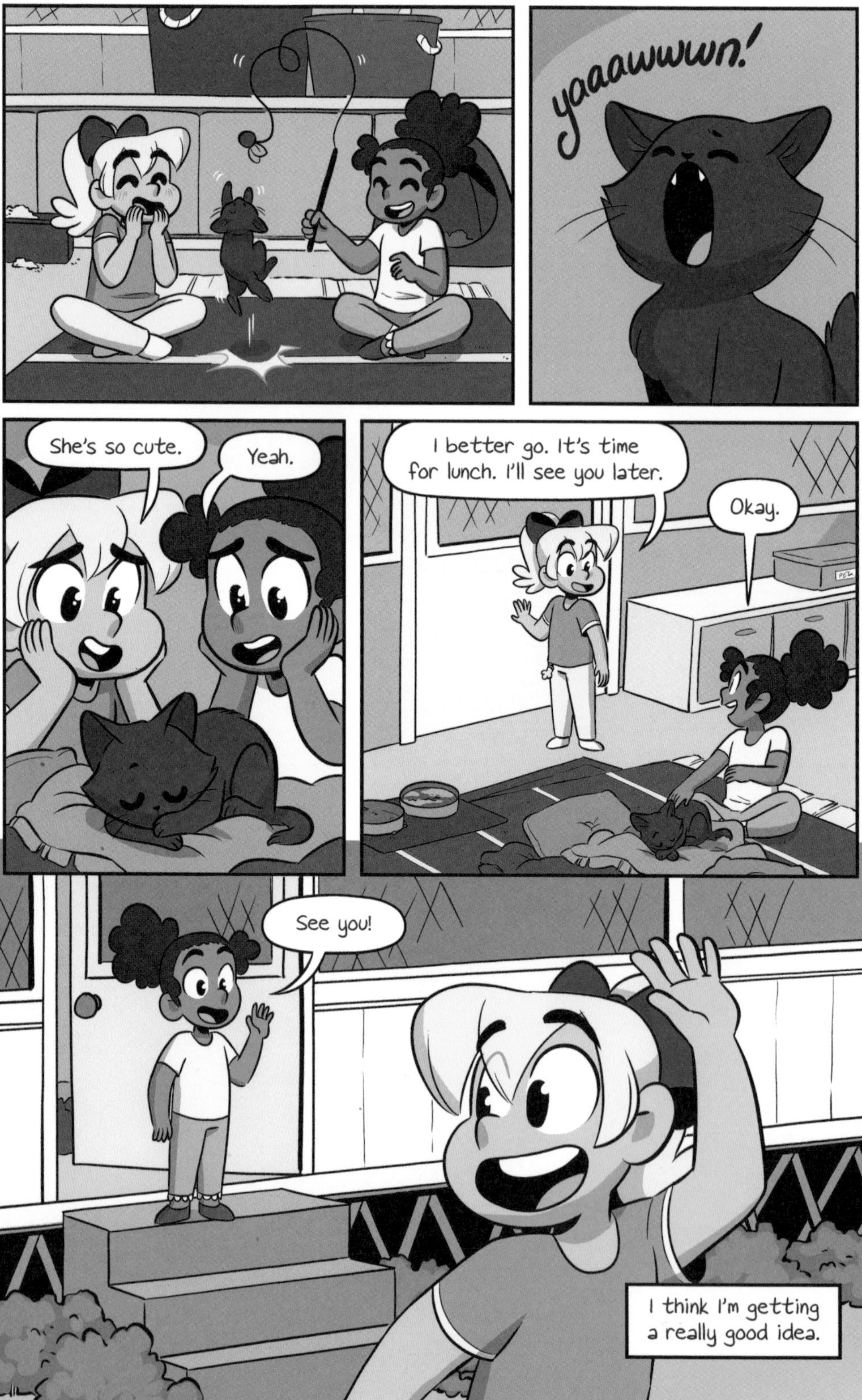
yaaawwwn!
She's so cute.
Yeah.
I better go. It's time for lunch. I'll see you later.
Okay.
See you!
I think I'm getting a really good idea.

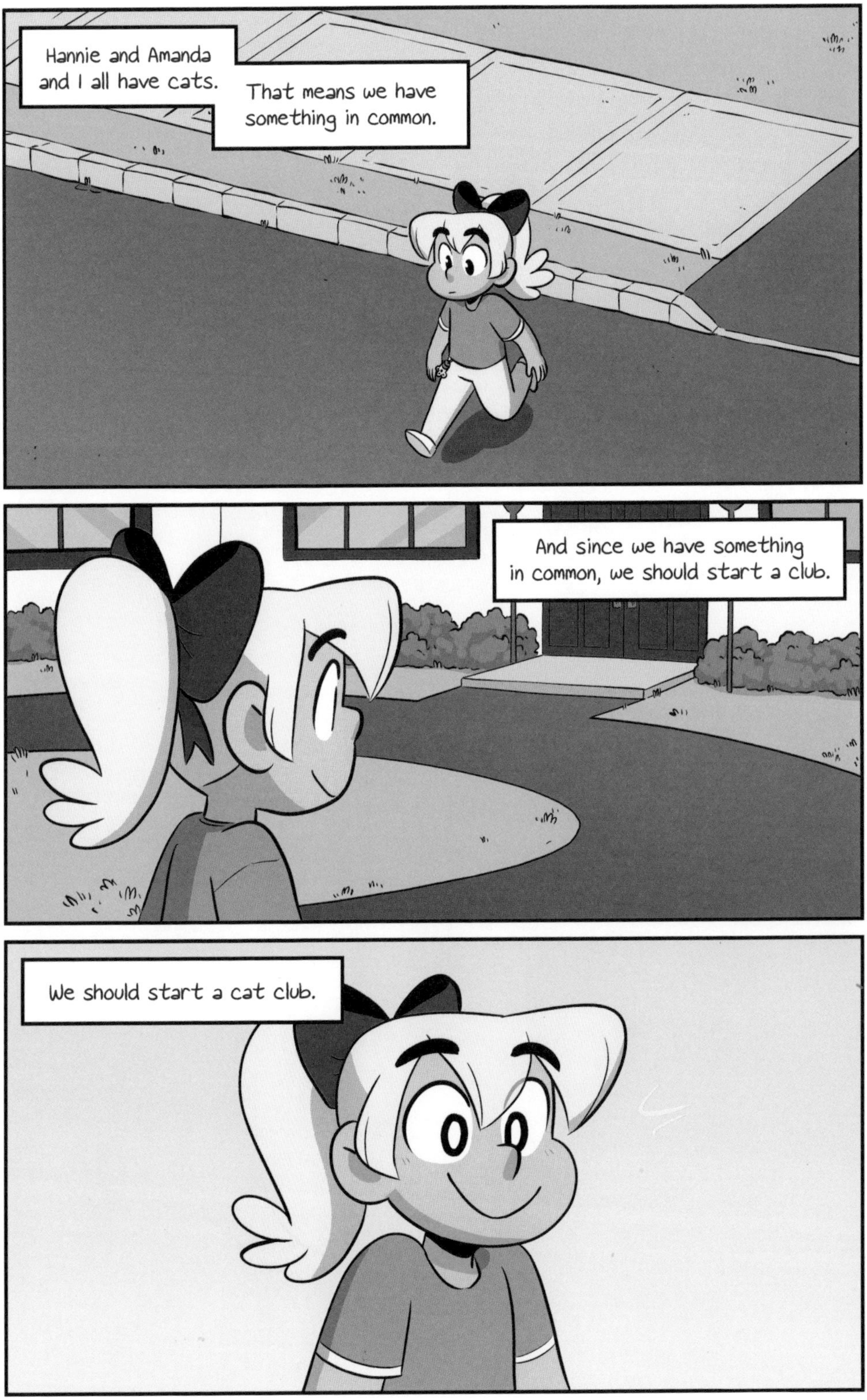
Hannie and Amanda and I all have cats.
That means we have something in common.
And since we have something in common, we should start a club.
We should start a cat club.

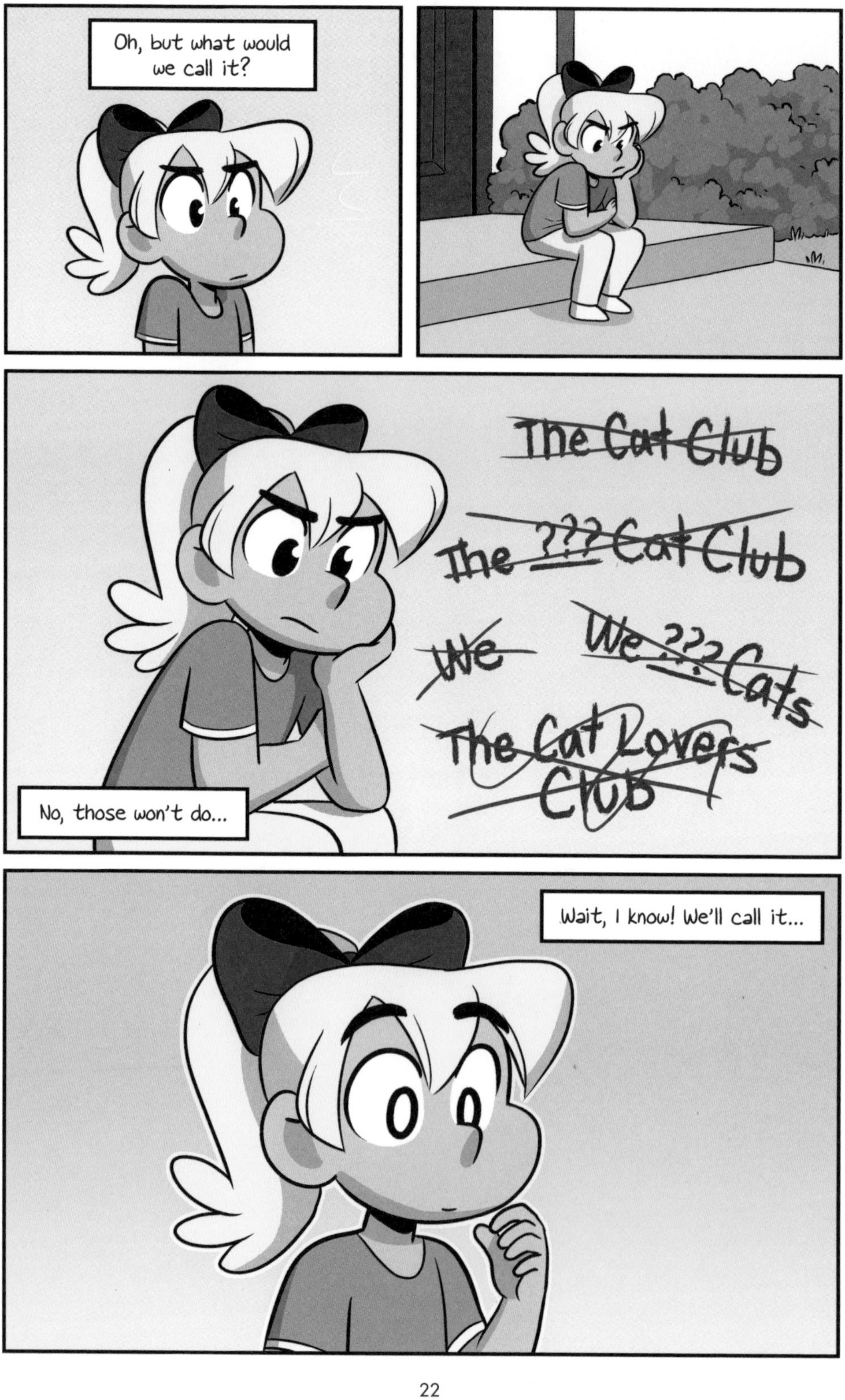
Oh, but what would we call it?
The Cat Club
The ??? Cat Club
We
We ??? Cats
The Cat Lovers Club
No, those won't do...
Wait, I know! We'll call it...

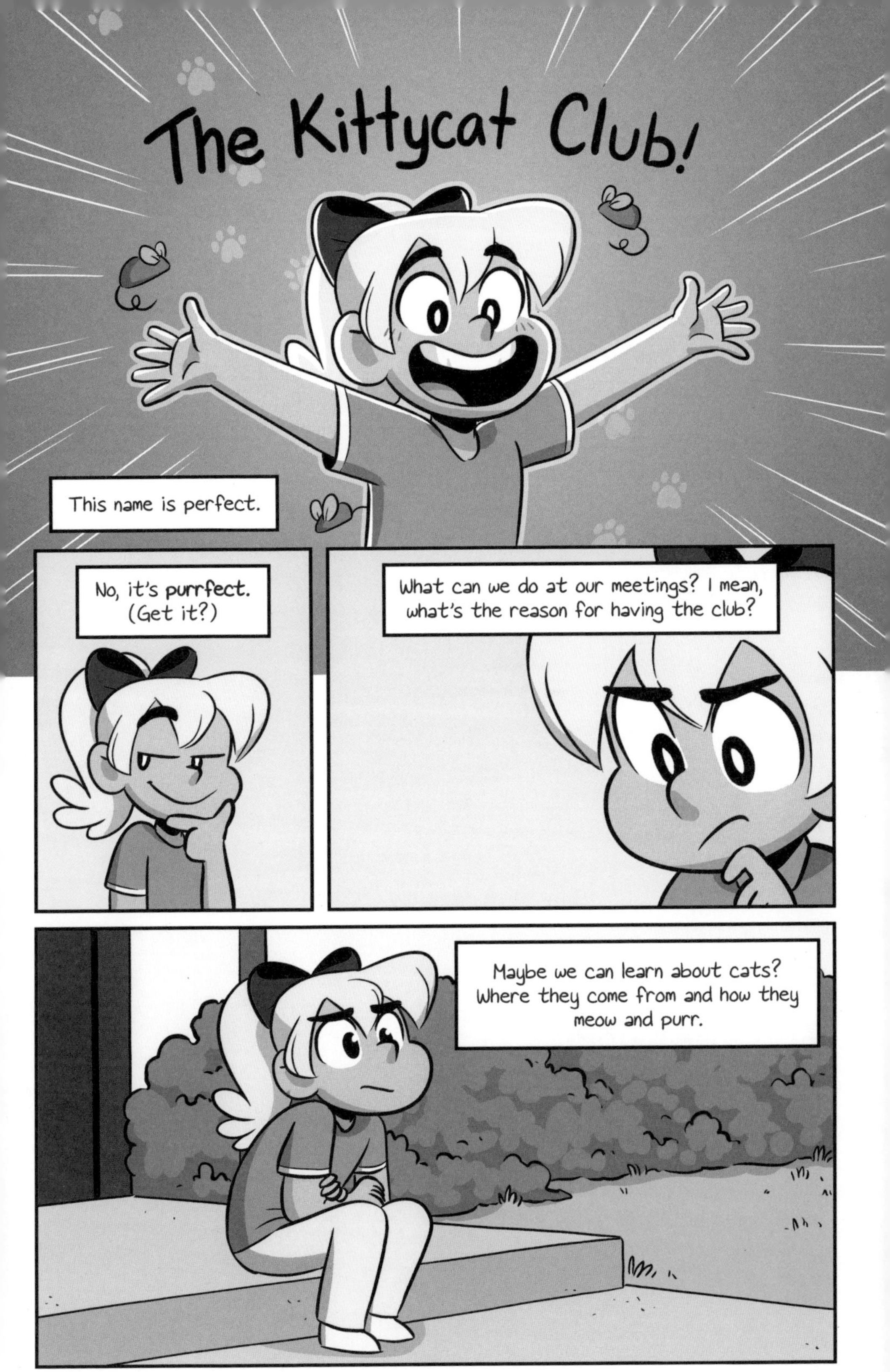
The Kittycat Club!
This name is perfect.
No, it's purrfect. (Get it?)
What can we do at our meetings? I mean, what's the reason for having the club?
Maybe we can learn about cats? Where they come from and how they meow and purr.

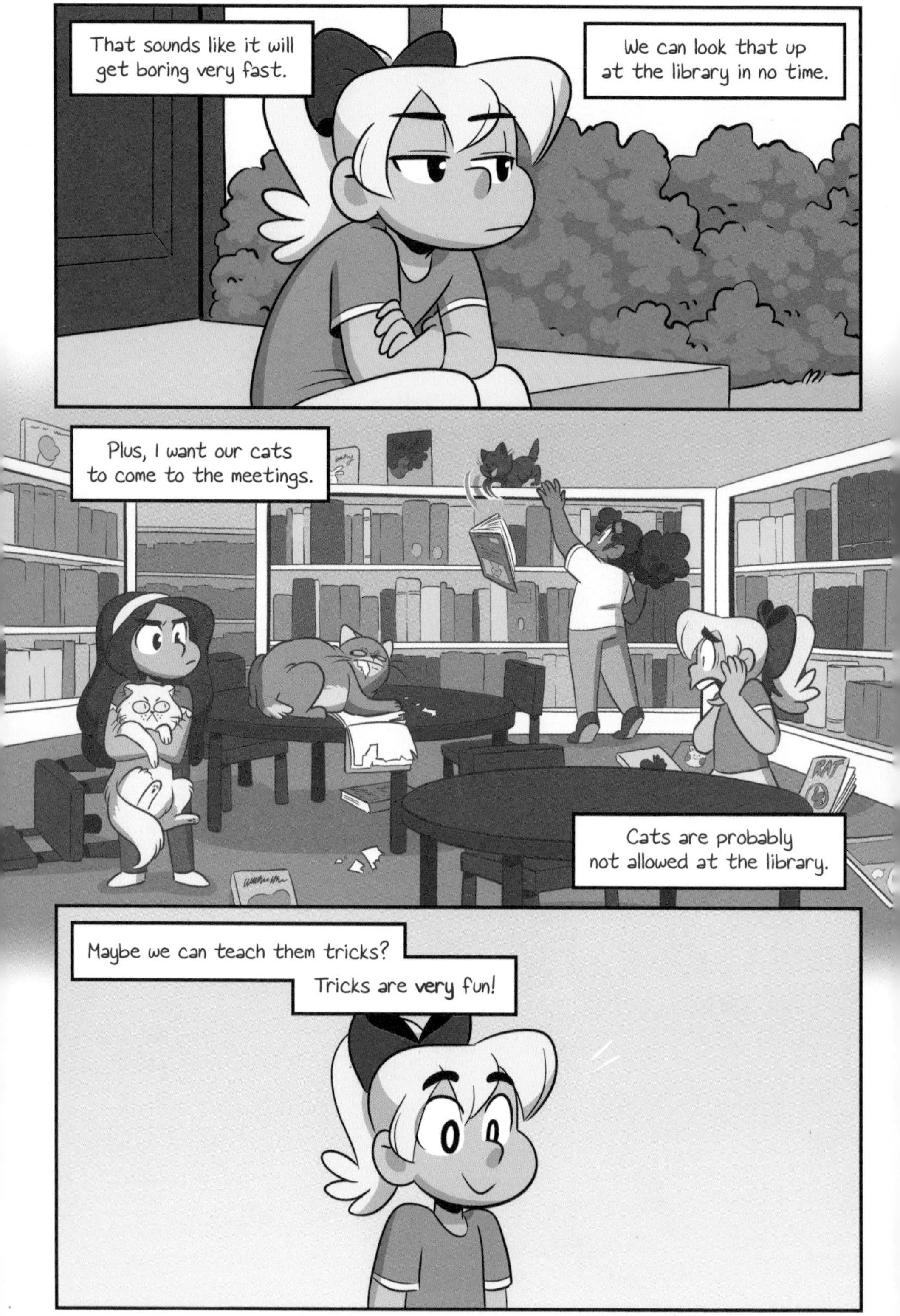
That sounds like it will get boring very fast.
We can look that up at the library in no time.
Plus, I want our cats to come to the meetings.
RAT
Cats are probably not allowed at the library.
Maybe we can teach them tricks?
Tricks are **very** fun!

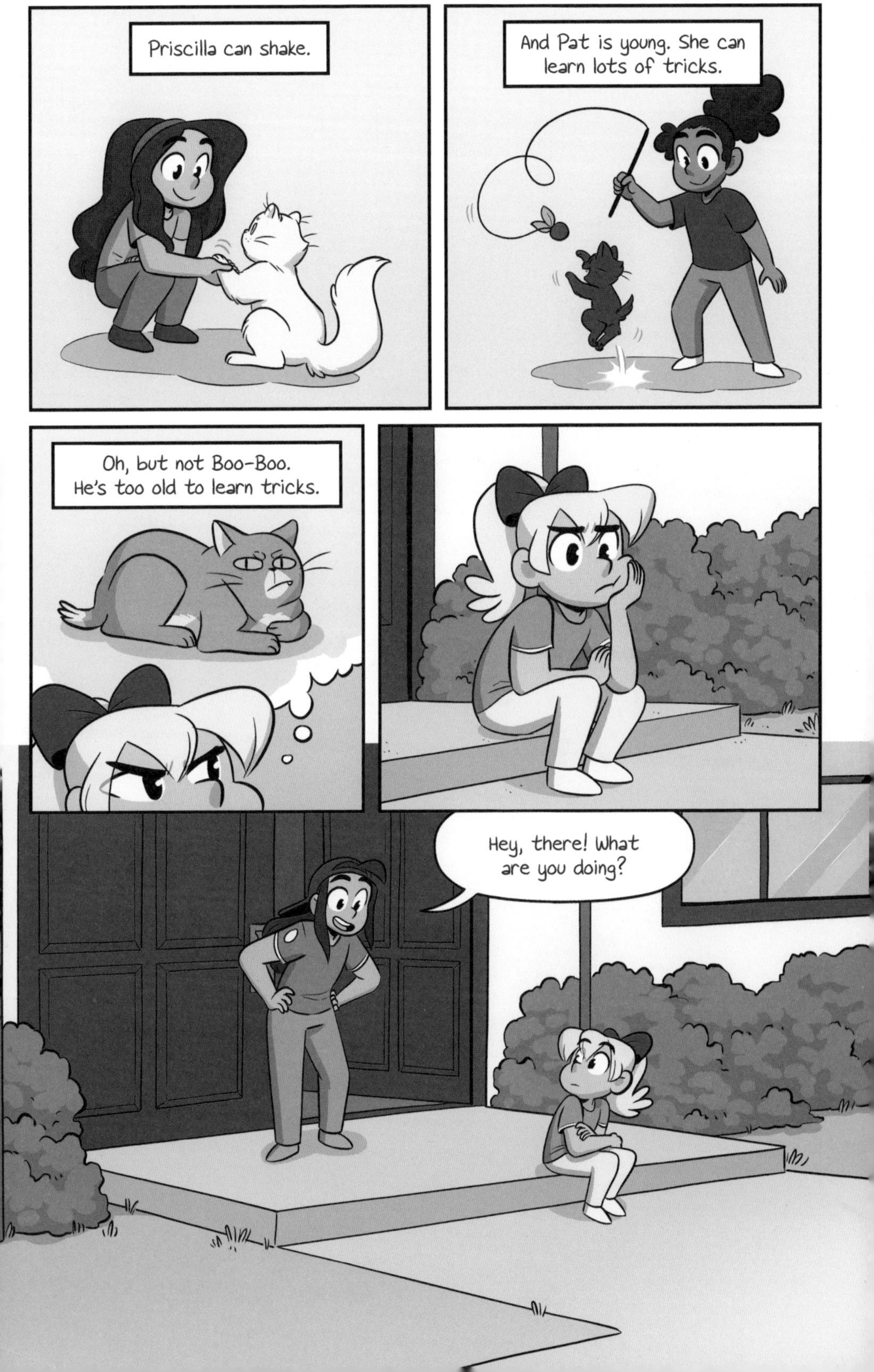
Priscilla can shake.
And Pat is young. She can learn lots of tricks.
Oh, but not Boo-Boo. He's too old to learn tricks.
Hey, there! What are you doing?

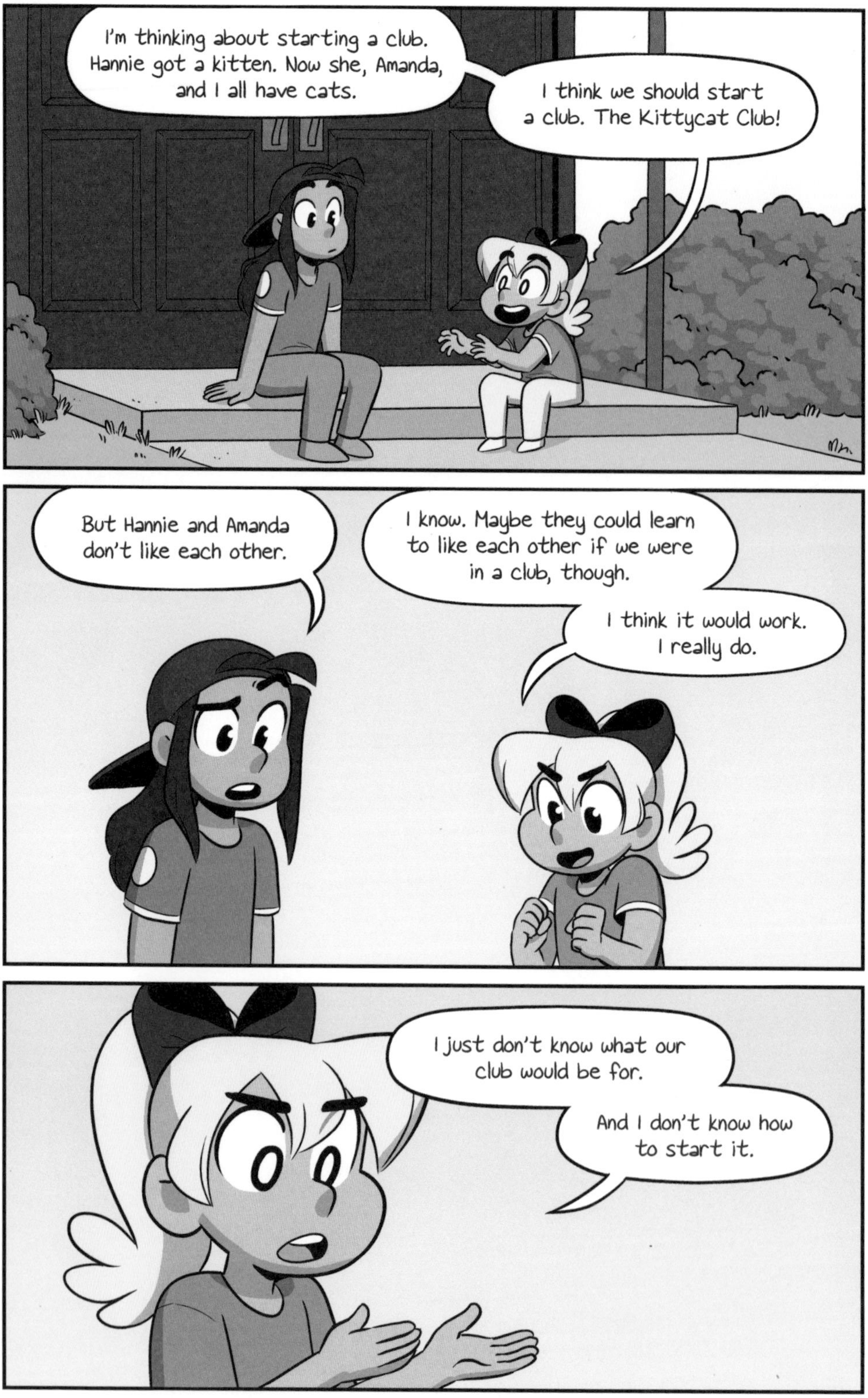
I'm thinking about starting a club. Hannie got a kitten. Now she, Amanda, and I all have cats.
I think we should start a club. The Kittycat Club!
But Hannie and Amanda don't like each other.
I know. Maybe they could learn to like each other if we were in a club, though.
I think it would work. I really do.
I just don't know what our club would be for.
And I don't know how to start it.

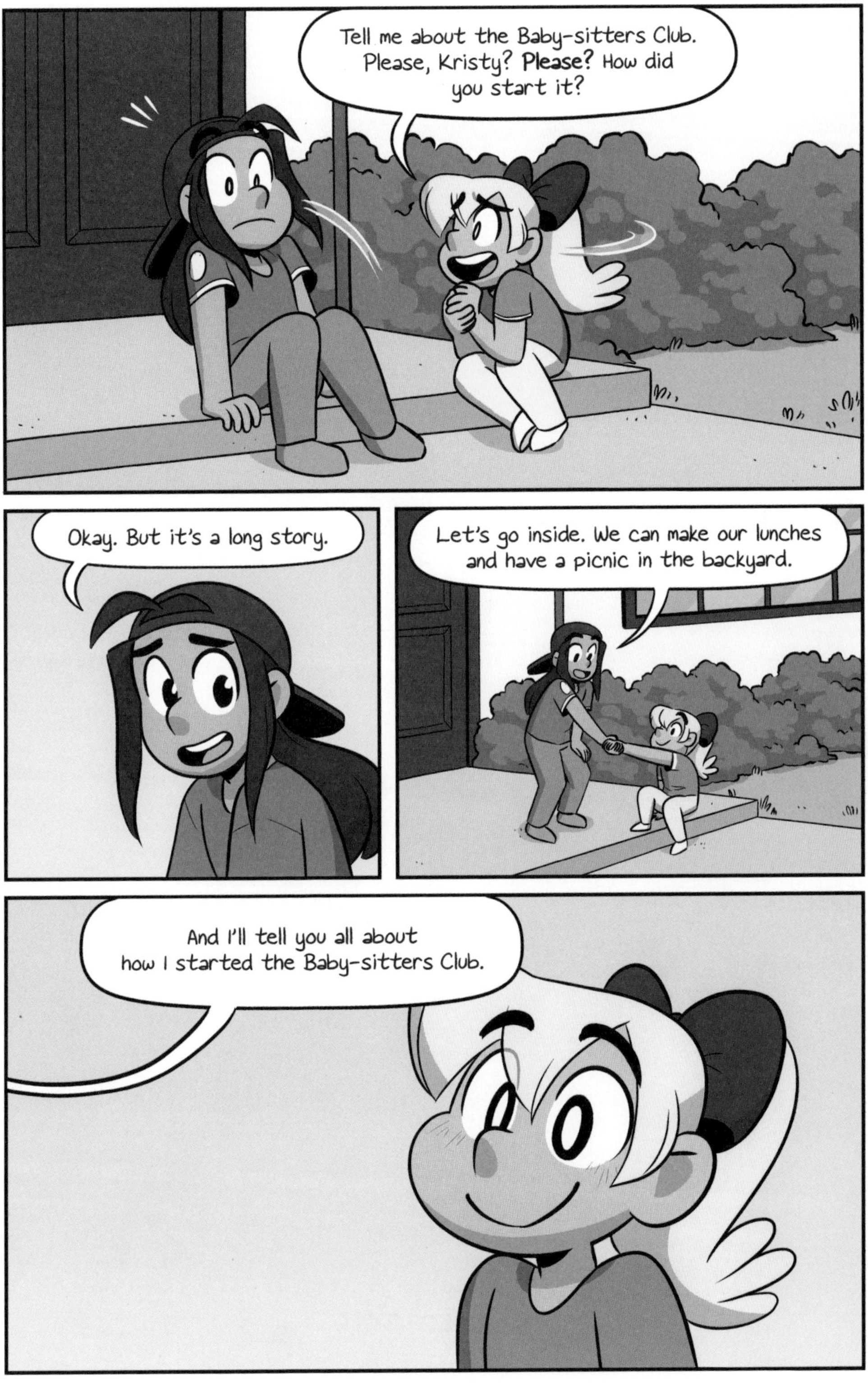
Tell me about the Baby-sitters Club. Please, Kristy? **Please?** How did you start it?
Okay. But it's a long story.
Let's go inside. We can make our lunches and have a picnic in the backyard.
And I'll tell you all about how I started the Baby-sitters Club.

CHAPTER 3

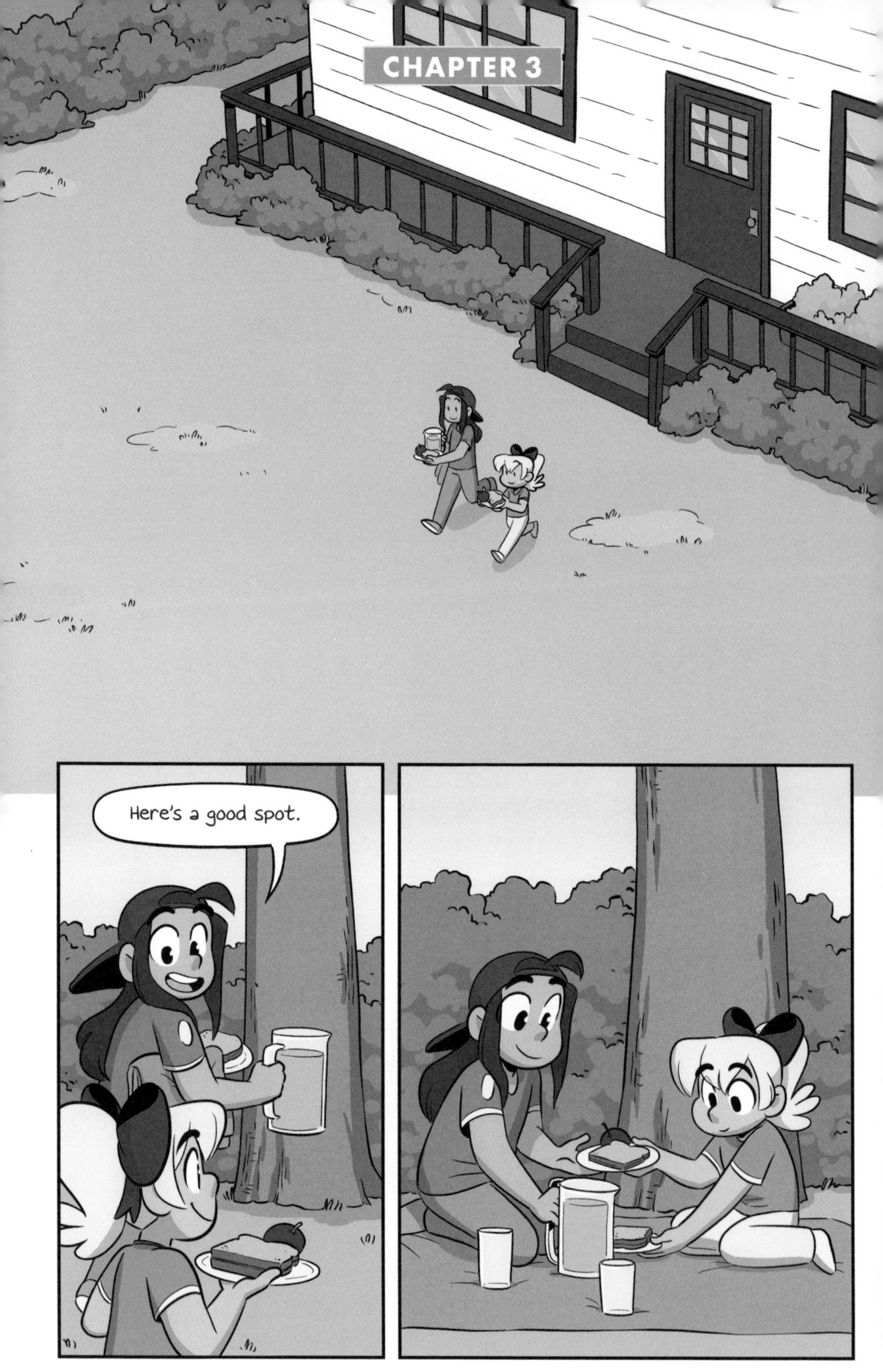
Here's a good spot.

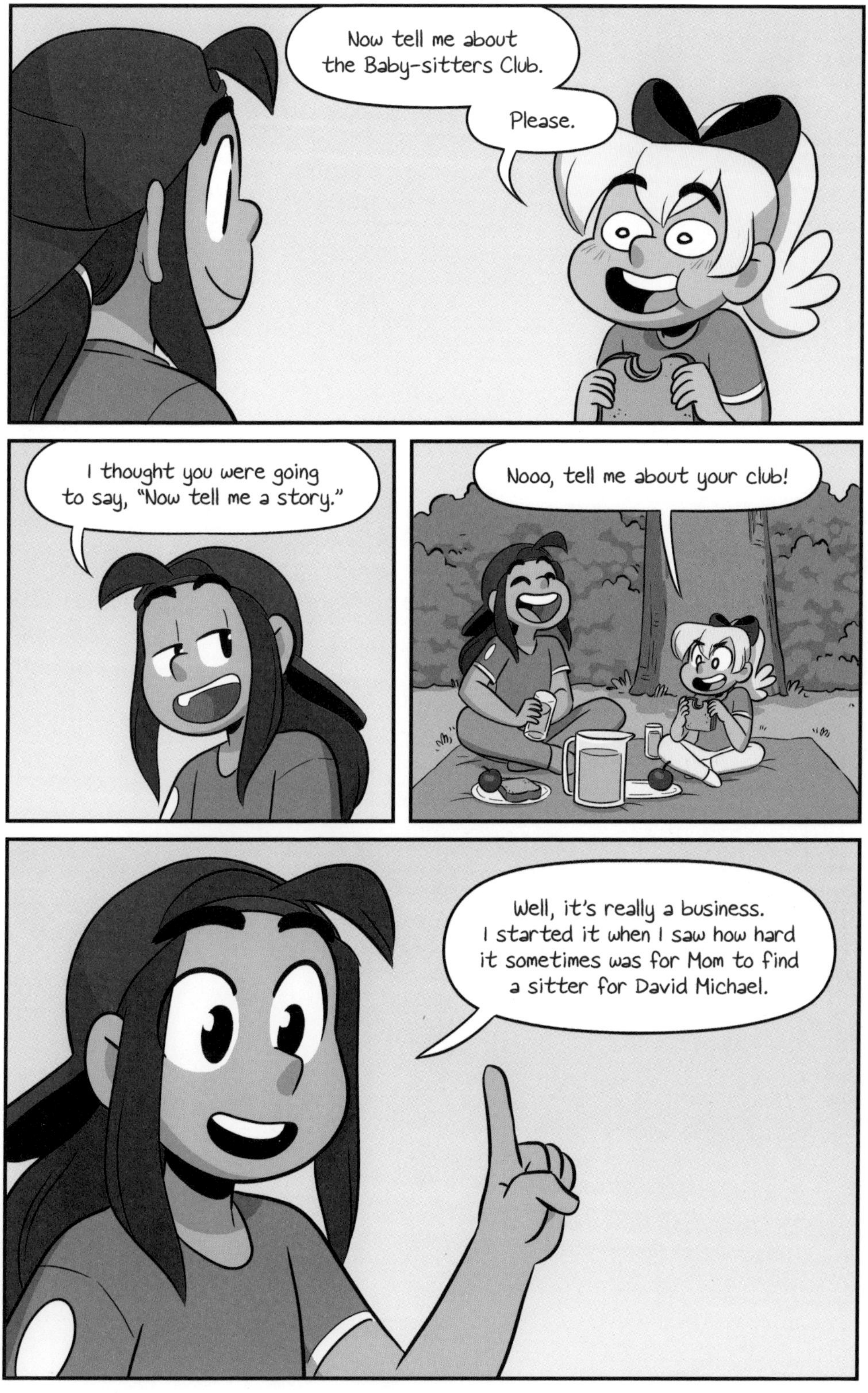
Now tell me about the Baby-sitters Club.
Please.
I thought you were going to say, "Now tell me a story."
Nooo, tell me about your club!
Well, it's really a business. I started it when I saw how hard it sometimes was for Mom to find a sitter for David Michael.

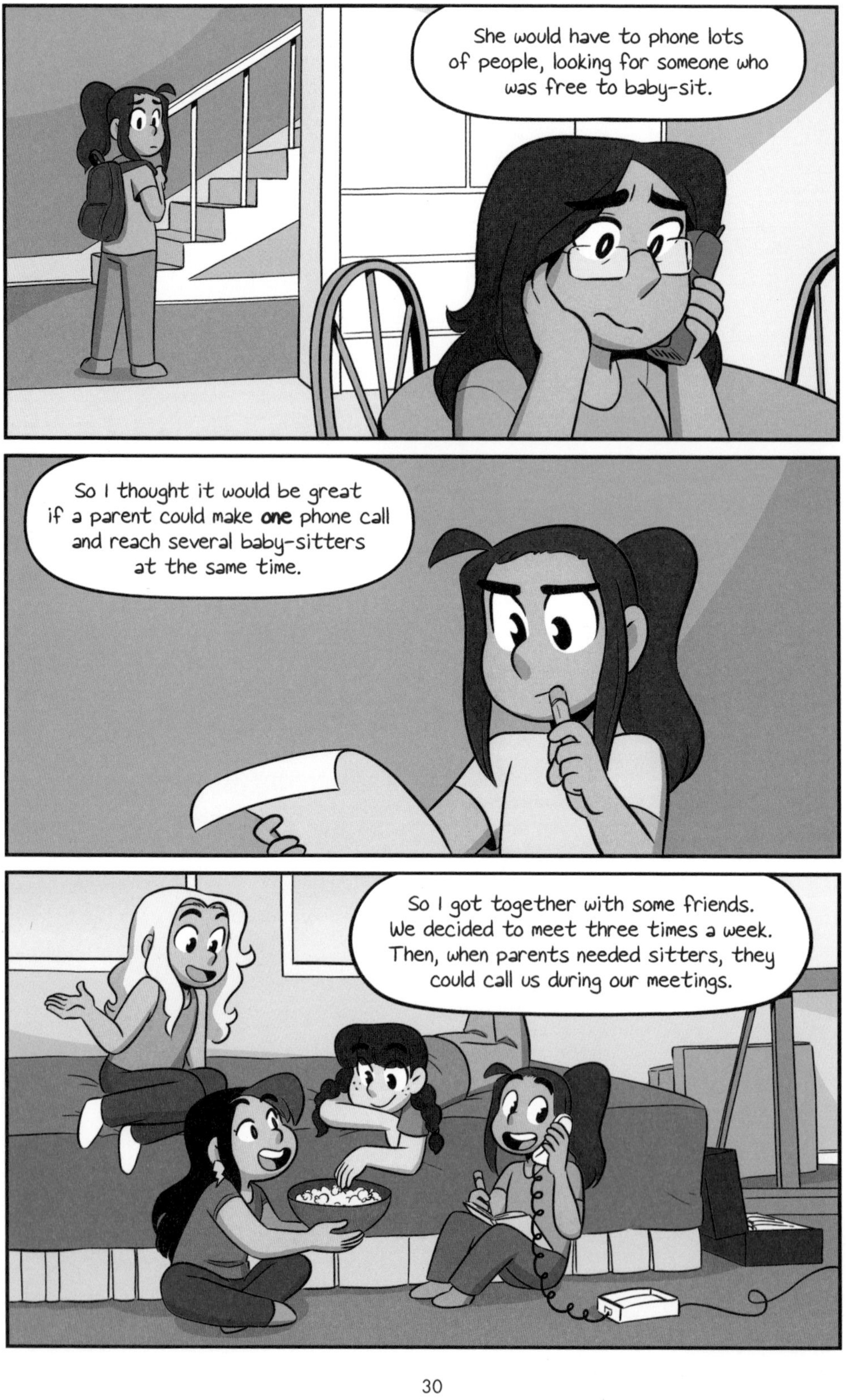
She would have to phone lots of people, looking for someone who was free to baby-sit.
So I thought it would be great if a parent could make **one** phone call and reach several baby-sitters at the same time.
So I got together with some friends. We decided to meet three times a week. Then, when parents needed sitters, they could call us during our meetings.

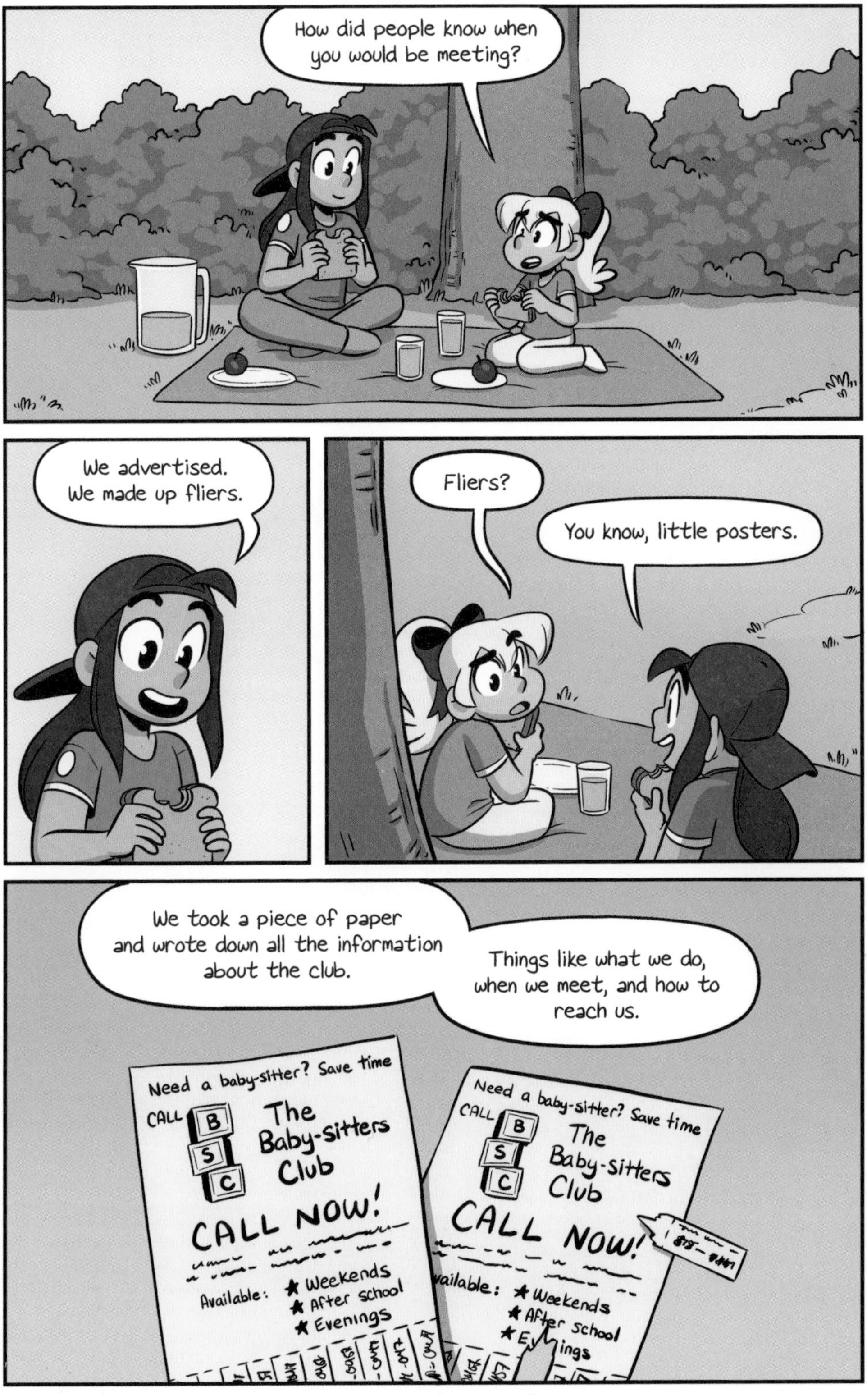
How did people know when you would be meeting?
We advertised. We made up fliers.
Fliers?
You know, little posters.
We took a piece of paper and wrote down all the information about the club.
Things like what we do, when we meet, and how to reach us.
Need a baby-sitter? Save time
CALL
B
S
C
The Baby-sitters Club
CALL NOW!
Available: ★ Weekends ★ After School ★ Evenings
Need a baby-sitter? Save time
CALL
B
S
C
The Baby-sitters Club
CALL NOW!
★ Weekends
★ After School

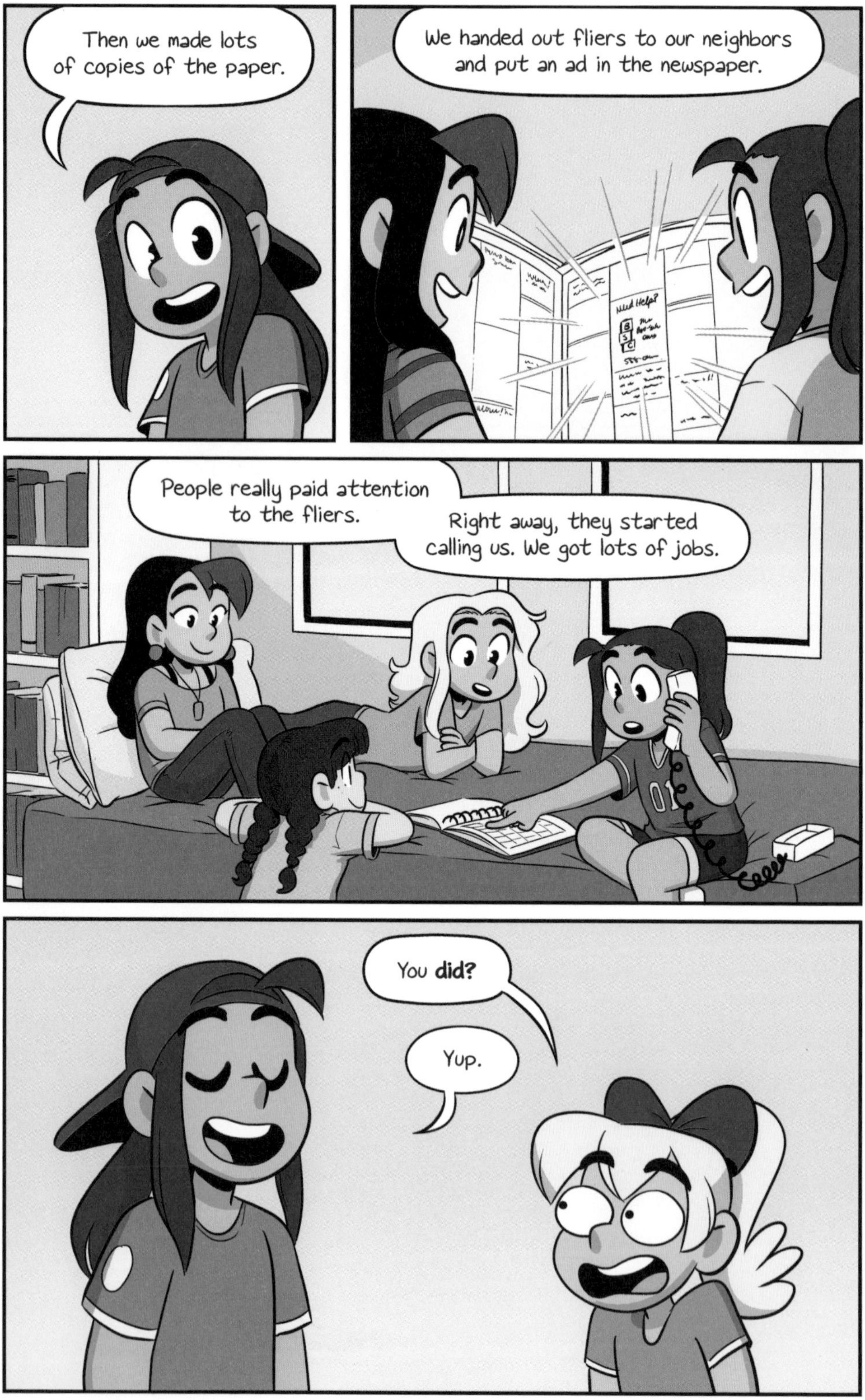
Then we made lots of copies of the paper.
We handed out fliers to our neighbors and put an ad in the newspaper.
People really paid attention to the fliers.
Right away, they started calling us. We got lots of jobs.
You **did?**
Yup.

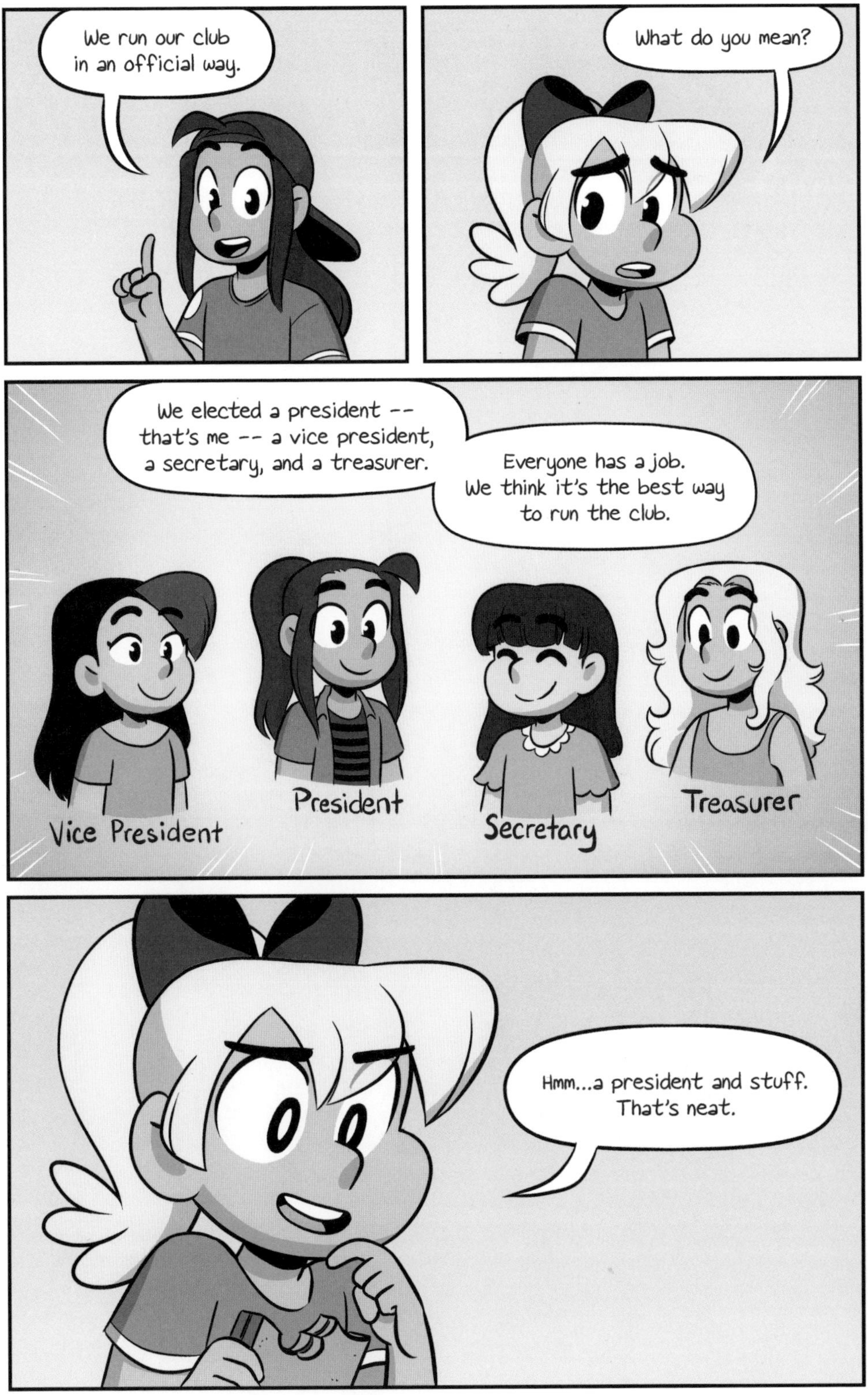
We run our club in an official way.
What do you mean?
We elected a president -- that's me -- a vice president, a secretary, and a treasurer.
Everyone has a job. We think it's the best way to run the club.
Vice President
President
Secretary
Treasurer
Hmm...a president and stuff. That's neat.

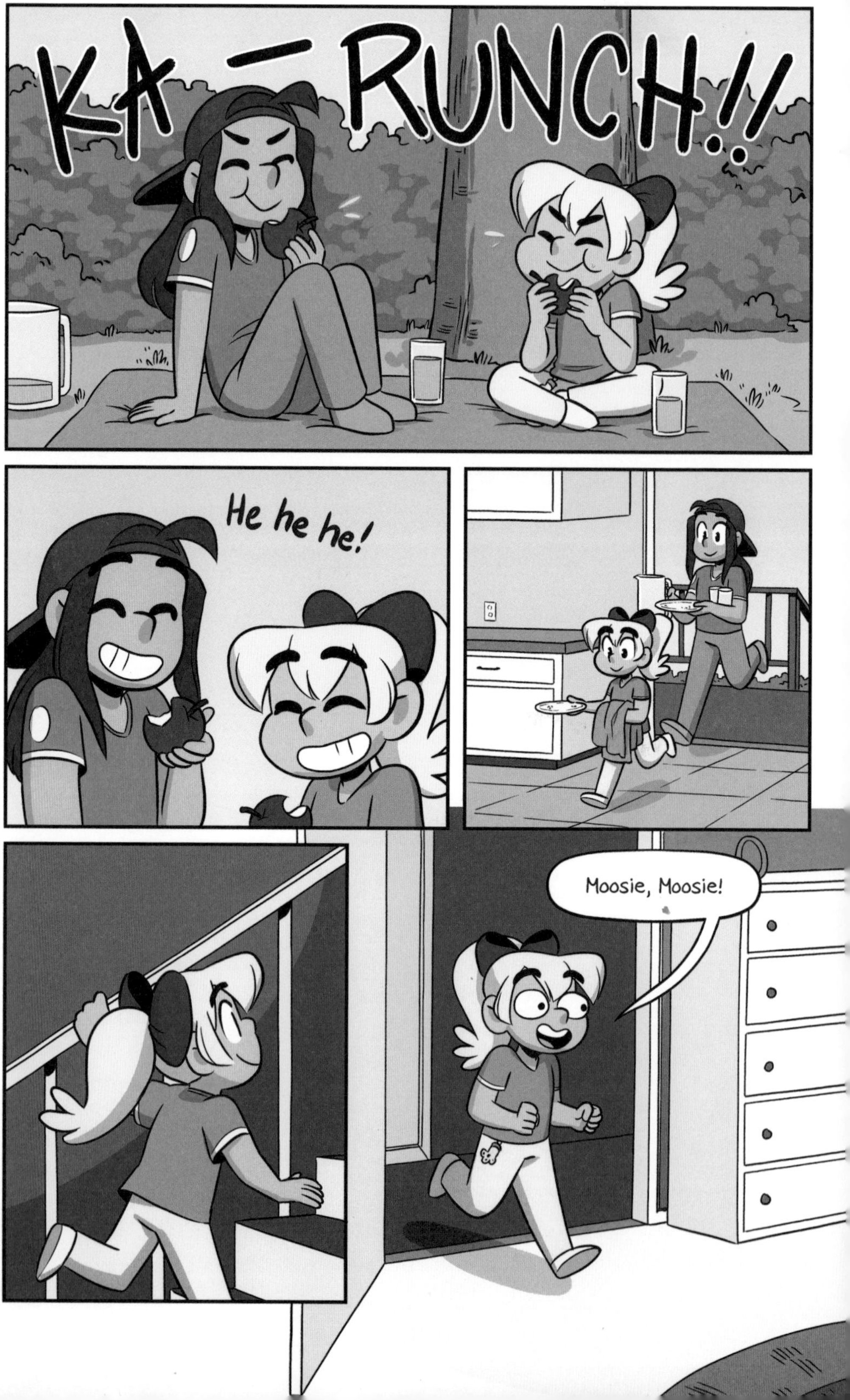
KA-RUNCH!!
He he he!
Moosie, Moosie!

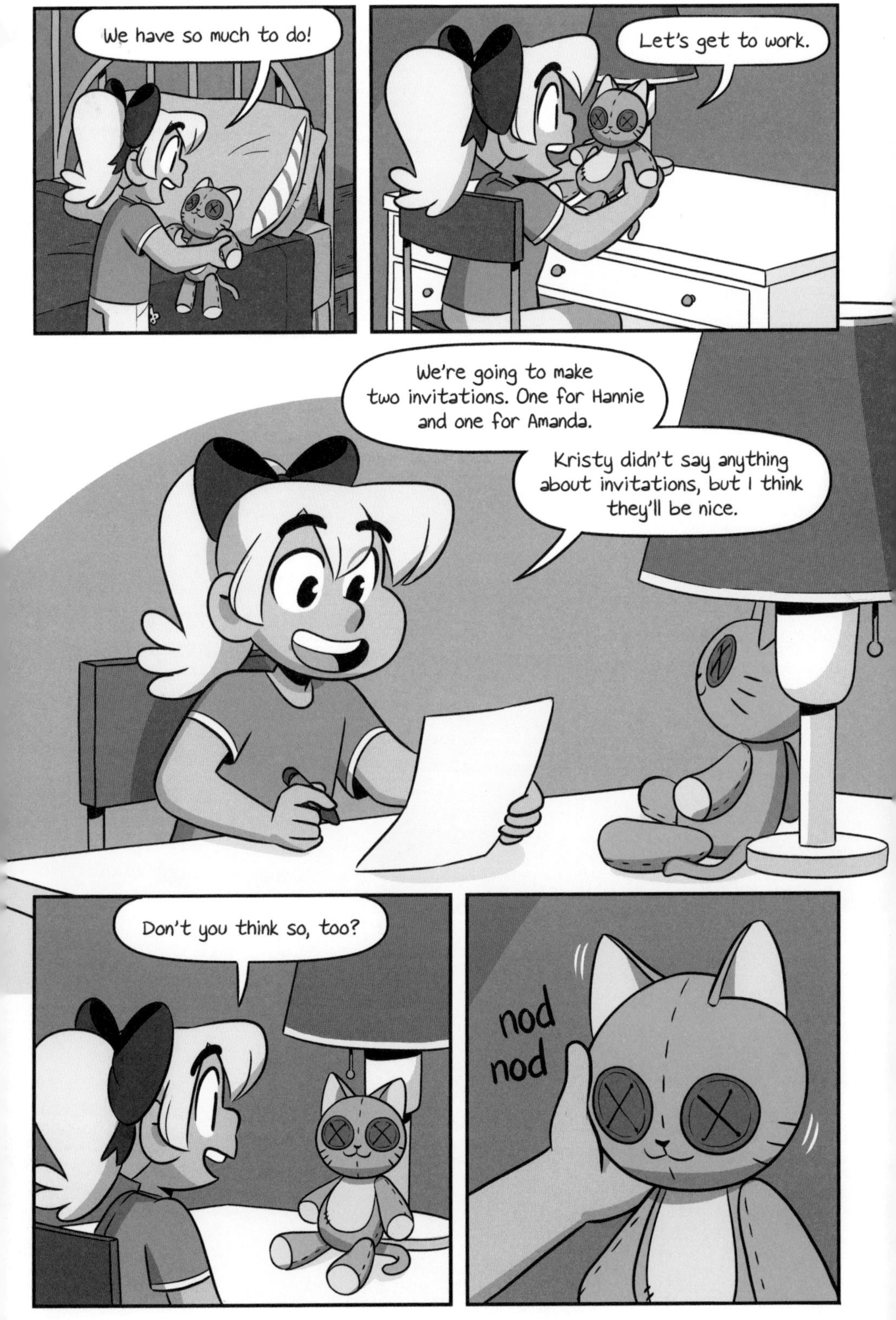
We have so much to do!
Let's get to work.
We're going to make two invitations. One for Hannie and one for Amanda.
Kristy didn't say anything about invitations, but I think they'll be nice.
Don't you think so, too?
nod nod

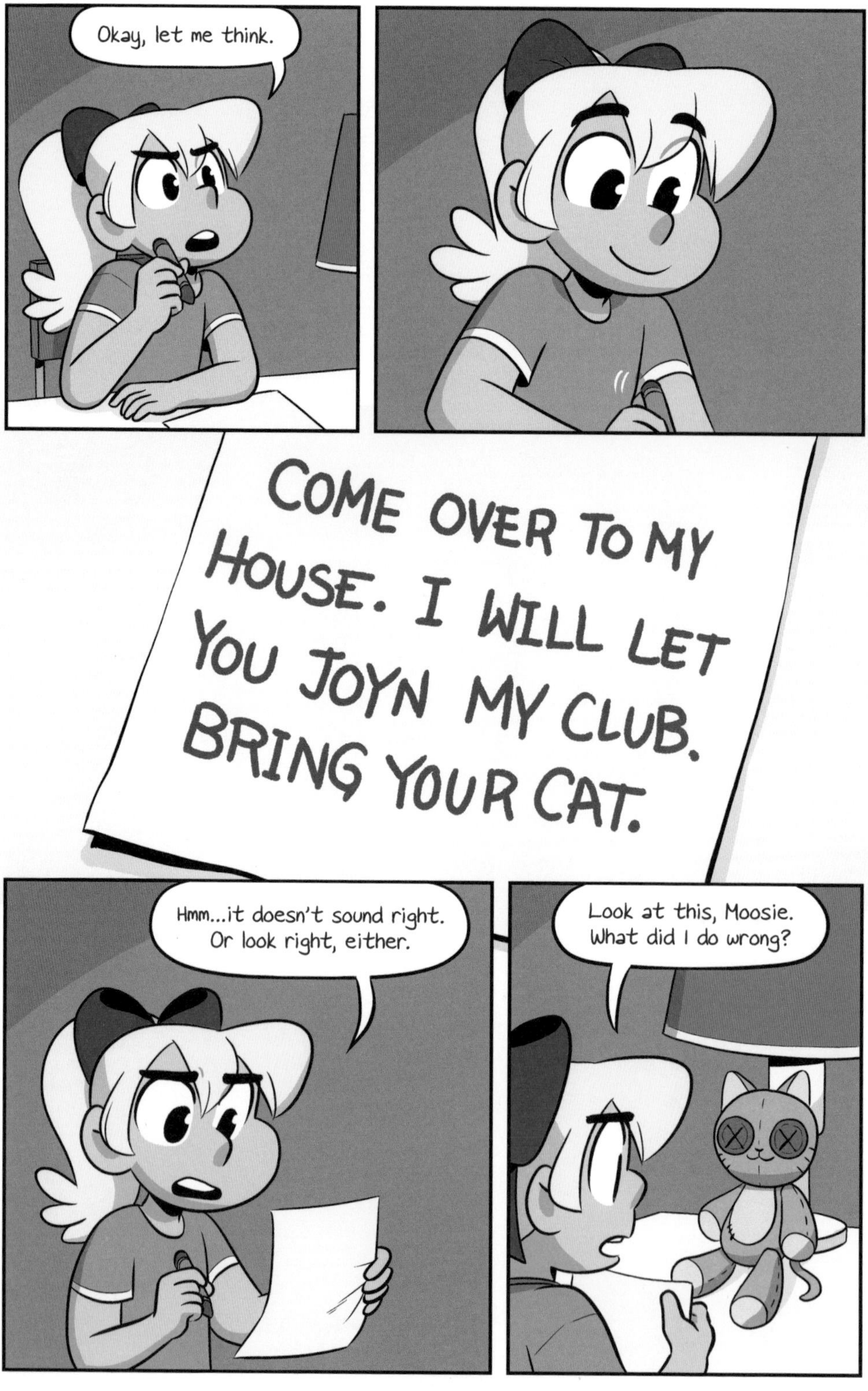
Okay, let me think.
COME OVER TO MY HOUSE. I WILL LET YOU JOYN MY CLUB. BRING YOUR CAT.
Hmm...it doesn't sound right. Or look right, either.
Look at this, Moosie. What did I do wrong?

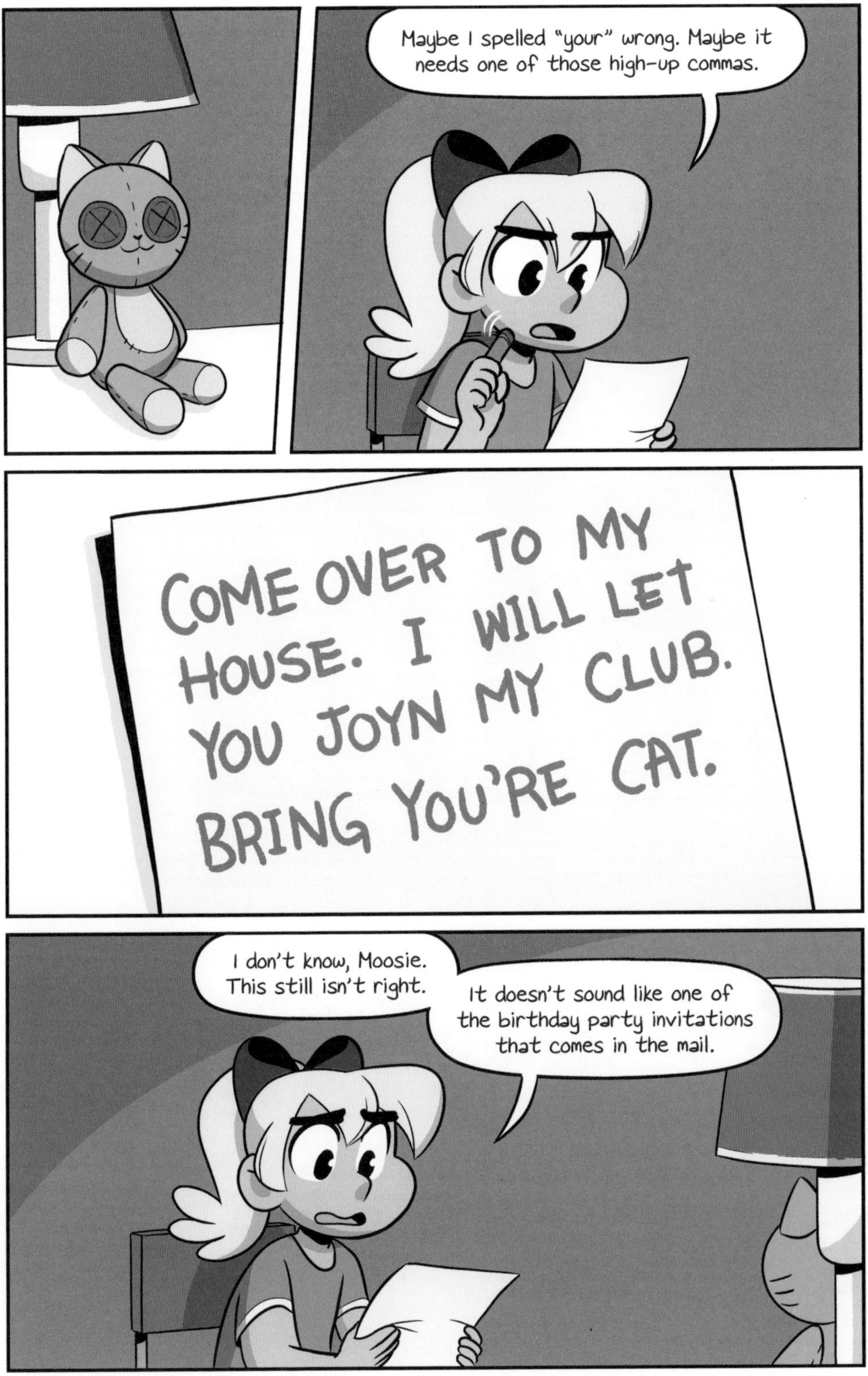
Maybe I spelled "your" wrong. Maybe it needs one of those high-up commas.
COME OVER TO MY HOUSE. I WILL LET YOU JOYN MY CLUB. BRING YOU'RE CAT.
I don't know, Moosie. This still isn't right.
It doesn't sound like one of the birthday party invitations that comes in the mail.

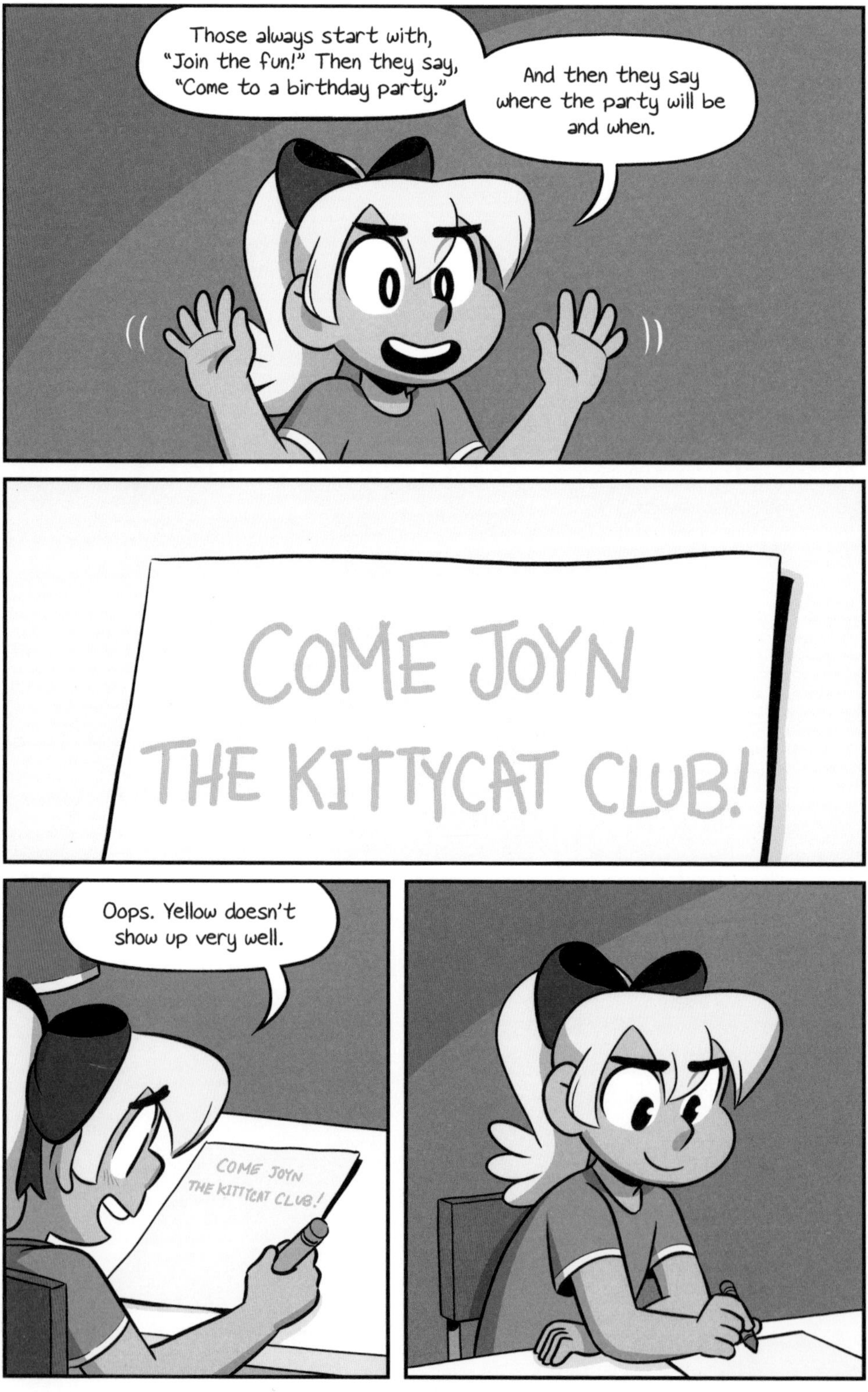

Those always start with, "Join the fun!" Then they say, "Come to a birthday party."
And then they say where the party will be and when.
COME JOYN THE KITTYCAT CLUB!
Oops. Yellow doesn't show up very well.
COME JOYN THE KITTYCAT CLUB!

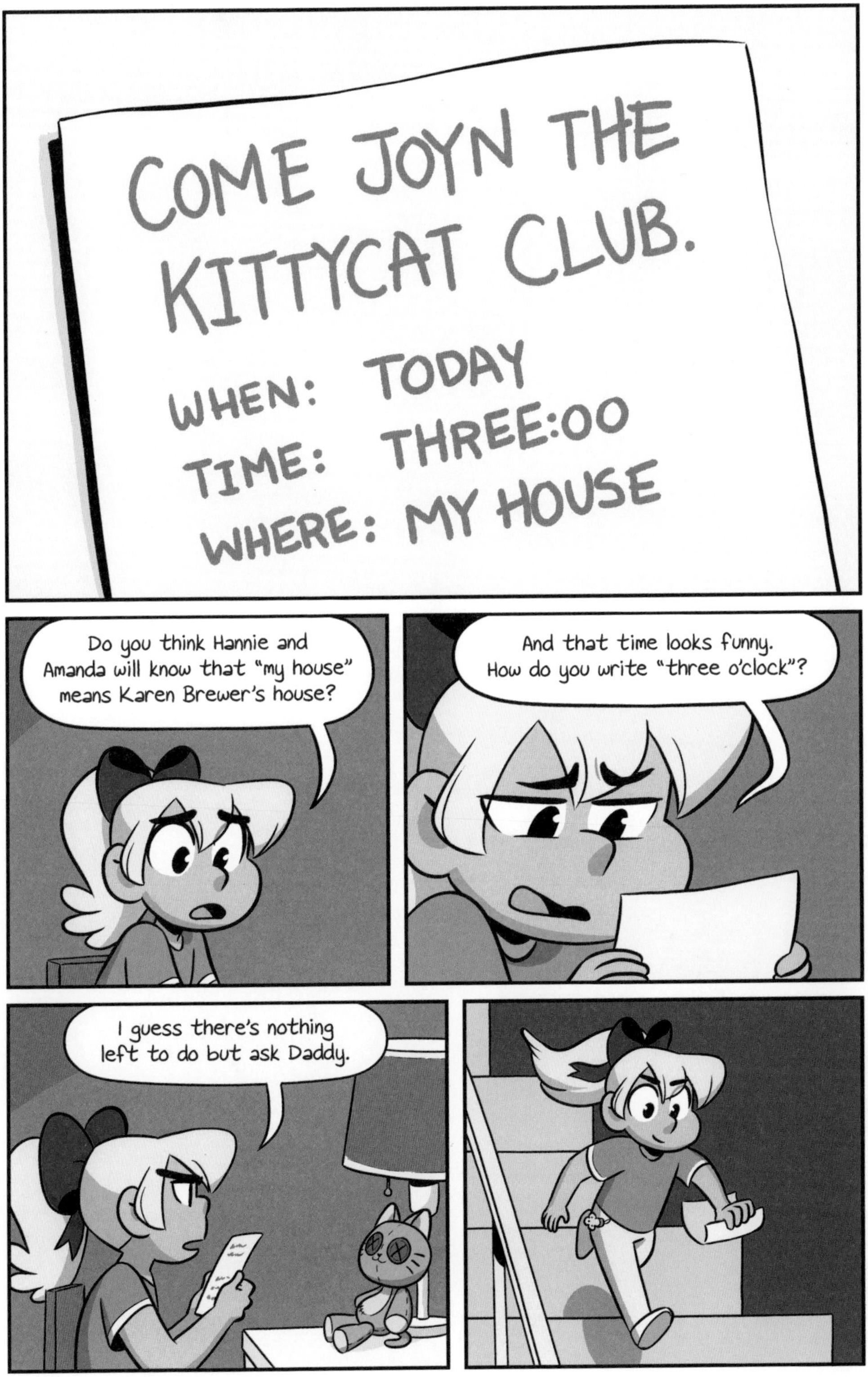
COME JOYN THE KITTYCAT CLUB.
WHEN: TODAY
TIME: THREE:00
WHERE: MY HOUSE
Do you think Hannie and Amanda will know that "my house" means Karen Brewer's house?
And that time looks funny. How do you write "three o'clock"?
I guess there's nothing left to do but ask Daddy.

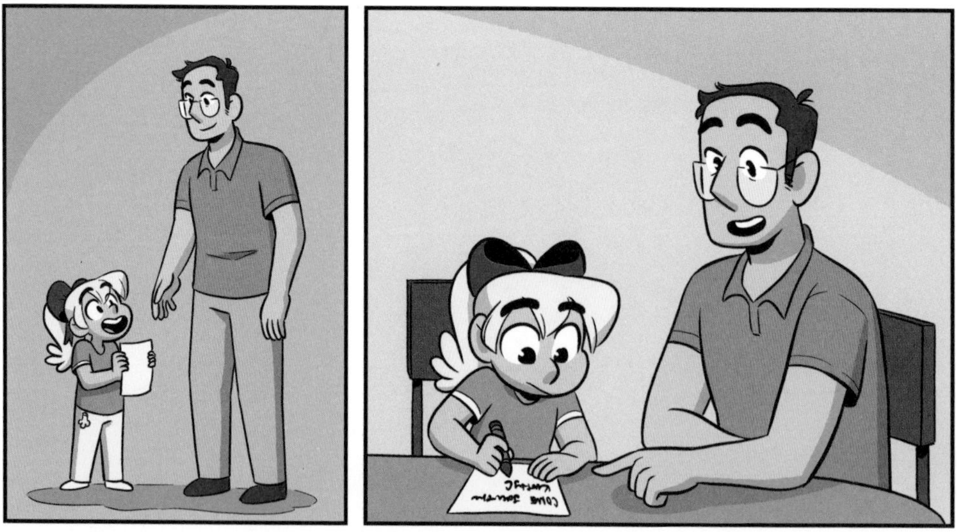

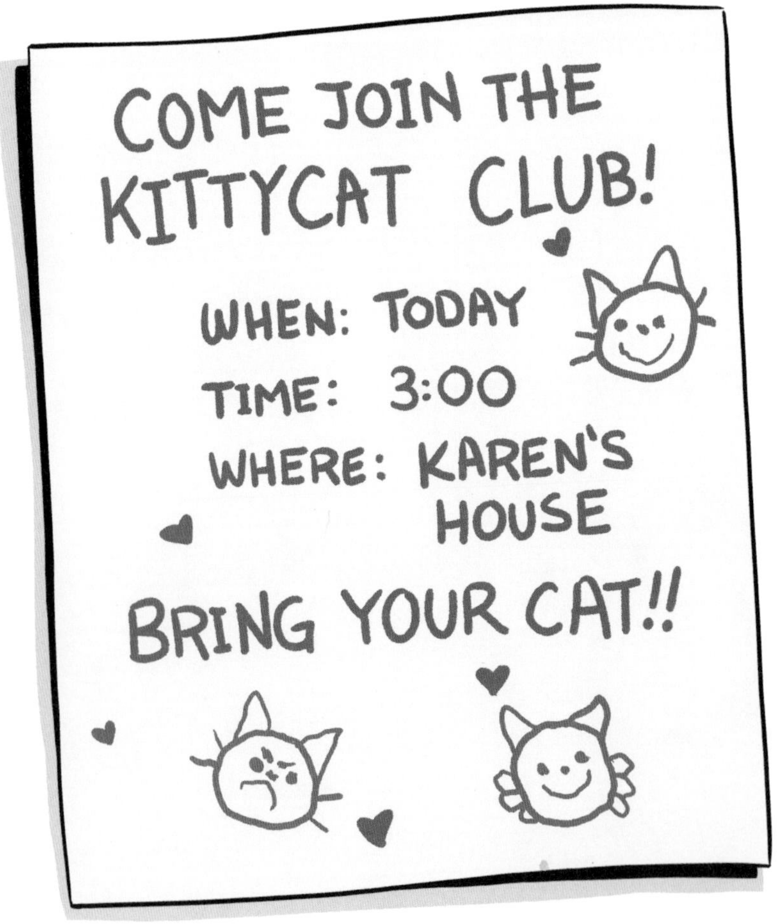
COME JOIN THE KITTYCAT CLUB!
WHEN: TODAY
TIME: 3:00
WHERE: KAREN'S HOUSE
BRING YOUR CAT!!

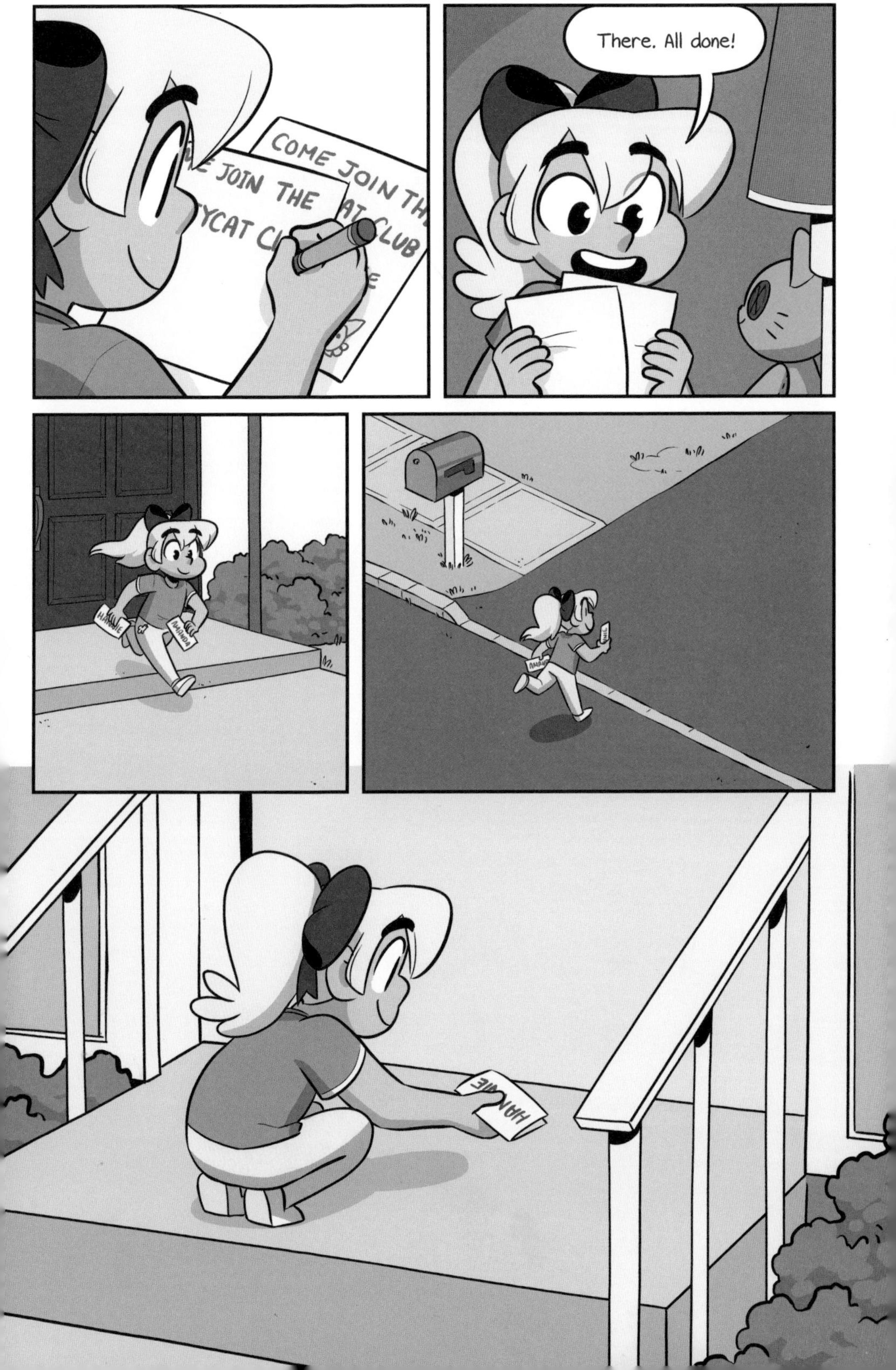

There. All done!
HANNIE
AMANDA

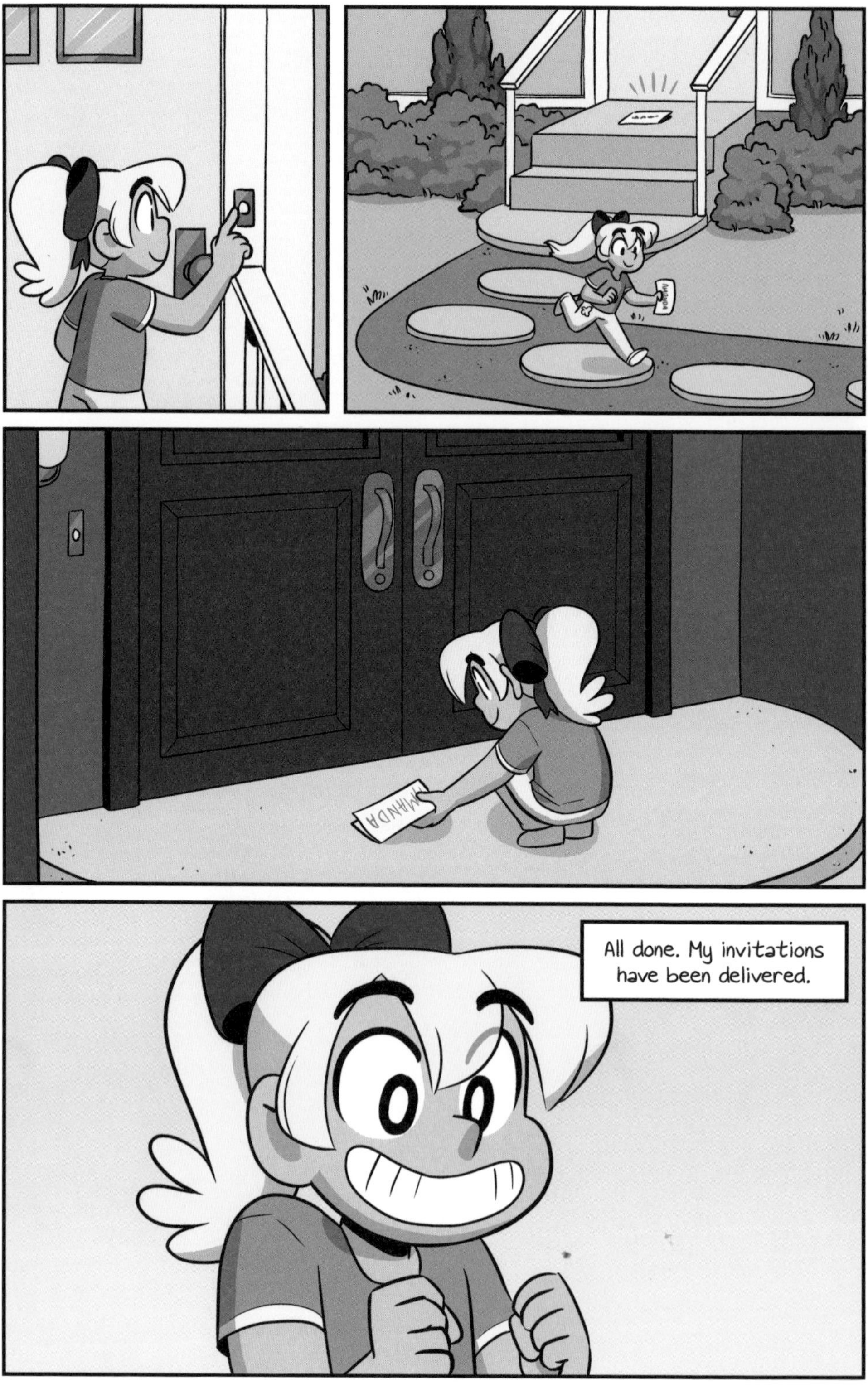
All done. My invitations have been delivered.

CHAPTER 4

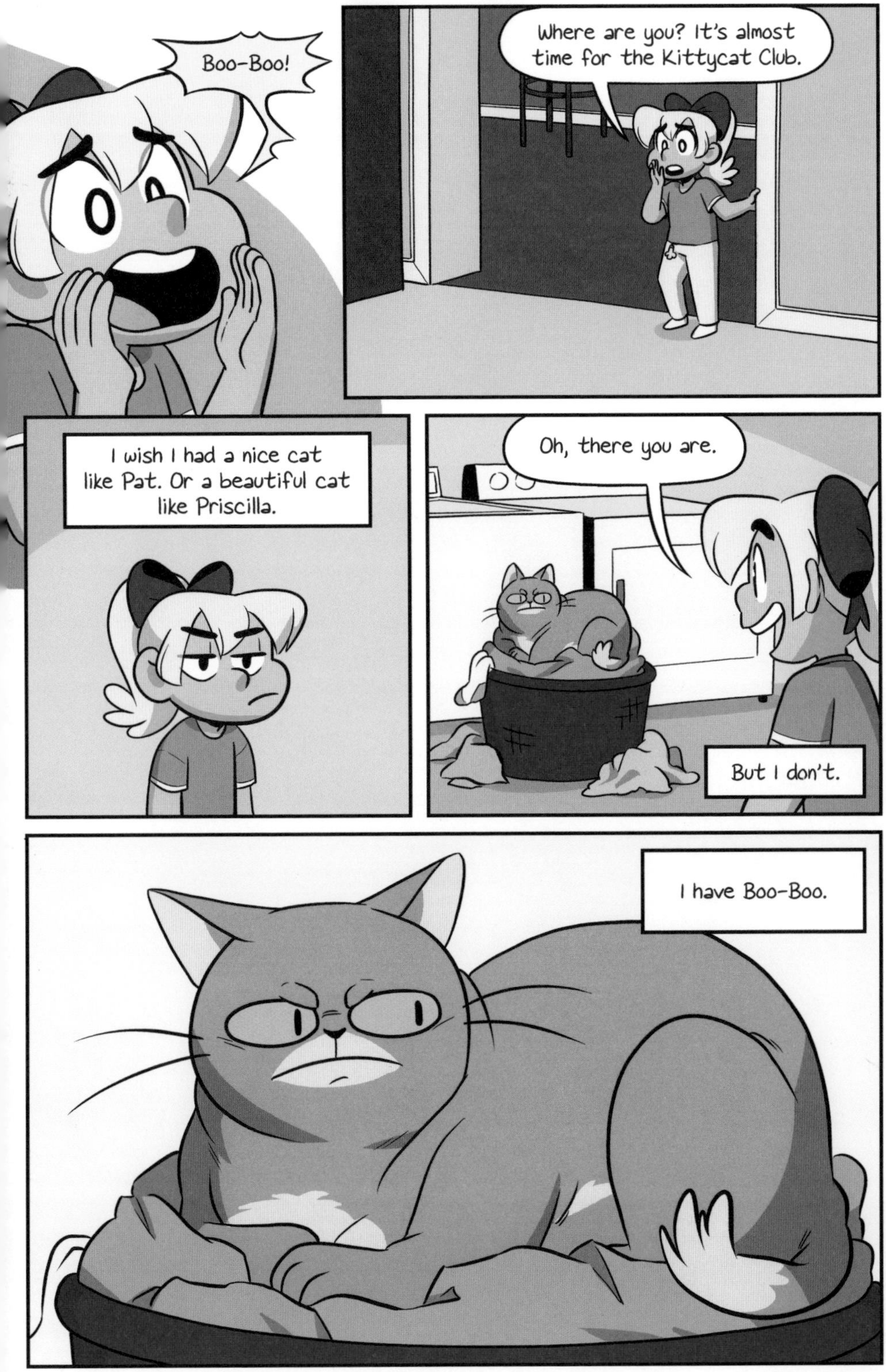
Boo-Boo!
Where are you? It's almost time for the Kittycat Club.
I wish I had a nice cat like Pat. Or a beautiful cat like Priscilla.
Oh, there you are.
But I don't.
I have Boo-Boo.

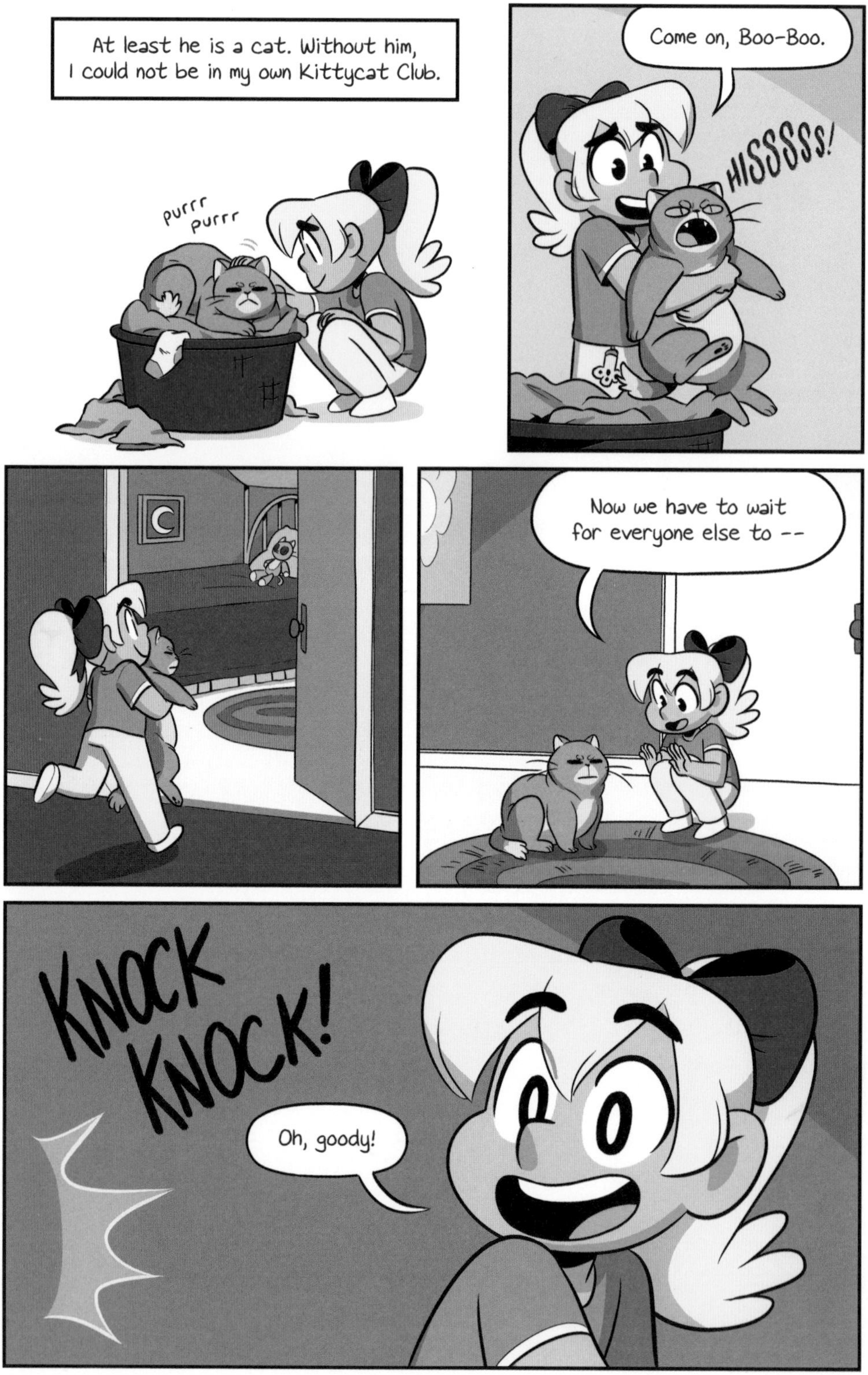

At least he is a cat. Without him, I could not be in my own Kittycat Club.
purrr purrr
Come on, Boo-Boo.
HISSSSS!
Now we have to wait for everyone else to --
KNOCK KNOCK!
Oh, goody!

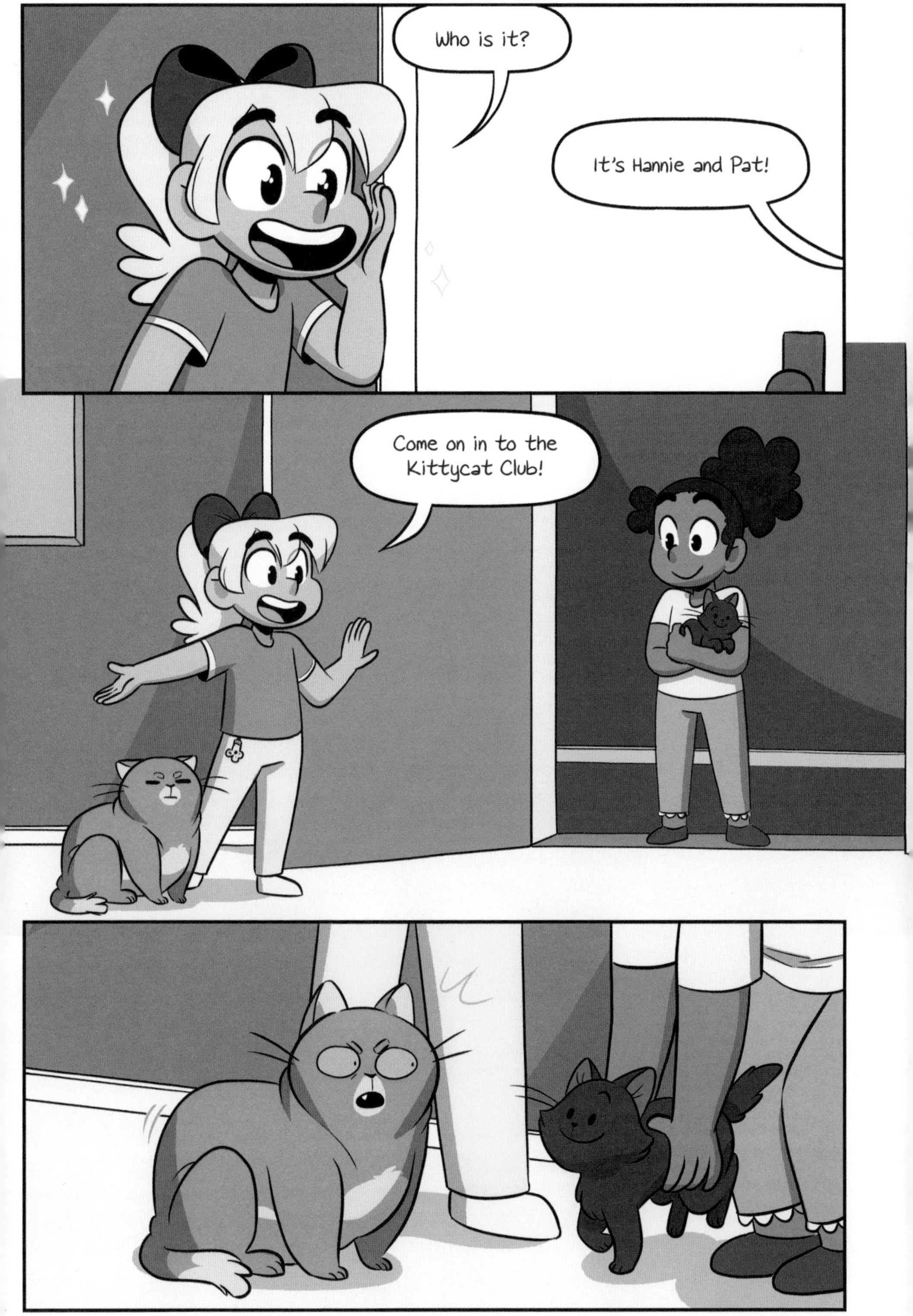
Who is it?
It's Hannie and Pat!
Come on in to the Kittycat Club!

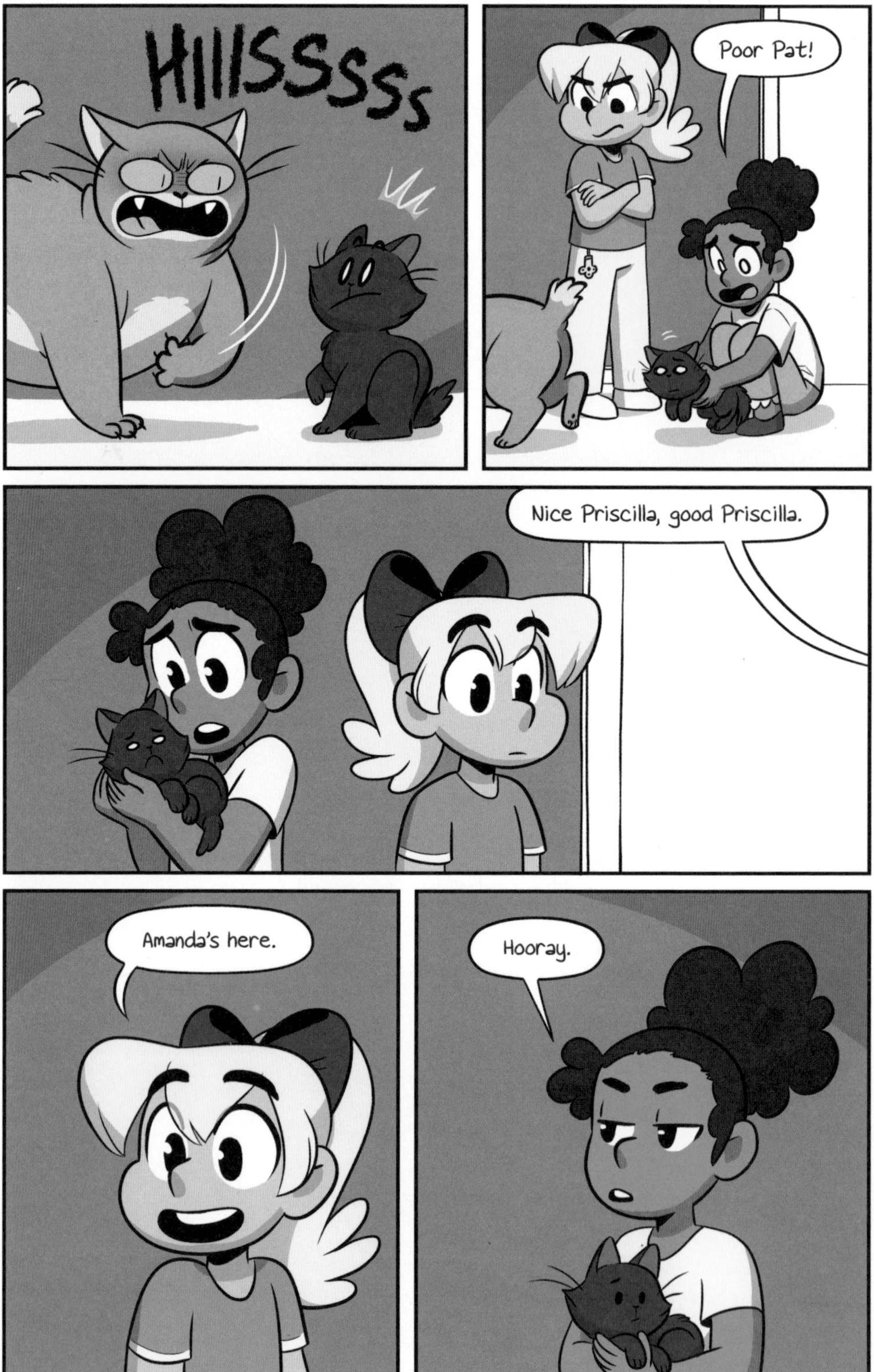
HIIISSSSSS
Poor Pat!
Nice Priscilla, good Priscilla.
Amanda's here.
Hooray.

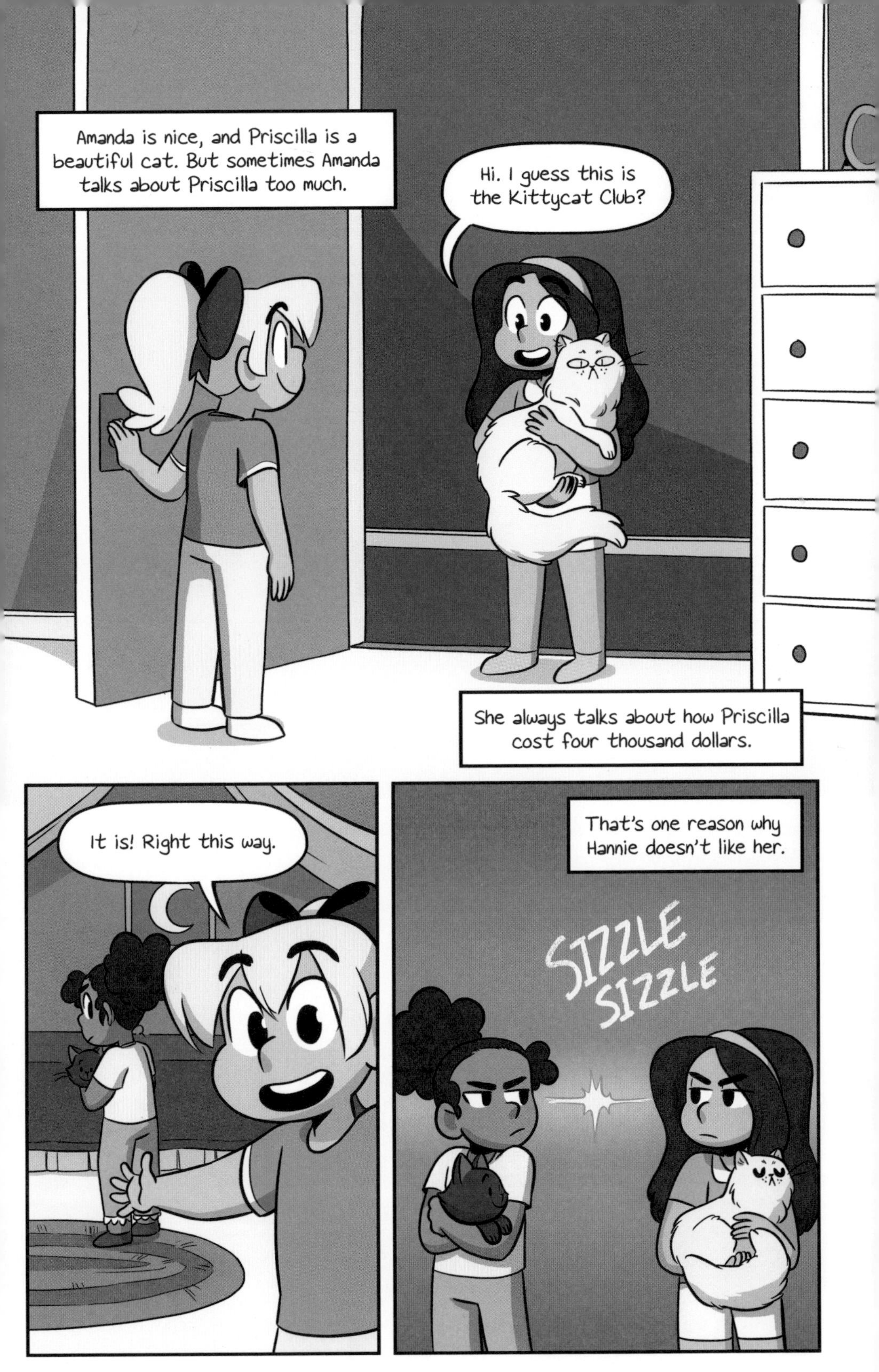
Amanda is nice, and Priscilla is a beautiful cat. But sometimes Amanda talks about Priscilla too much.
Hi. I guess this is the Kittycat Club?
She always talks about how Priscilla cost four thousand dollars.
It is! Right this way.
That's one reason why Hannie doesn't like her.
SIZZLE
SIZZLE

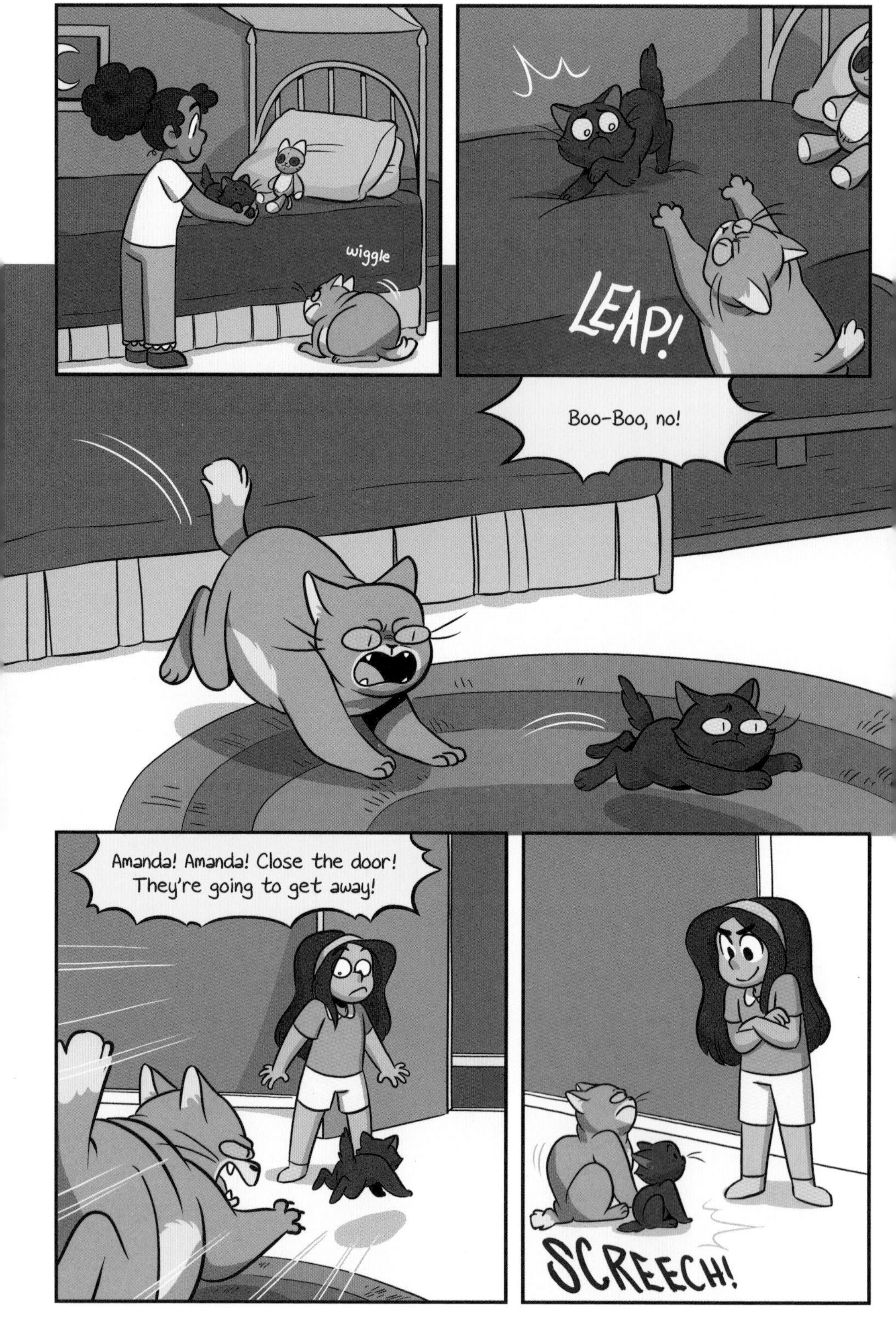
wiggle
LEAP!
Boo-Boo, no!
Amanda! Amanda! Close the door! They're going to get away!
SCREECH!

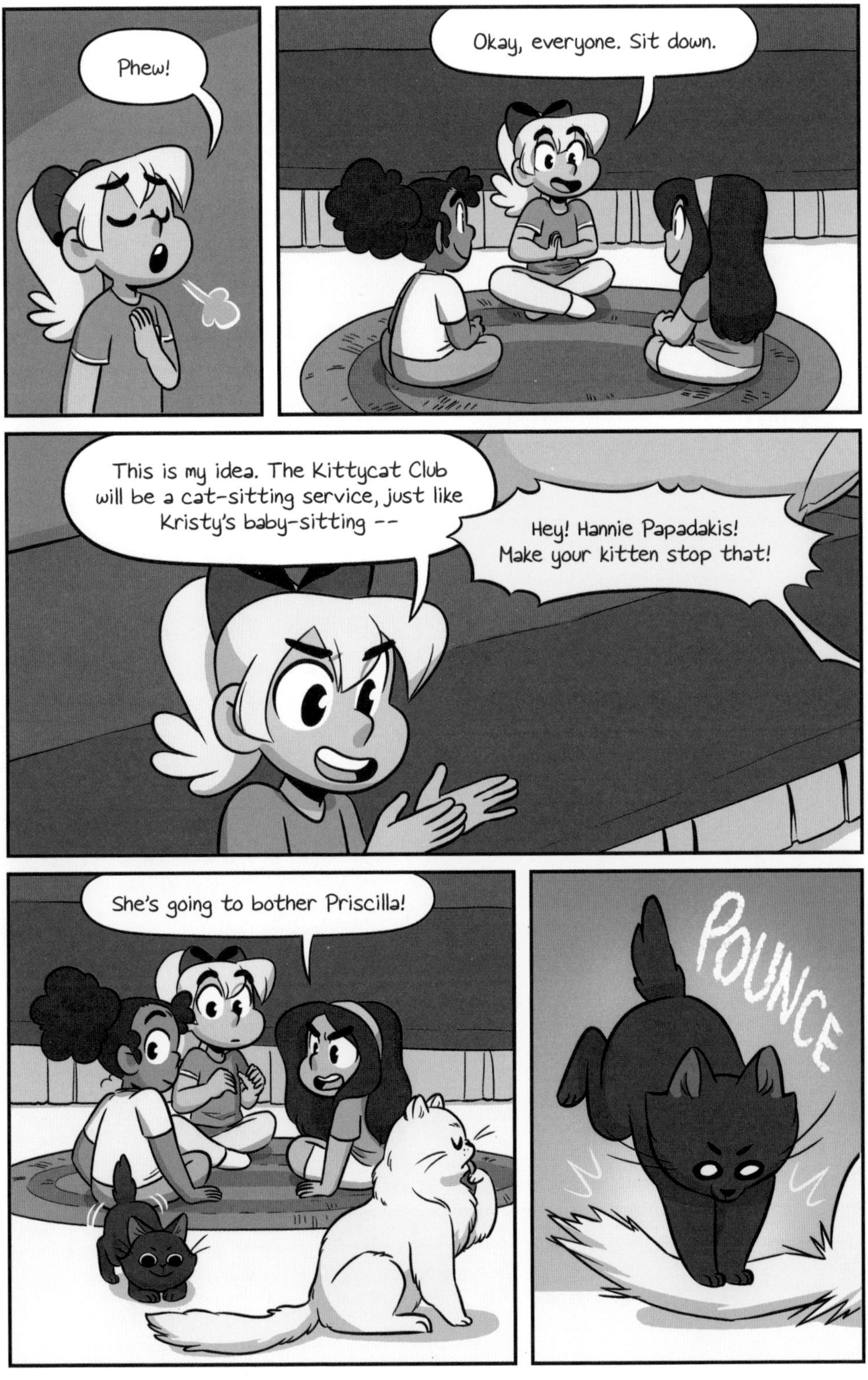
Phew!
Okay, everyone. Sit down.
This is my idea. The Kittycat Club will be a cat-sitting service, just like Kristy's baby-sitting --
Hey! Hannie Papadakis! Make your kitten stop that!
She's going to bother Priscilla!
POUNCE

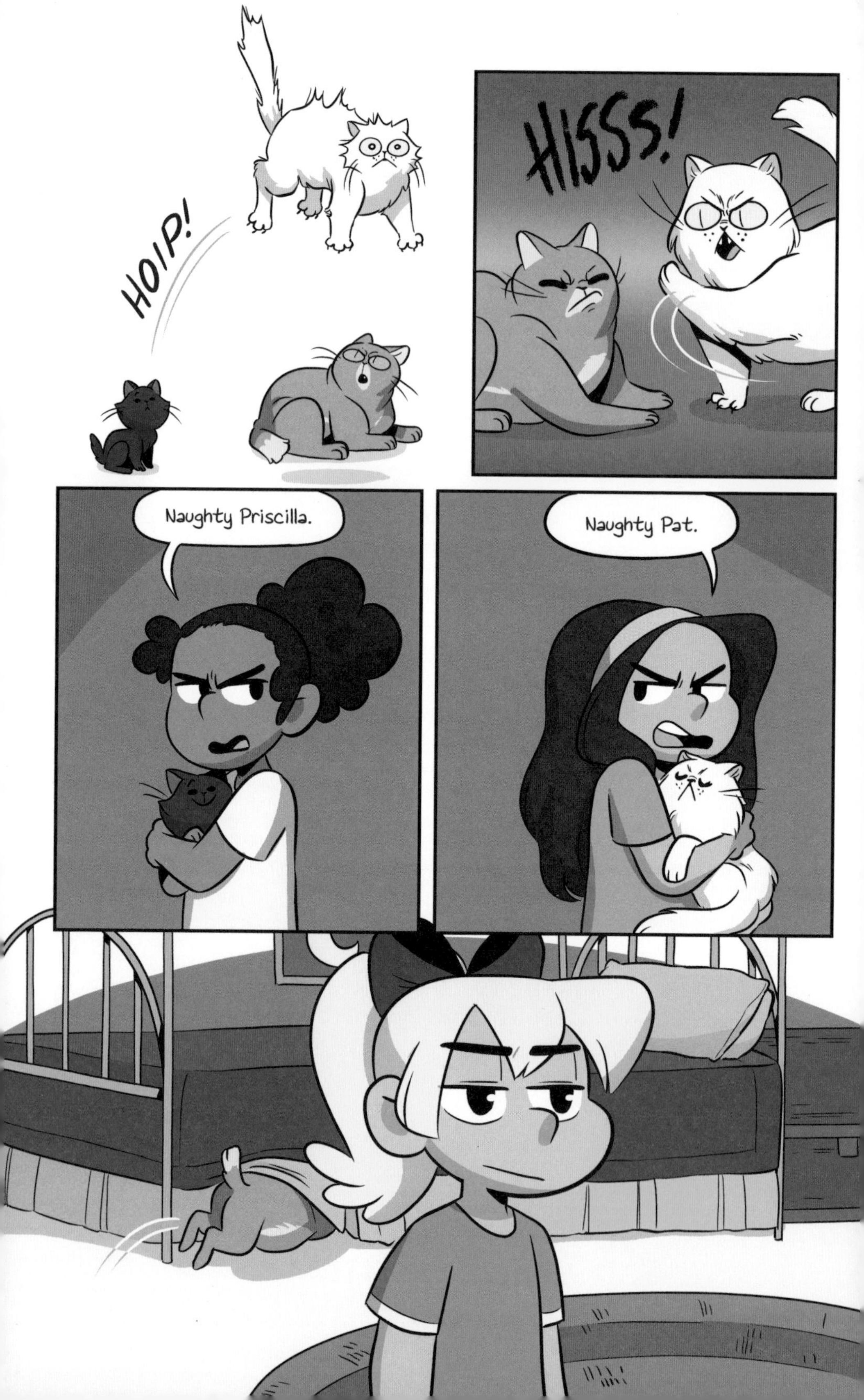
HOIP!
HISSS!
Naughty Priscilla.
Naughty Pat.

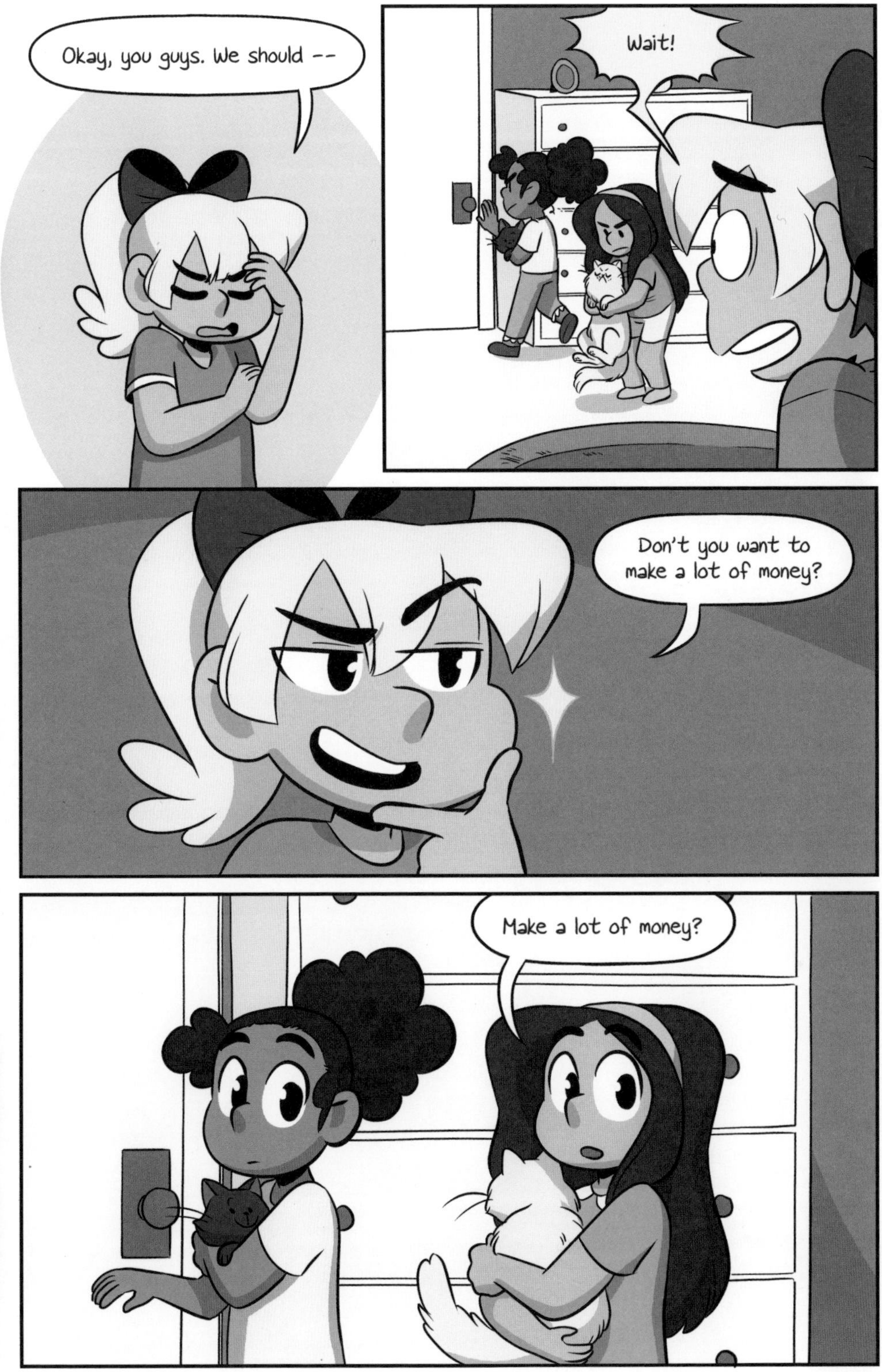
Okay, you guys. We should --
Wait!
Don't you want to make a lot of money?
Make a lot of money?

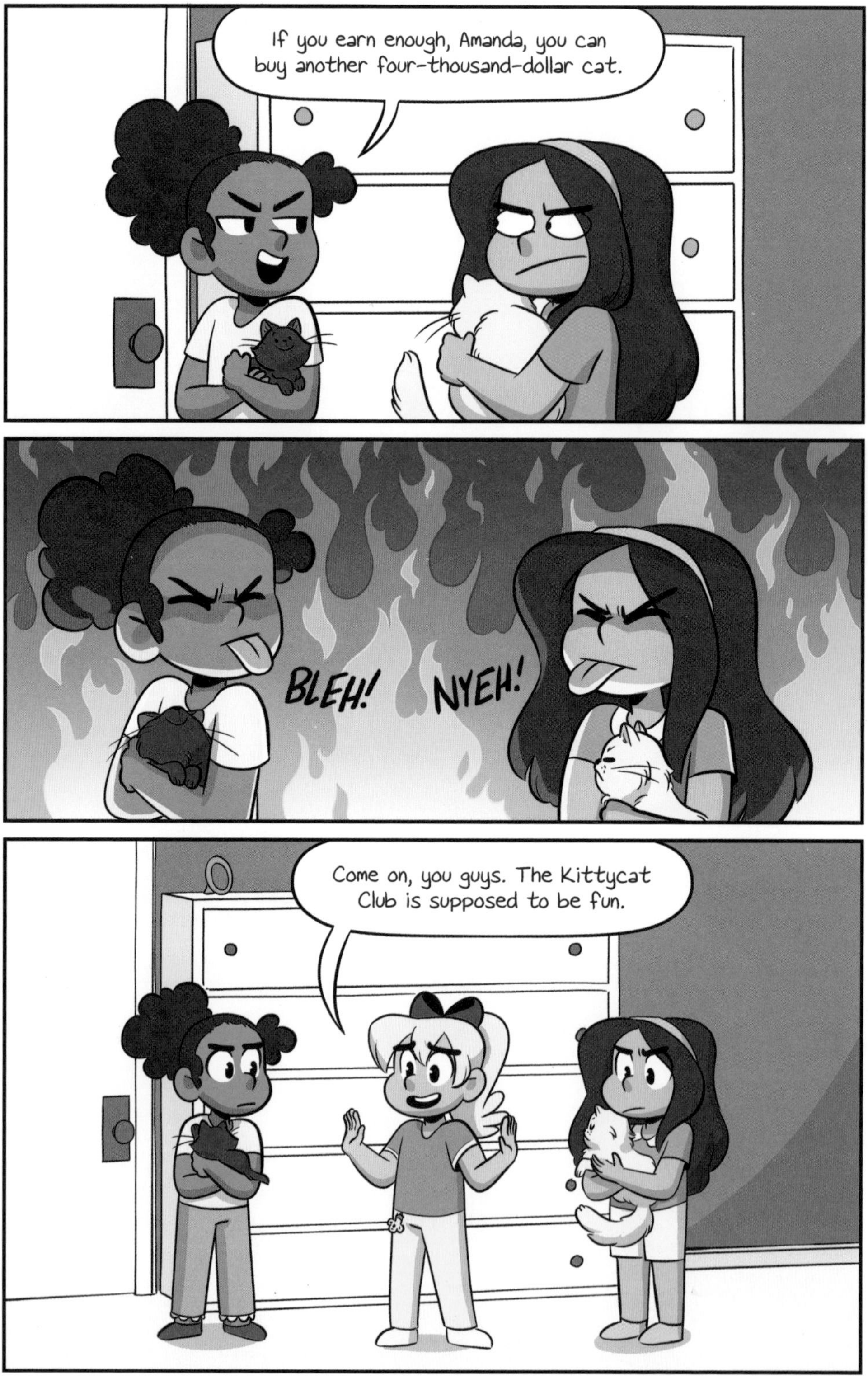
If you earn enough, Amanda, you can buy another four-thousand-dollar cat.
BLEH!
NYEH!
Come on, you guys. The Kittycat Club is supposed to be fun.

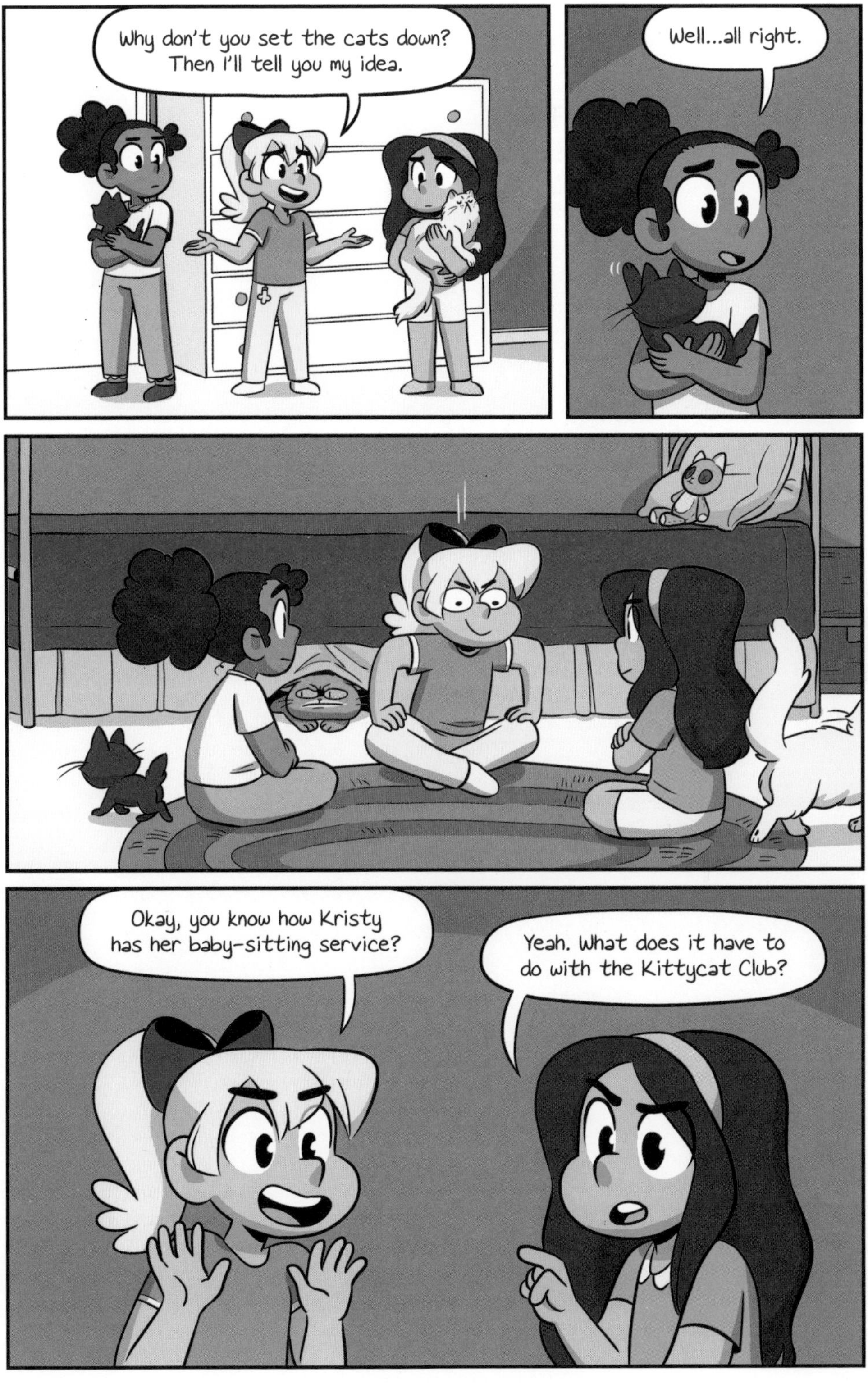
Why don't you set the cats down? Then I'll tell you my idea.
Well...all right.
Okay, you know how Kristy has her baby-sitting service?
Yeah. What does it have to do with the Kittycat Club?

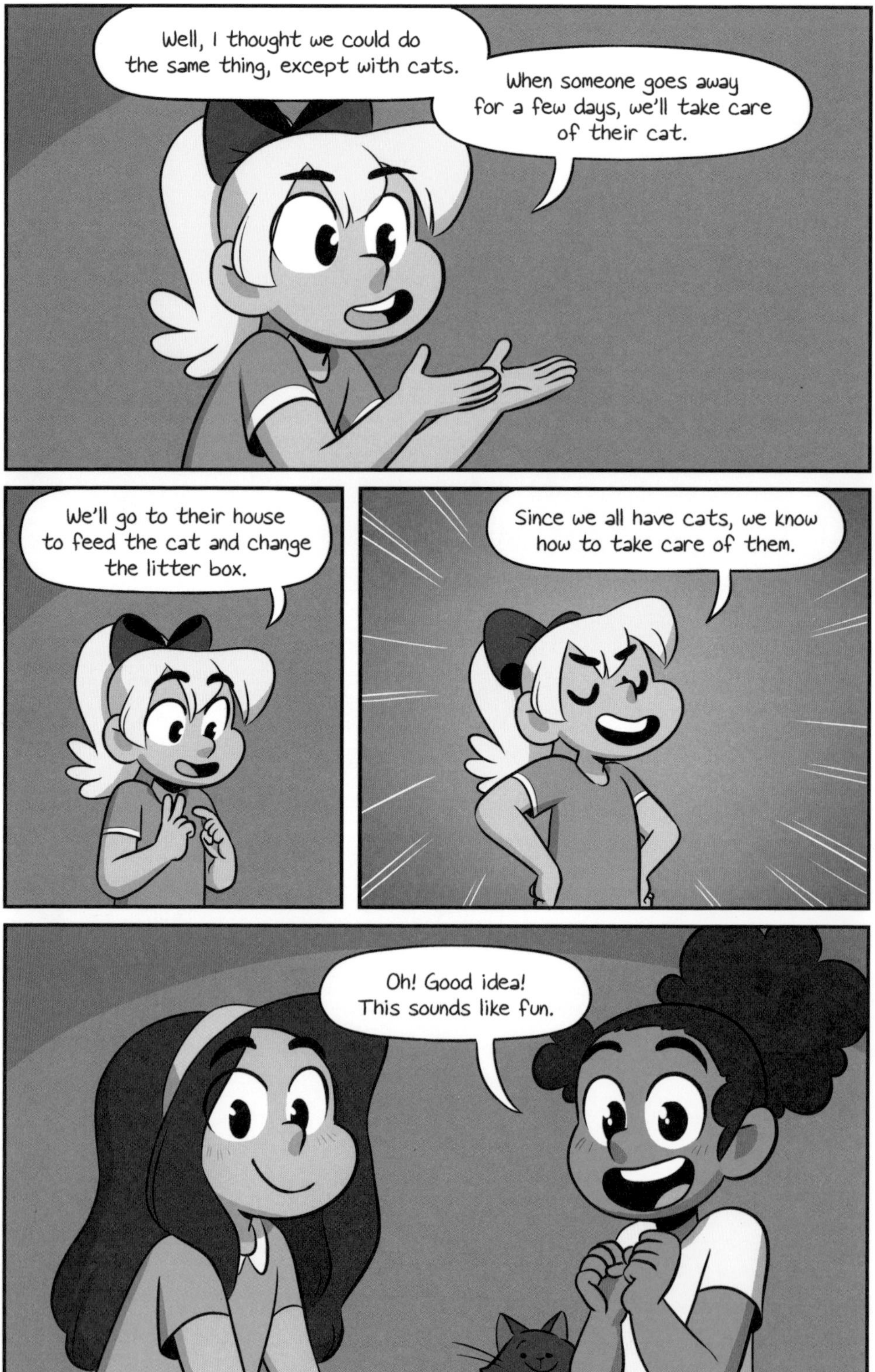
Well, I thought we could do the same thing, except with cats.
When someone goes away for a few days, we'll take care of their cat.
We'll go to their house to feed the cat and change the litter box.
Since we all have cats, we know how to take care of them.
Oh! Good idea! This sounds like fun.

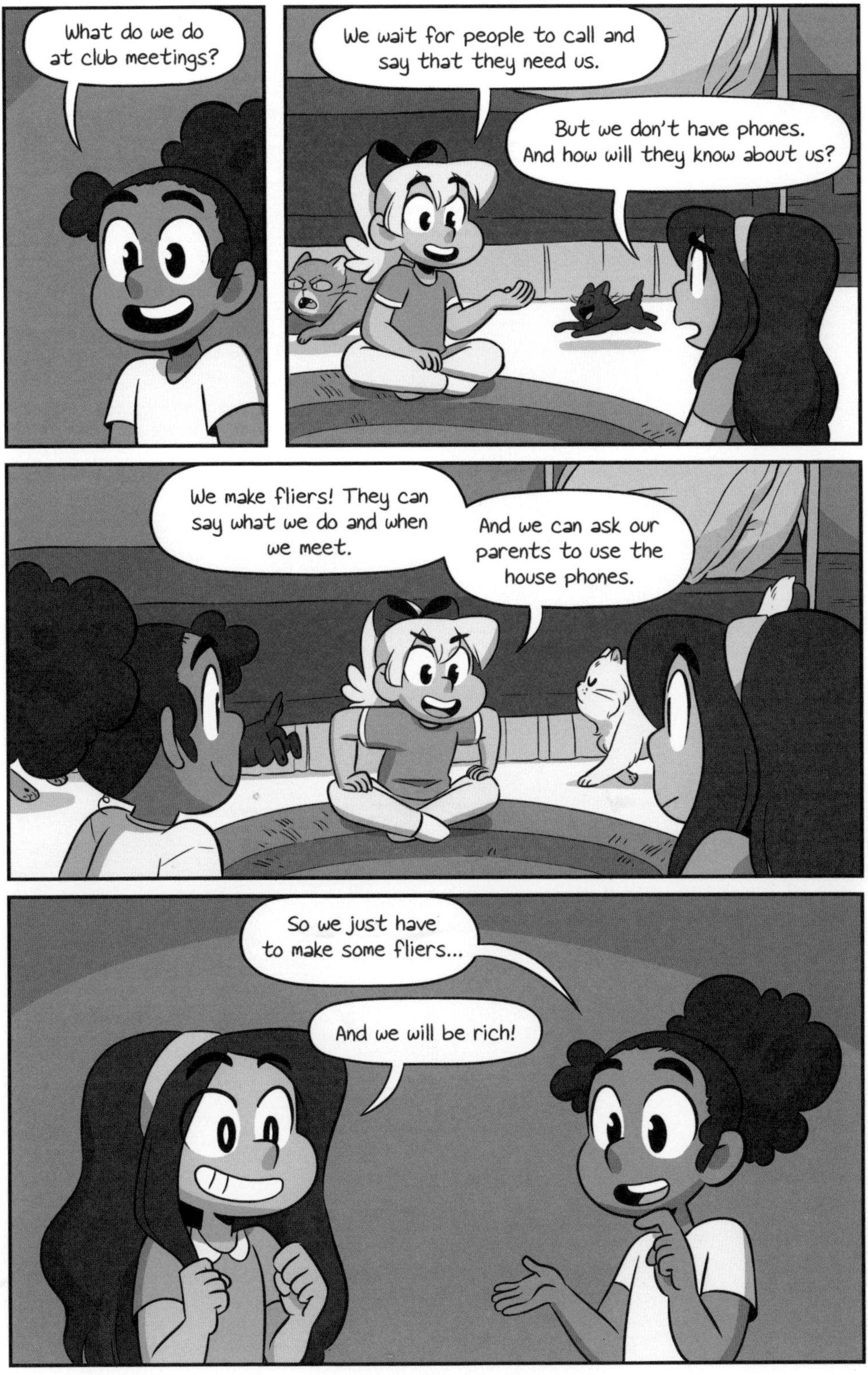
What do we do at club meetings?
We wait for people to call and say that they need us.
But we don't have phones. And how will they know about us?
We make fliers! They can say what we do and when we meet.
And we can ask our parents to use the house phones.
So we just have to make some fliers...
And we will be rich!

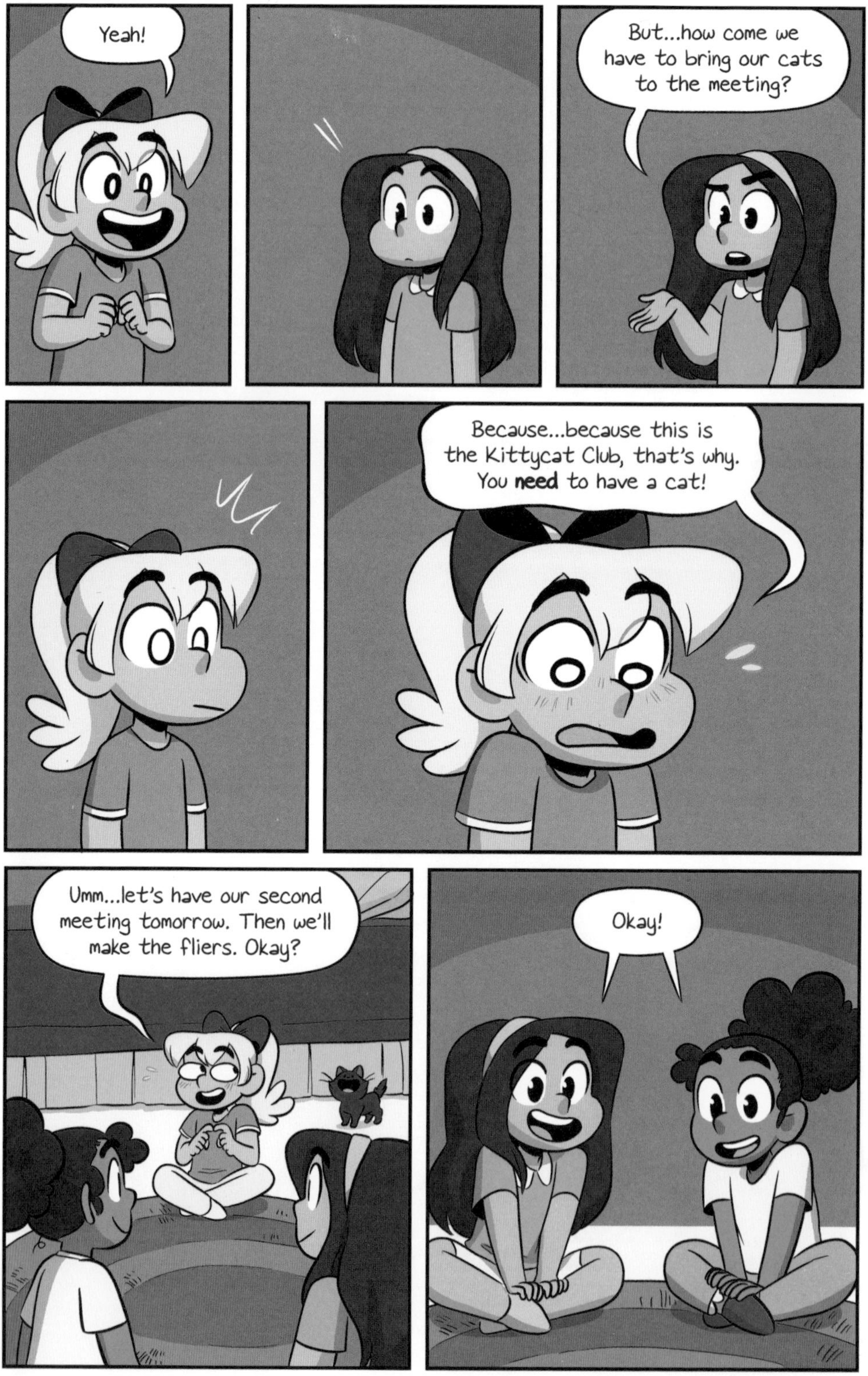
Yeah!
But...how come we have to bring our cats to the meeting?
Because...because this is the Kittycat Club, that's why. You **need** to have a cat!
Umm...let's have our second meeting tomorrow. Then we'll make the fliers. Okay?
Okay!

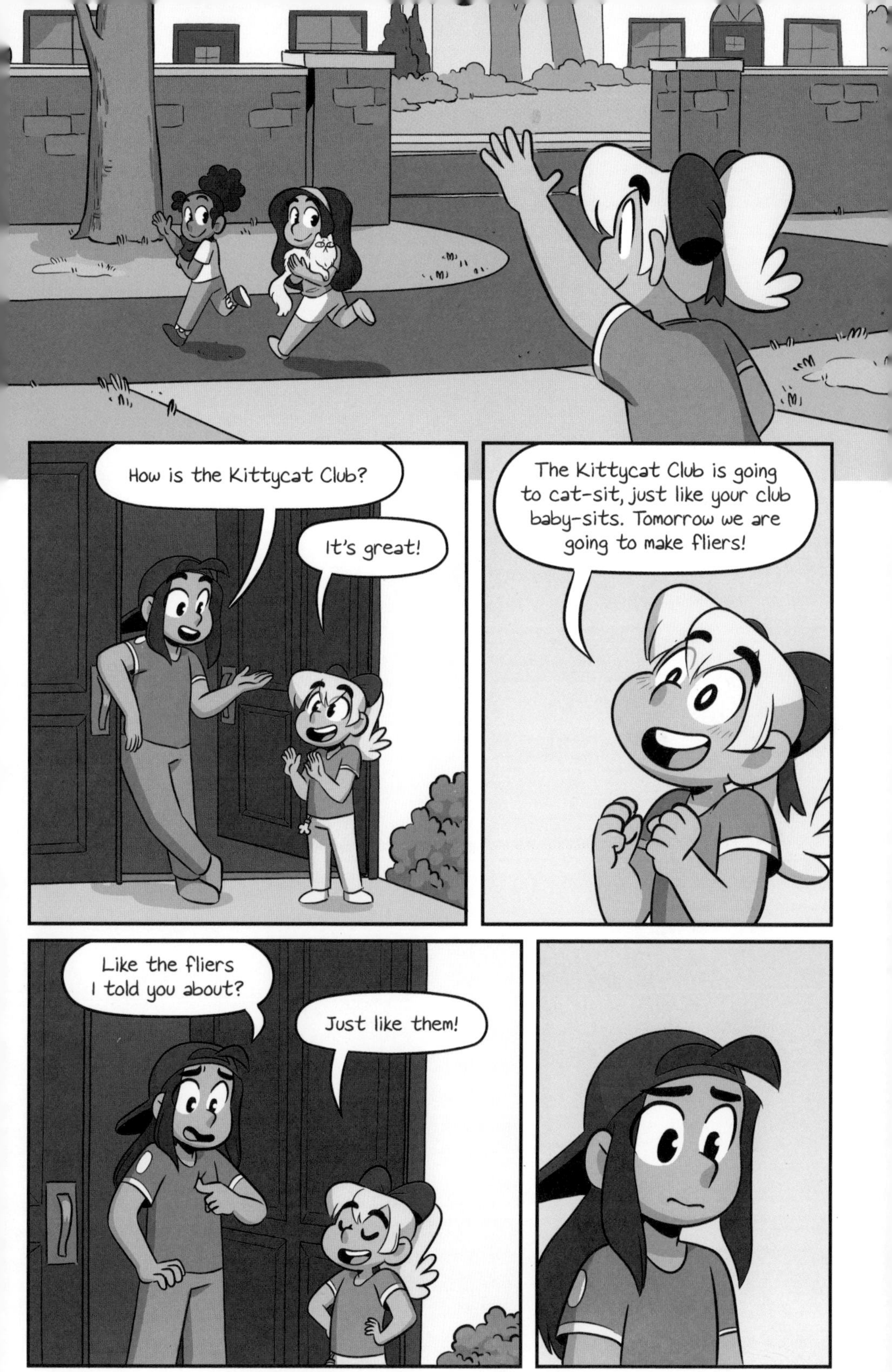
How is the Kittycat Club?
It's great!
The Kittycat Club is going to cat-sit, just like your club baby-sits. Tomorrow we are going to make fliers!
Like the fliers I told you about?
Just like them!

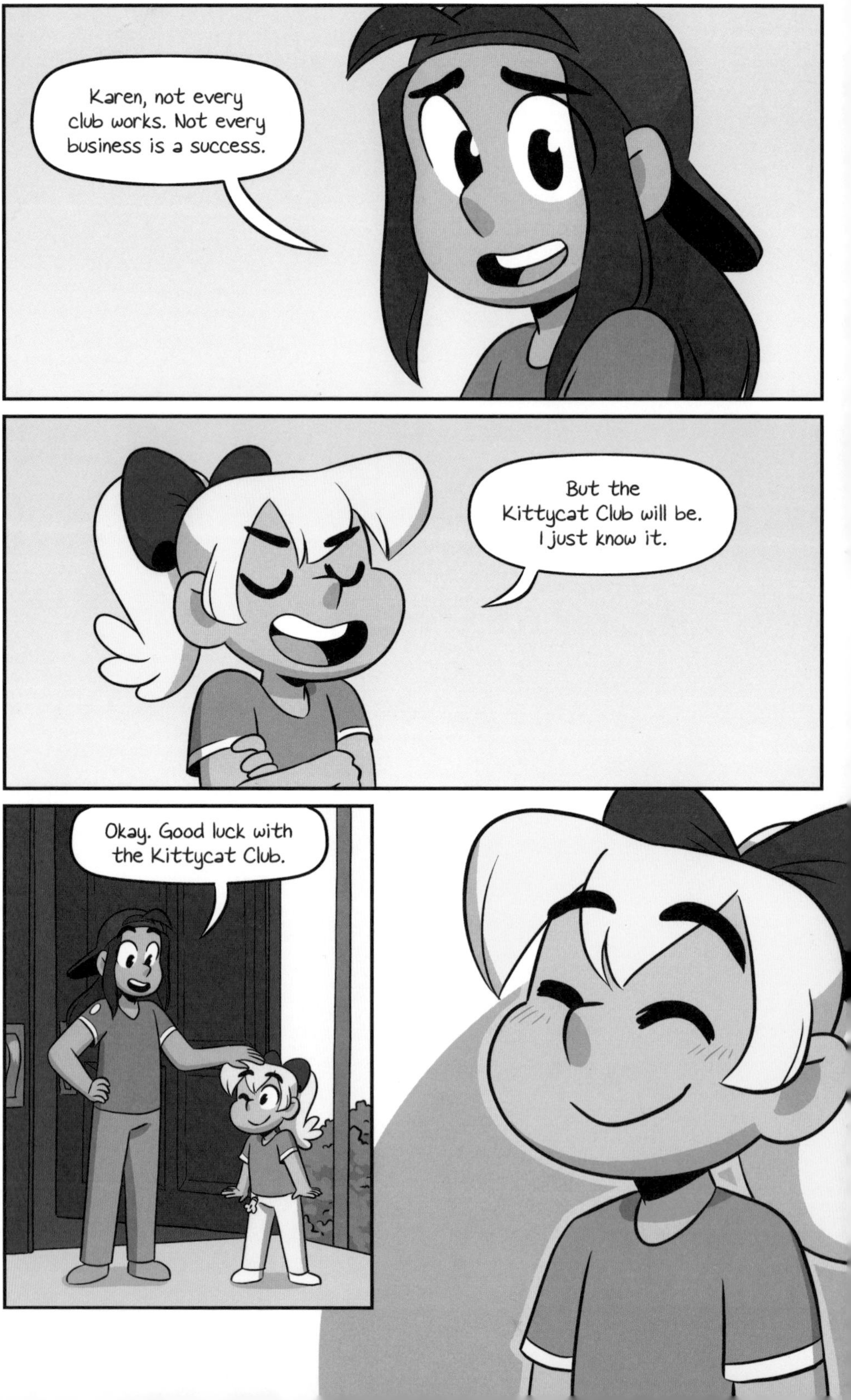
Karen, not every club works. Not every business is a success.
But the Kittycat Club will be. I just know it.
Okay. Good luck with the Kittycat Club.

CHAPTER 5

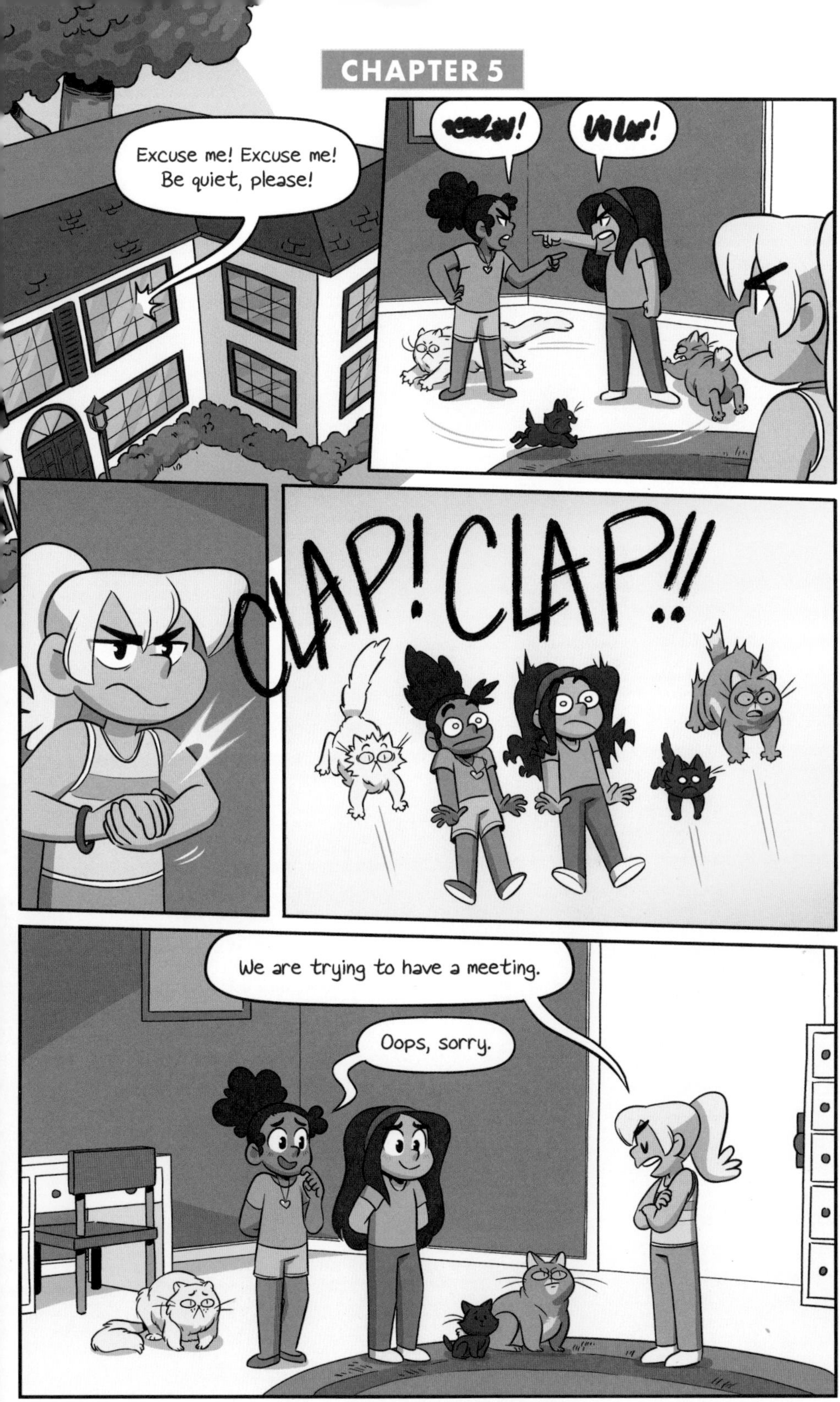
Excuse me! Excuse me! Be quiet, please!
CLAP! CLAP!!
We are trying to have a meeting.
Oops, sorry.

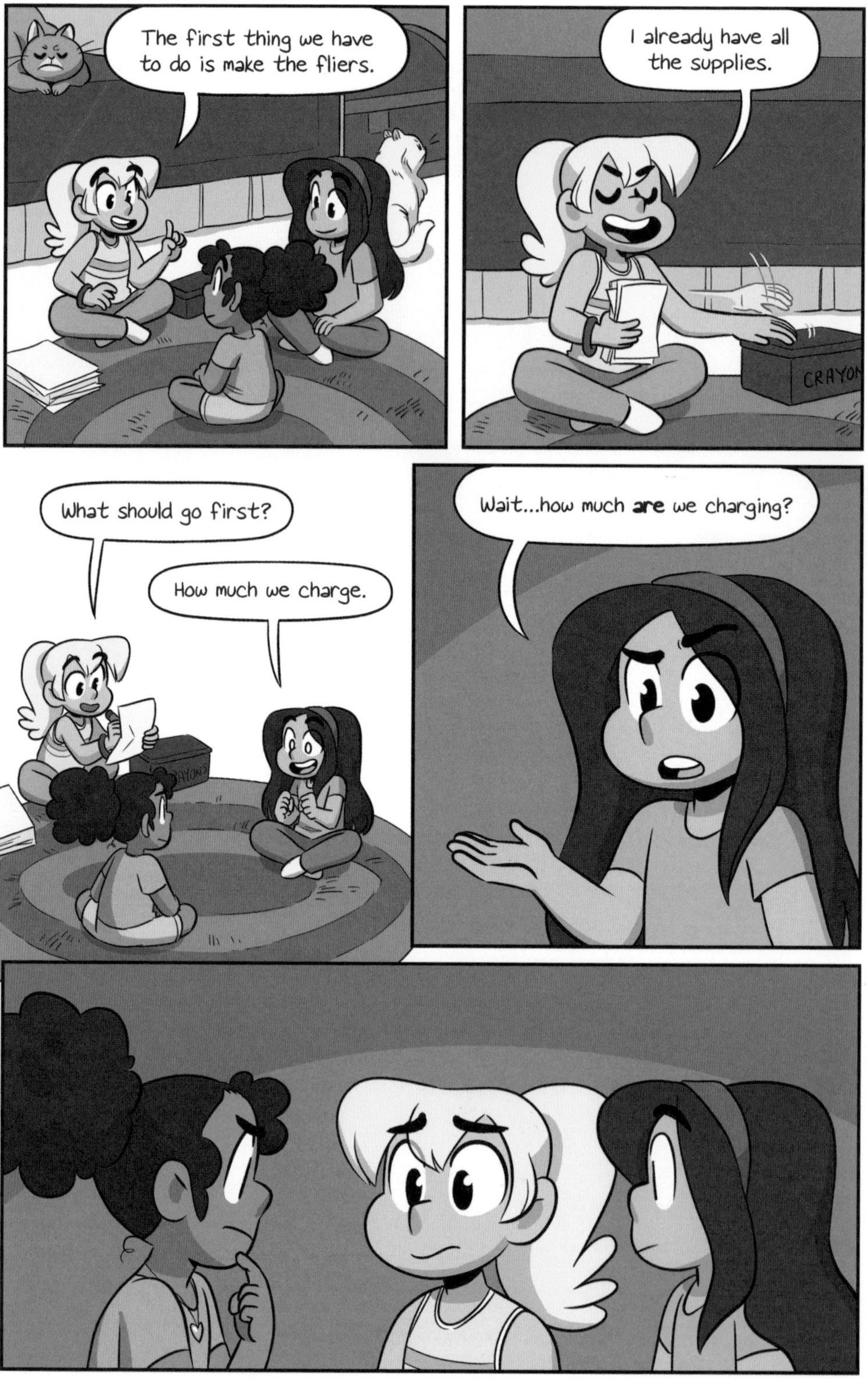
The first thing we have to do is make the fliers.
I already have all the supplies.
CRAYONS
What should go first?
How much we charge.
Wait...how much **are** we charging?

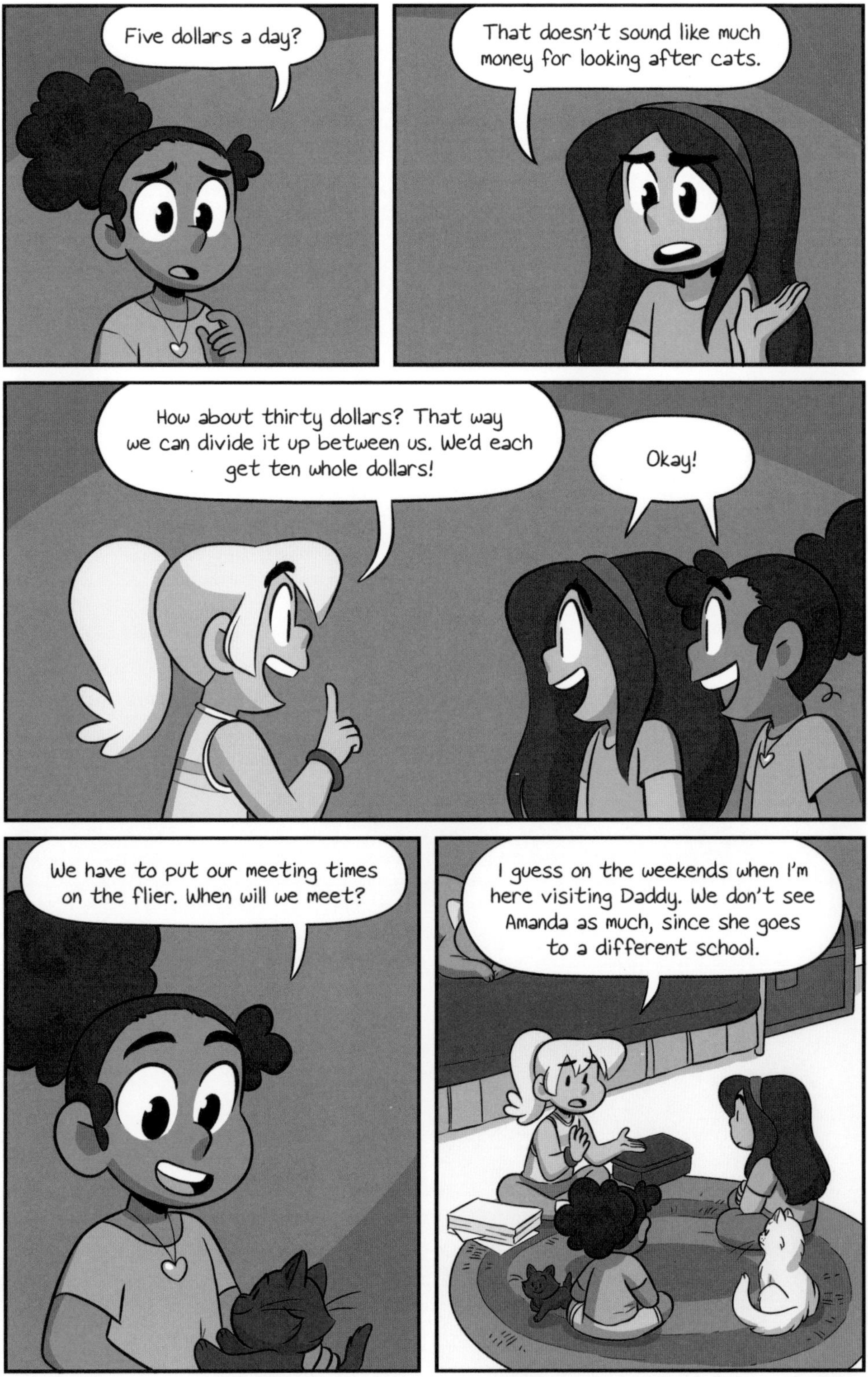
Five dollars a day?
That doesn't sound like much money for looking after cats.
How about thirty dollars? That way we can divide it up between us. We'd each get ten whole dollars!
Okay!
We have to put our meeting times on the flier. When will we meet?
I guess on the weekends when I'm here visiting Daddy. We don't see Amanda as much, since she goes to a different school.

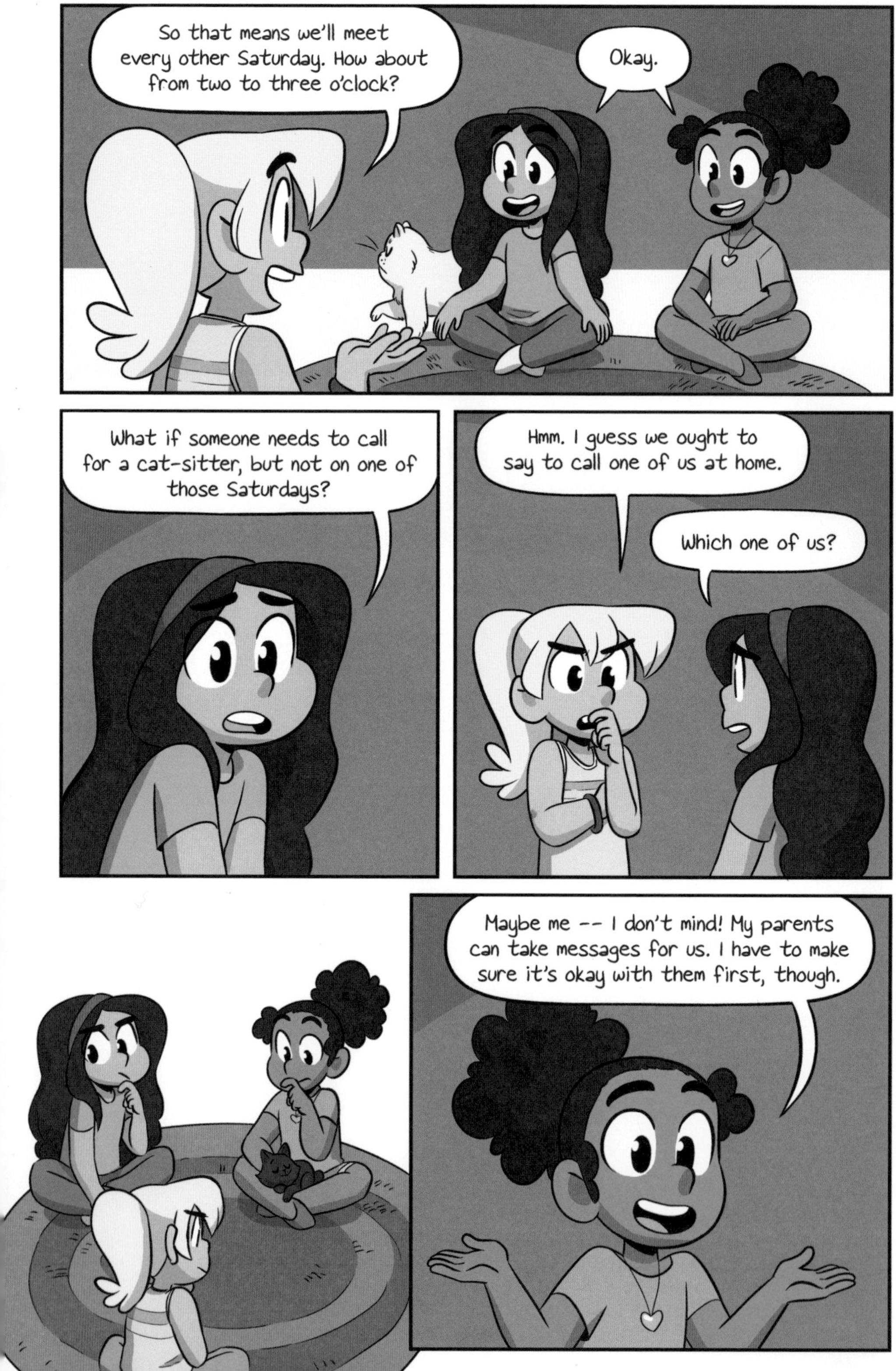

So that means we'll meet every other Saturday. How about from two to three o'clock?
Okay.
What if someone needs to call for a cat-sitter, but not on one of those Saturdays?
Hmm. I guess we ought to say to call one of us at home.
Which one of us?
Maybe me -- I don't mind! My parents can take messages for us. I have to make sure it's okay with them first, though.

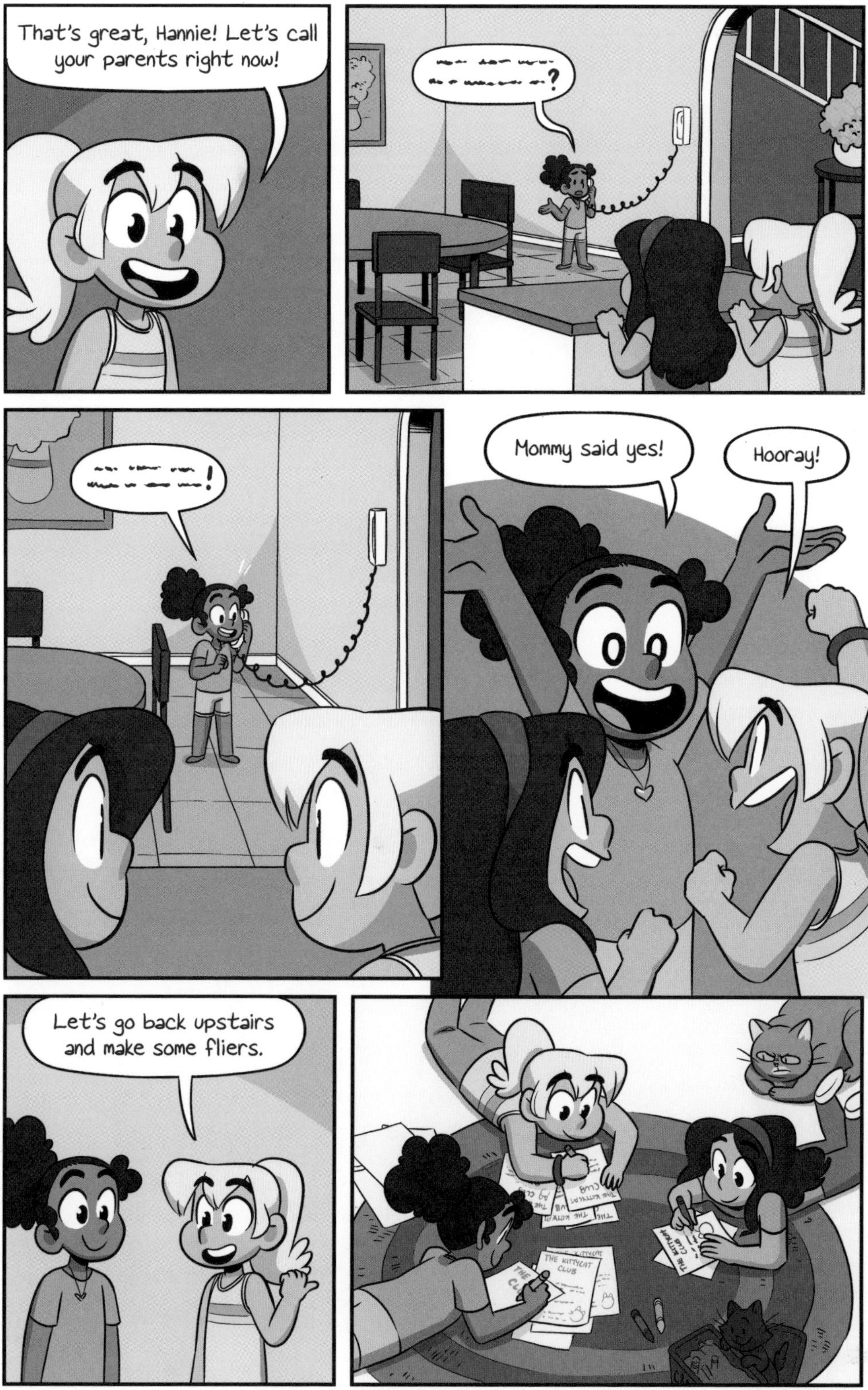
That's great, Hannie! Let's call your parents right now!
Mommy said yes!
Hooray!
Let's go back upstairs and make some fliers.
THE KITTYCAT CLUB

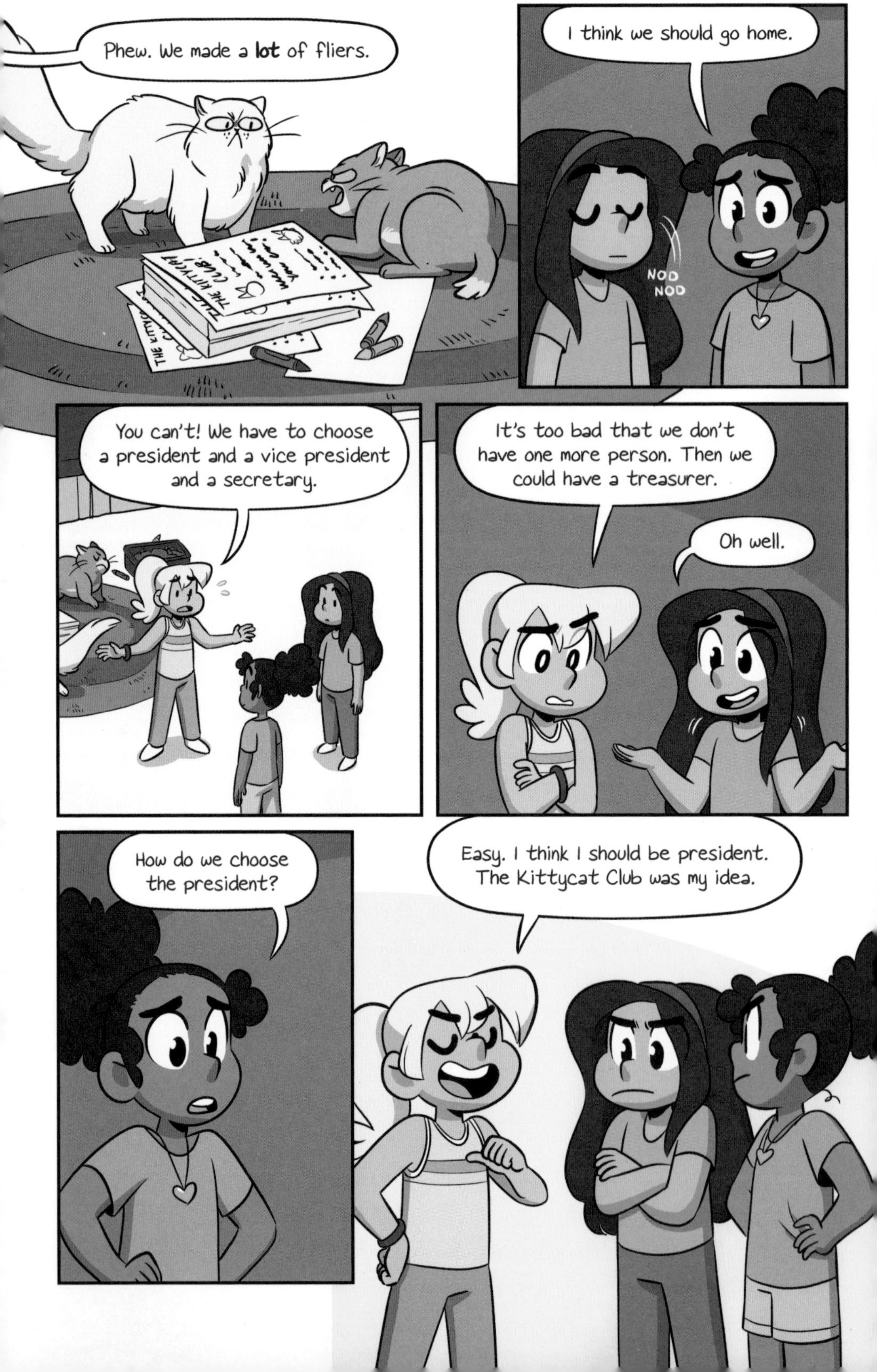
Phew. We made a **lot** of fliers.
THE KITTYCAT CLUB!
I think we should go home.
NOD NOD
You can't! We have to choose a president and a vice president and a secretary.
It's too bad that we don't have one more person. Then we could have a treasurer.
Oh well.
How do we choose the president?
Easy. I think I should be president. The Kittycat Club was my idea.

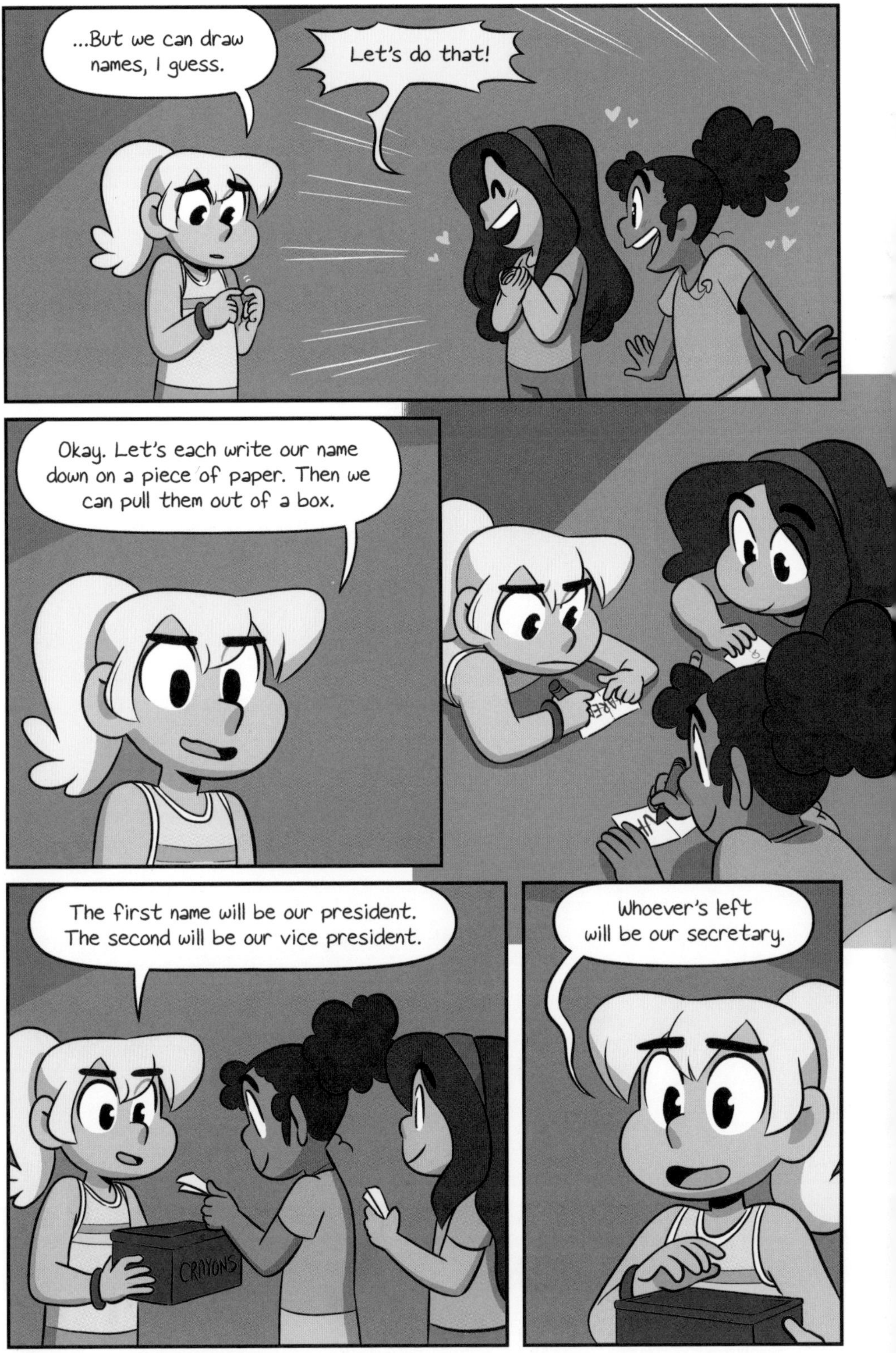
...But we can draw names, I guess.
Let's do that!
Okay. Let's each write our name down on a piece of paper. Then we can pull them out of a box.
The first name will be our president. The second will be our vice president.
CRAYONS
Whoever's left will be our secretary.

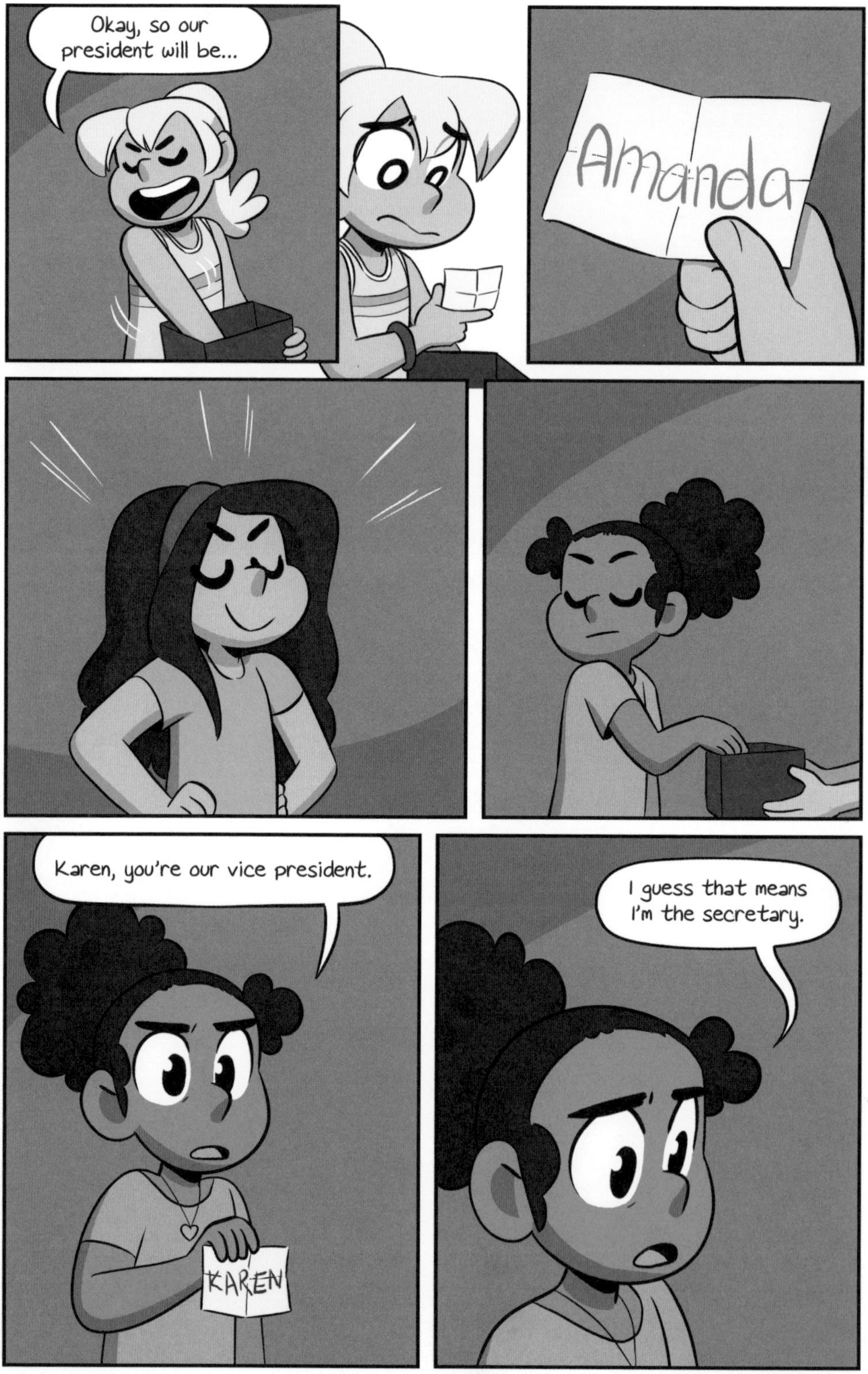
Okay, so our president will be...
Amanda
Karen, you're our vice president.
KAREN
I guess that means I'm the secretary.

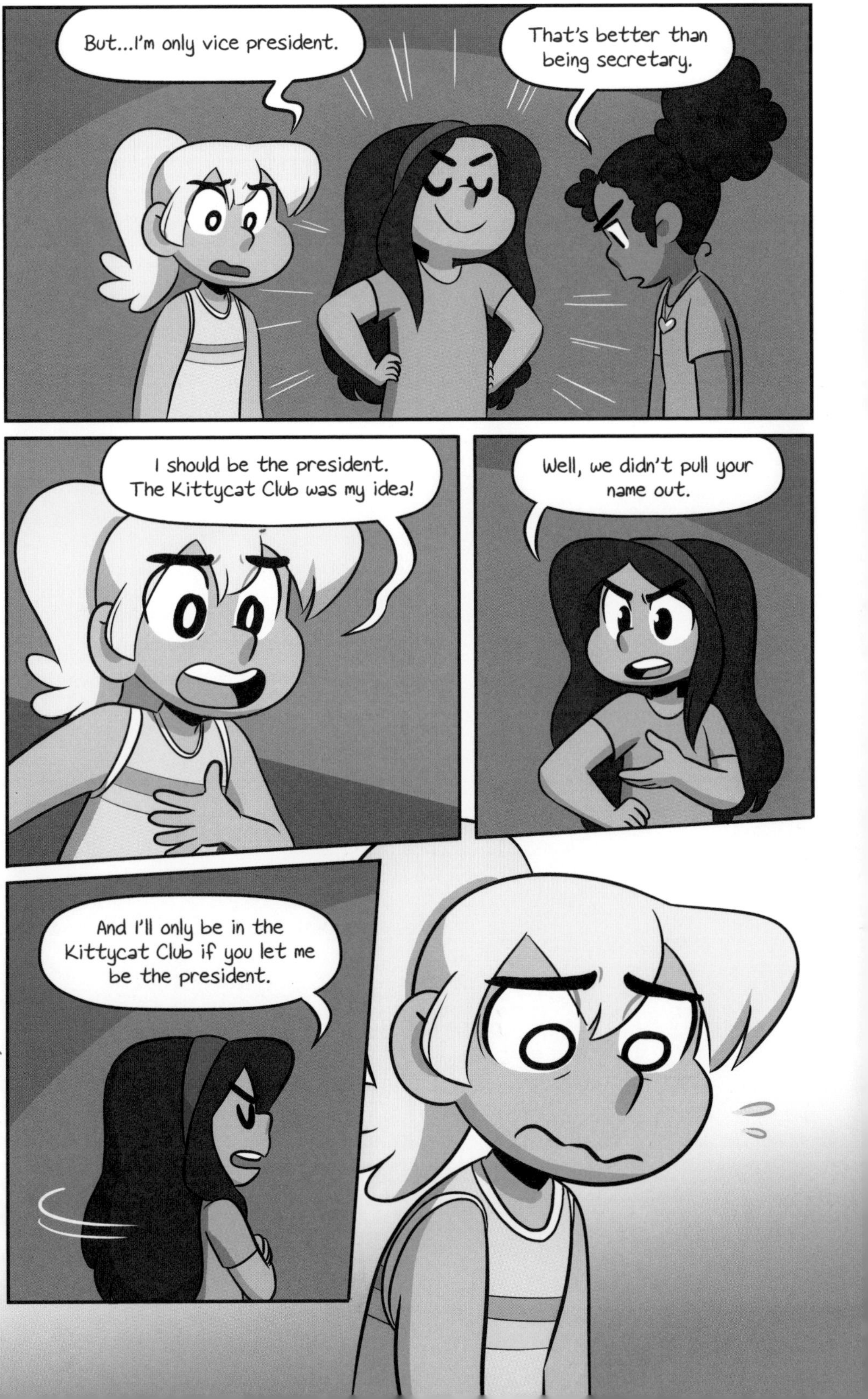
But...I'm only vice president.
That's better than being secretary.
I should be the president. The Kittycat Club was my idea!
Well, we didn't pull your name out.
And I'll only be in the Kittycat Club if you let me be the president.

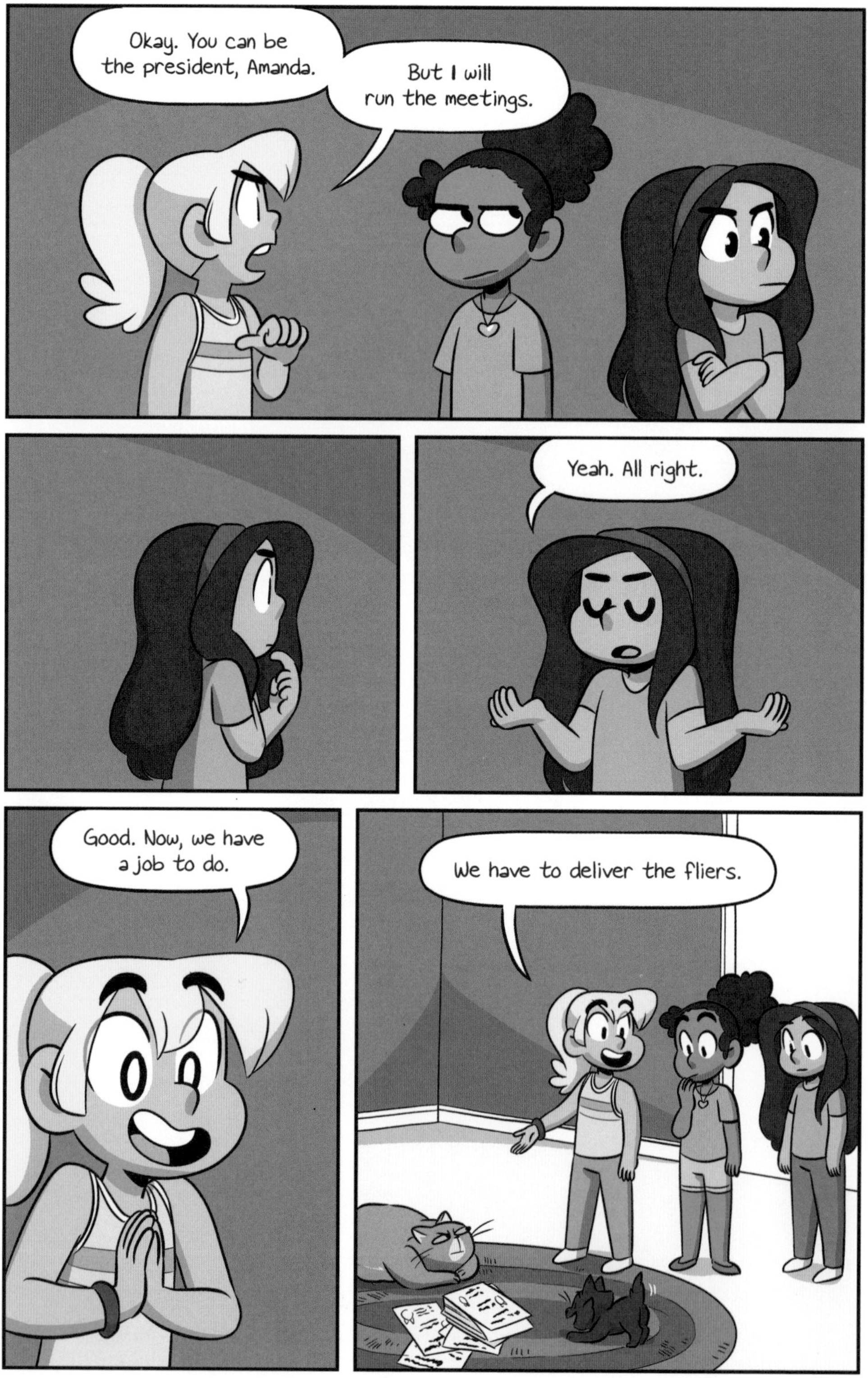
Okay. You can be the president, Amanda.
But I will run the meetings.
Yeah. All right.
Good. Now, we have a job to do.
We have to deliver the fliers.

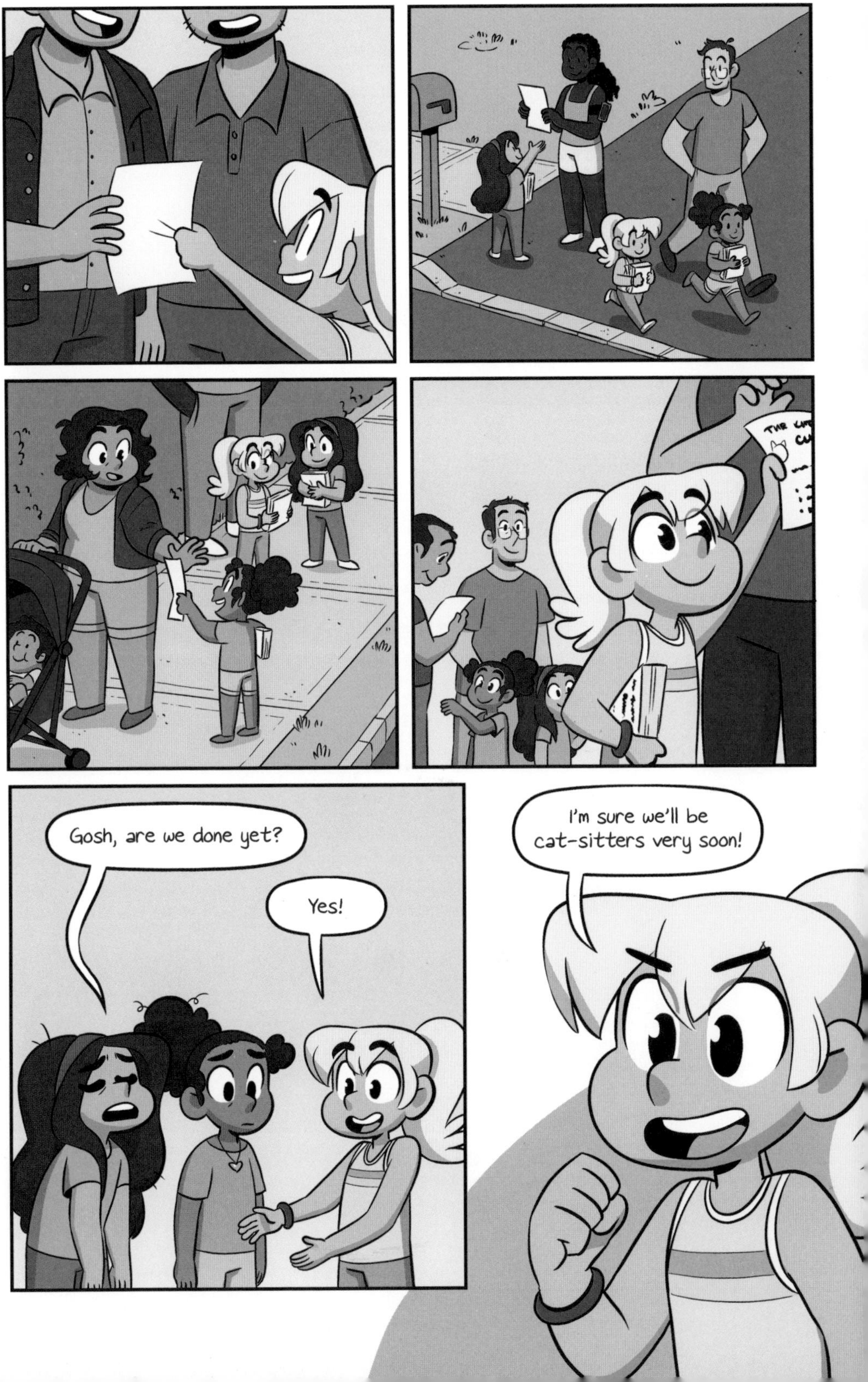
Gosh, are we done yet?
Yes!
I'm sure we'll be cat-sitters very soon!

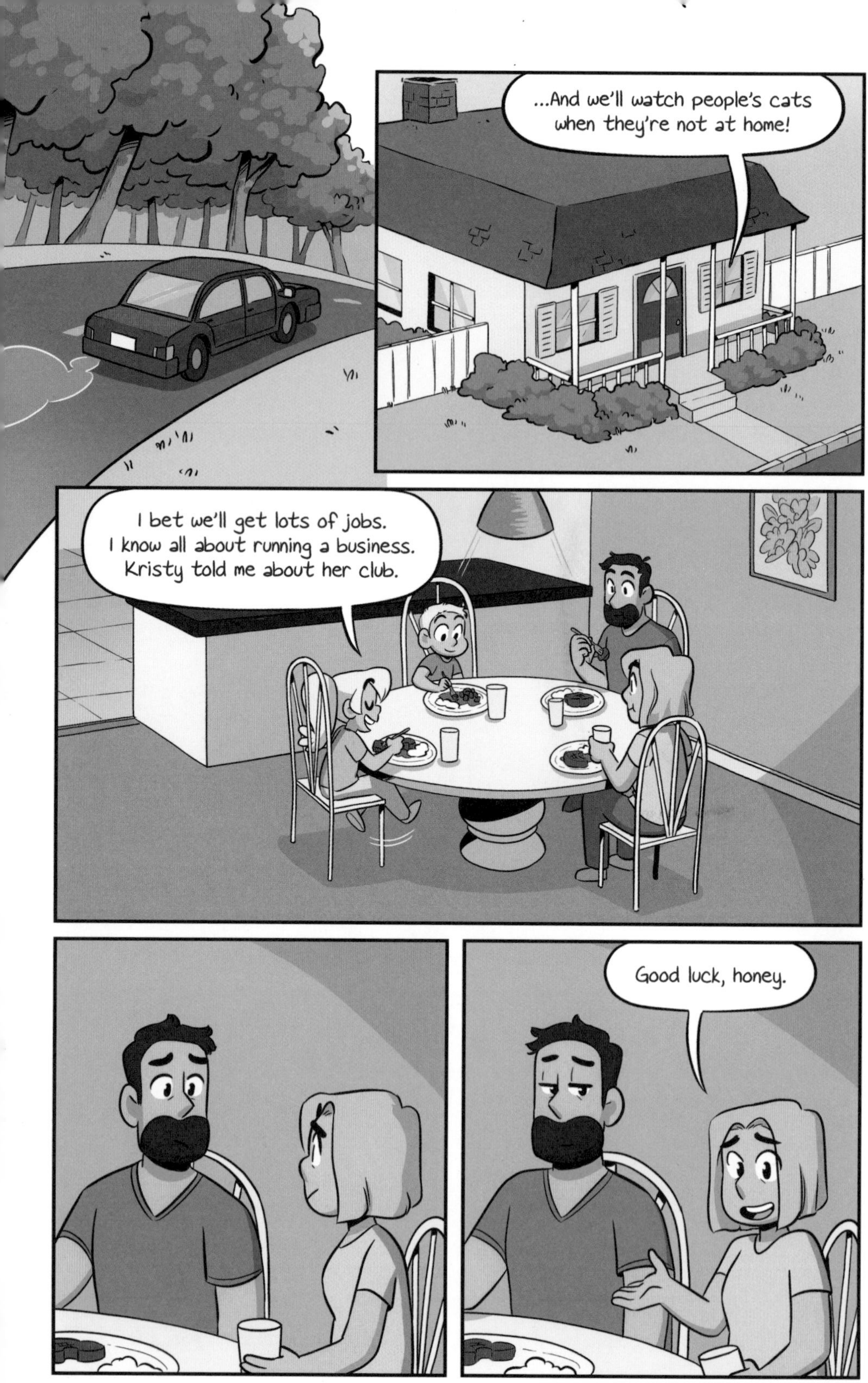
...And we'll watch people's cats when they're not at home!
I bet we'll get lots of jobs. I know all about running a business. Kristy told me about her club.
Good luck, honey.

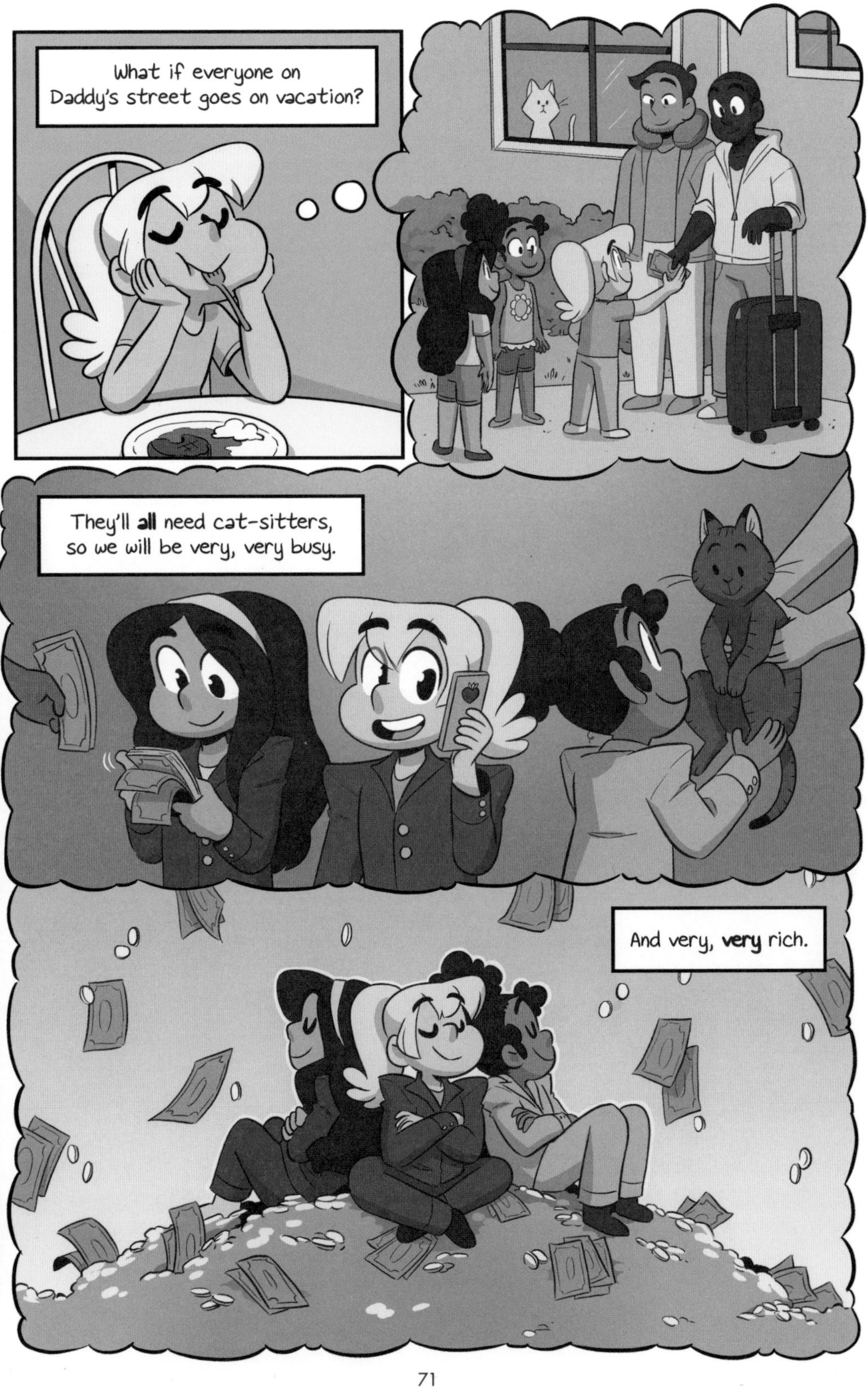
What if everyone on Daddy's street goes on vacation?
They'll **all** need cat-sitters, so we will be very, very busy.
And very, **very** rich.

CHAPTER 6

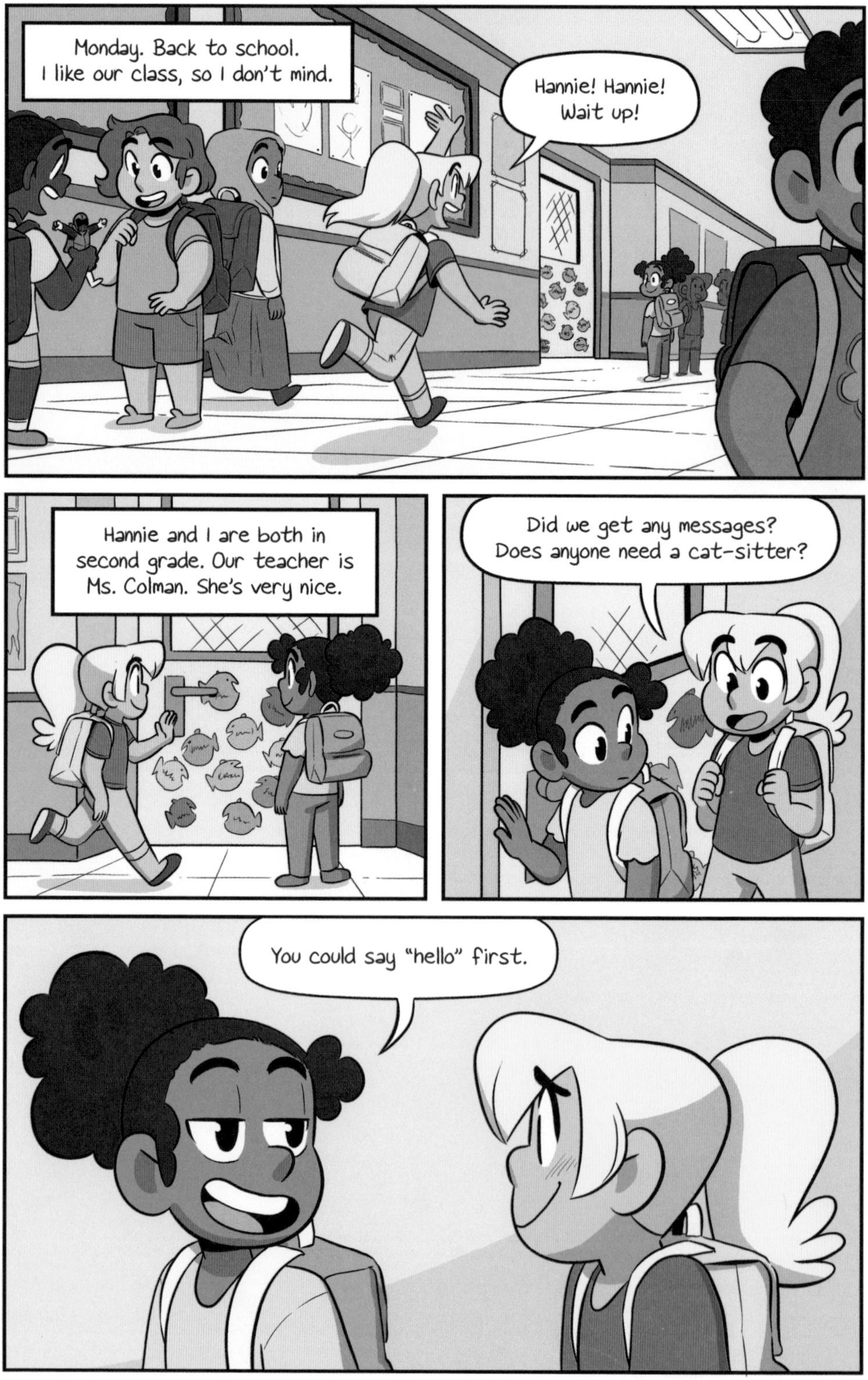
Monday. Back to school.
I like our class, so I don't mind.
Hannie! Hannie!
Wait up!
Hannie and I are both in
second grade. Our teacher is
Ms. Colman. She's very nice.
Did we get any messages?
Does anyone need a cat-sitter?
You could say "hello" first.

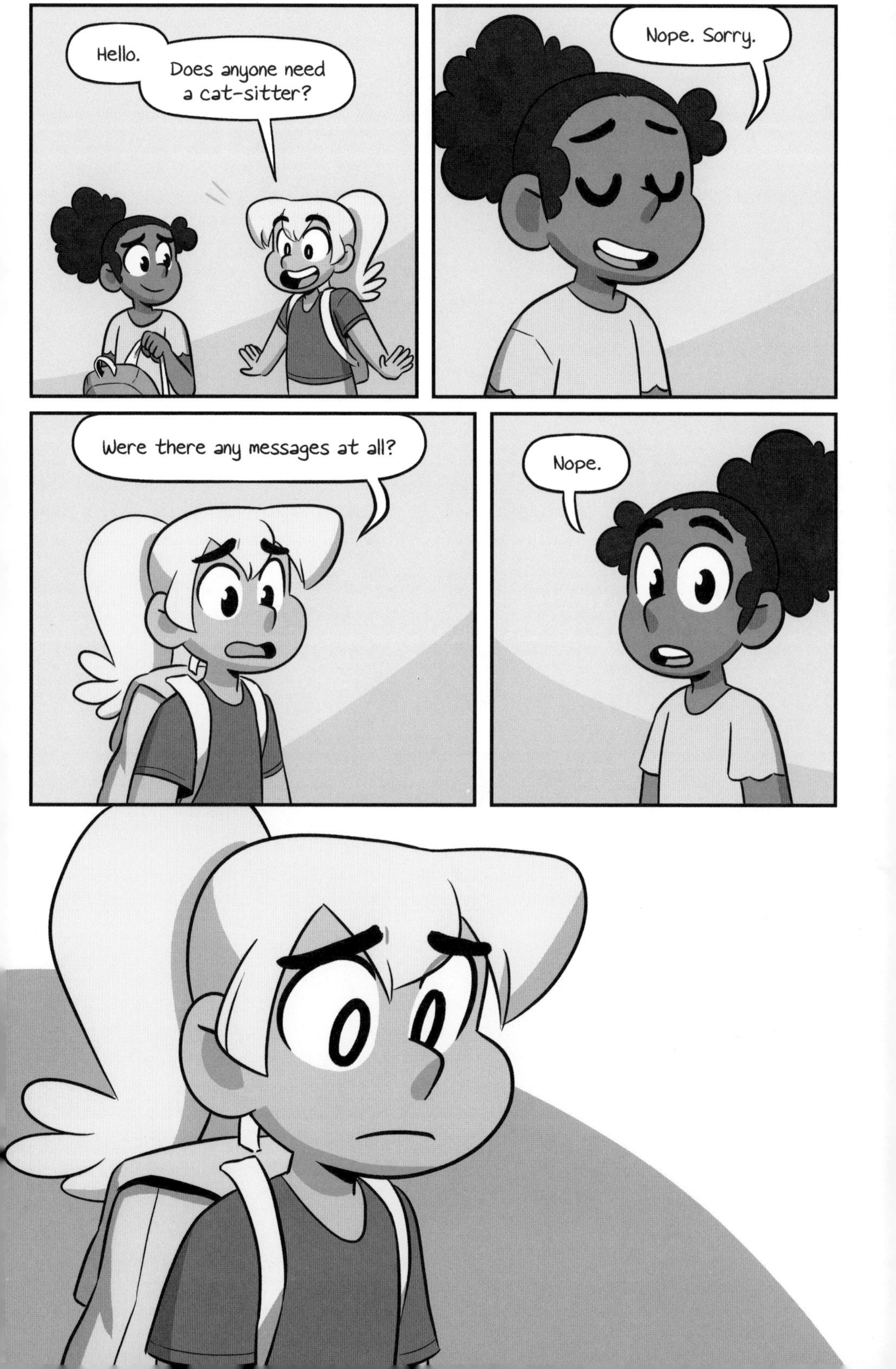
Hello.
Does anyone need a cat-sitter?
Nope. Sorry.
Were there any messages at all?
Nope.

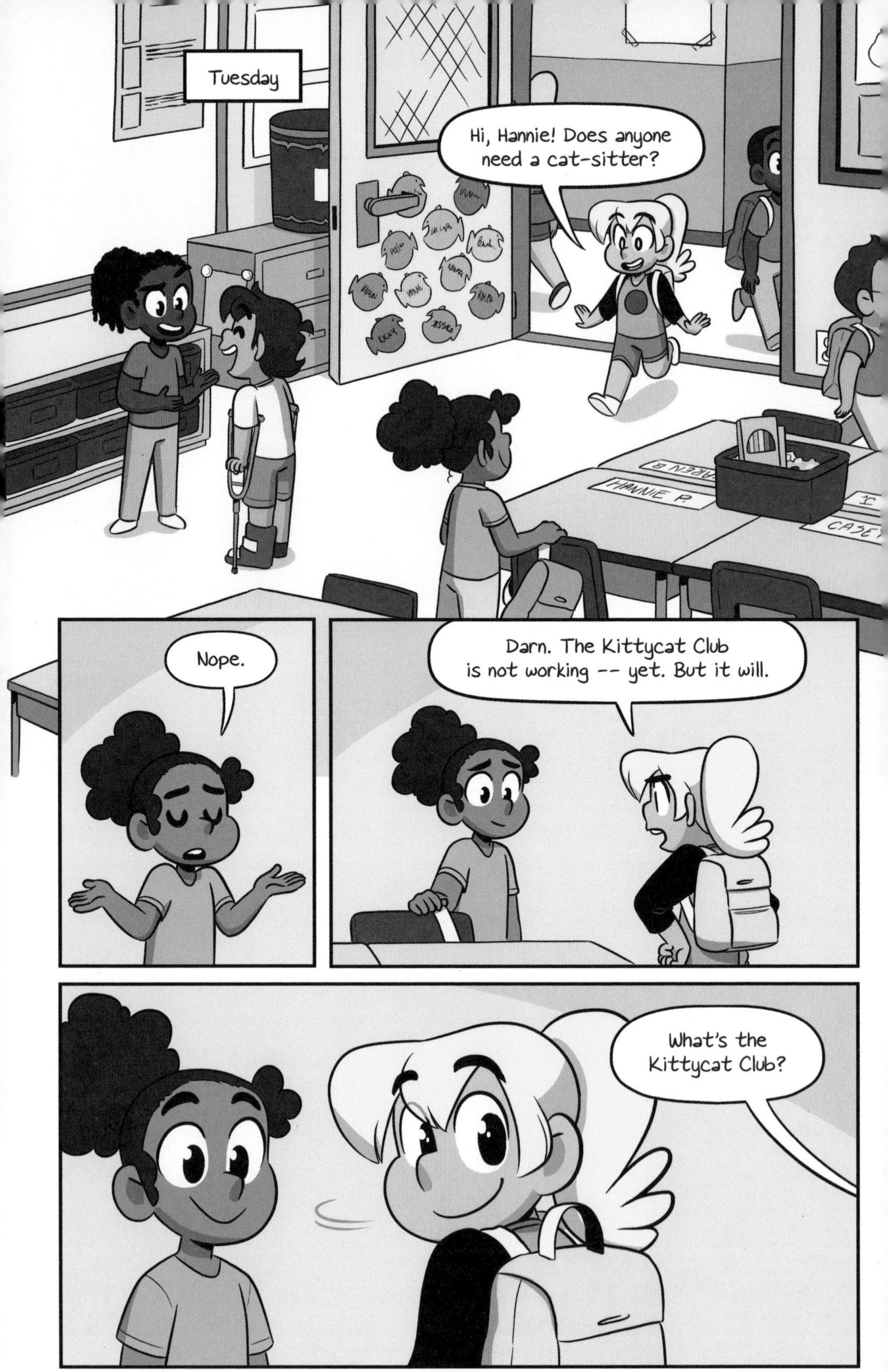
Tuesday
Hi, Hannie! Does anyone need a cat-sitter?
HANNIE P.
Nope.
Darn. The Kittycat Club is not working -- yet. But it will.
What's the Kittycat Club?

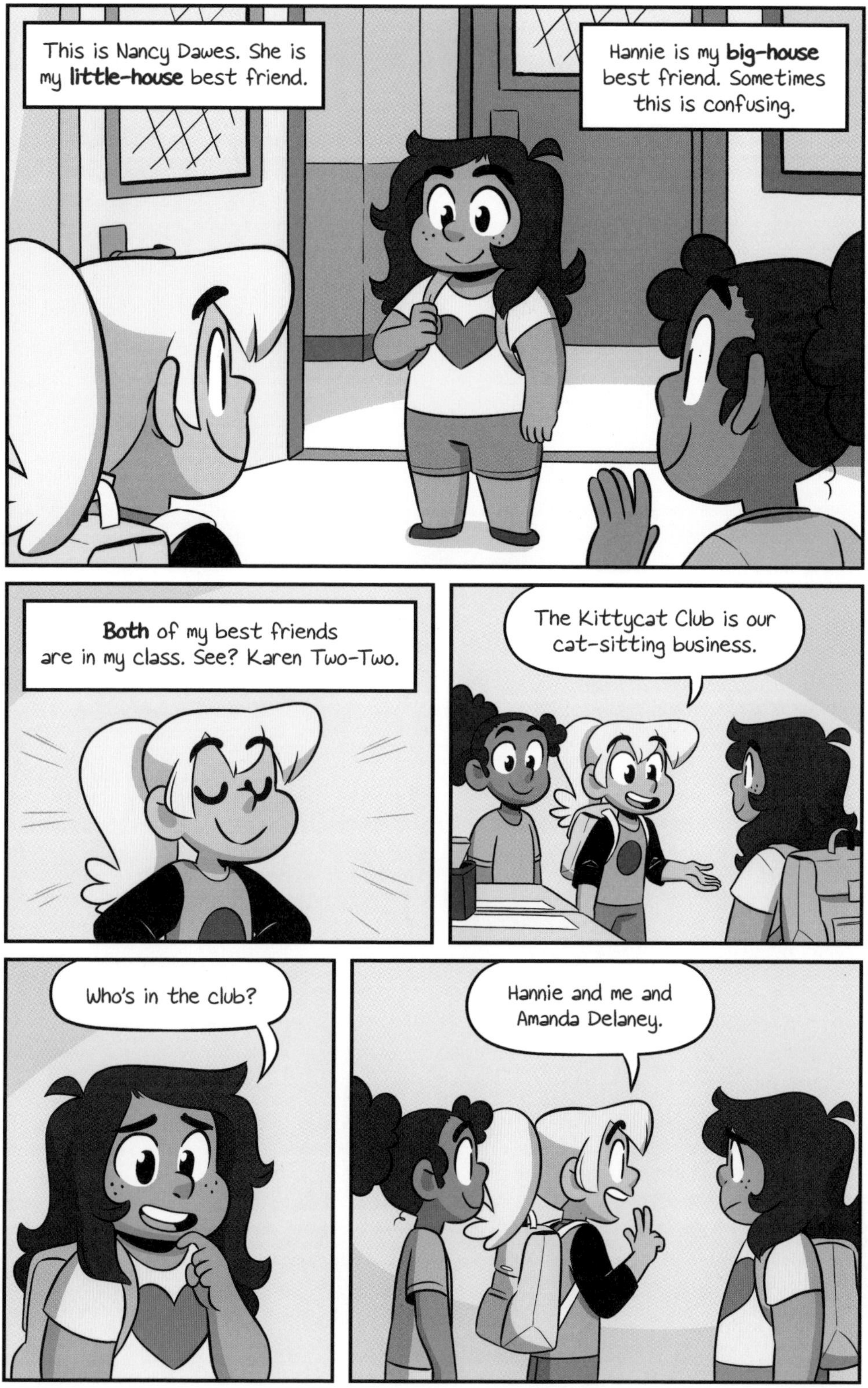
This is Nancy Dawes. She is my **little-house** best friend.
Hannie is my **big-house** best friend. Sometimes this is confusing.
Both of my best friends are in my class. See? Karen Two-Two.
The Kittycat Club is our cat-sitting business.
Who's in the club?
Hannie and me and Amanda Delaney.

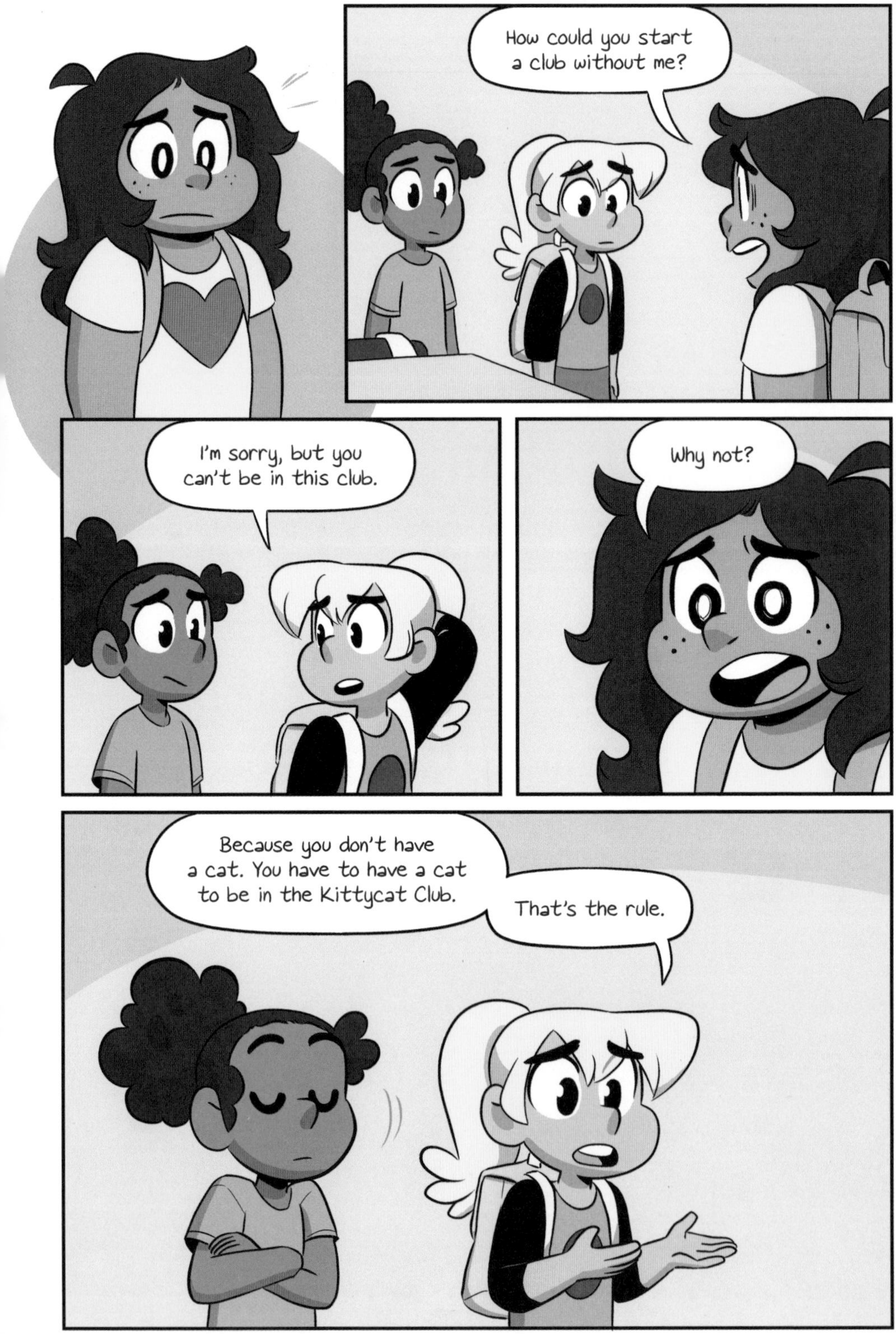
How could you start a club without me?
I'm sorry, but you can't be in this club.
Why not?
Because you don't have a cat. You have to have a cat to be in the Kittycat Club.
That's the rule.

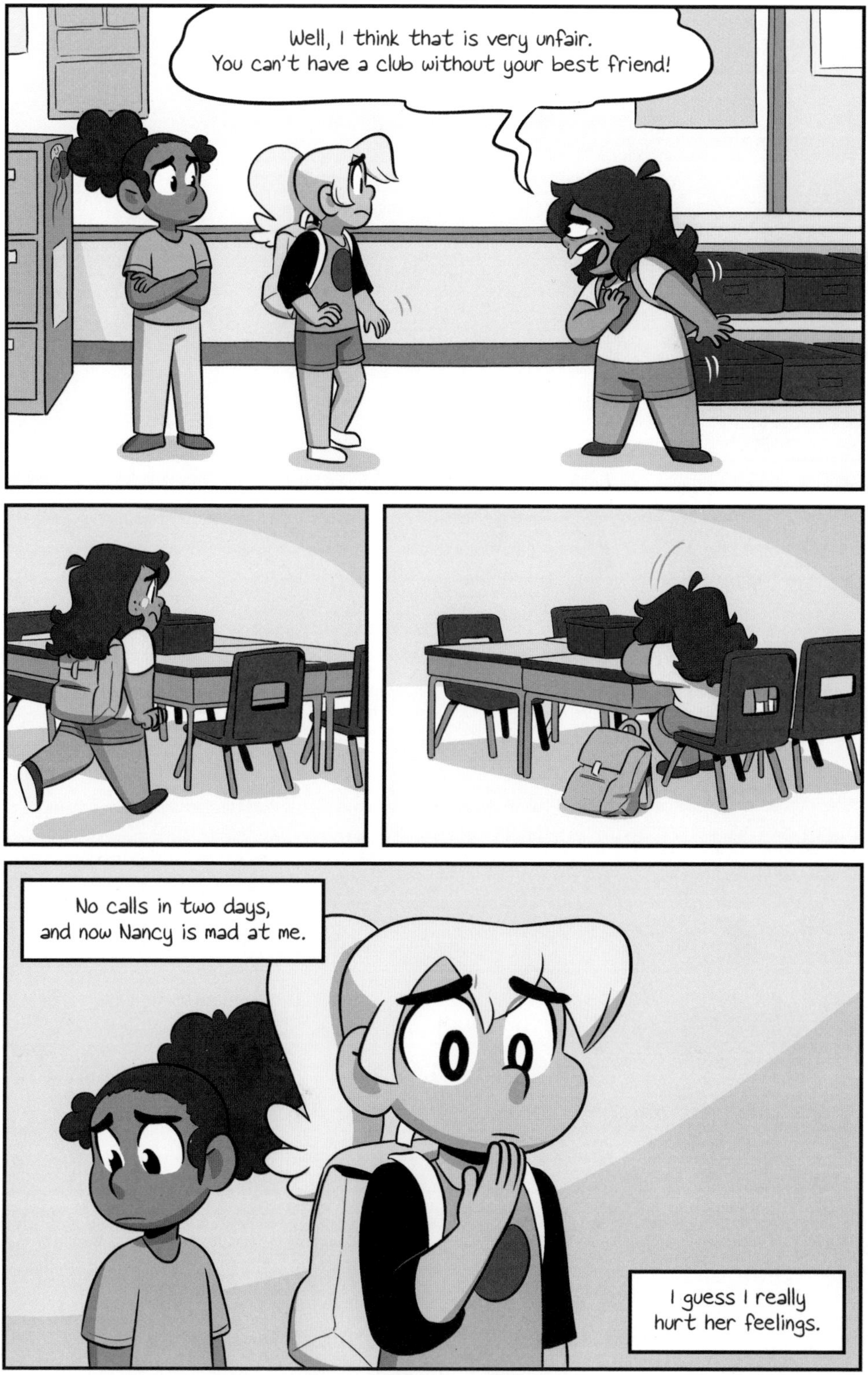
Well, I think that is very unfair.
You can't have a club without your best friend!
No calls in two days,
and now Nancy is mad at me.
I guess I really
hurt her feelings.

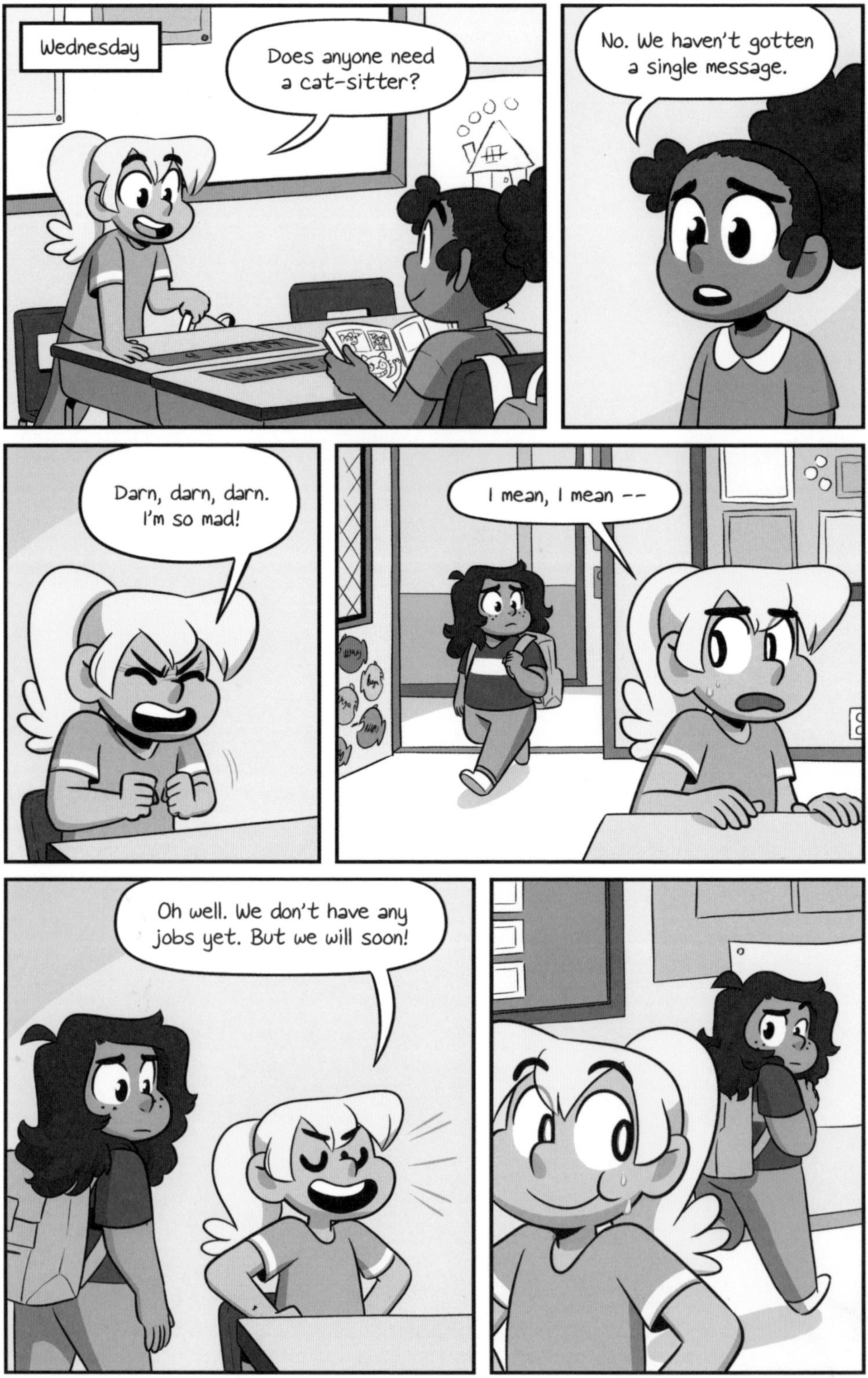
Wednesday
Does anyone need a cat-sitter?
No. We haven't gotten a single message.
Darn, darn, darn. I'm so mad!
I mean, I mean --
Oh well. We don't have any jobs yet. But we will soon!

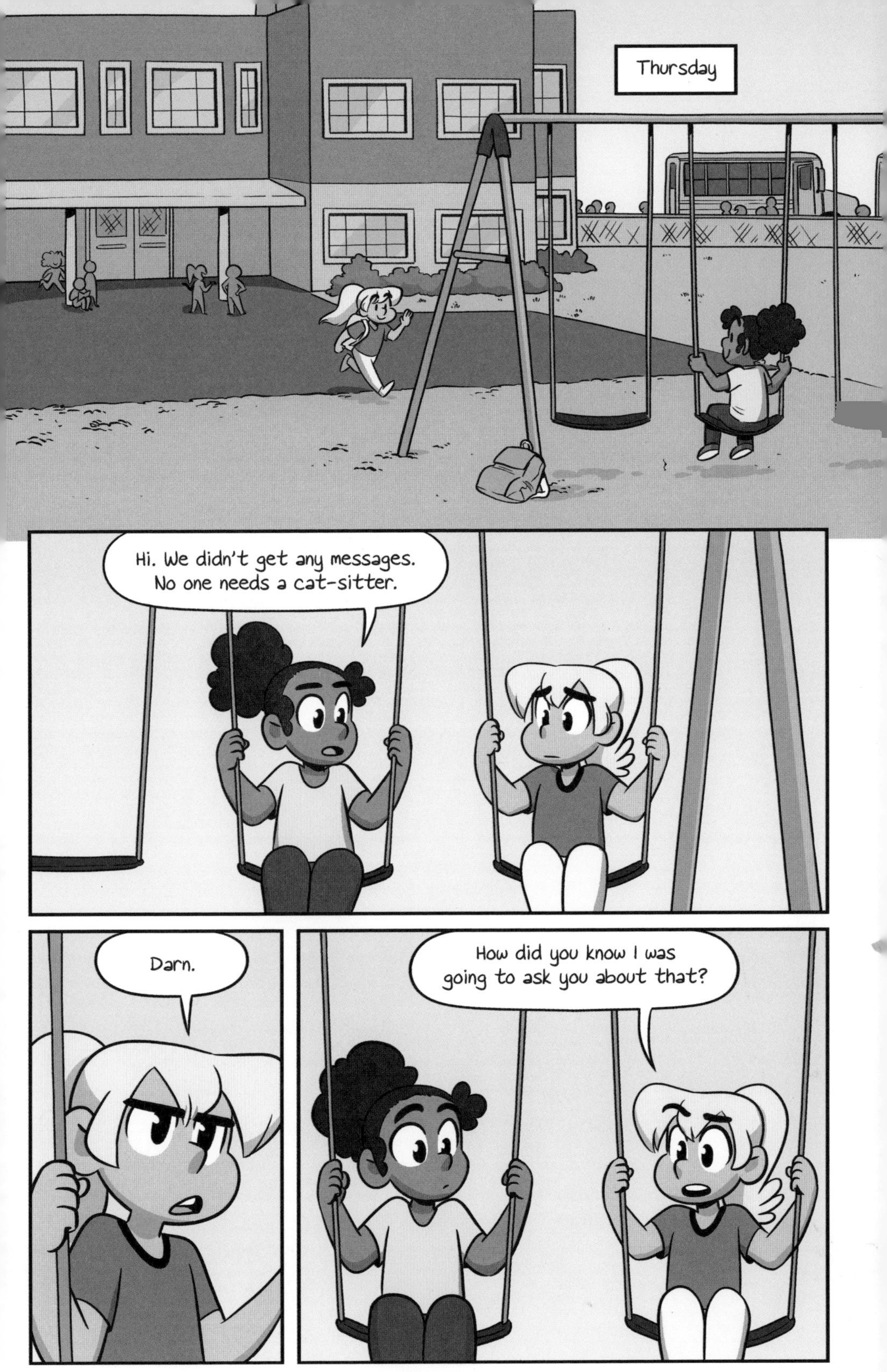
Thursday
Hi. We didn't get any messages. No one needs a cat-sitter.
Darn.
How did you know I was going to ask you about that?

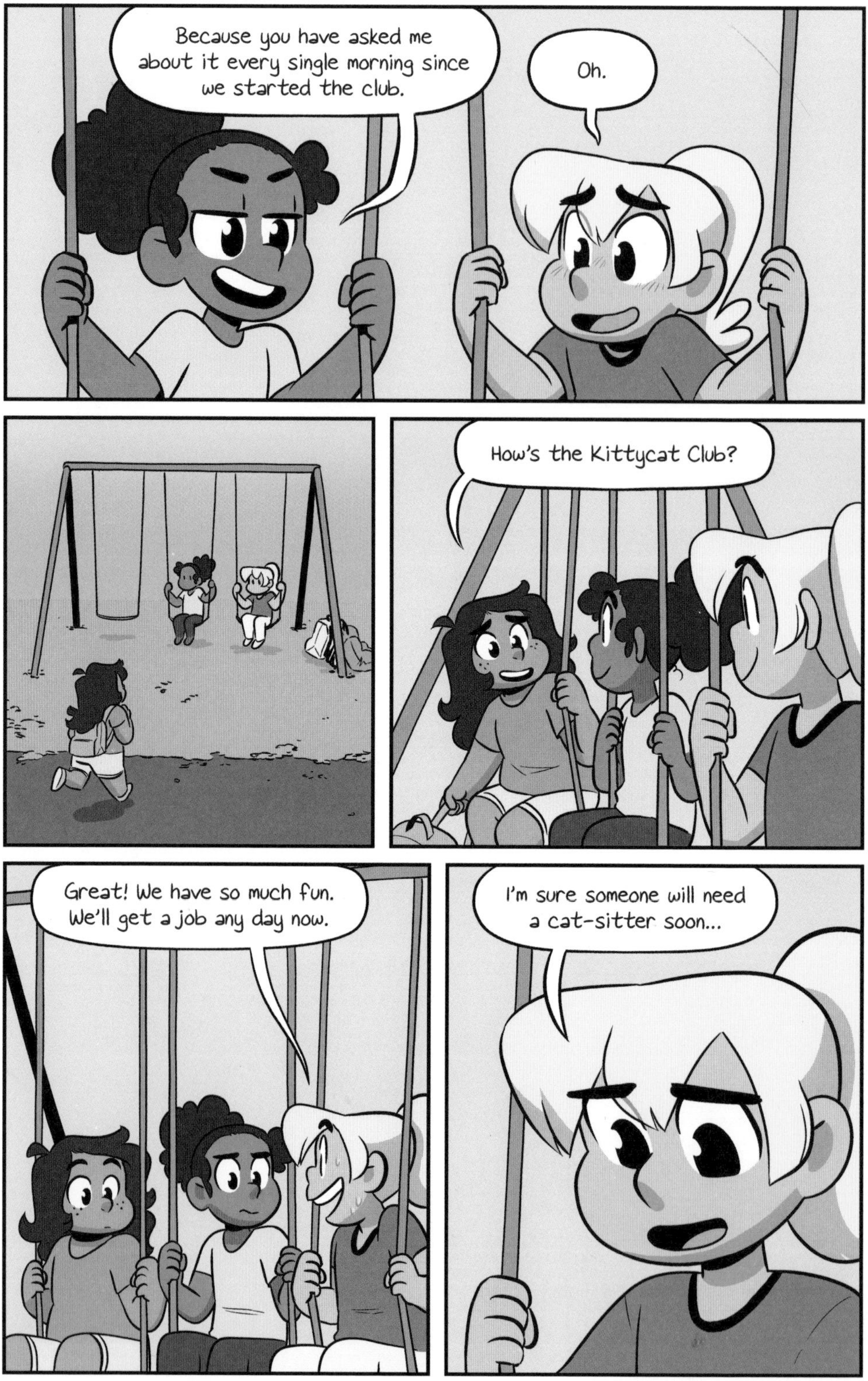
Because you have asked me about it every single morning since we started the club.
Oh.
How's the Kittycat Club?
Great! We have so much fun. We'll get a job any day now.
I'm sure someone will need a cat-sitter soon...

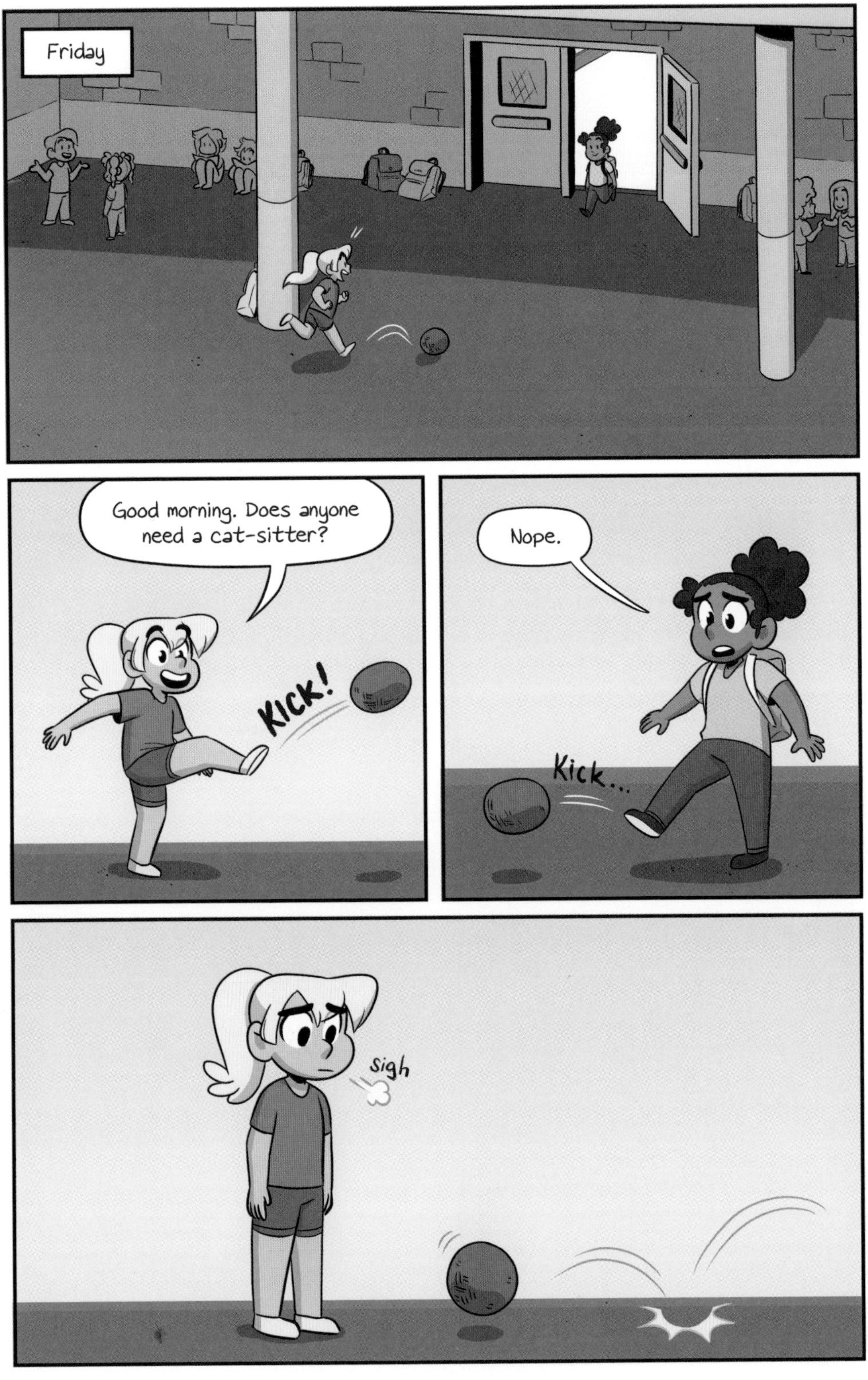

Friday
Good morning. Does anyone need a cat-sitter?
KICK!
Nope.
Kick...
sigh

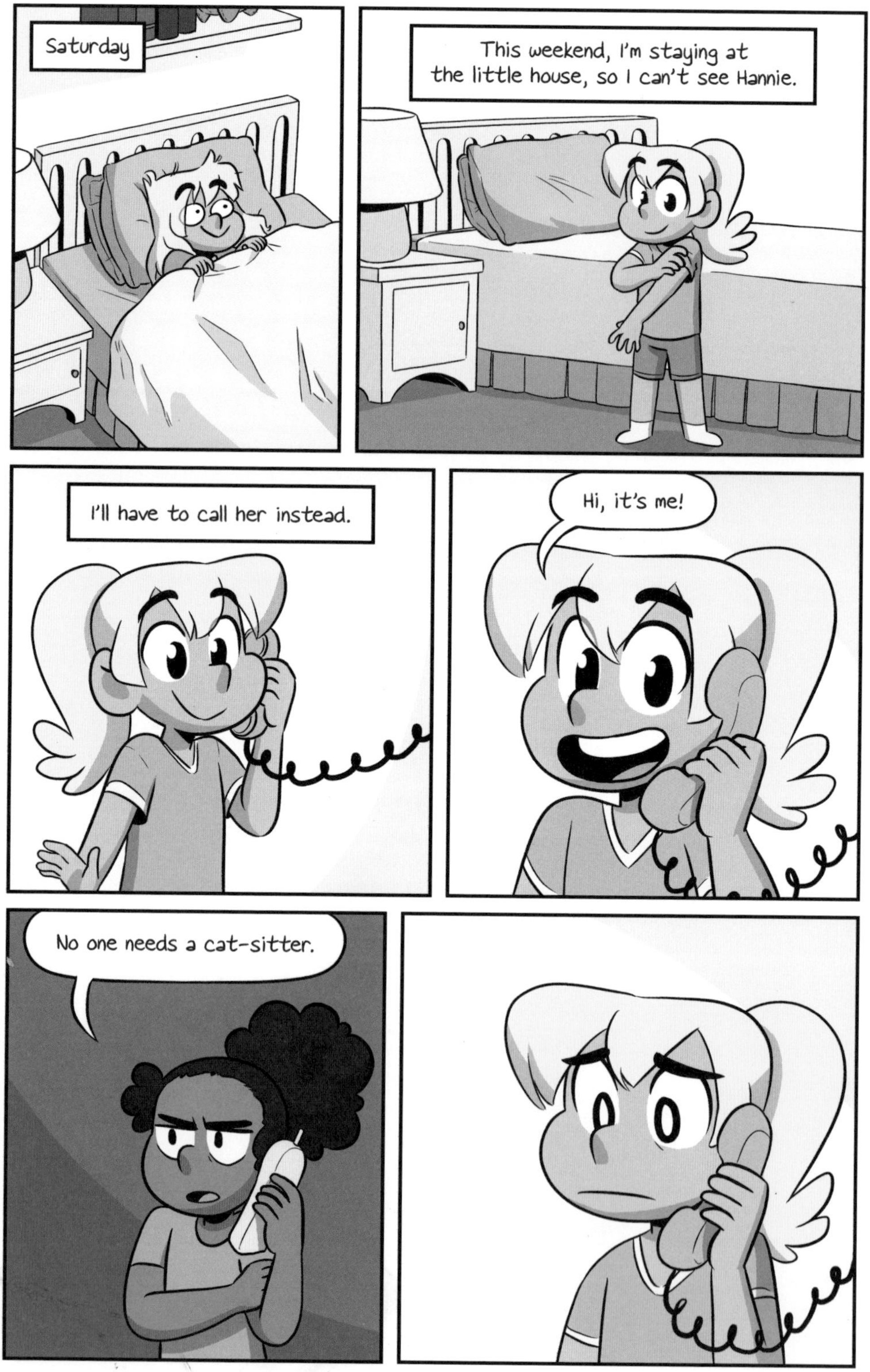
Saturday
This weekend, I'm staying at the little house, so I can't see Hannie.
I'll have to call her instead.
Hi, it's me!
No one needs a cat-sitter.

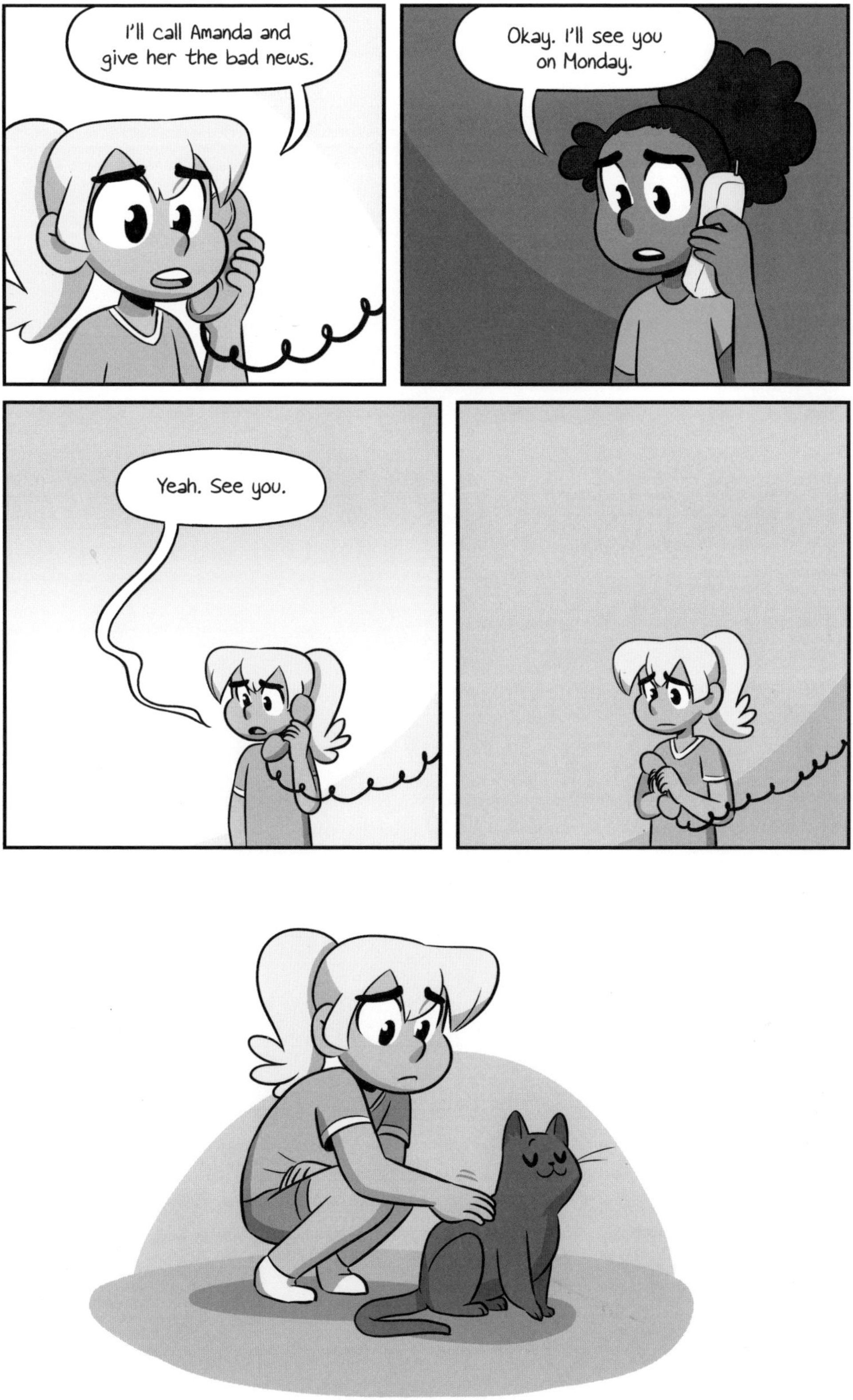
I'll call Amanda and give her the bad news.
Okay. I'll see you on Monday.
Yeah. See you.

CHAPTER 7

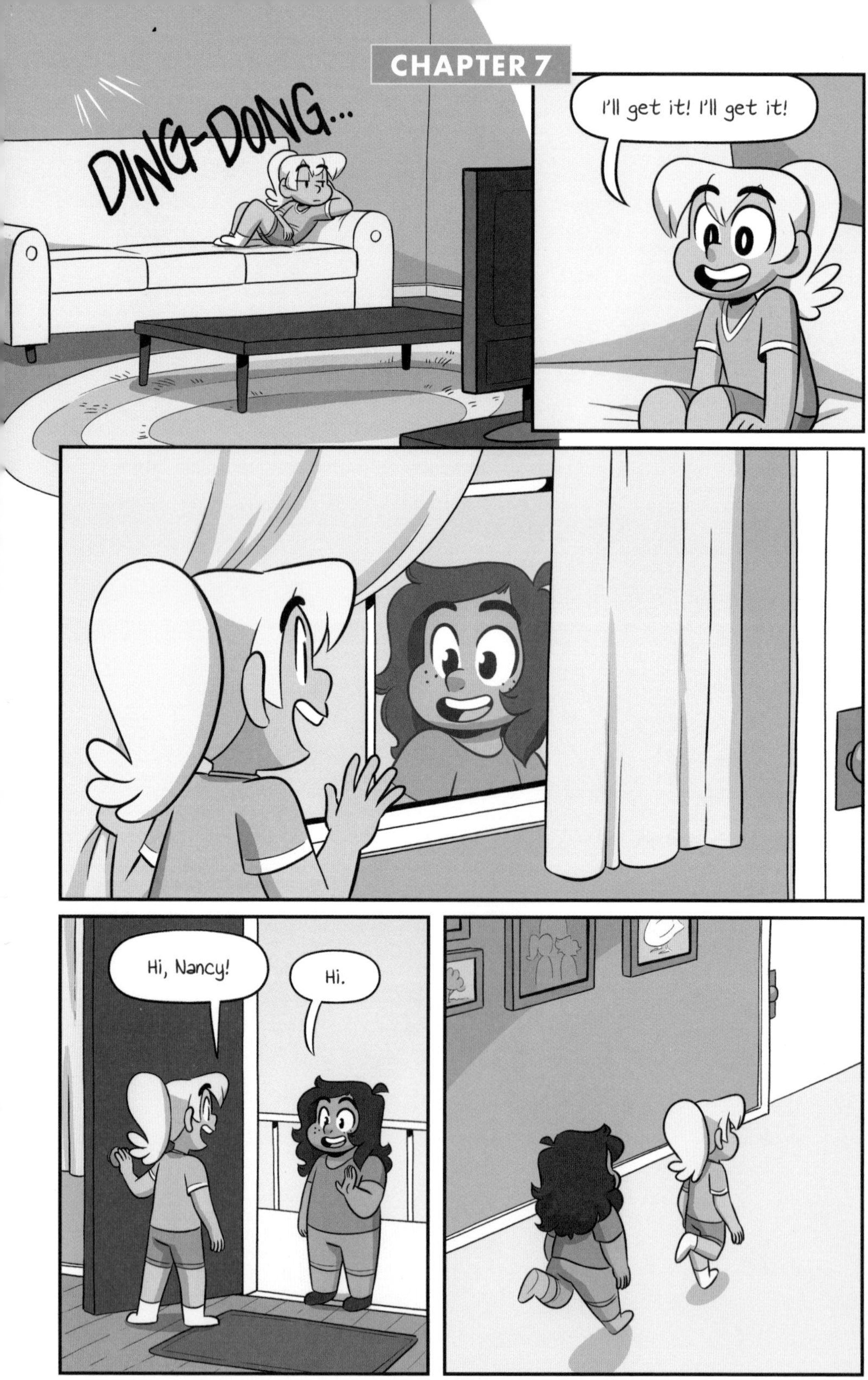
DING-DONG...
I'll get it! I'll get it!
Hi, Nancy!
Hi.

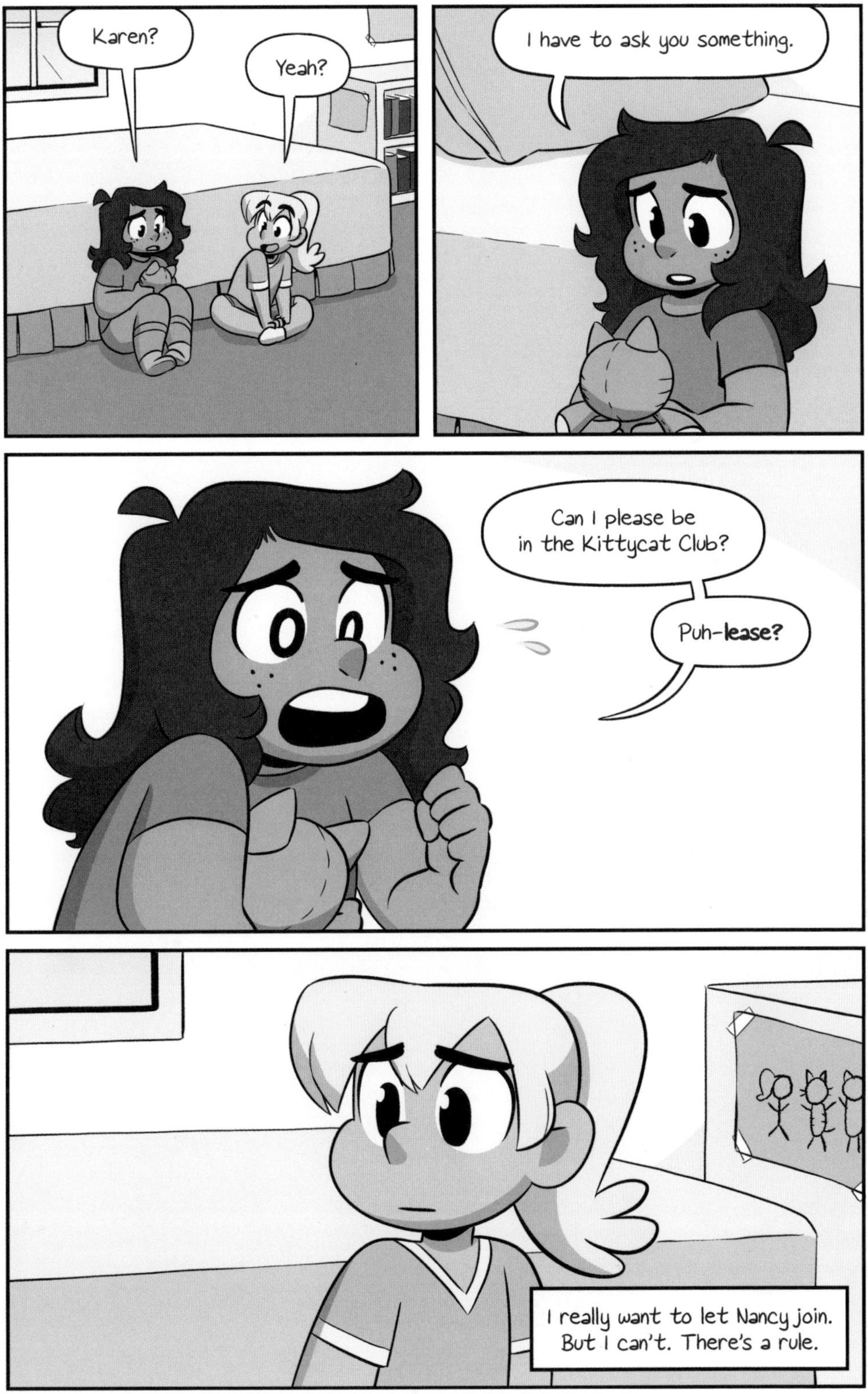
Karen?
Yeah?
I have to ask you something.
Can I please be in the Kittycat Club?
Puh-**lease?**
I really want to let Nancy join. But I can't. There's a rule.

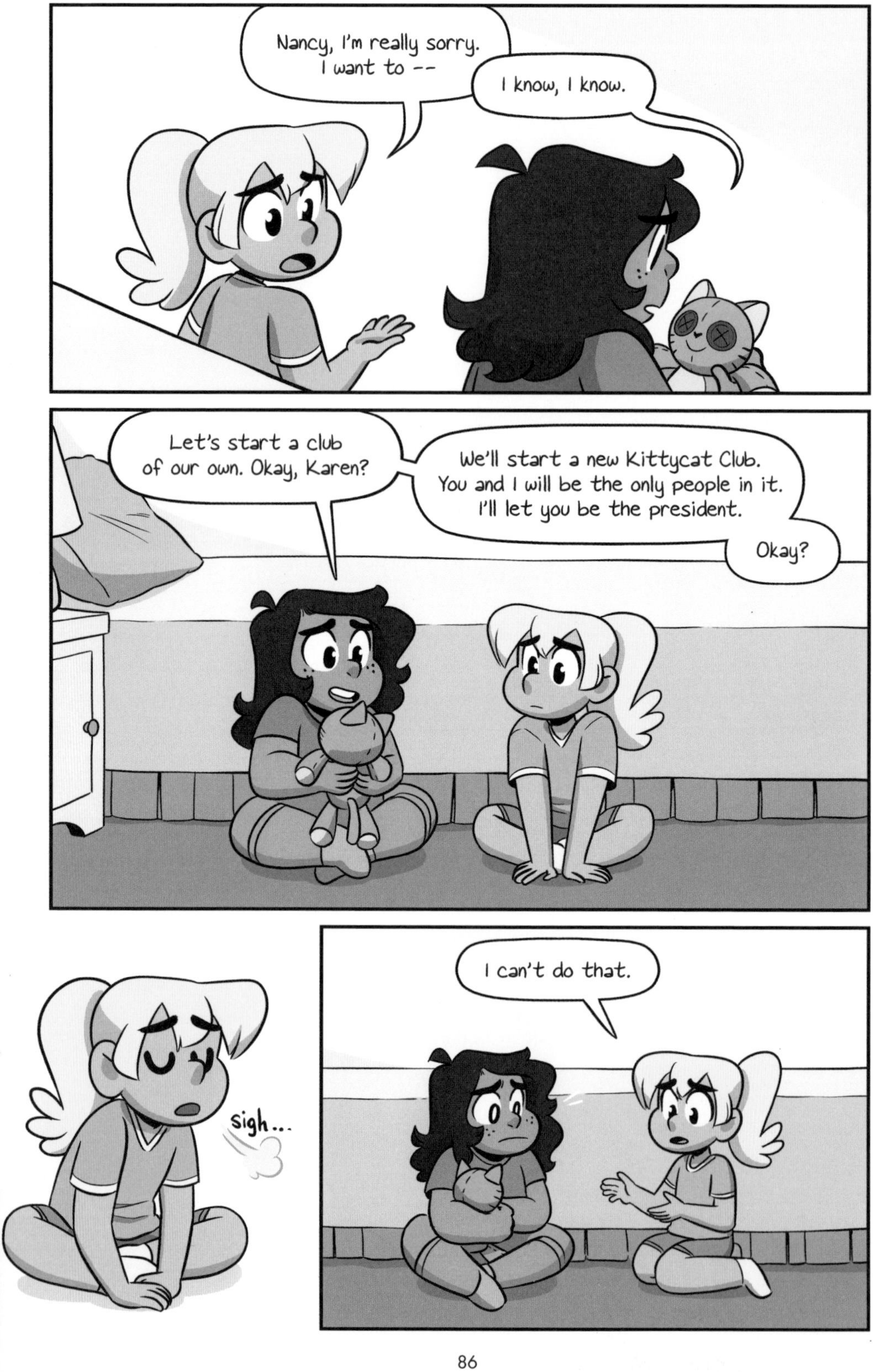
Nancy, I'm really sorry. I want to --
I know, I know.
Let's start a club of our own. Okay, Karen?
We'll start a new Kittycat Club. You and I will be the only people in it. I'll let you be the president.
Okay?
sigh...
I can't do that.

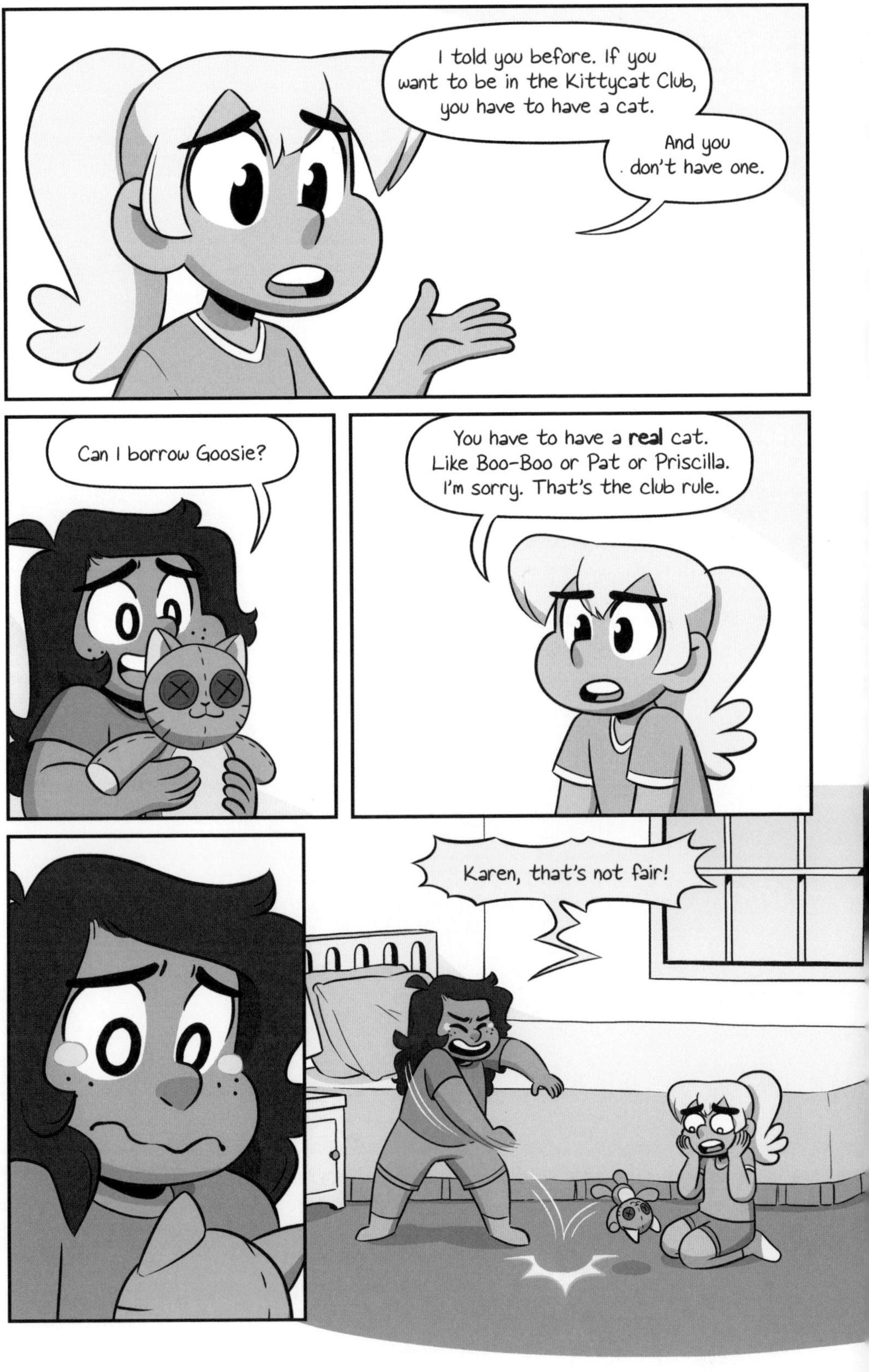
I told you before. If you want to be in the Kittycat Club, you have to have a cat.
And you don't have one.
Can I borrow Goosie?
You have to have a **real** cat. Like Boo-Boo or Pat or Priscilla. I'm sorry. That's the club rule.
Karen, that's not fair!

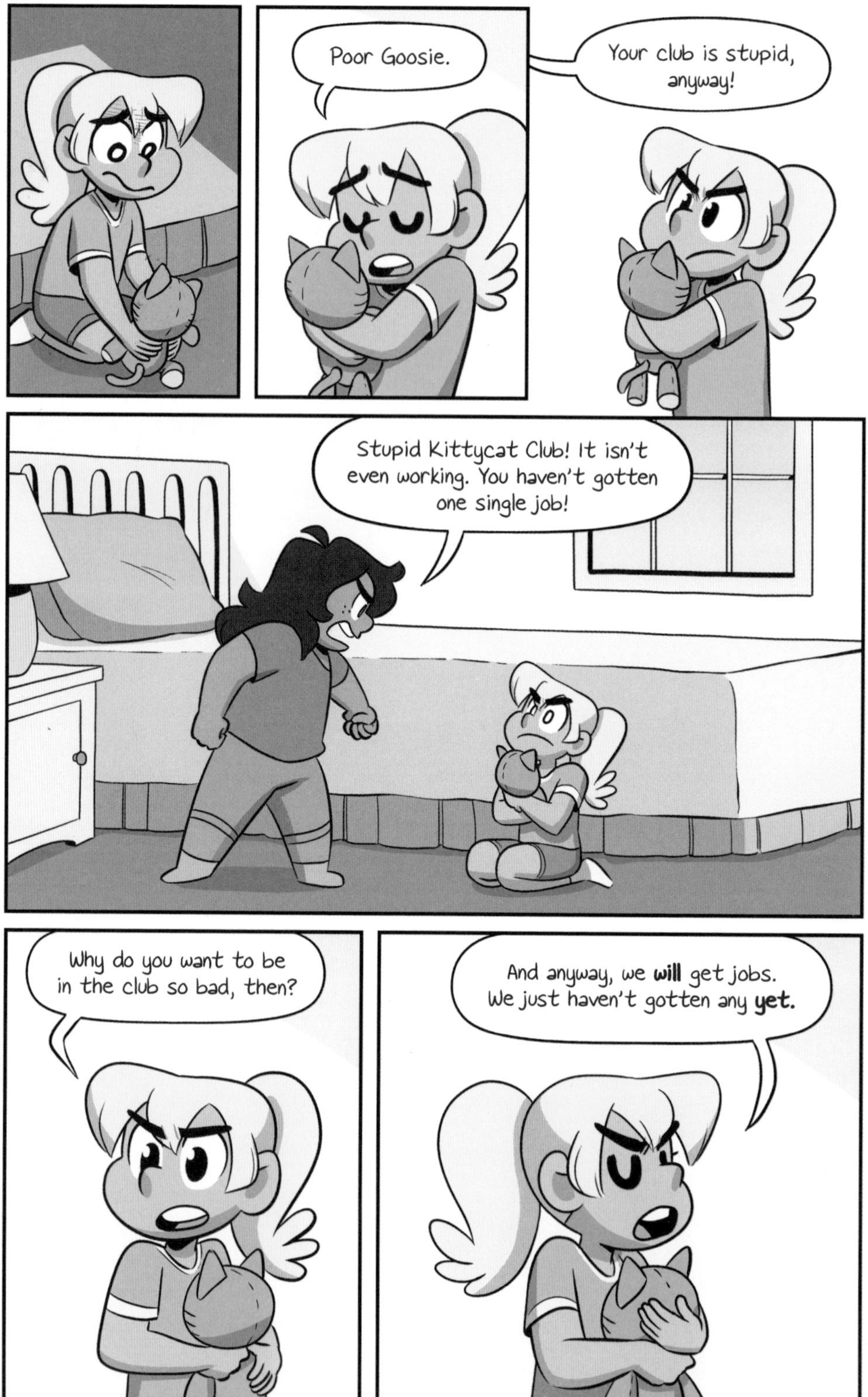
Poor Goosie.
Your club is stupid, anyway!
Stupid Kittycat Club! It isn't even working. You haven't gotten one single job!
Why do you want to be in the club so bad, then?
And anyway, we **will** get jobs. We just haven't gotten any **yet.**

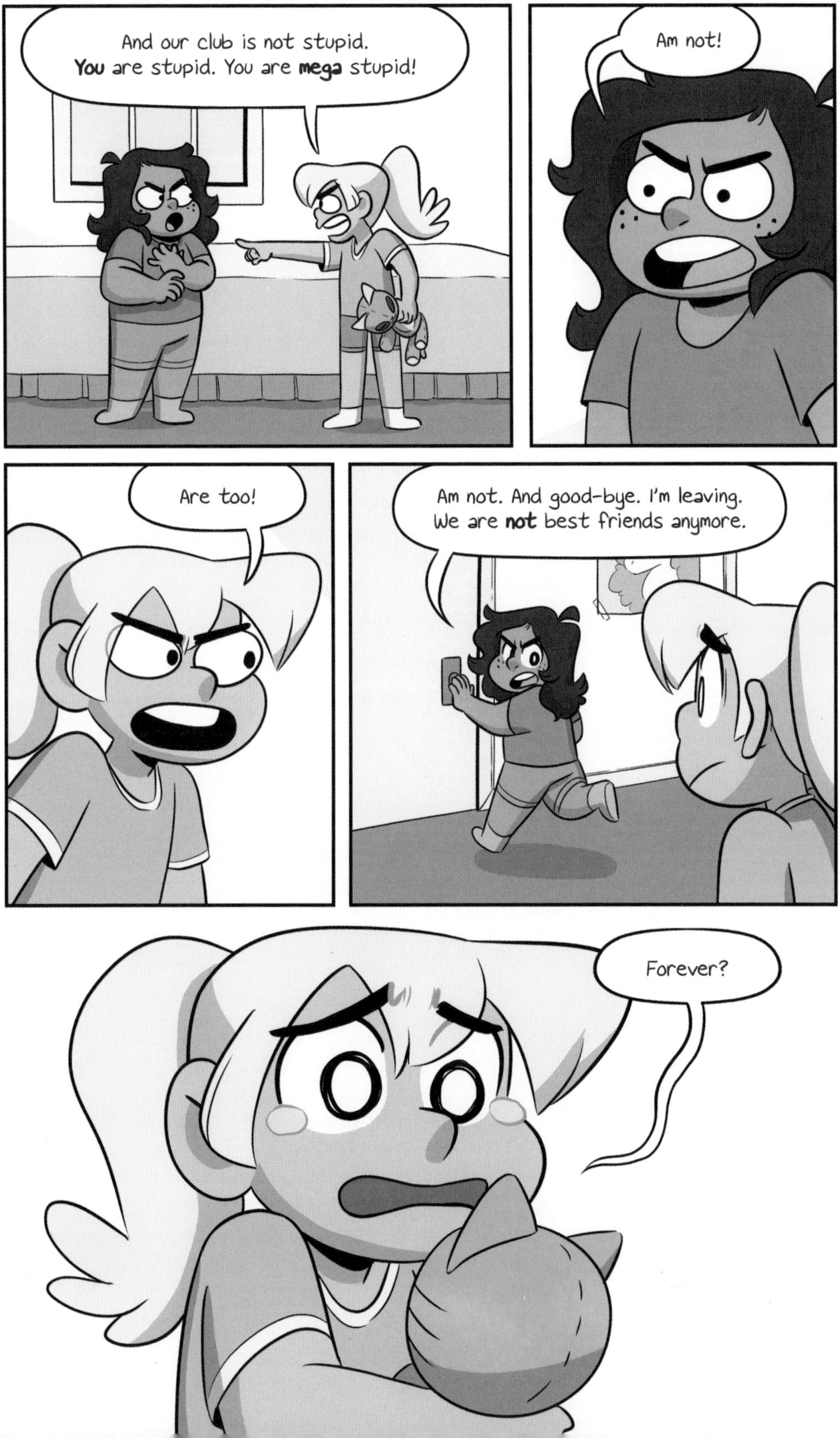
And our club is not stupid.
You are stupid. You are **mega** stupid!
Am not!
Are too!
Am not. And good-bye. I'm leaving.
We are **not** best friends anymore.
Forever?

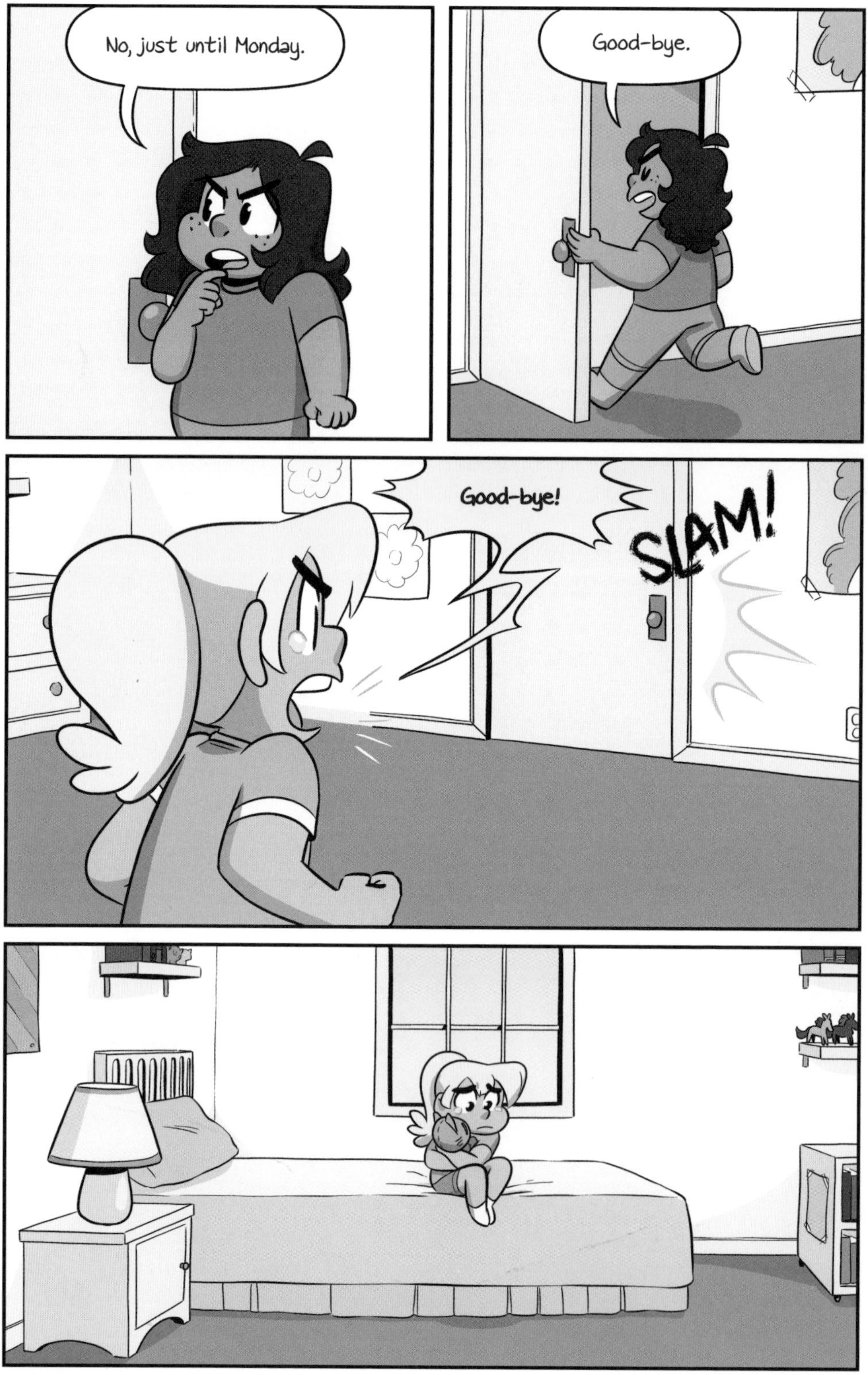
No, just until Monday.
Good-bye.
Good-bye!
SLAM!

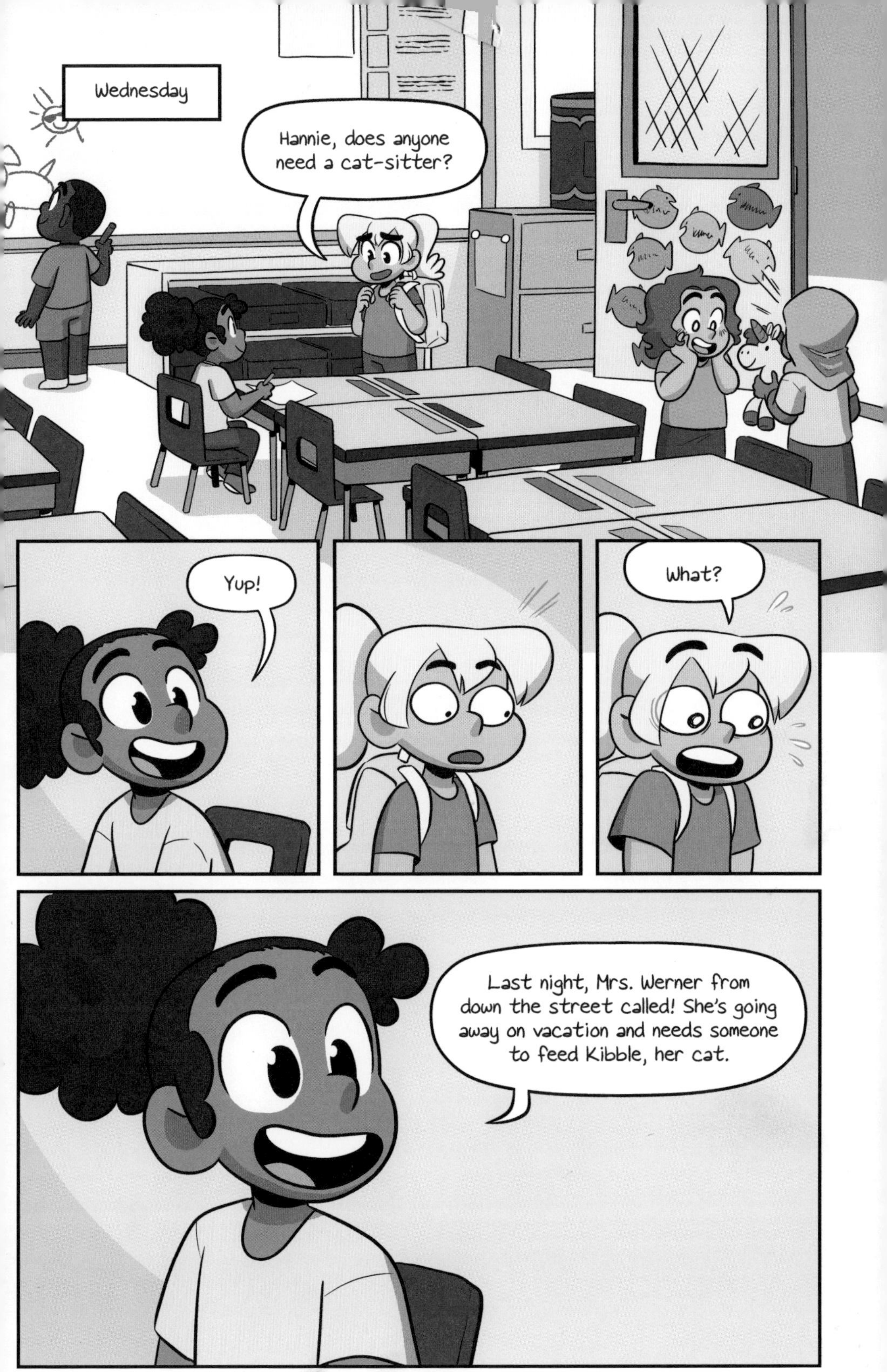
Wednesday
Hannie, does anyone need a cat-sitter?
Yup!
What?
Last night, Mrs. Werner from down the street called! She's going away on vacation and needs someone to feed Kibble, her cat.

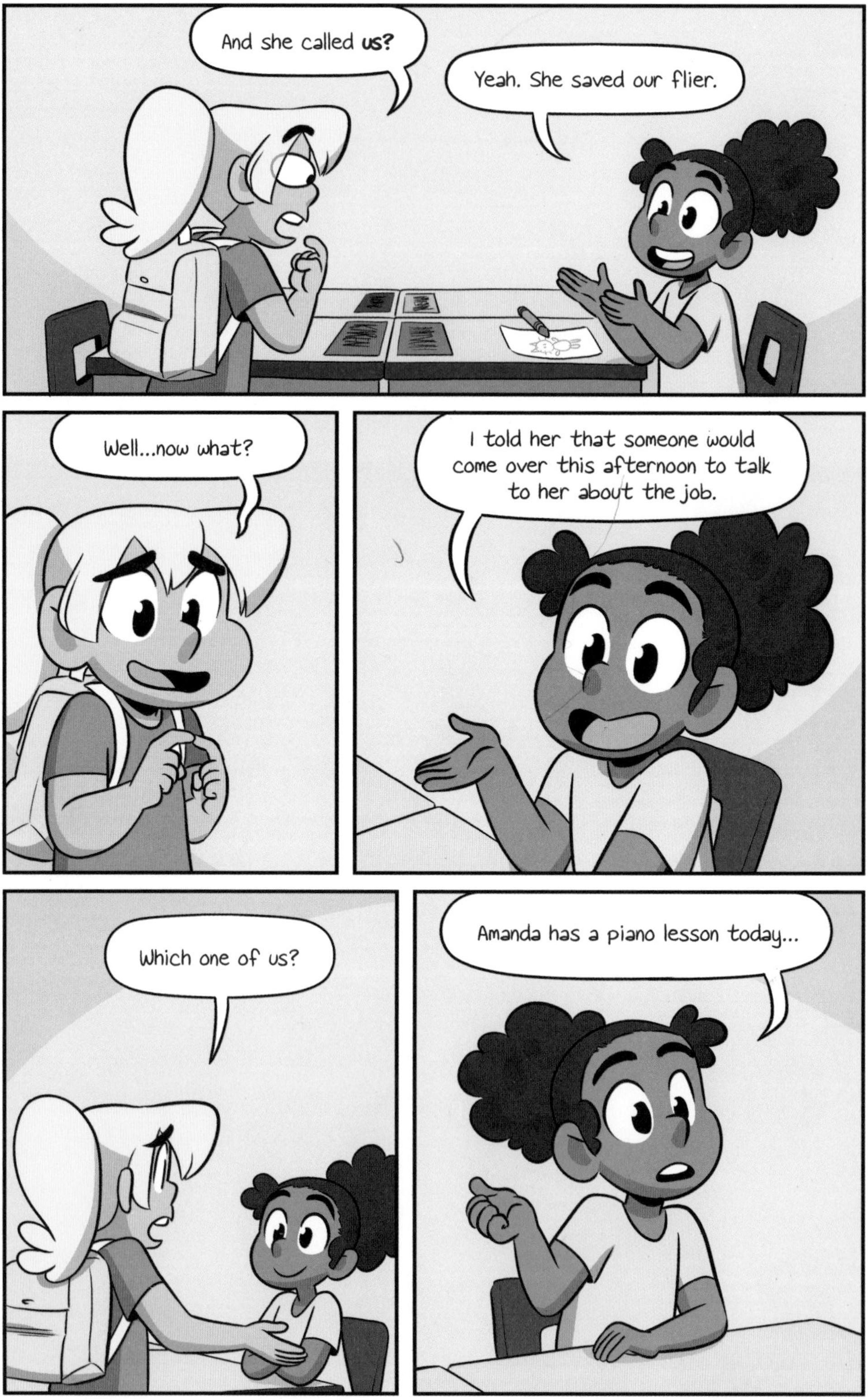
And she called **us?**
Yeah. She saved our flier.
Well...now what?
I told her that someone would come over this afternoon to talk to her about the job.
Which one of us?
Amanda has a piano lesson today...

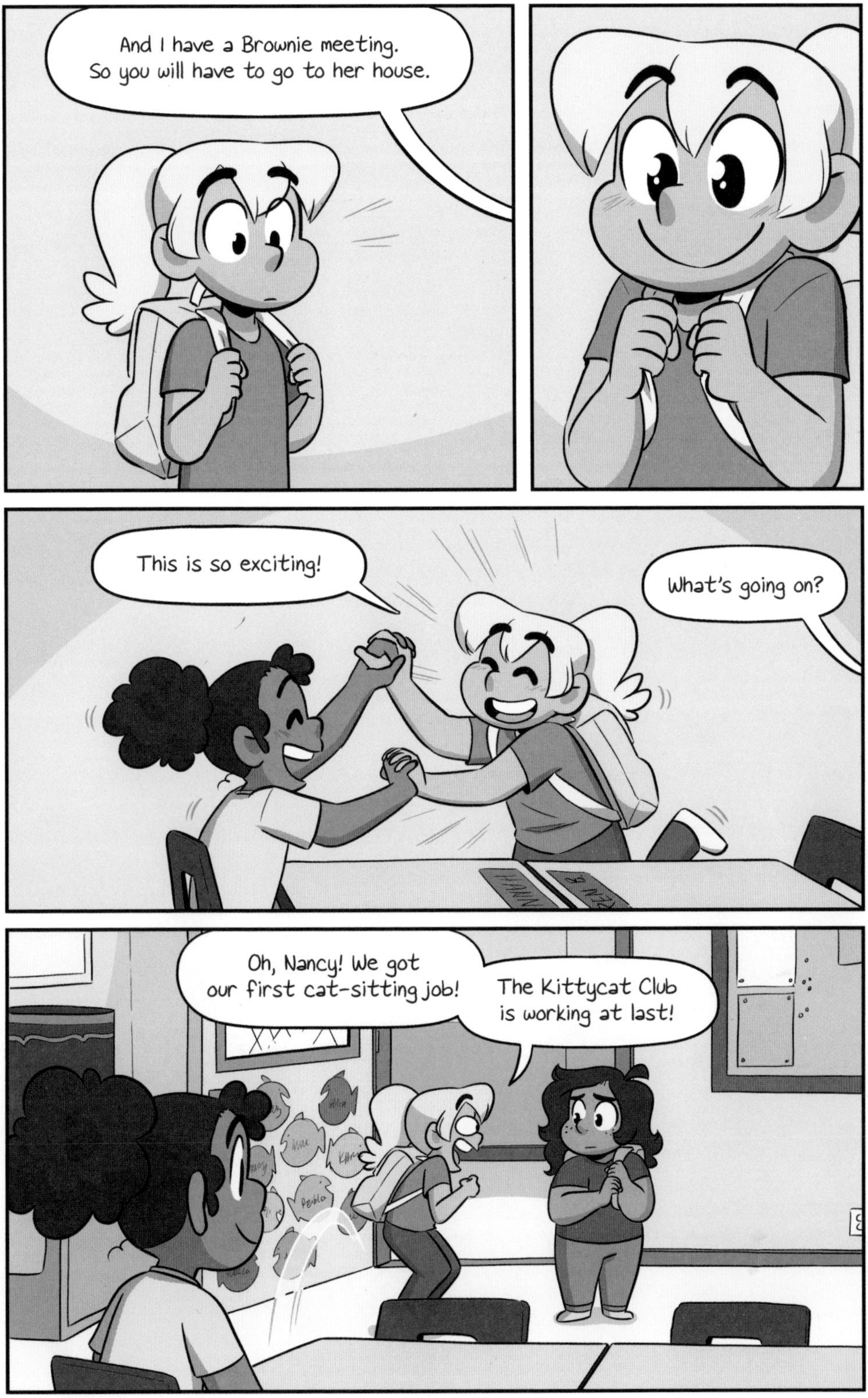
And I have a Brownie meeting. So you will have to go to her house.
This is so exciting!
What's going on?
Oh, Nancy! We got our first cat-sitting job!
The Kittycat Club is working at last!

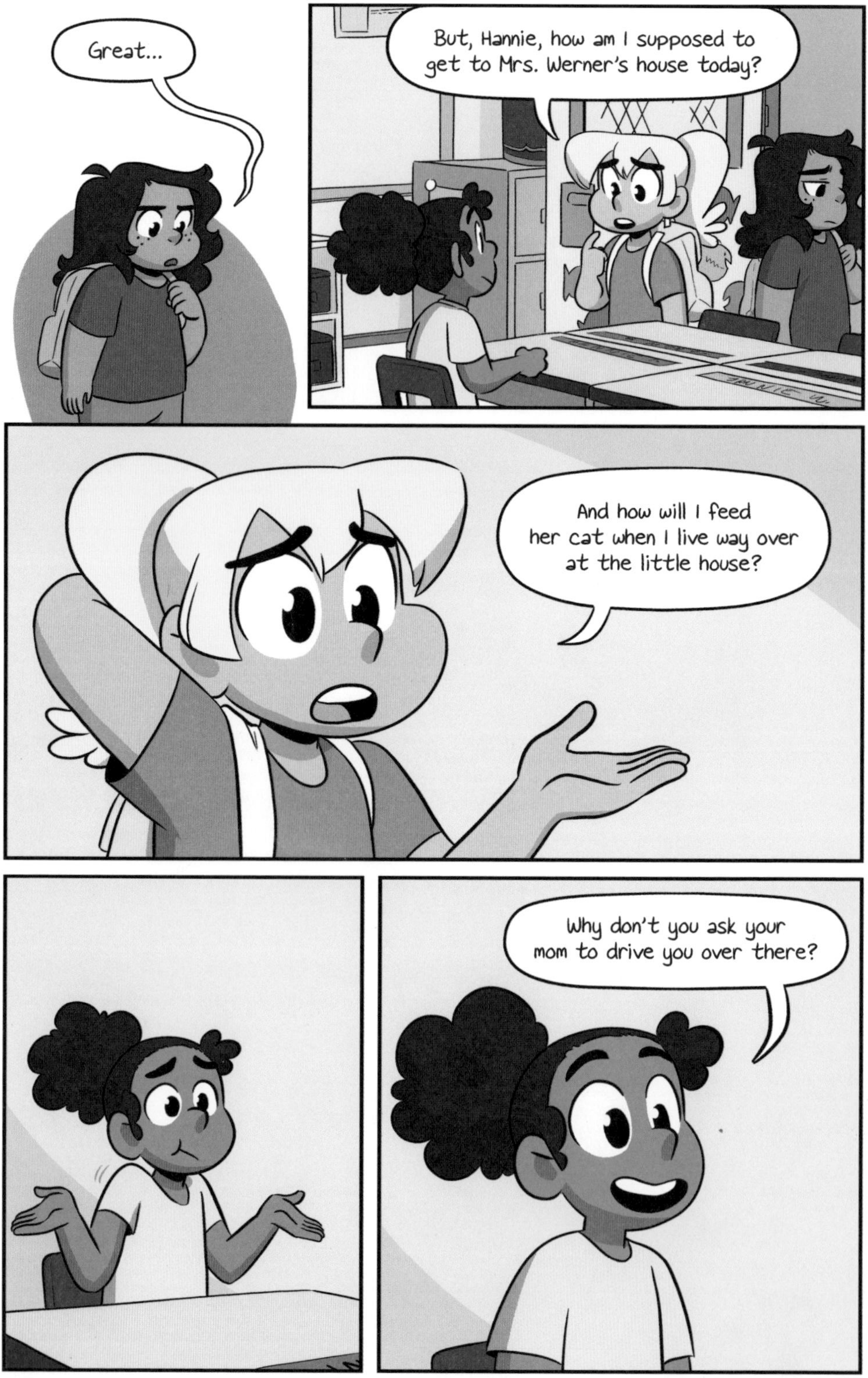
Great...
But, Hannie, how am I supposed to get to Mrs. Werner's house today?
And how will I feed her cat when I live way over at the little house?
Why don't you ask your mom to drive you over there?

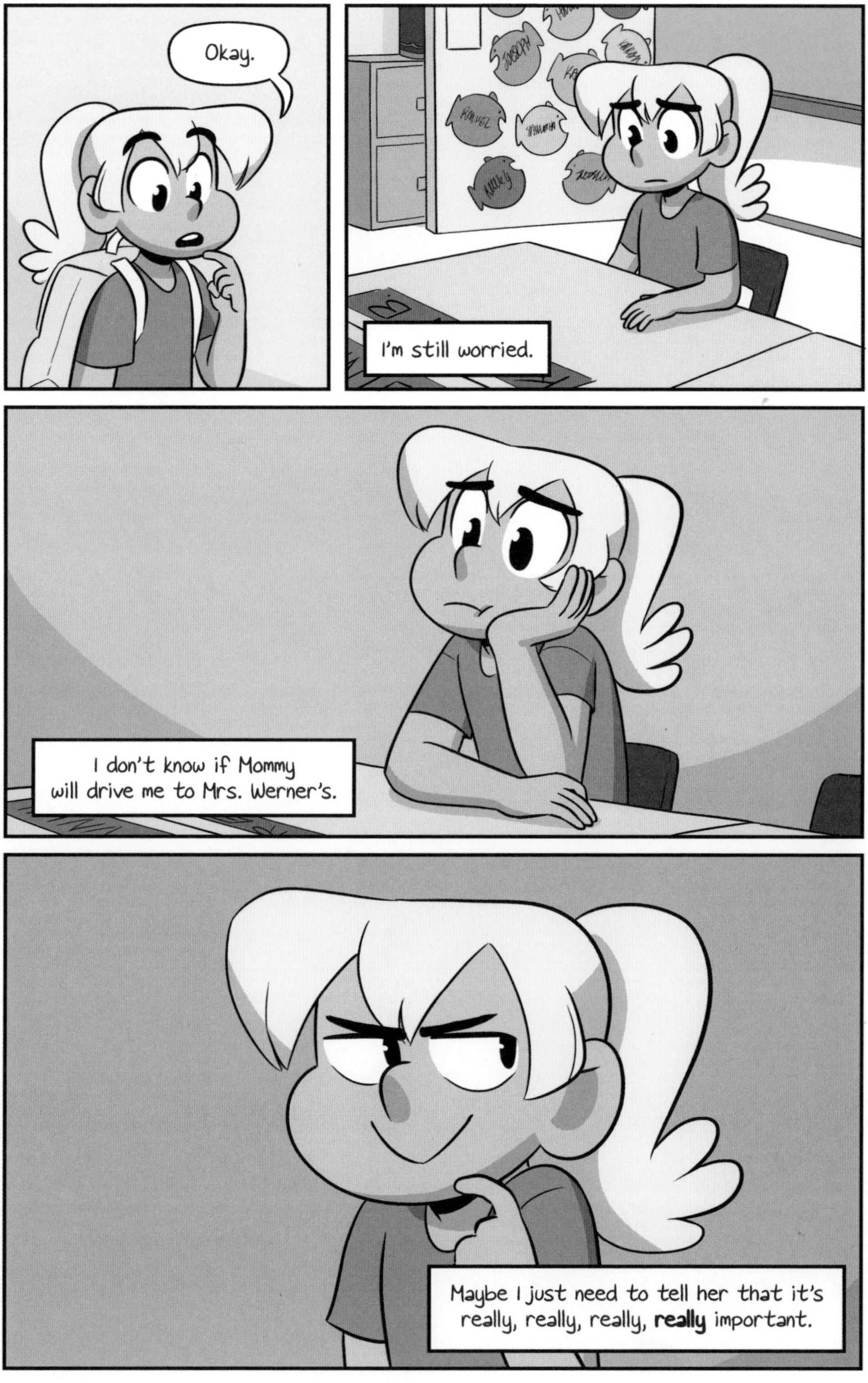
Okay.
I'm still worried.
I don't know if Mommy will drive me to Mrs. Werner's.
Maybe I just need to tell her that it's really, really, really, **really** important.

CHAPTER 8

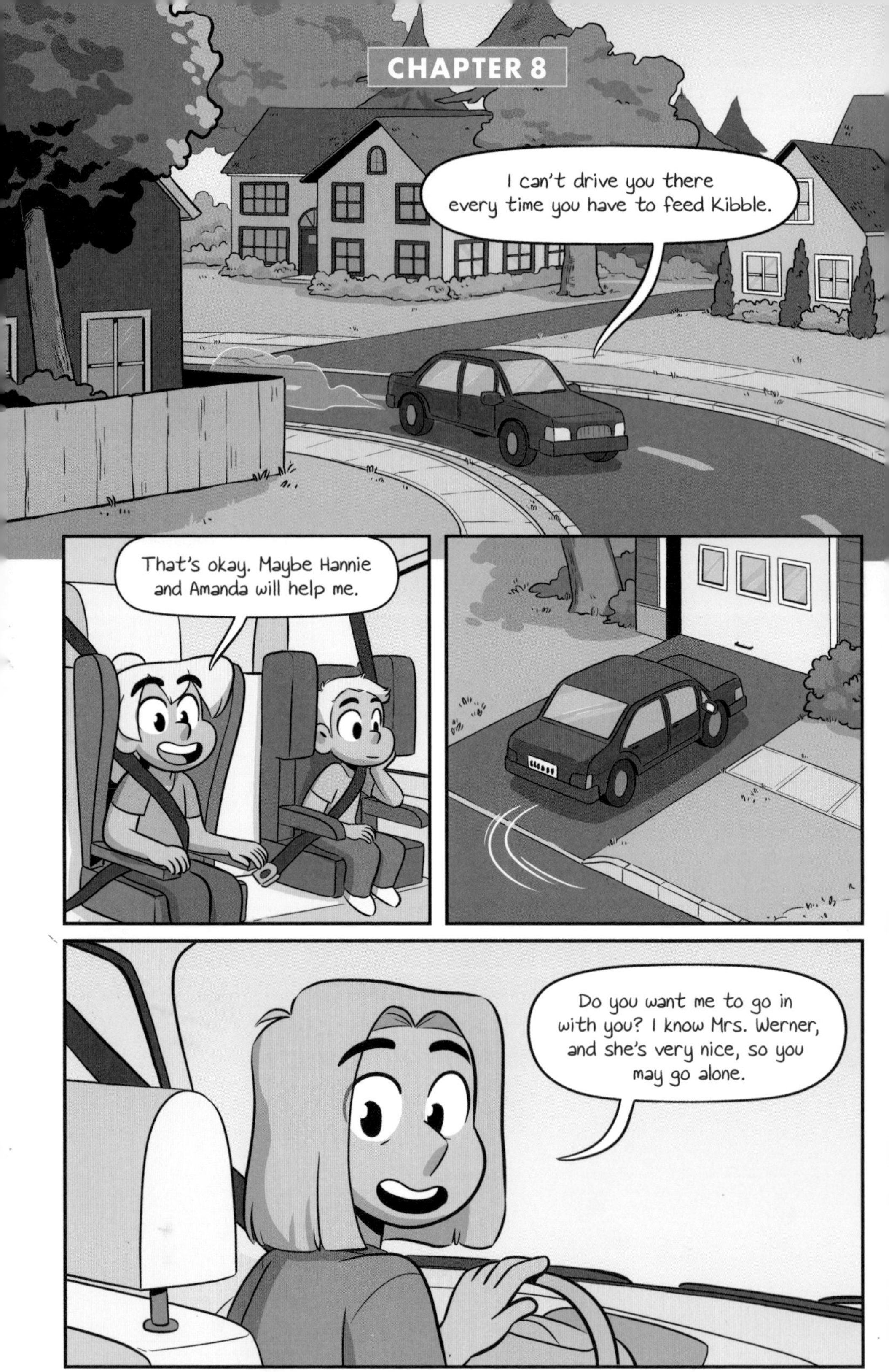
I can't drive you there every time you have to feed Kibble.
That's okay. Maybe Hannie and Amanda will help me.
Do you want me to go in with you? I know Mrs. Werner, and she's very nice, so you may go alone.

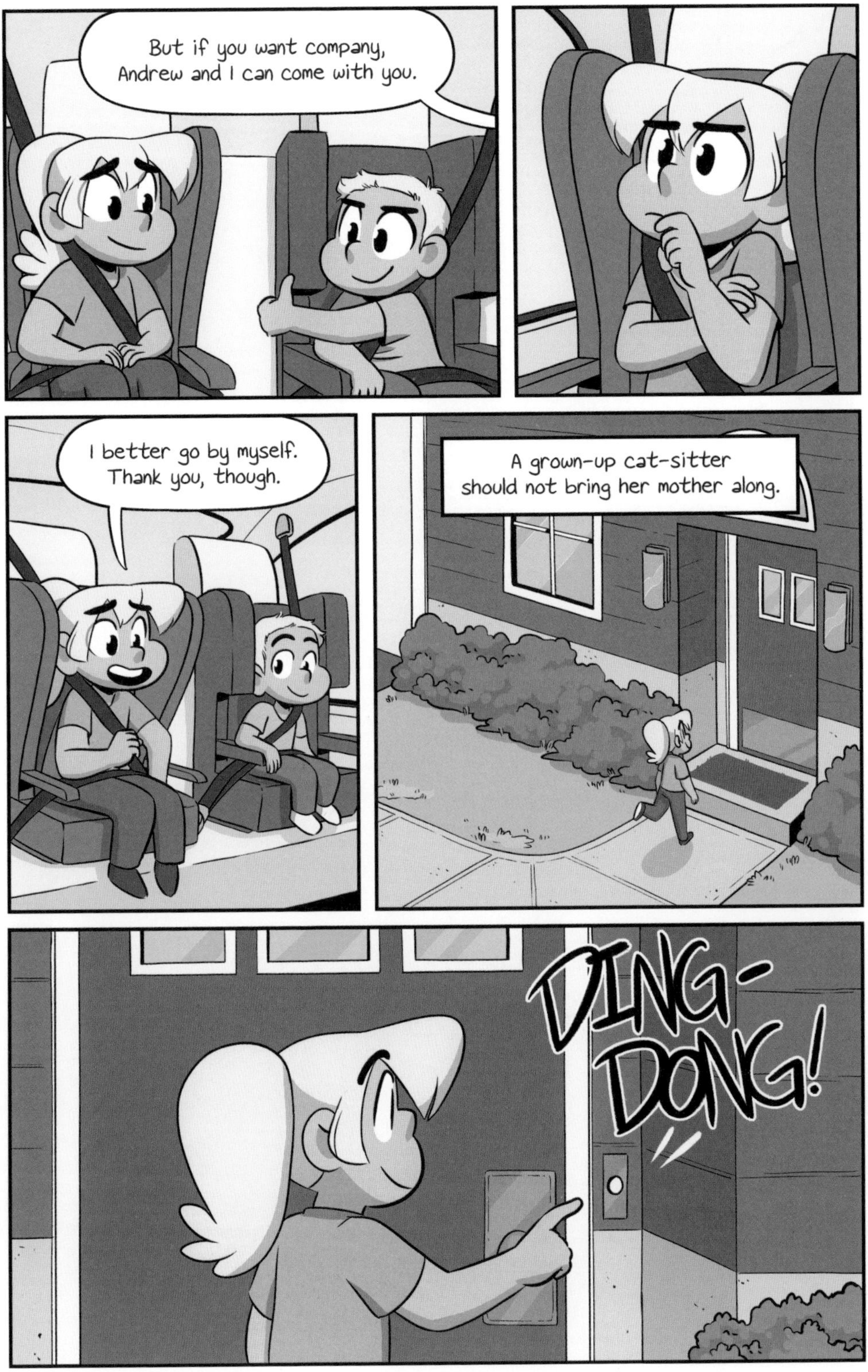
But if you want company, Andrew and I can come with you.
I better go by myself. Thank you, though.
A grown-up cat-sitter should not bring her mother along.
DING-DONG!

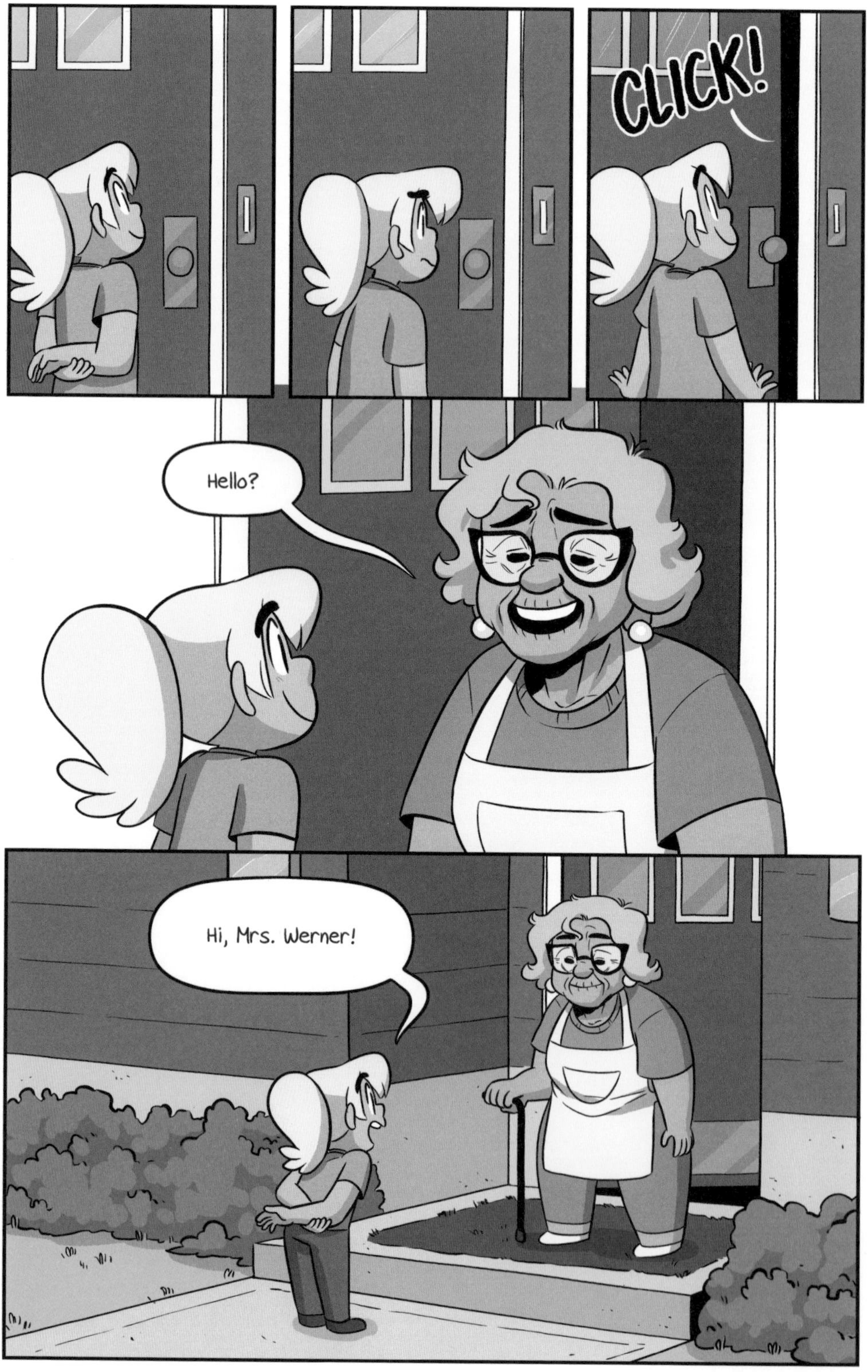
CLICK!
Hello?
Hi, Mrs. Werner!

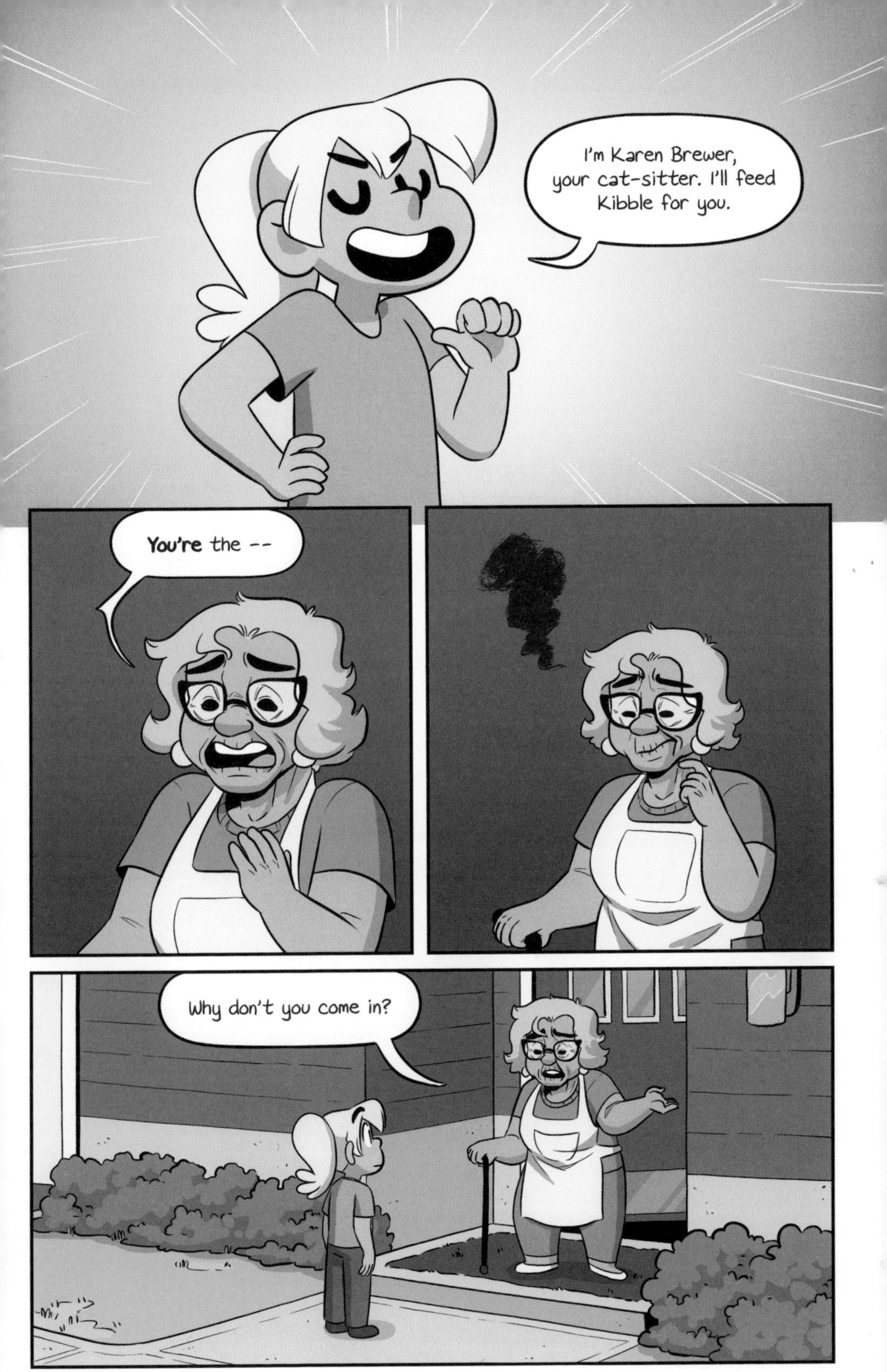
I'm Karen Brewer, your cat-sitter. I'll feed Kibble for you.
You're the --
Why don't you come in?

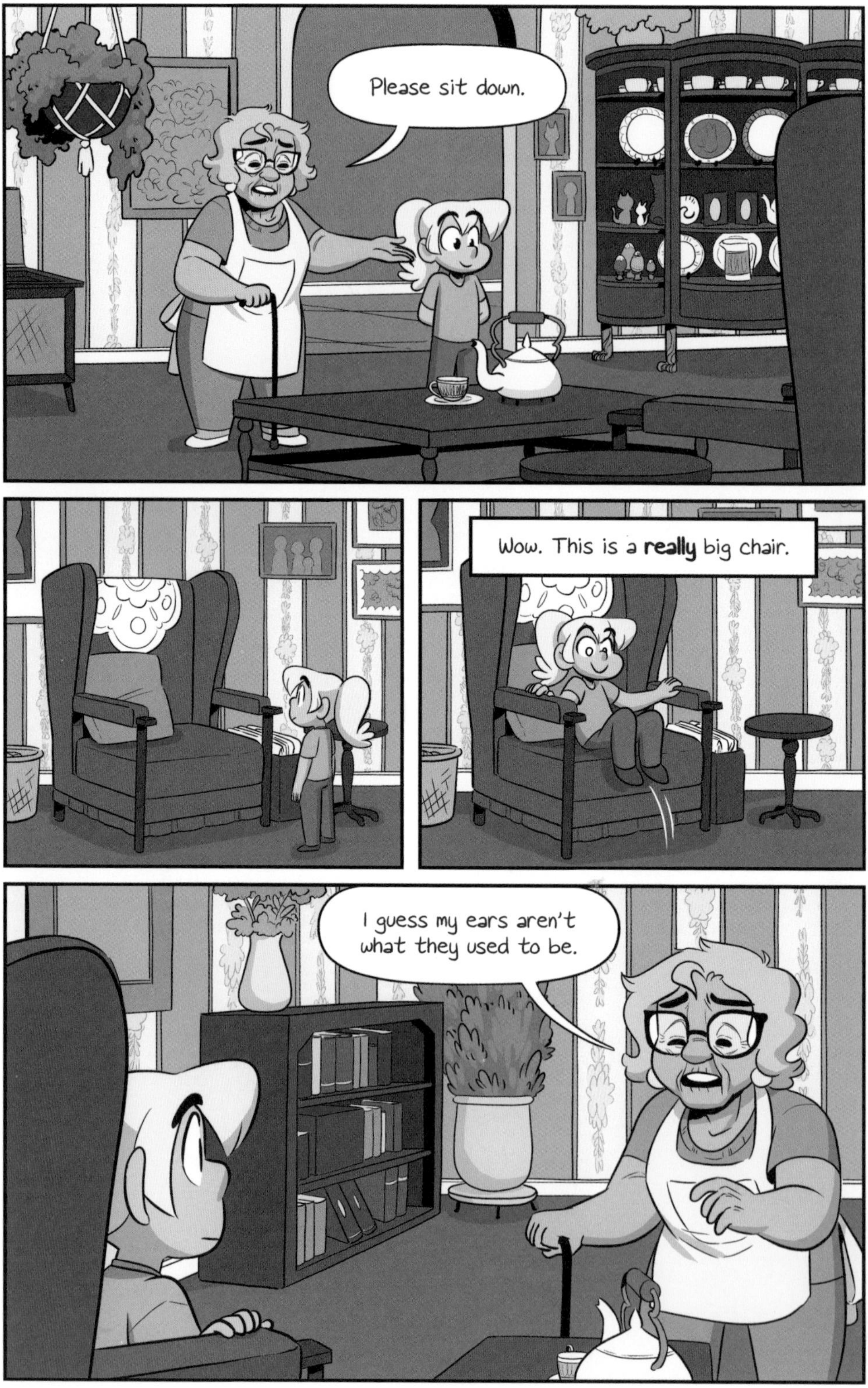
Please sit down.
Wow. This is a **really** big chair.
I guess my ears aren't what they used to be.

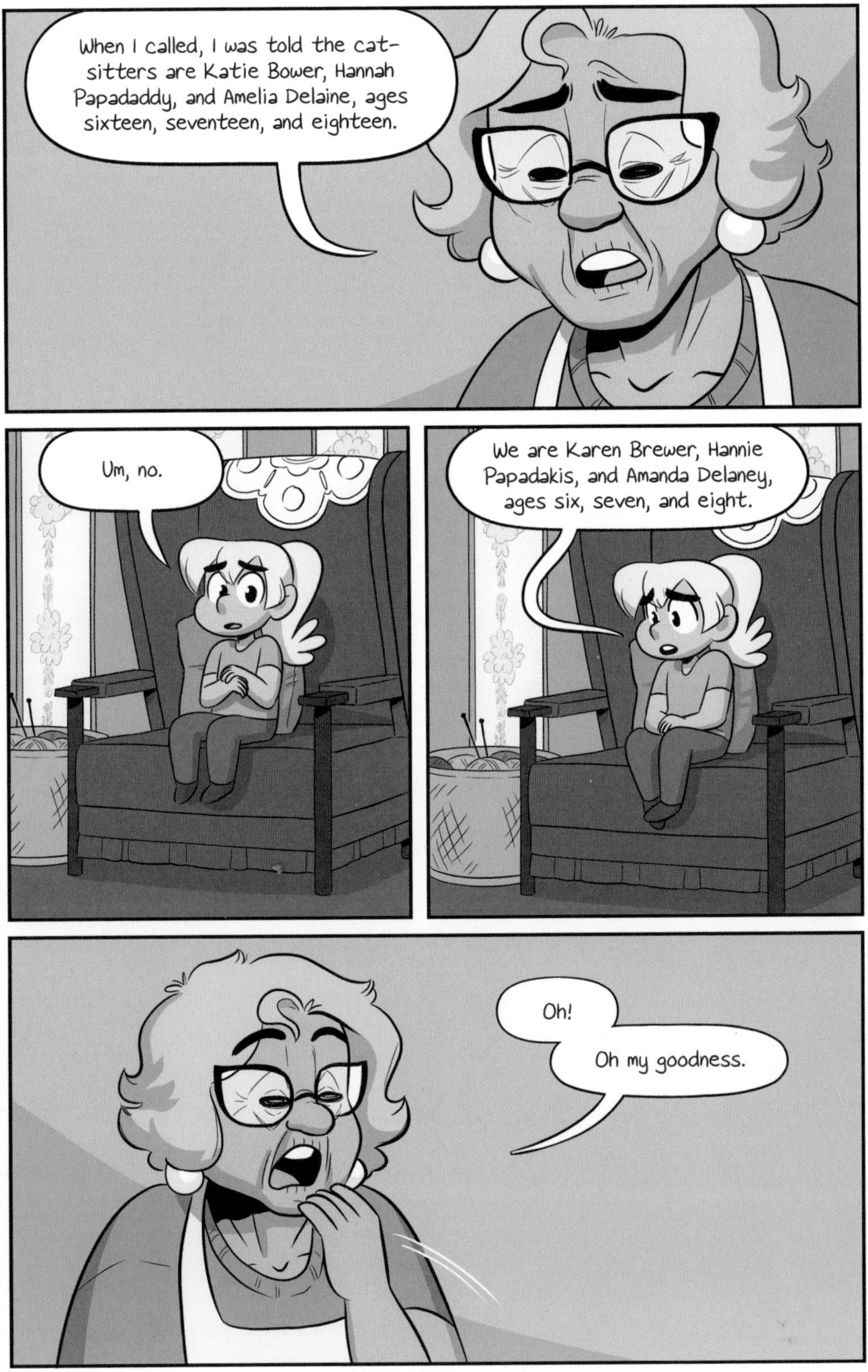

When I called, I was told the cat-sitters are Katie Bower, Hannah Papadaddy, and Amelia Delaine, ages sixteen, seventeen, and eighteen.
Um, no.
We are Karen Brewer, Hannie Papadakis, and Amanda Delaney, ages six, seven, and eight.
Oh!
Oh my goodness.

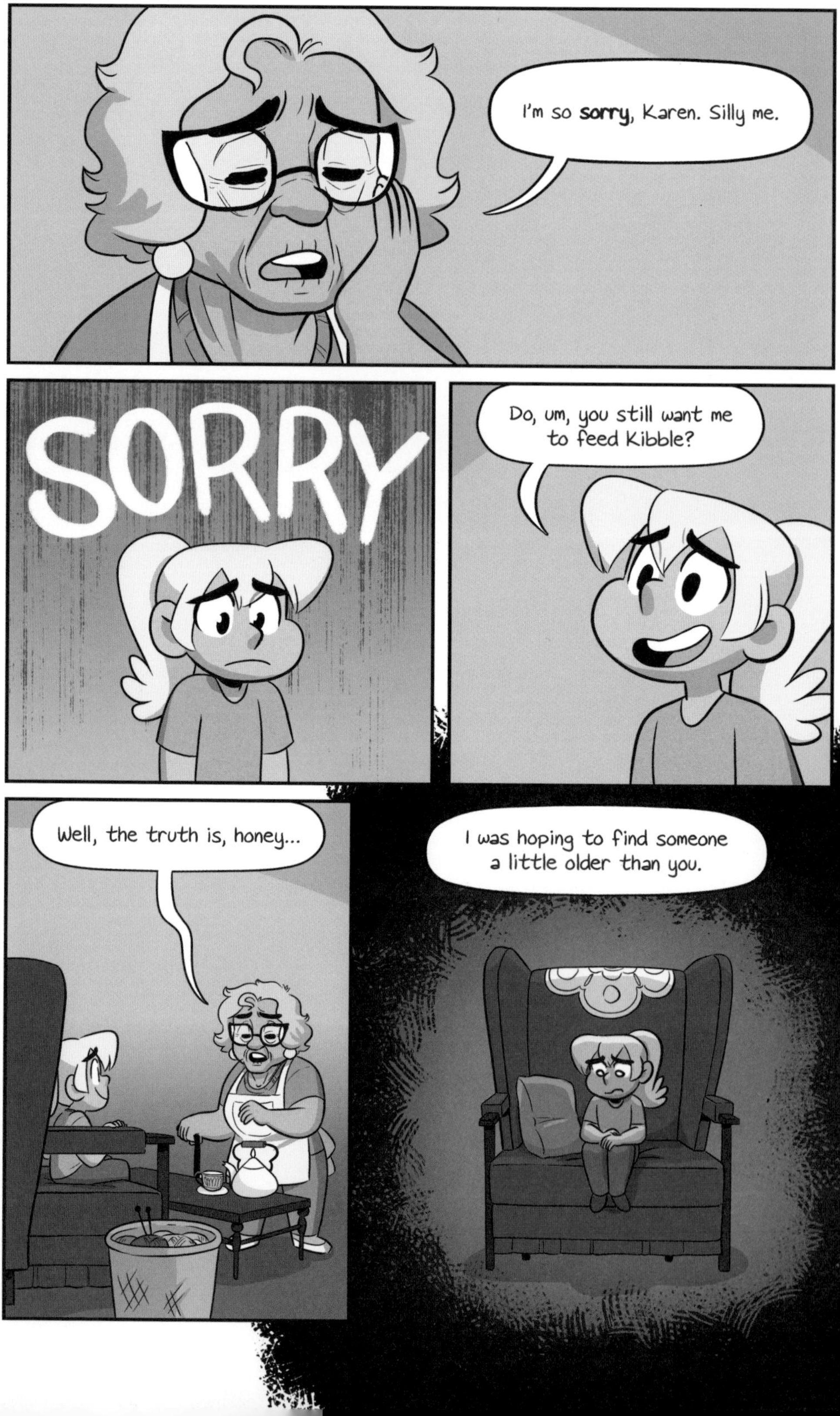
I'm so **sorry**, Karen. Silly me.
SORRY
Do, um, you still want me to feed Kibble?
Well, the truth is, honey...
I was hoping to find someone a little older than you.

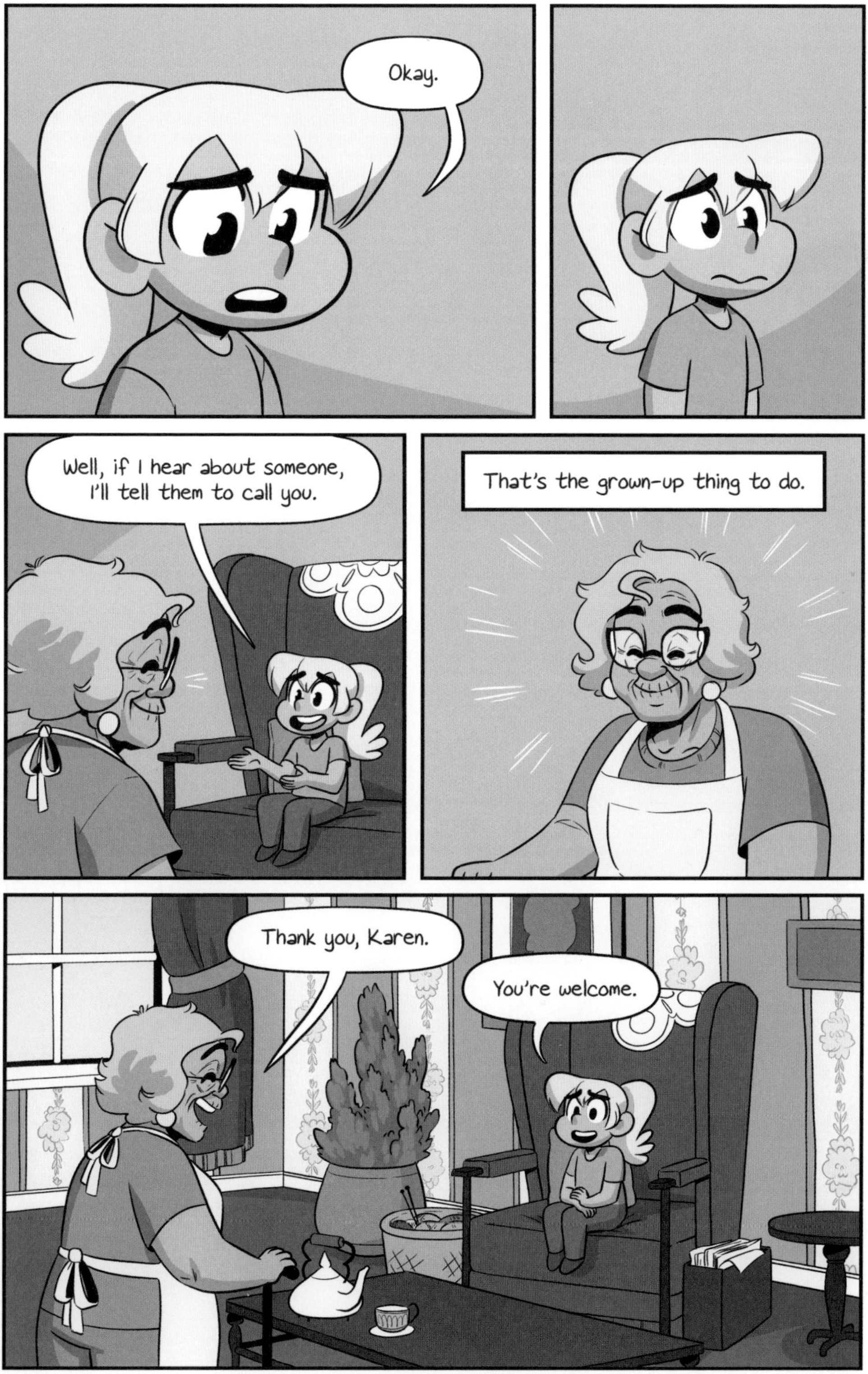
Okay.
Well, if I hear about someone, I'll tell them to call you.
That's the grown-up thing to do.
Thank you, Karen.
You're welcome.

KAYLEIGH

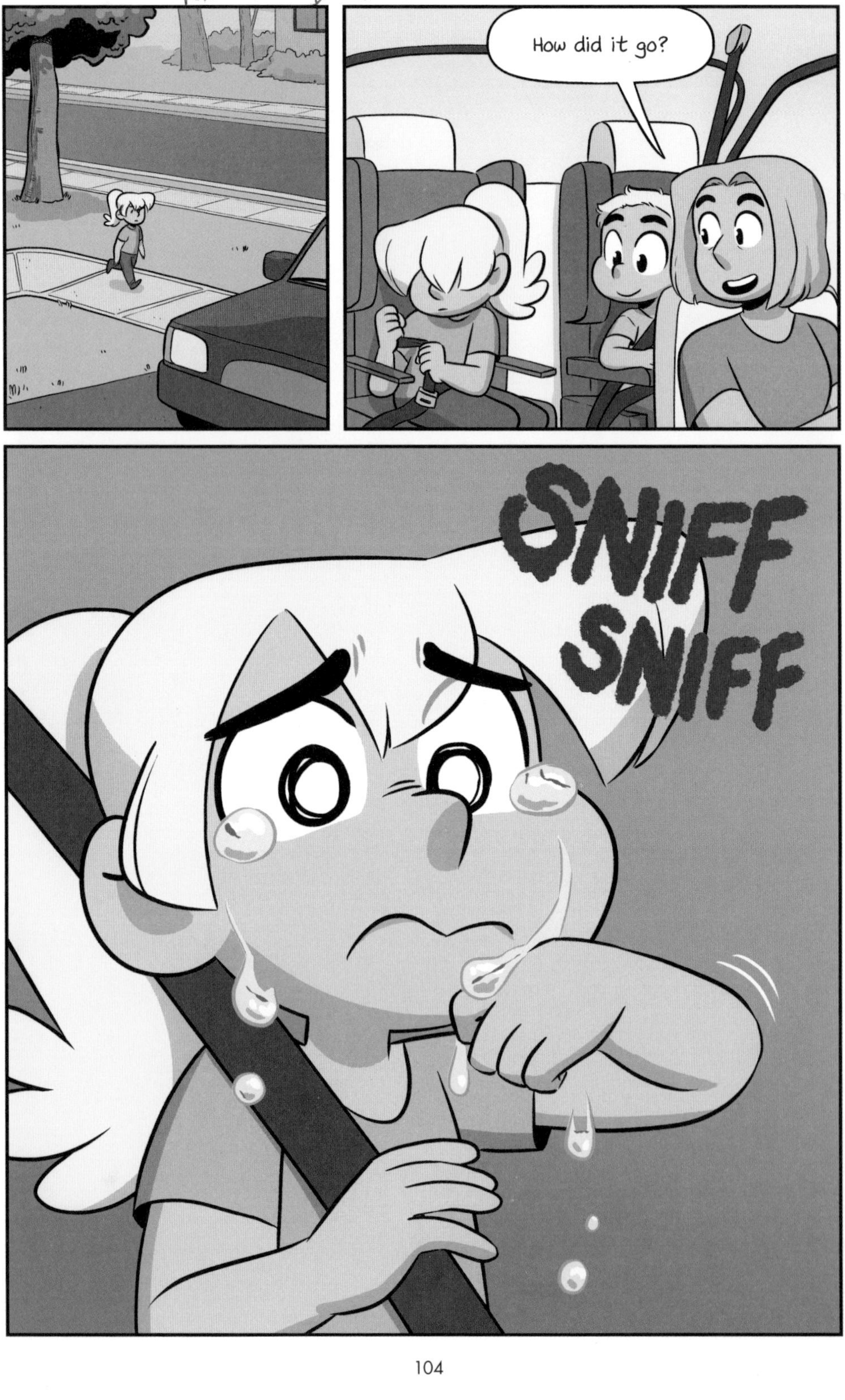
How did it go?
SNIFF
SNIFF

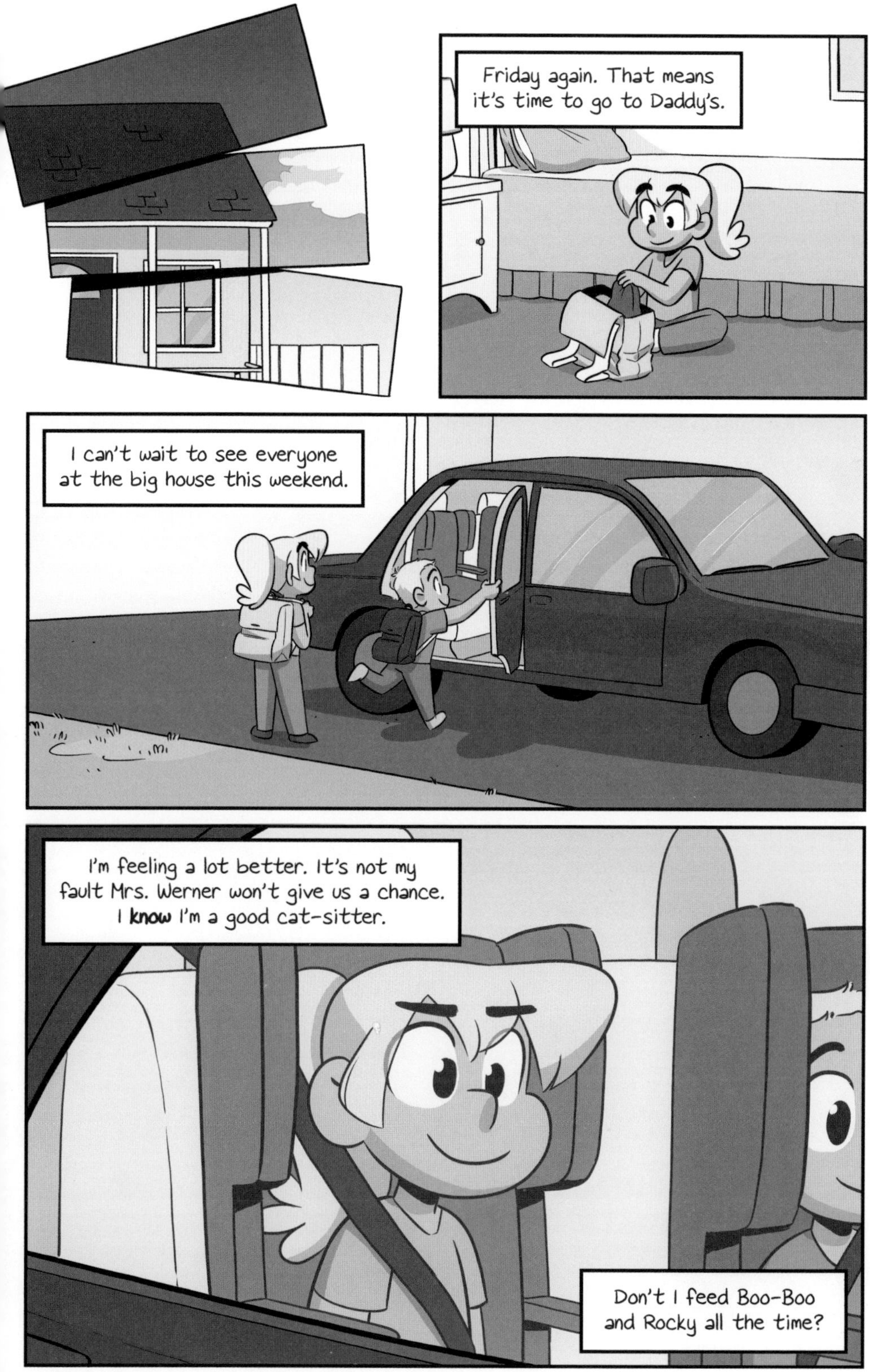
Friday again. That means it's time to go to Daddy's.
I can't wait to see everyone at the big house this weekend.
I'm feeling a lot better. It's not my fault Mrs. Werner won't give us a chance. I **know** I'm a good cat-sitter.
Don't I feed Boo-Boo and Rocky all the time?

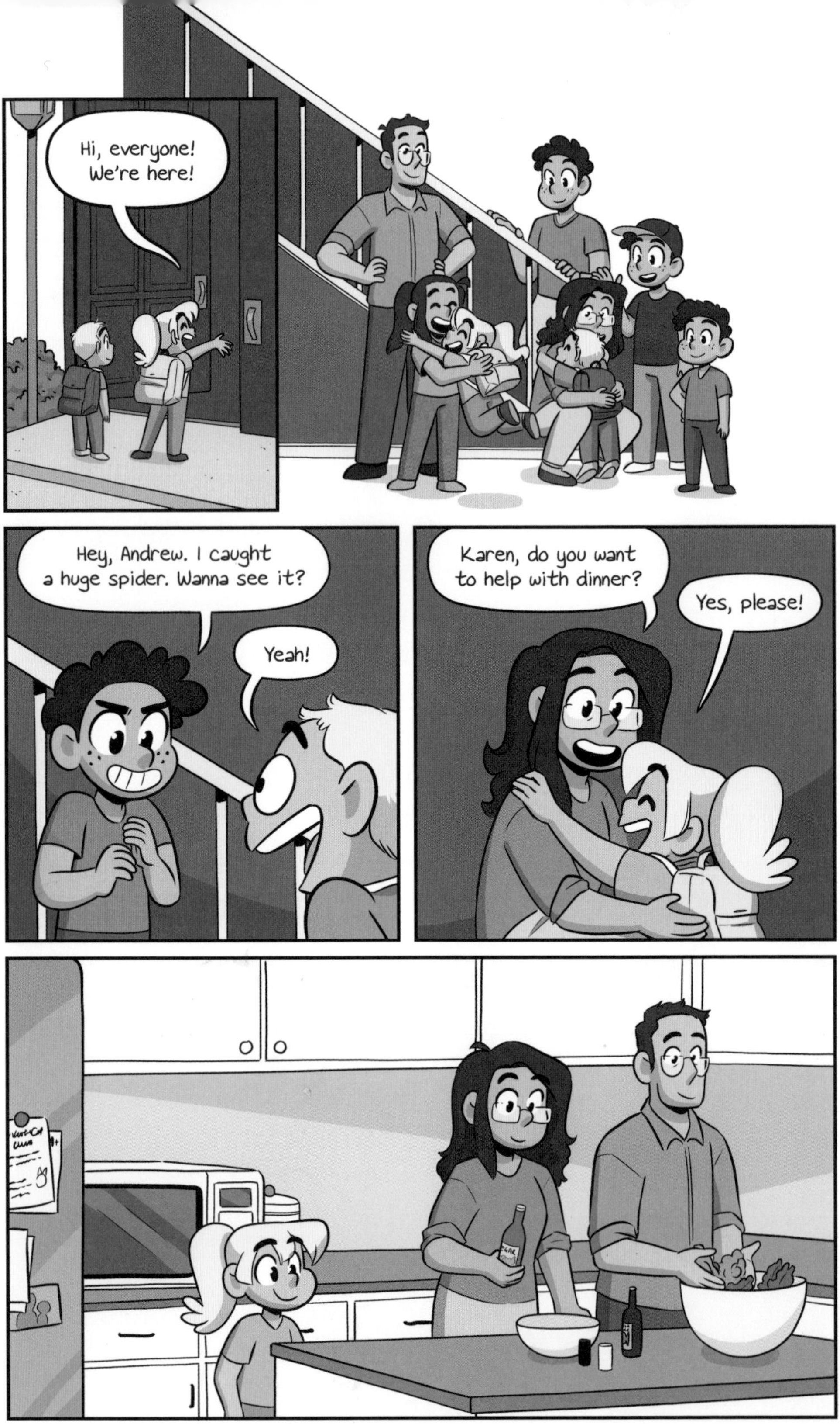
Hi, everyone! We're here!
Hey, Andrew. I caught a huge spider. Wanna see it?
Yeah!
Karen, do you want to help with dinner?
Yes, please!

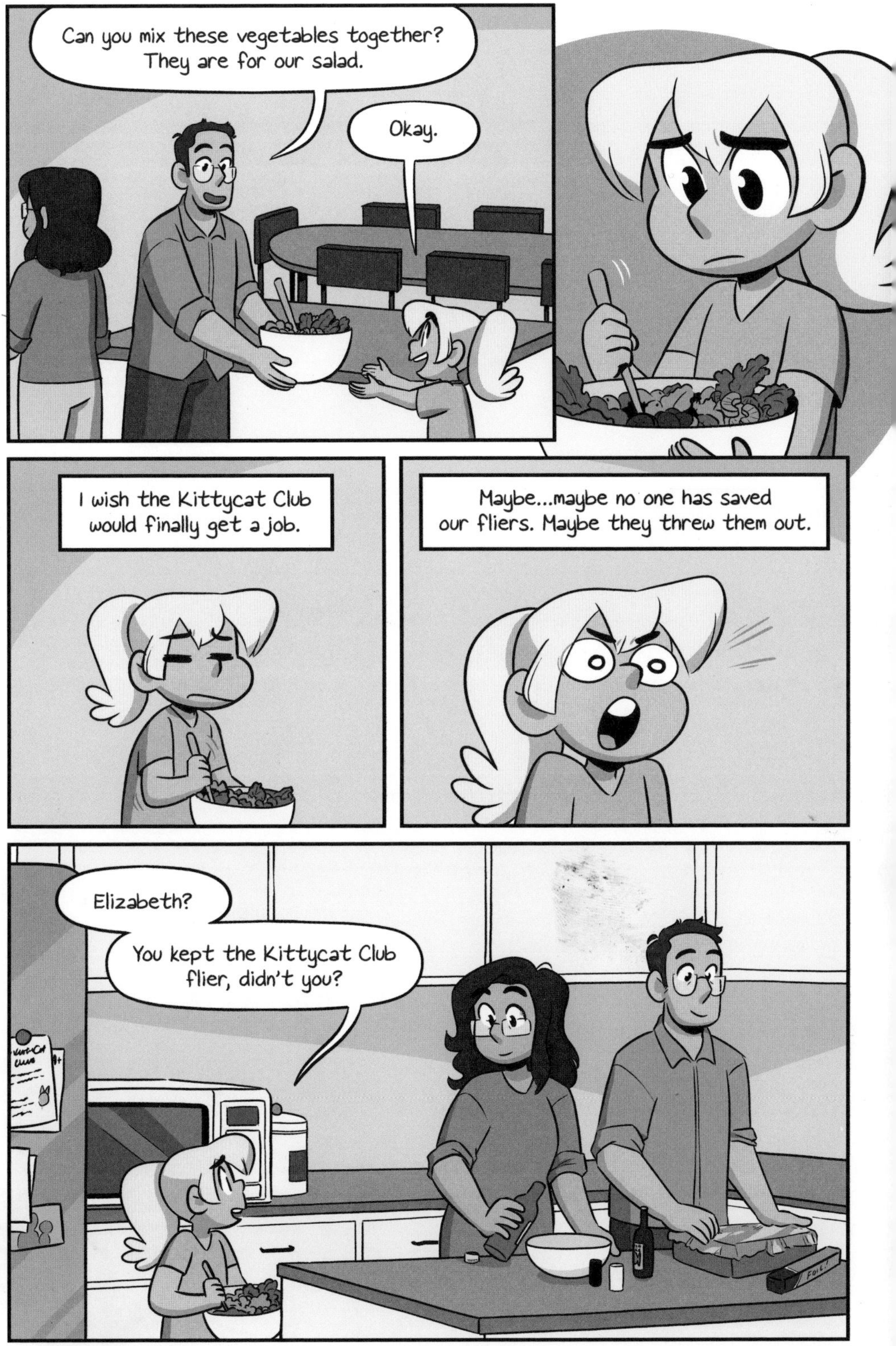
Can you mix these vegetables together? They are for our salad.
Okay.
I wish the Kittycat Club would finally get a job.
Maybe...maybe no one has saved our fliers. Maybe they threw them out.
Elizabeth?
You kept the Kittycat Club flier, didn't you?

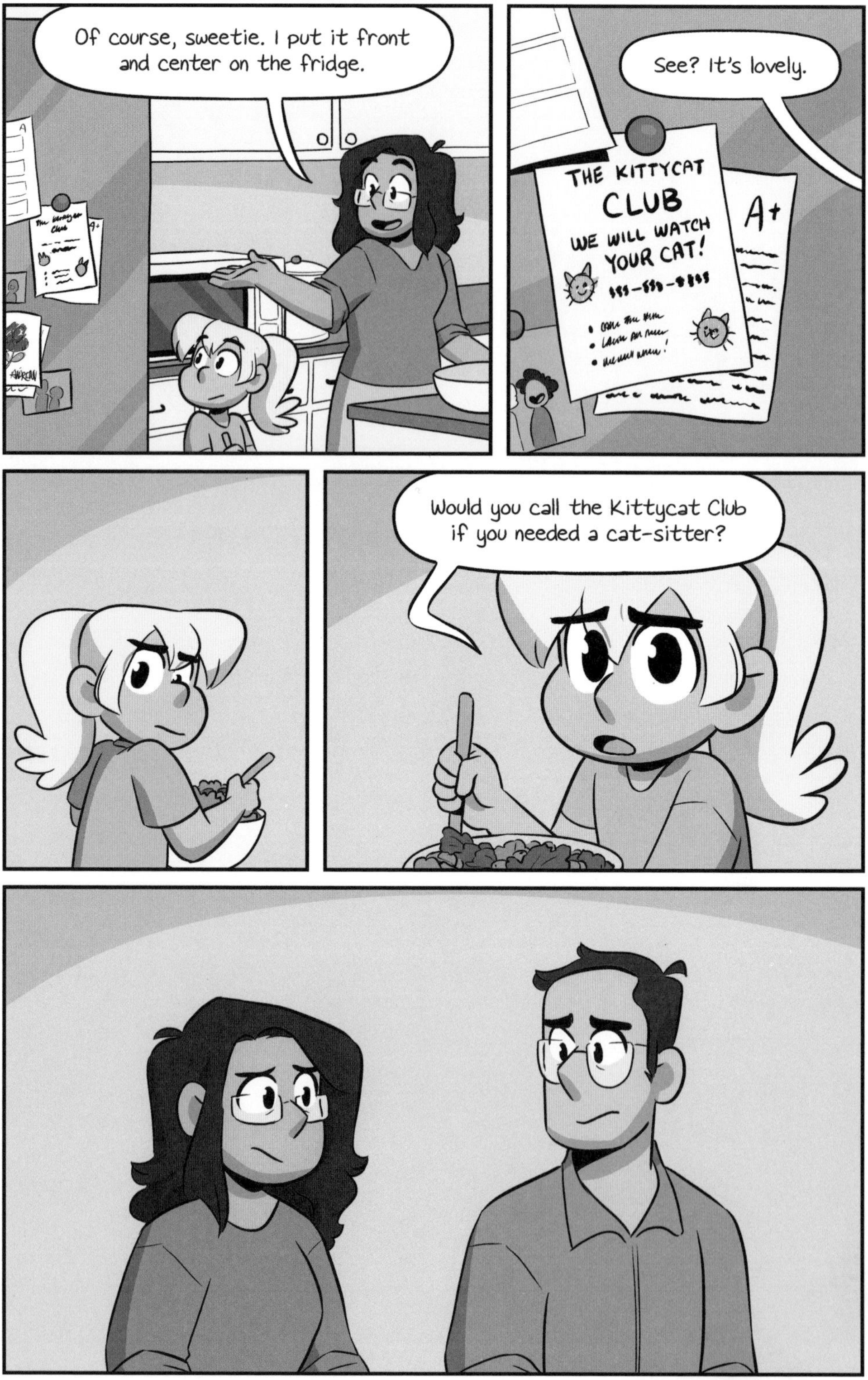
Of course, sweetie. I put it front and center on the fridge.
See? It's lovely.
THE KITTYCAT CLUB
WE WILL WATCH YOUR CAT!
A+
Would you call the Kittycat Club if you needed a cat-sitter?

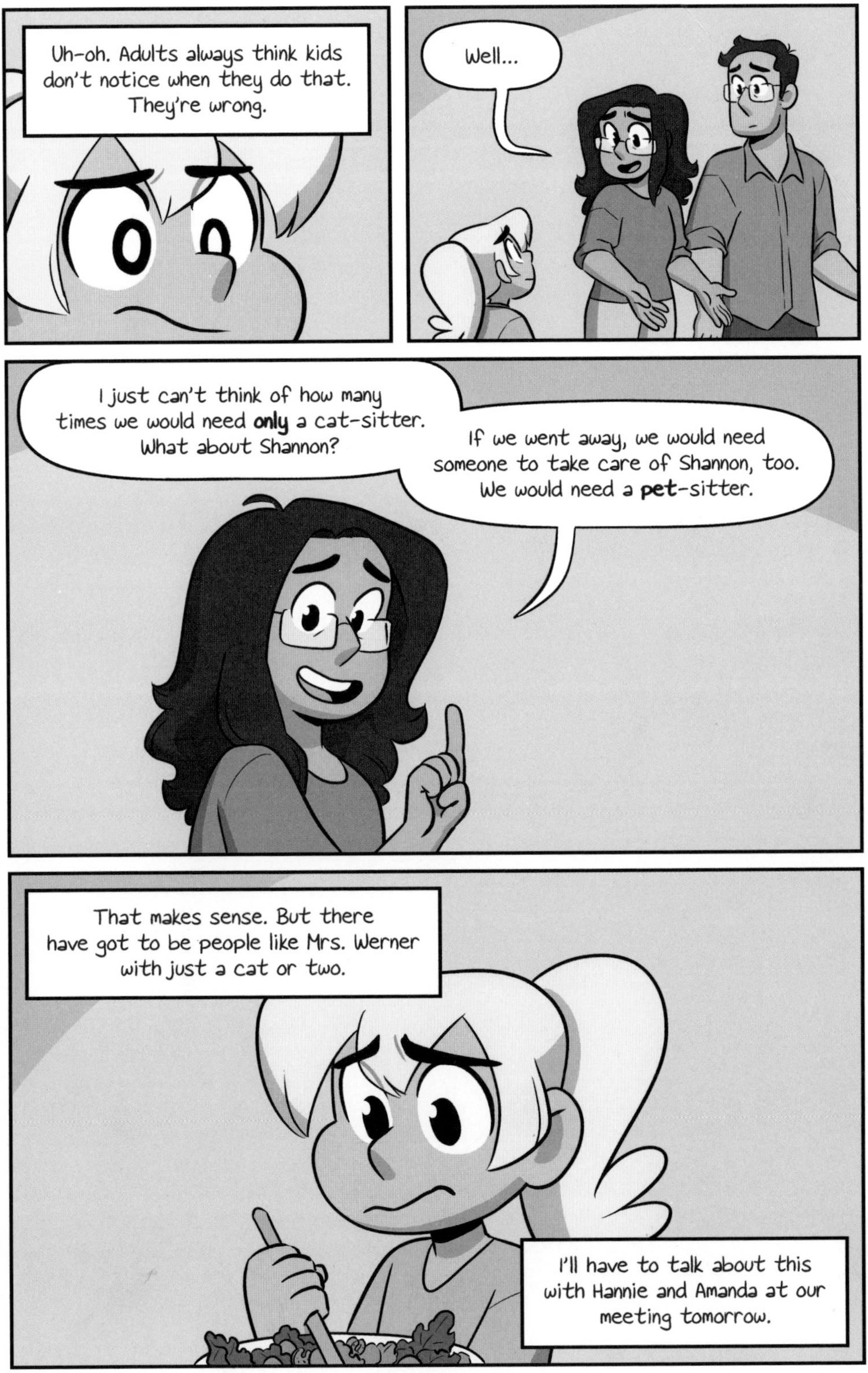
Uh-oh. Adults always think kids don't notice when they do that. They're wrong.
Well...
I just can't think of how many times we would need **only** a cat-sitter. What about Shannon?
If we went away, we would need someone to take care of Shannon, too. We would need a **pet**-sitter.
That makes sense. But there have got to be people like Mrs. Werner with just a cat or two.
I'll have to talk about this with Hannie and Amanda at our meeting tomorrow.

CHAPTER 9

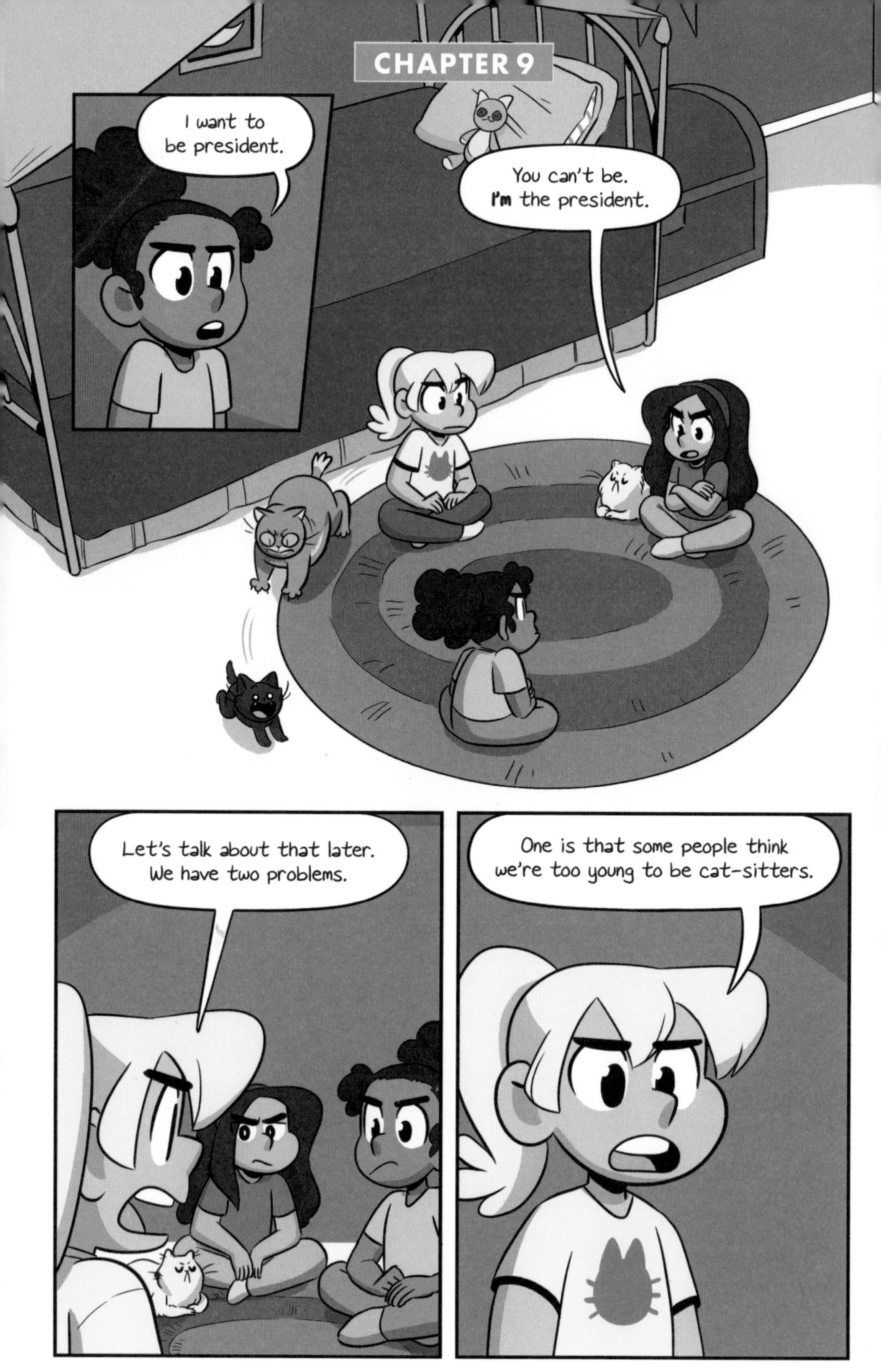
I want to be president.
You can't be. I'm the president.
Let's talk about that later. We have two problems.
One is that some people think we're too young to be cat-sitters.

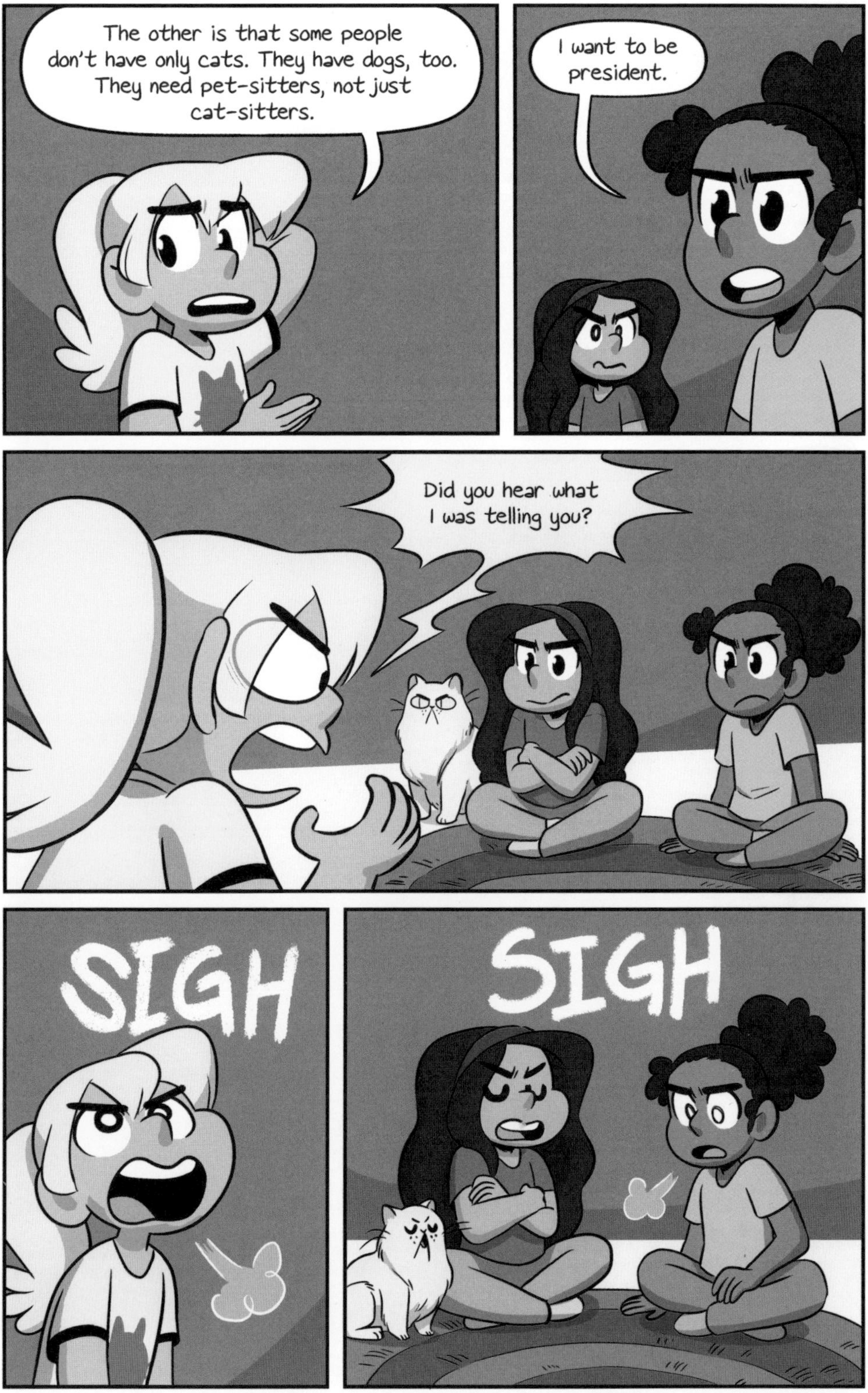
The other is that some people don't have only cats. They have dogs, too. They need pet-sitters, not just cat-sitters.
I want to be president.
Did you hear what I was telling you?
SIGH
SIGH

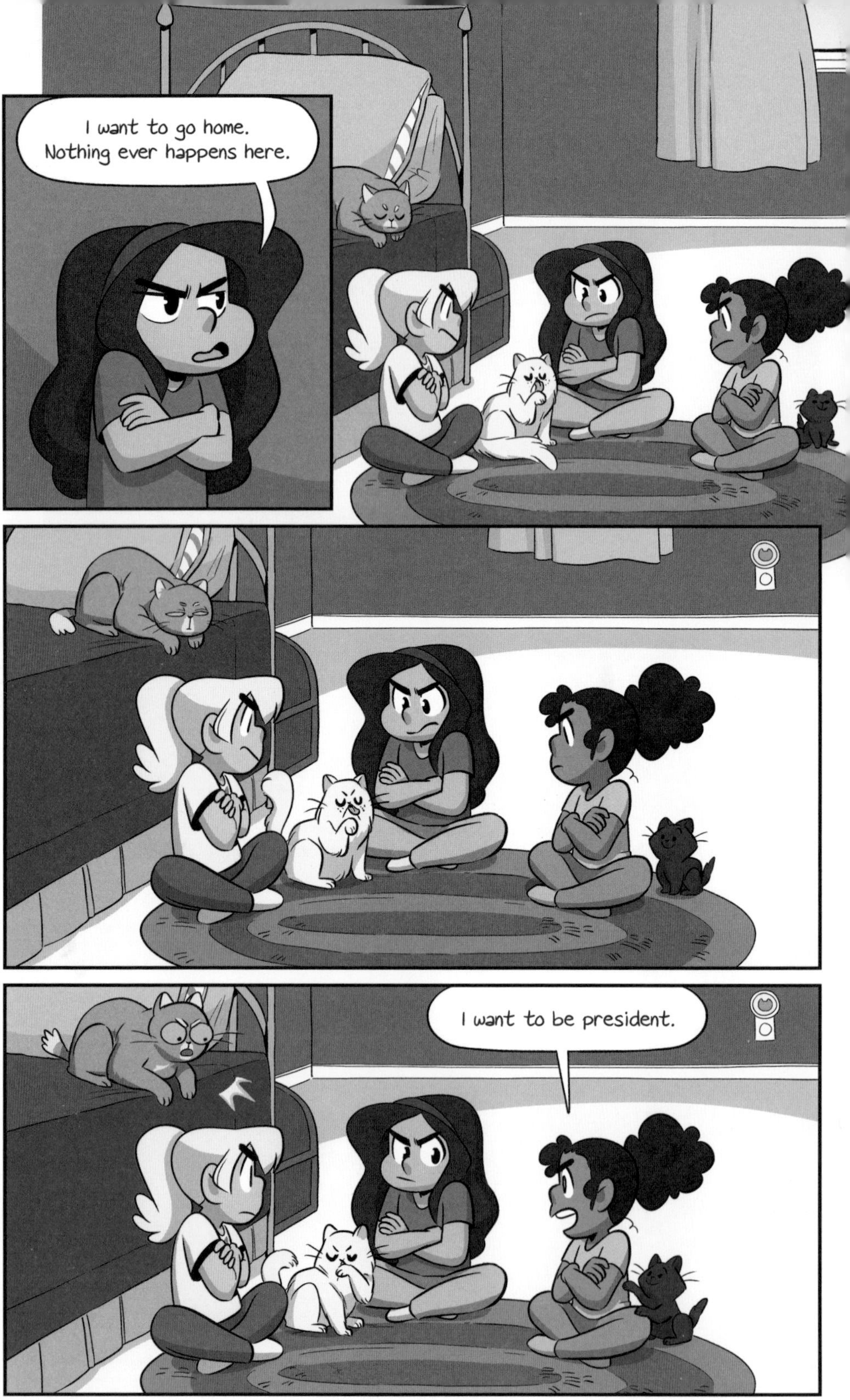
I want to go home.
Nothing ever happens here.
I want to be president.

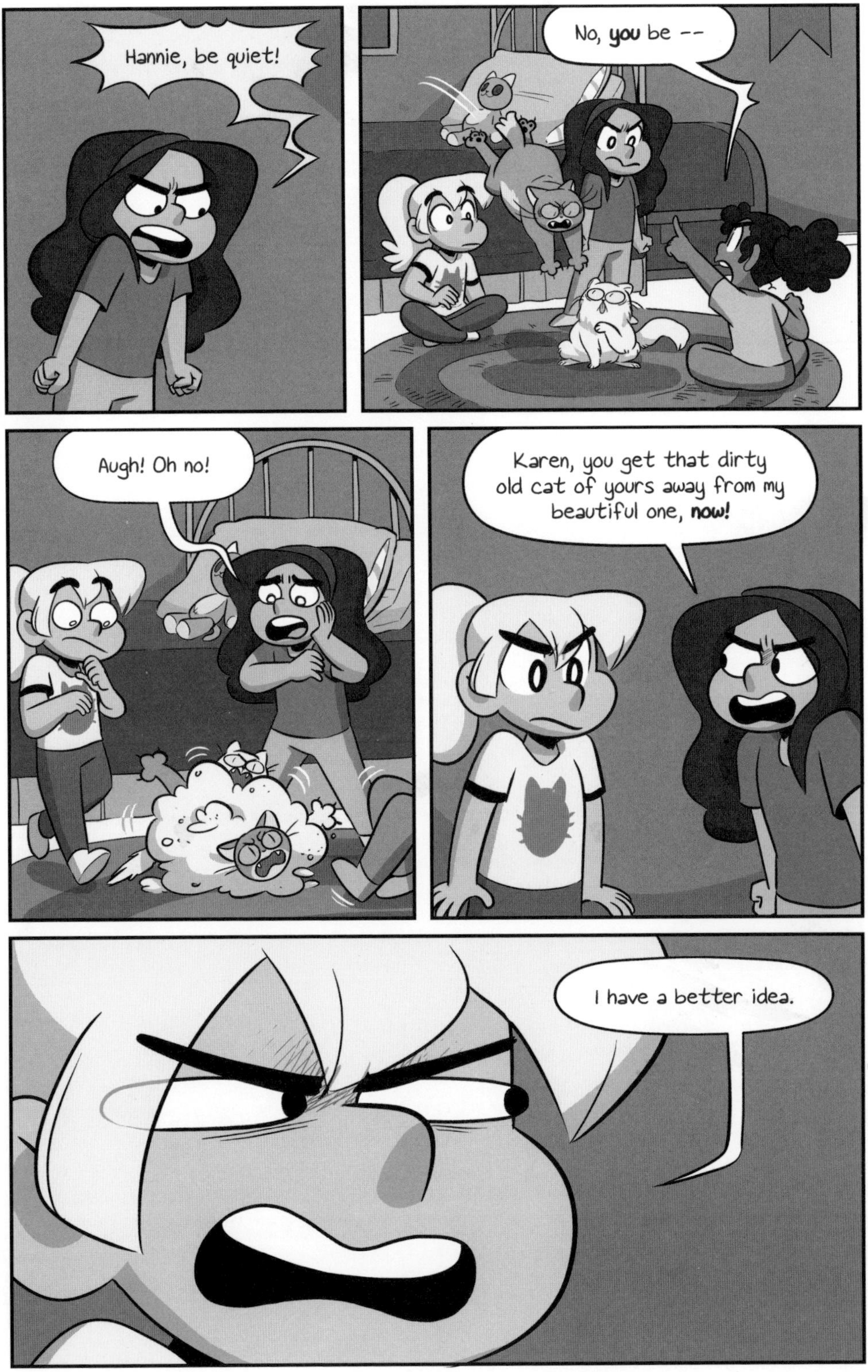
Hannie, be quiet!
No, **you** be --
Augh! Oh no!
Karen, you get that dirty old cat of yours away from my beautiful one, **now!**
I have a better idea.

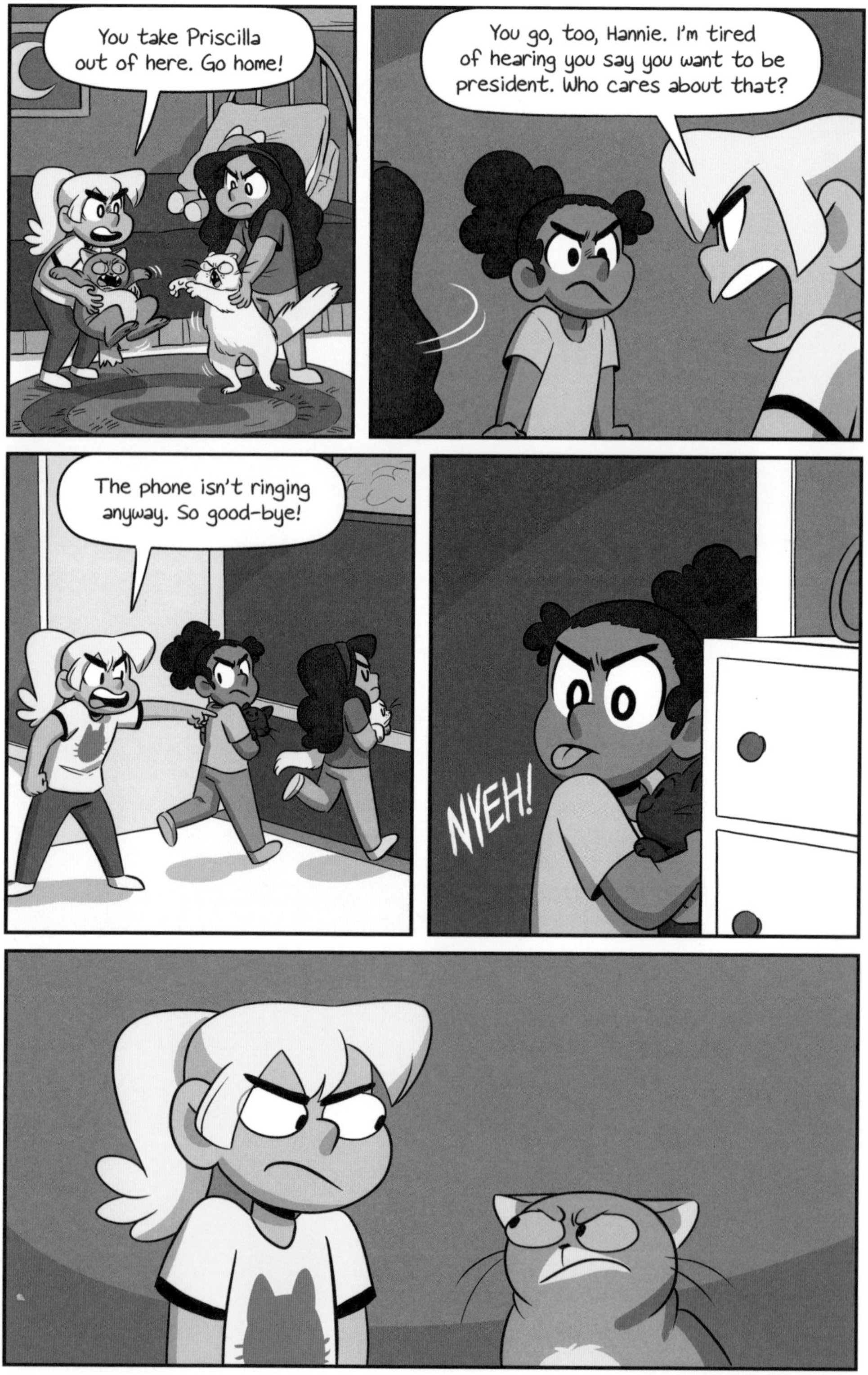
You take Priscilla out of here. Go home!
You go, too, Hannie. I'm tired of hearing you say you want to be president. Who cares about that?
The phone isn't ringing anyway. So good-bye!
NYEH!

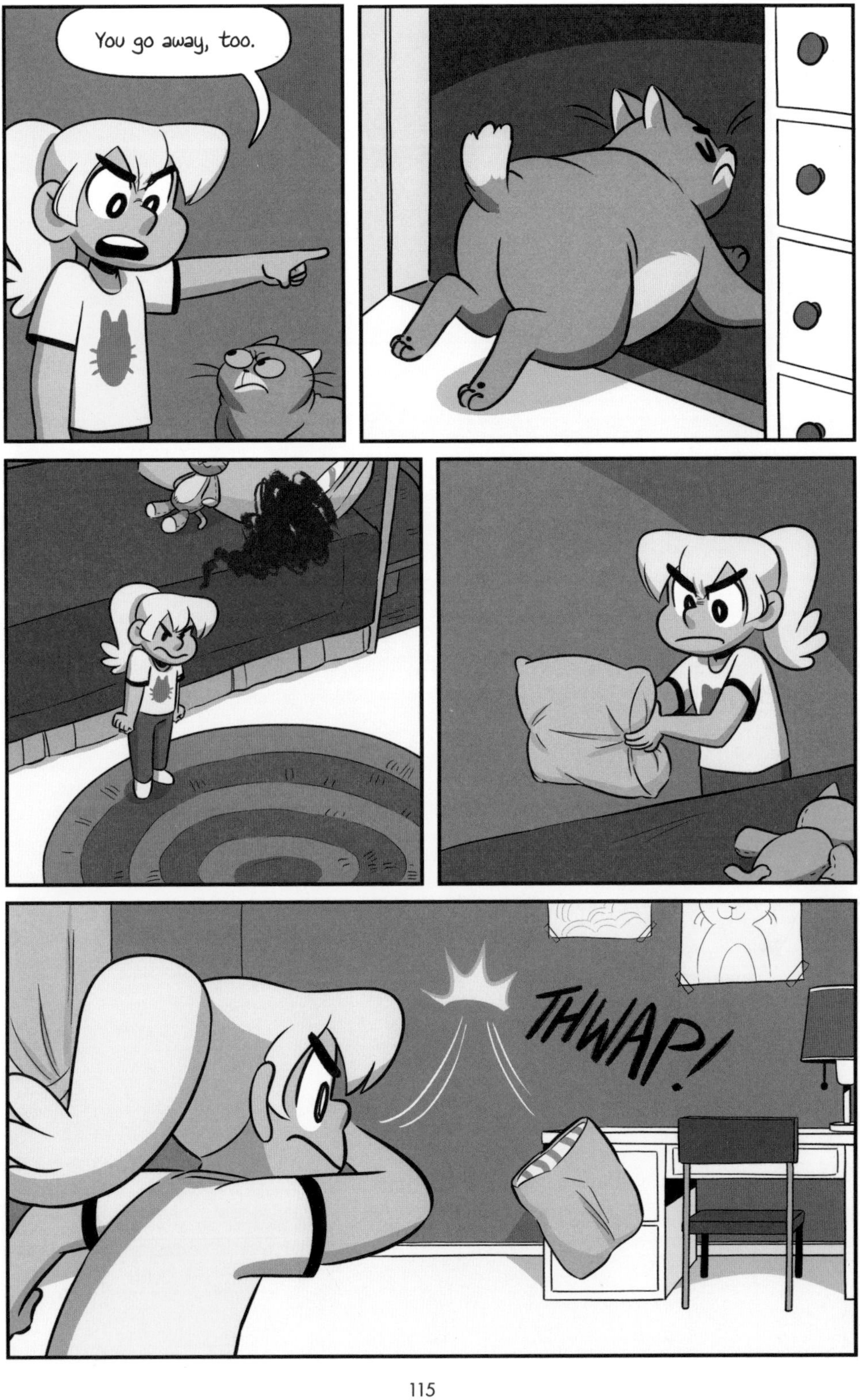
You go away, too.
THWAP!

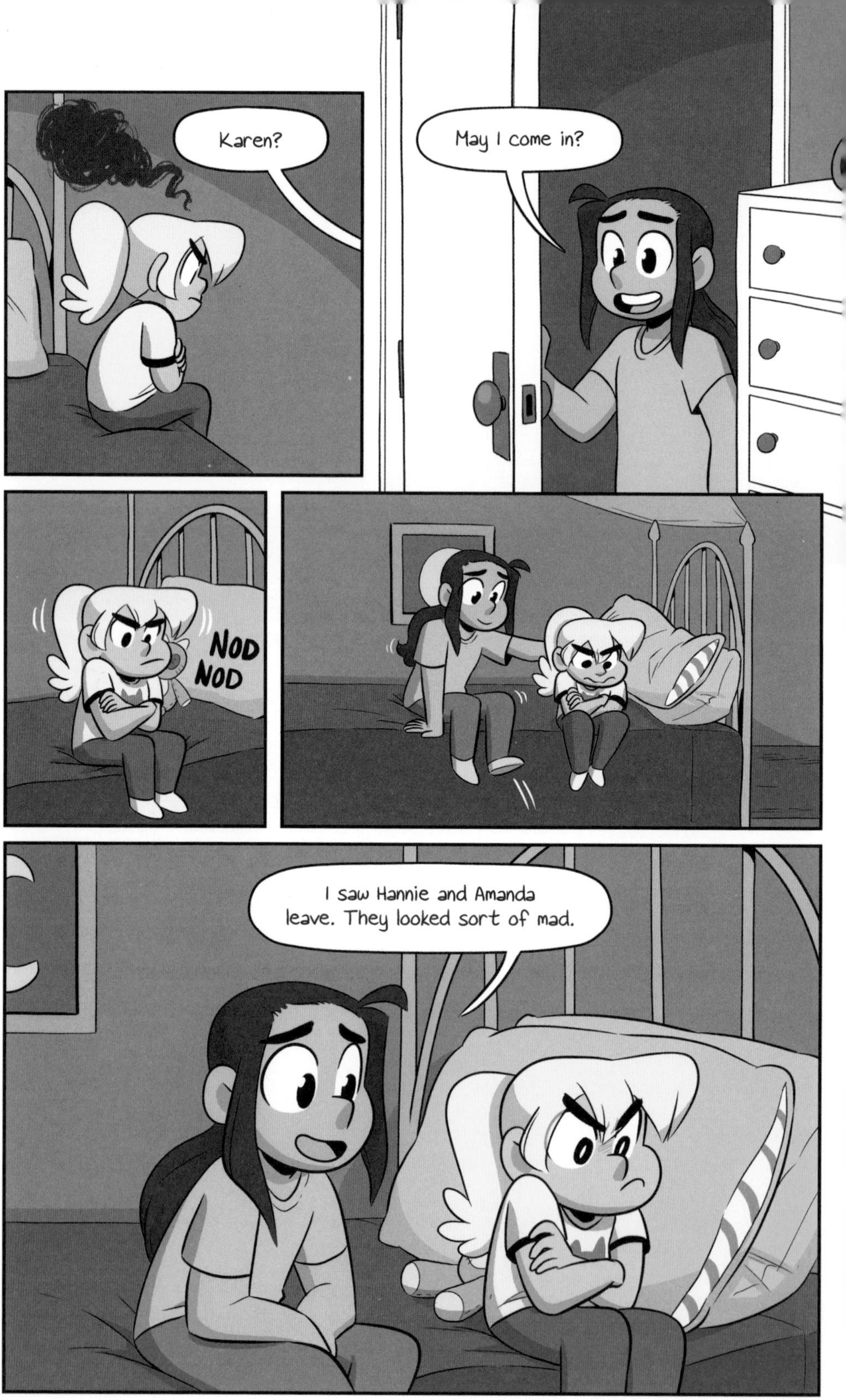
Karen?
May I come in?
NOD NOD
I saw Hannie and Amanda leave. They looked sort of mad.

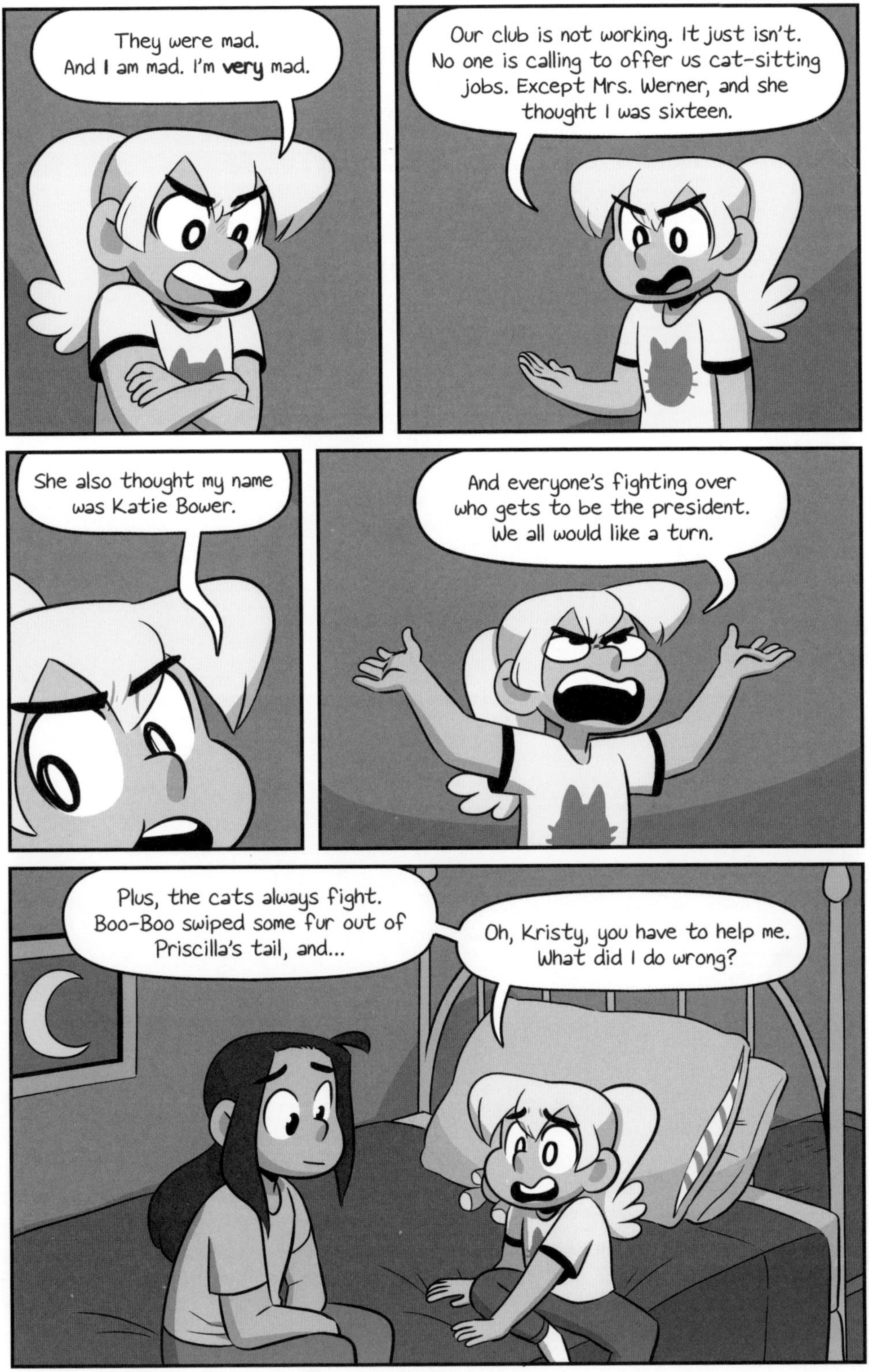
They were mad. And I am mad. I'm **very** mad.
Our club is not working. It just isn't. No one is calling to offer us cat-sitting jobs. Except Mrs. Werner, and she thought I was sixteen.
She also thought my name was Katie Bower.
And everyone's fighting over who gets to be the president. We all would like a turn.
Plus, the cats always fight. Boo-Boo swiped some fur out of Priscilla's tail, and...
Oh, Kristy, you have to help me. What did I do wrong?

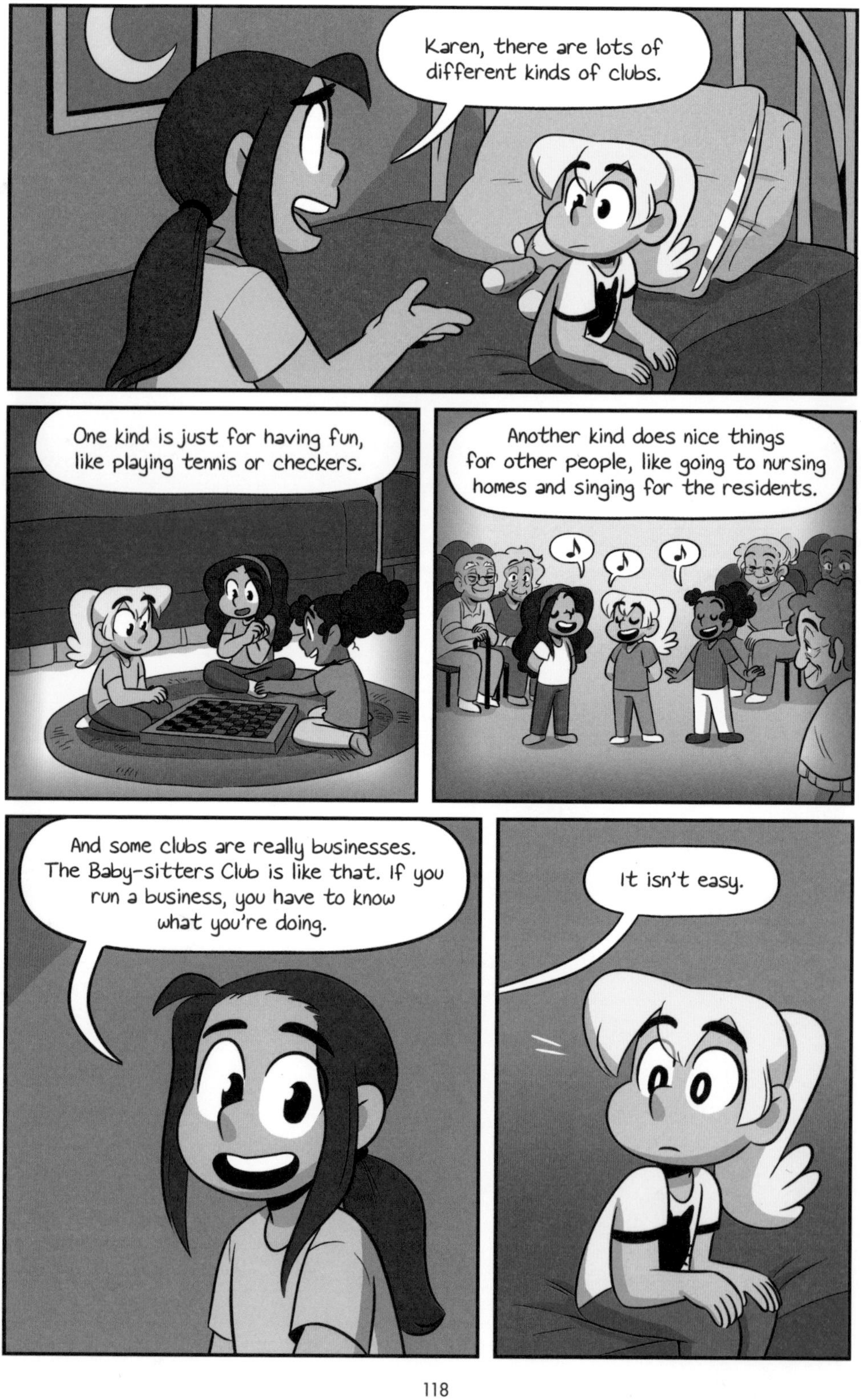
Karen, there are lots of different kinds of clubs.
One kind is just for having fun, like playing tennis or checkers.
Another kind does nice things for other people, like going to nursing homes and singing for the residents.
And some clubs are really businesses. The Baby-sitters Club is like that. If you run a business, you have to know what you're doing.
It isn't easy.

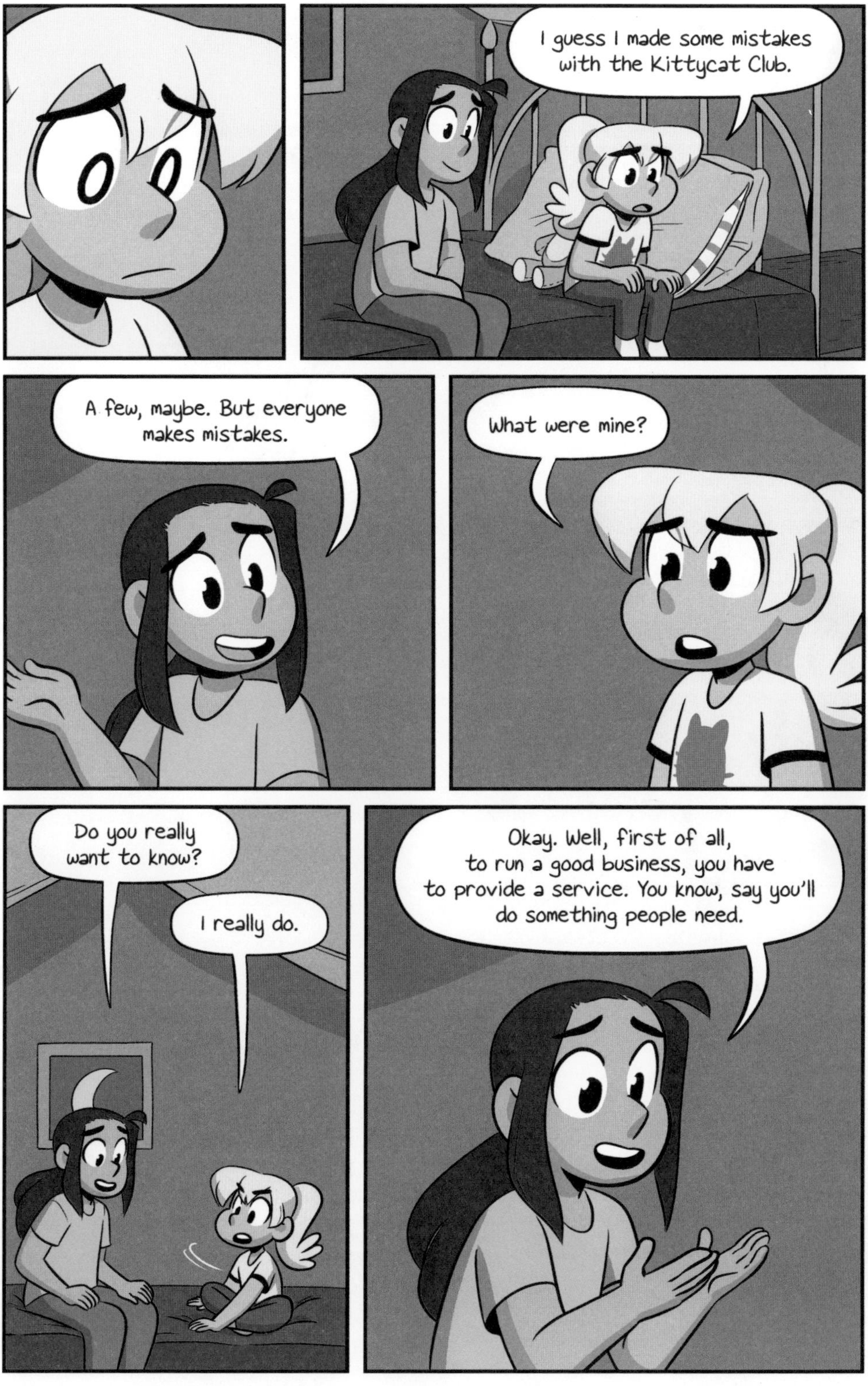
I guess I made some mistakes with the Kittycat Club.
A few, maybe. But everyone makes mistakes.
What were mine?
Do you really want to know?
I really do.
Okay. Well, first of all, to run a good business, you have to provide a service. You know, say you'll do something people need.

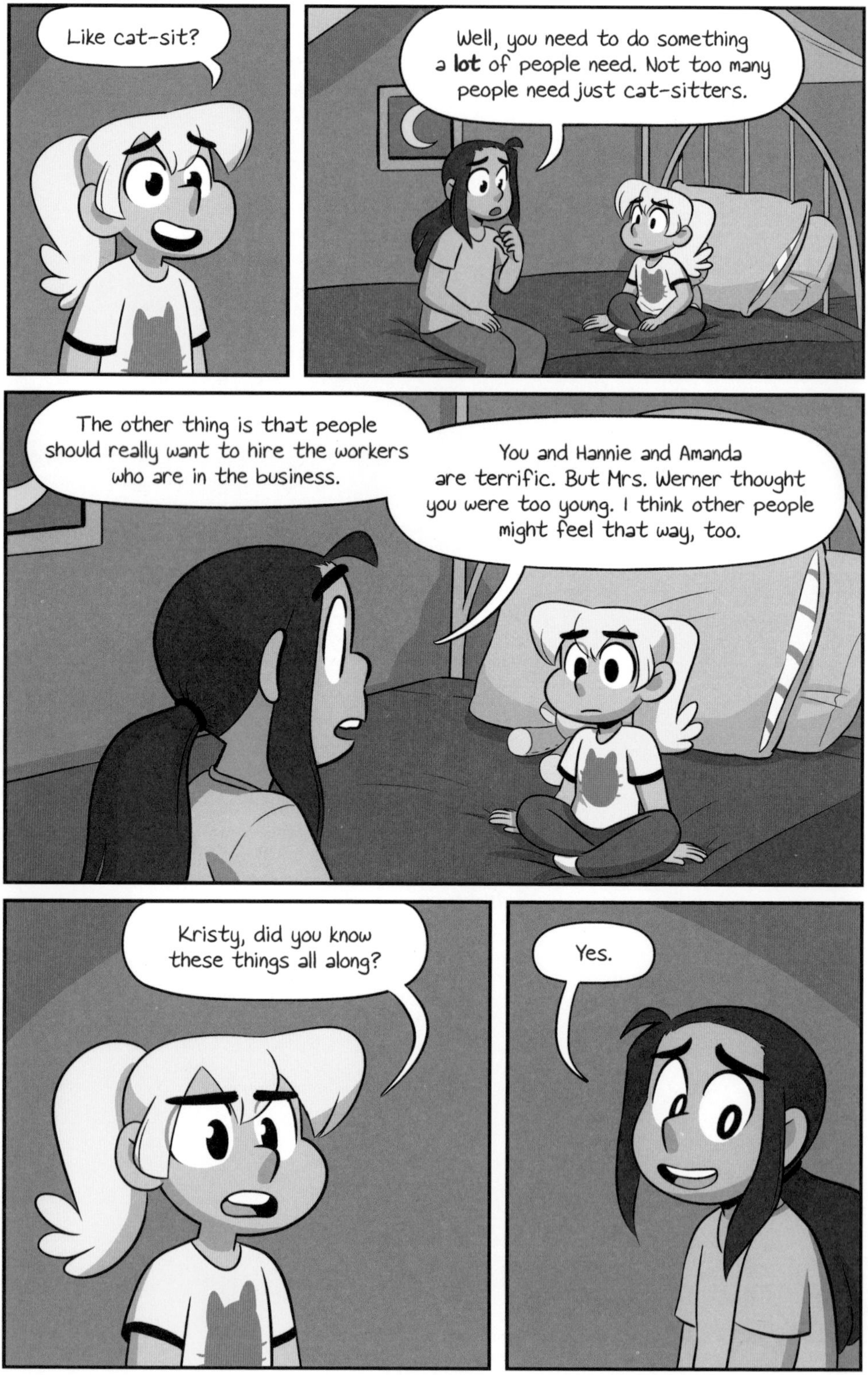
Like cat-sit?
Well, you need to do something a **lot** of people need. Not too many people need just cat-sitters.
The other thing is that people should really want to hire the workers who are in the business.
You and Hannie and Amanda are terrific. But Mrs. Werner thought you were too young. I think other people might feel that way, too.
Kristy, did you know these things all along?
Yes.

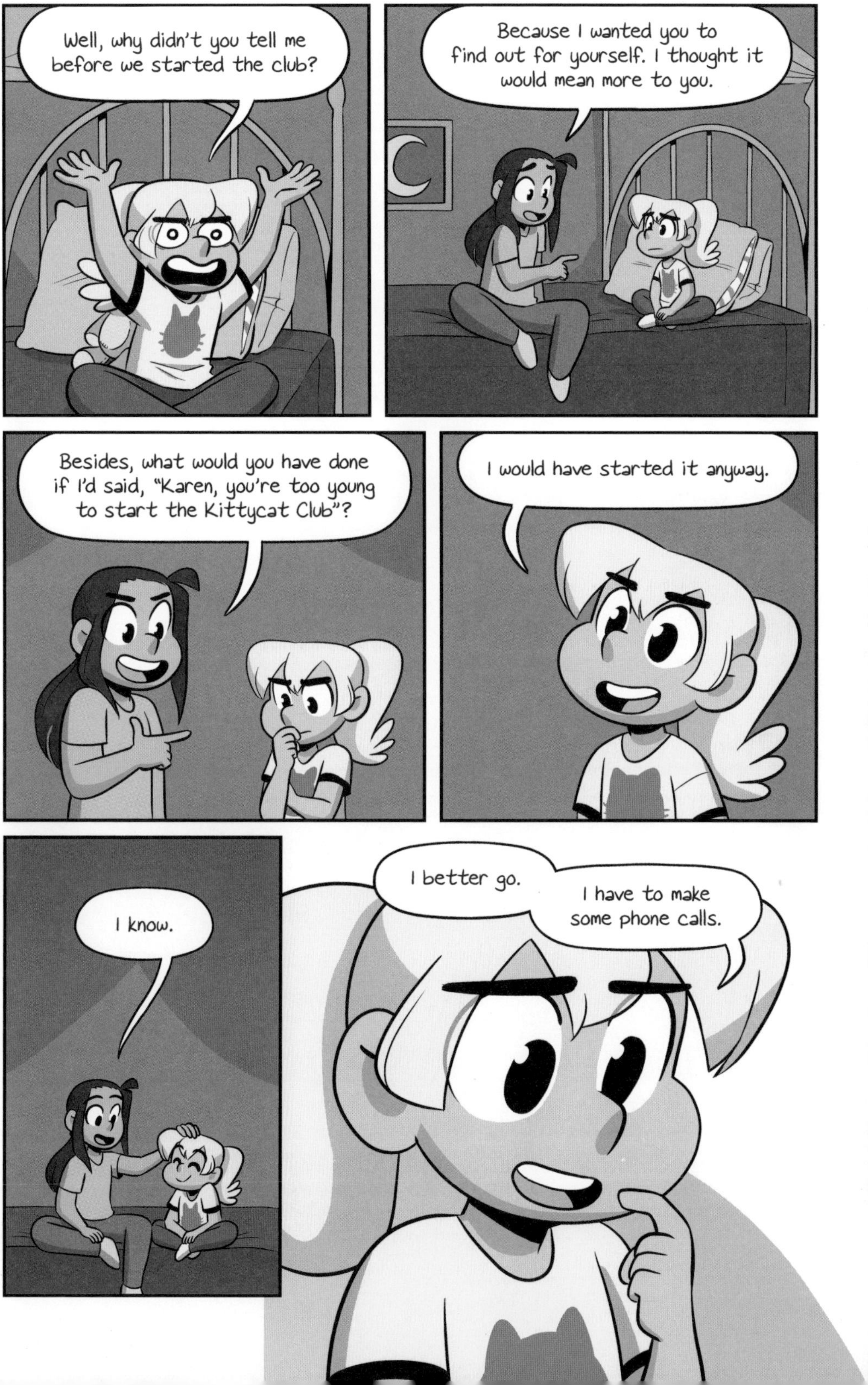

Well, why didn't you tell me before we started the club?
Because I wanted you to find out for yourself. I thought it would mean more to you.
Besides, what would you have done if I'd said, "Karen, you're too young to start the Kittycat Club"?
I would have started it anyway.
I know.
I better go.
I have to make some phone calls.

CHAPTER 10

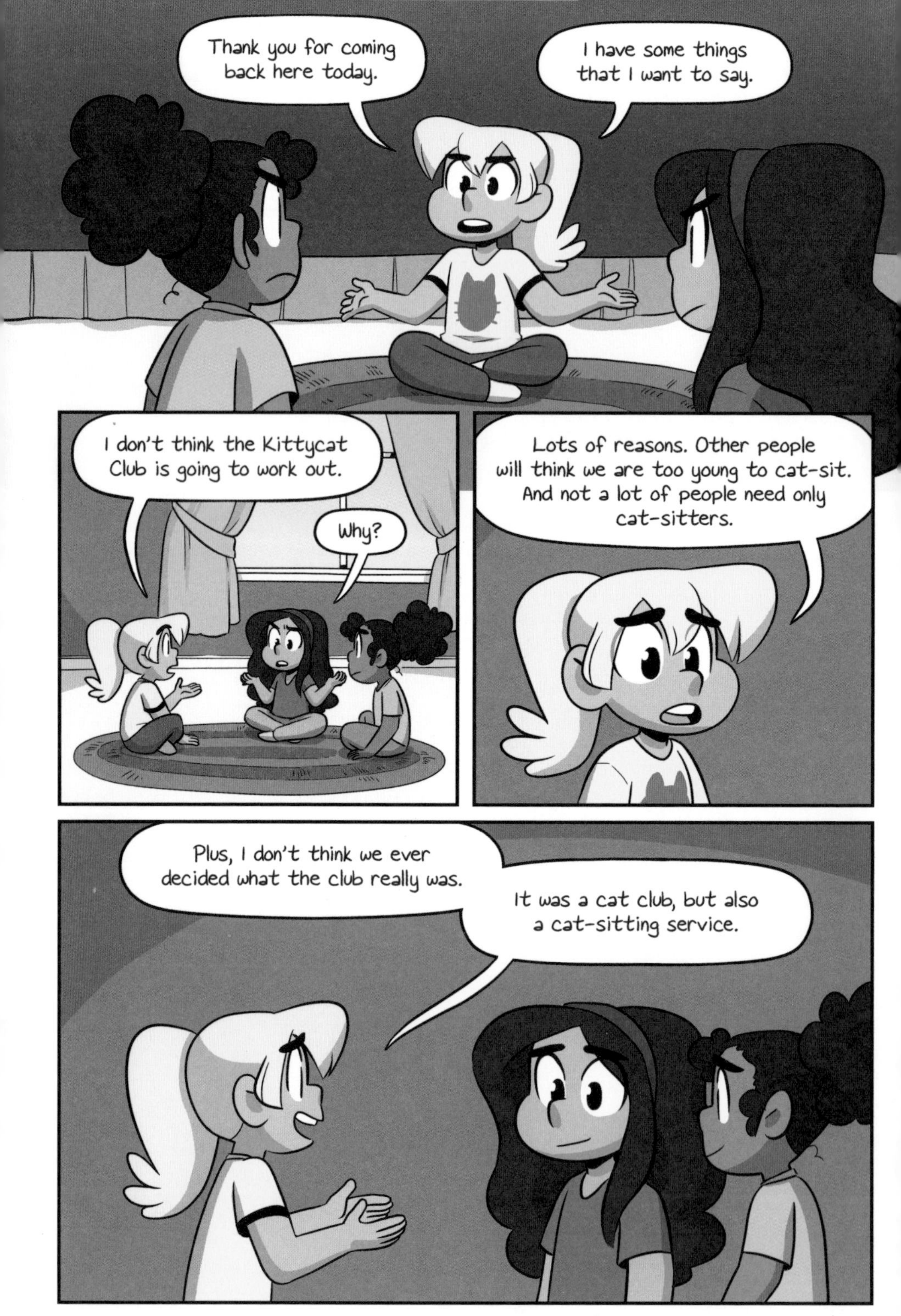

Thank you for coming back here today.
I have some things that I want to say.
I don't think the Kittycat Club is going to work out.
Why?
Lots of reasons. Other people will think we are too young to cat-sit. And not a lot of people need only cat-sitters.
Plus, I don't think we ever decided what the club really was.
It was a cat club, but also a cat-sitting service.

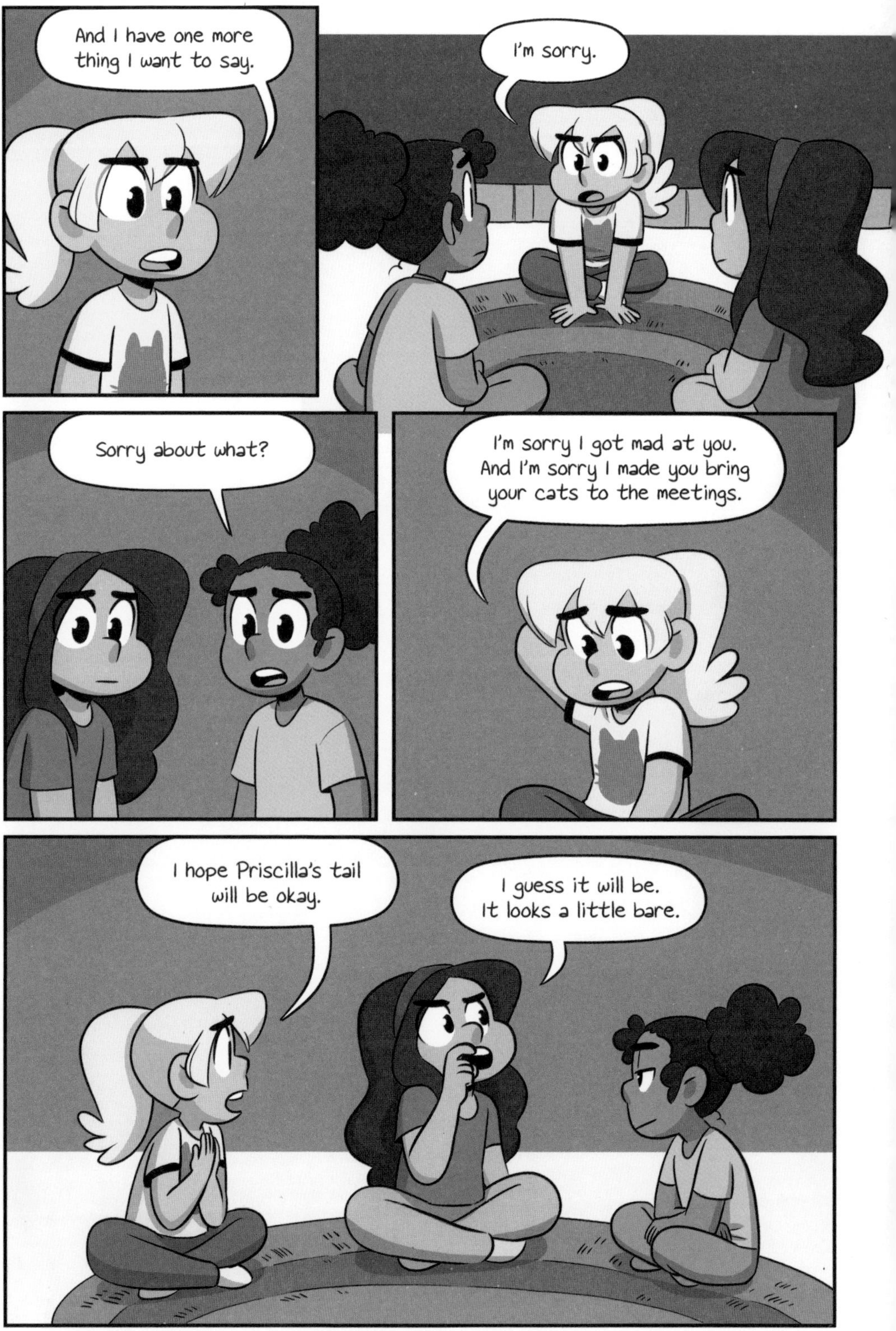
And I have one more thing I want to say.
I'm sorry.
Sorry about what?
I'm sorry I got mad at you. And I'm sorry I made you bring your cats to the meetings.
I hope Priscilla's tail will be okay.
I guess it will be. It looks a little bare.

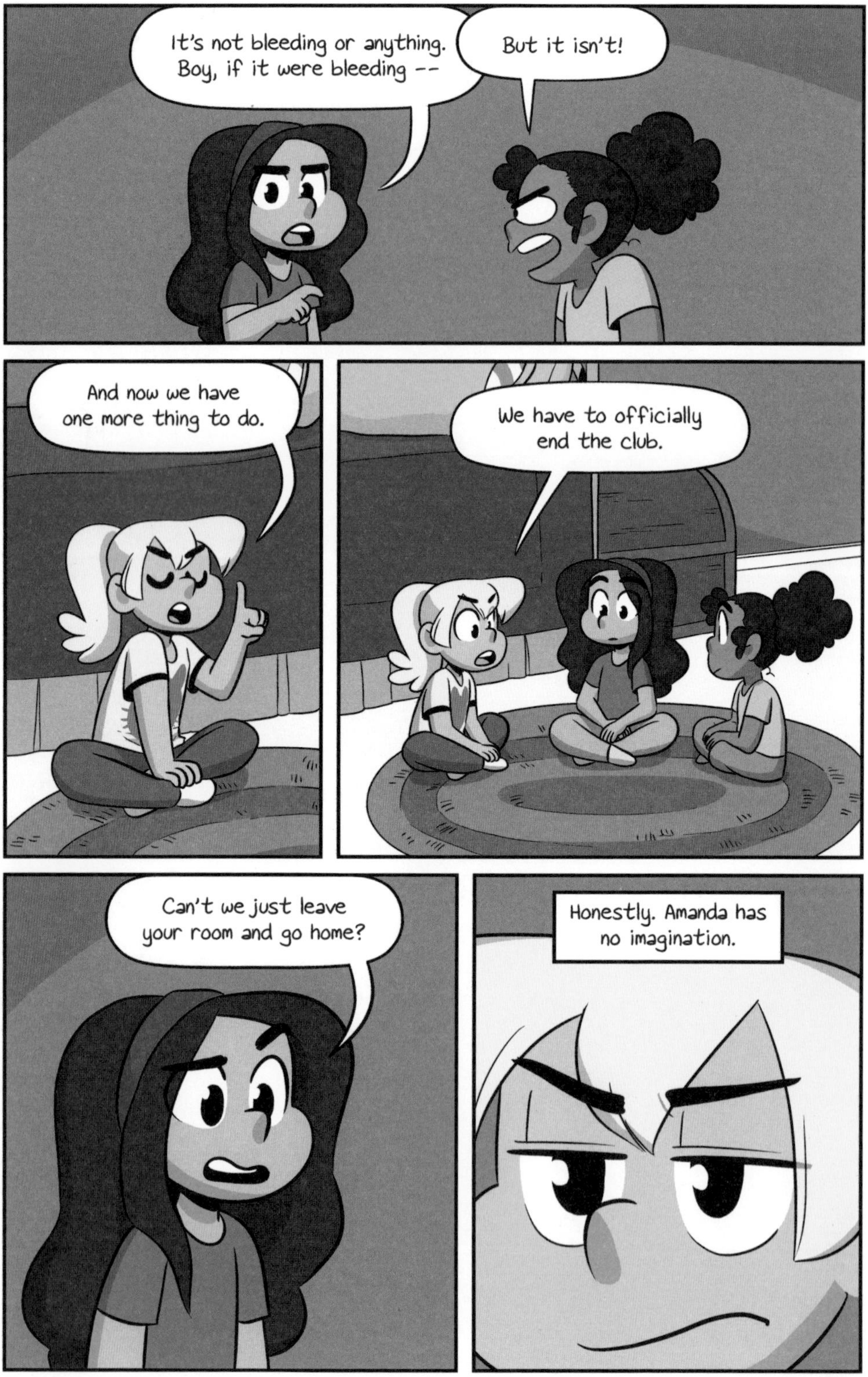
It's not bleeding or anything. Boy, if it were bleeding --
But it isn't!
And now we have one more thing to do.
We have to officially end the club.
Can't we just leave your room and go home?
Honestly. Amanda has no imagination.

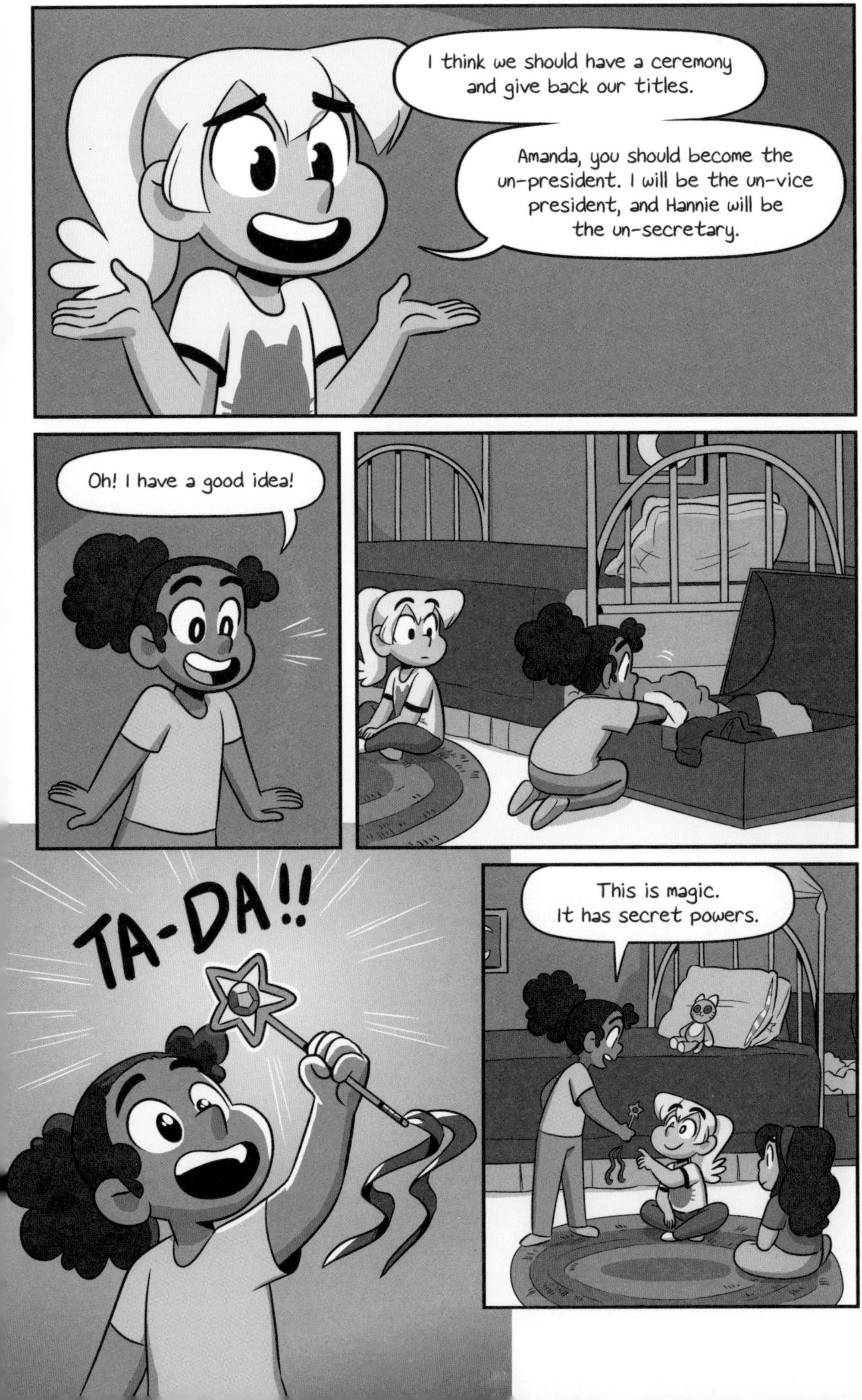

I think we should have a ceremony and give back our titles.
Amanda, you should become the un-president. I will be the un-vice president, and Hannie will be the un-secretary.
Oh! I have a good idea!
TA-DA!!
This is magic. It has secret powers.

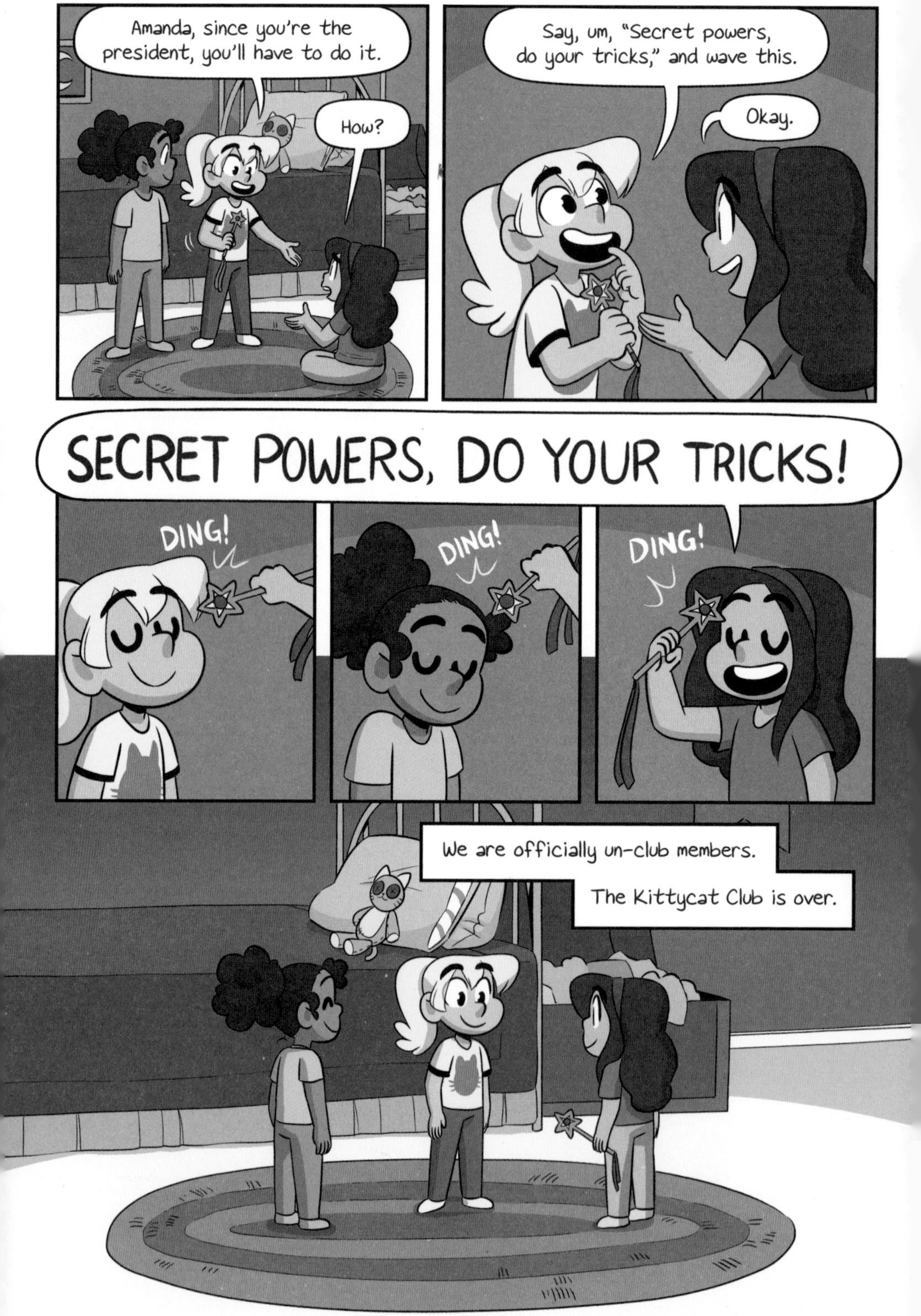
Amanda, since you're the president, you'll have to do it.
How?
Say, um, "Secret powers, do your tricks," and wave this.
Okay.
SECRET POWERS, DO YOUR TRICKS!
DING!
DING!
DING!
We are officially un-club members.
The Kittycat Club is over.

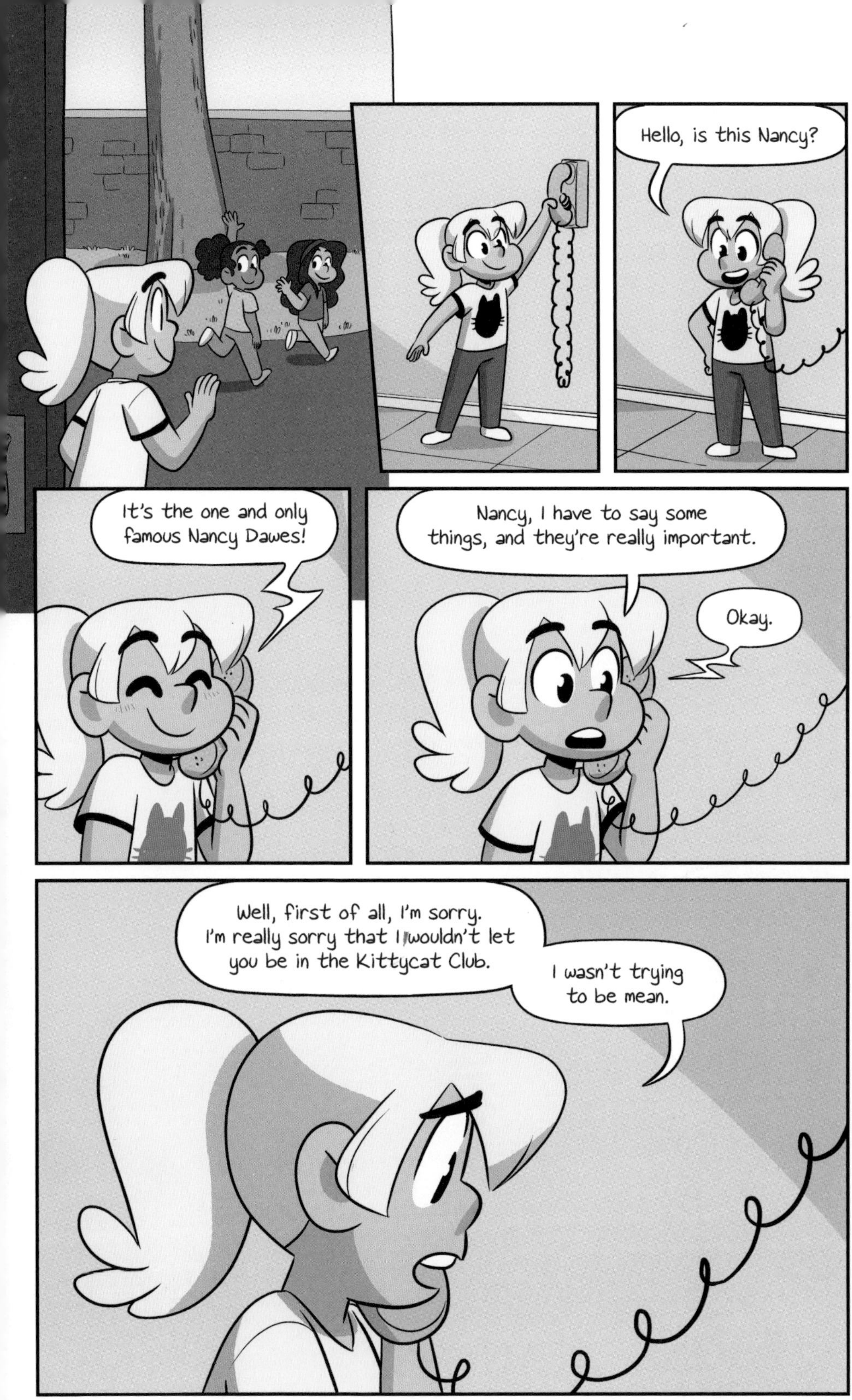
Hello, is this Nancy?
It's the one and only famous Nancy Dawes!
Nancy, I have to say some things, and they're really important.
Okay.
Well, first of all, I'm sorry. I'm really sorry that I wouldn't let you be in the Kittycat Club.
I wasn't trying to be mean.

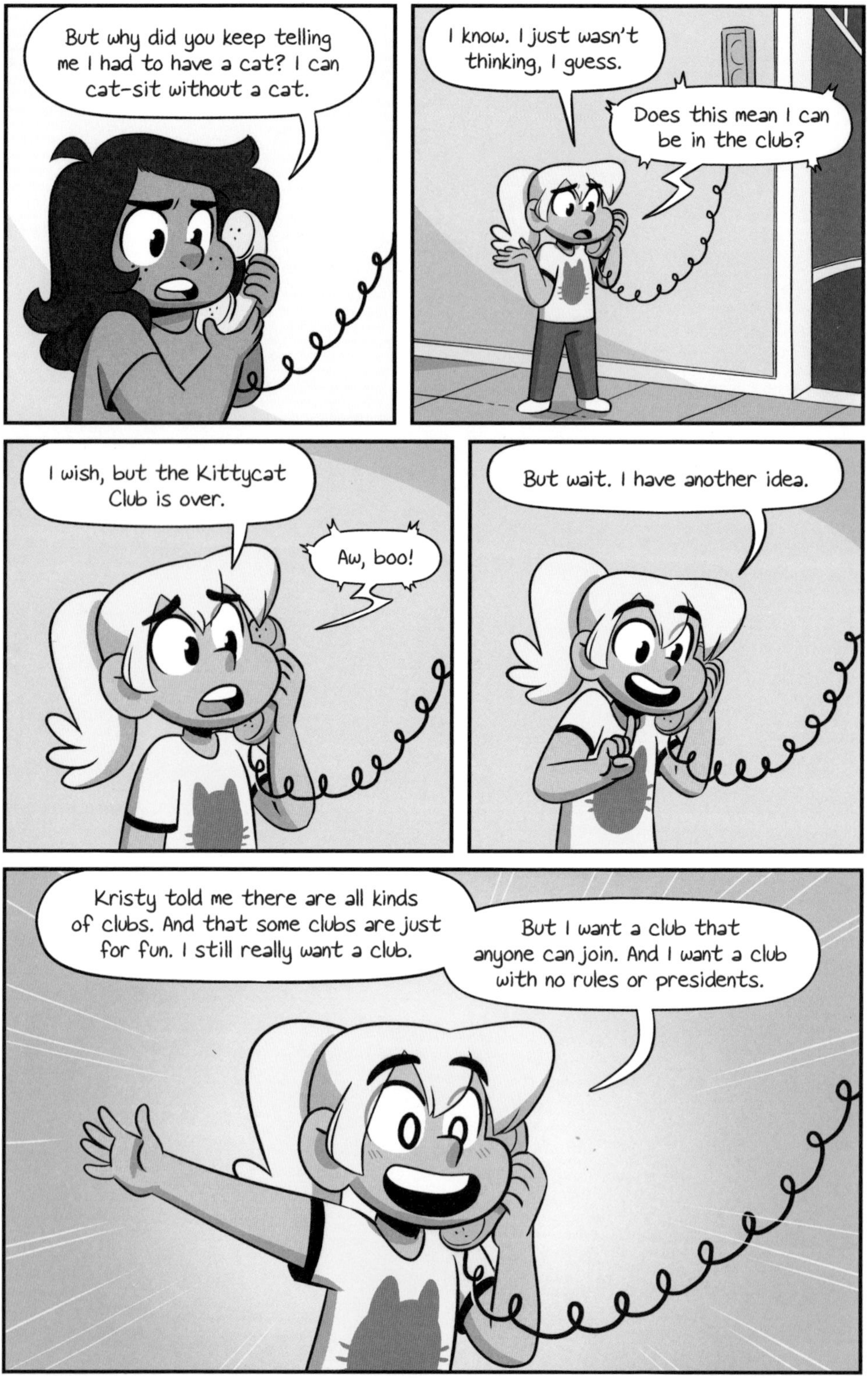
But why did you keep telling me I had to have a cat? I can cat-sit without a cat.
I know. I just wasn't thinking, I guess.
Does this mean I can be in the club?
I wish, but the Kittycat Club is over.
Aw, boo!
But wait. I have another idea.
Kristy told me there are all kinds of clubs. And that some clubs are just for fun. I still really want a club.
But I want a club that anyone can join. And I want a club with no rules or presidents.

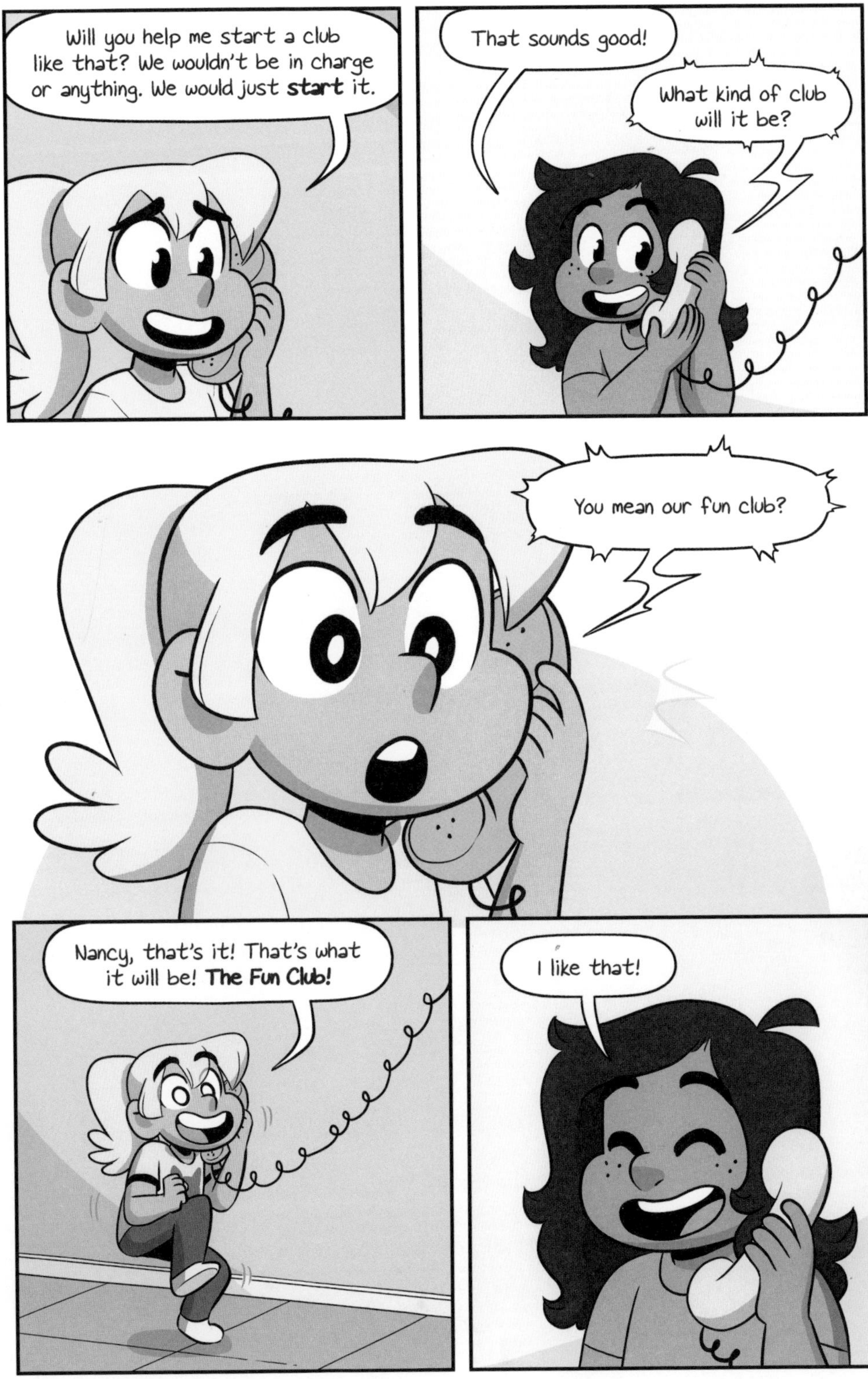
Will you help me start a club like that? We wouldn't be in charge or anything. We would just **start** it.
That sounds good!
What kind of club will it be?
You mean our fun club?
Nancy, that's it! That's what it will be! **The Fun Club!**
I like that!

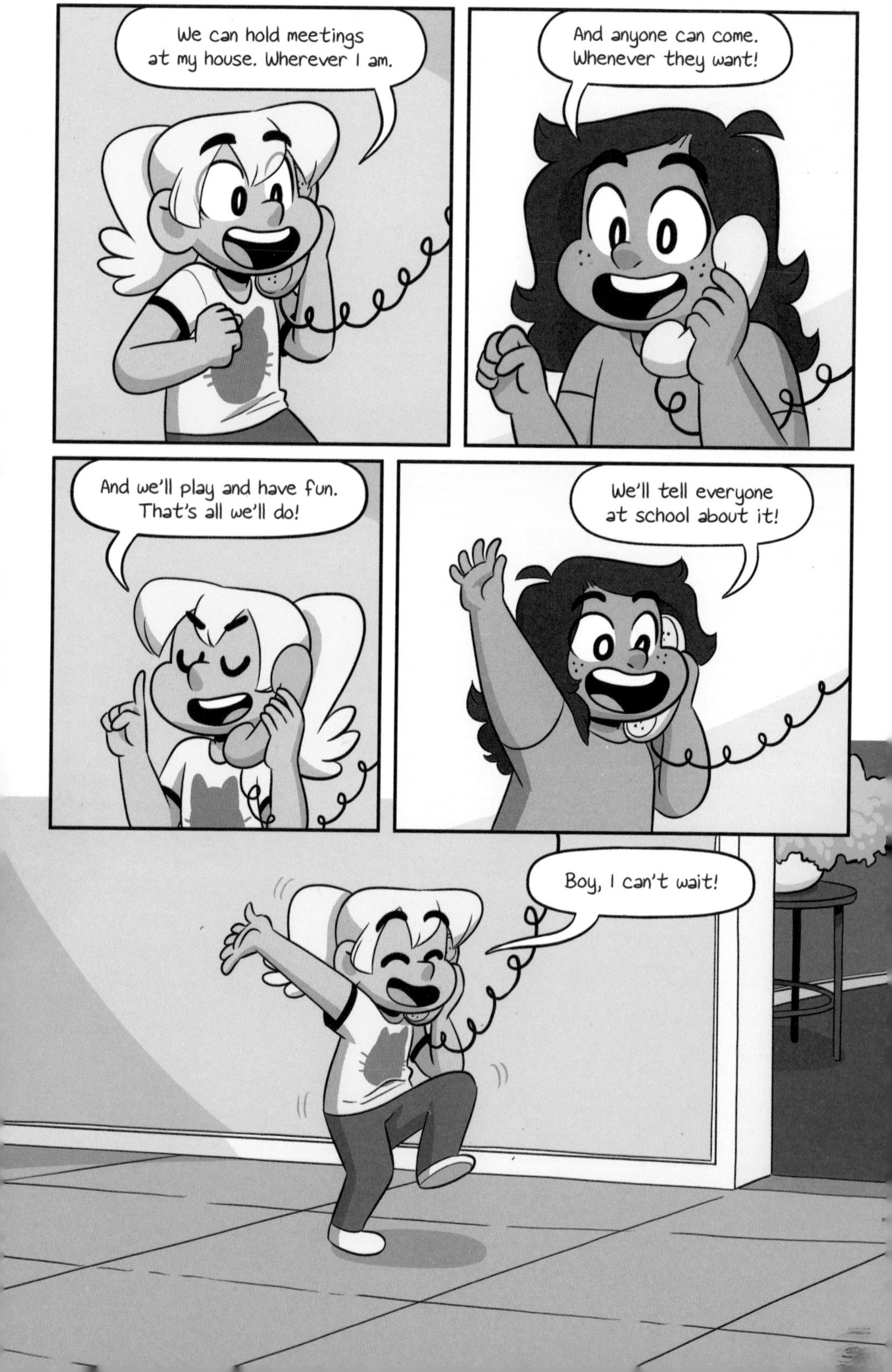
We can hold meetings at my house. Wherever I am.
And anyone can come. Whenever they want!
And we'll play and have fun. That's all we'll do!
We'll tell everyone at school about it!
Boy, I can't wait!

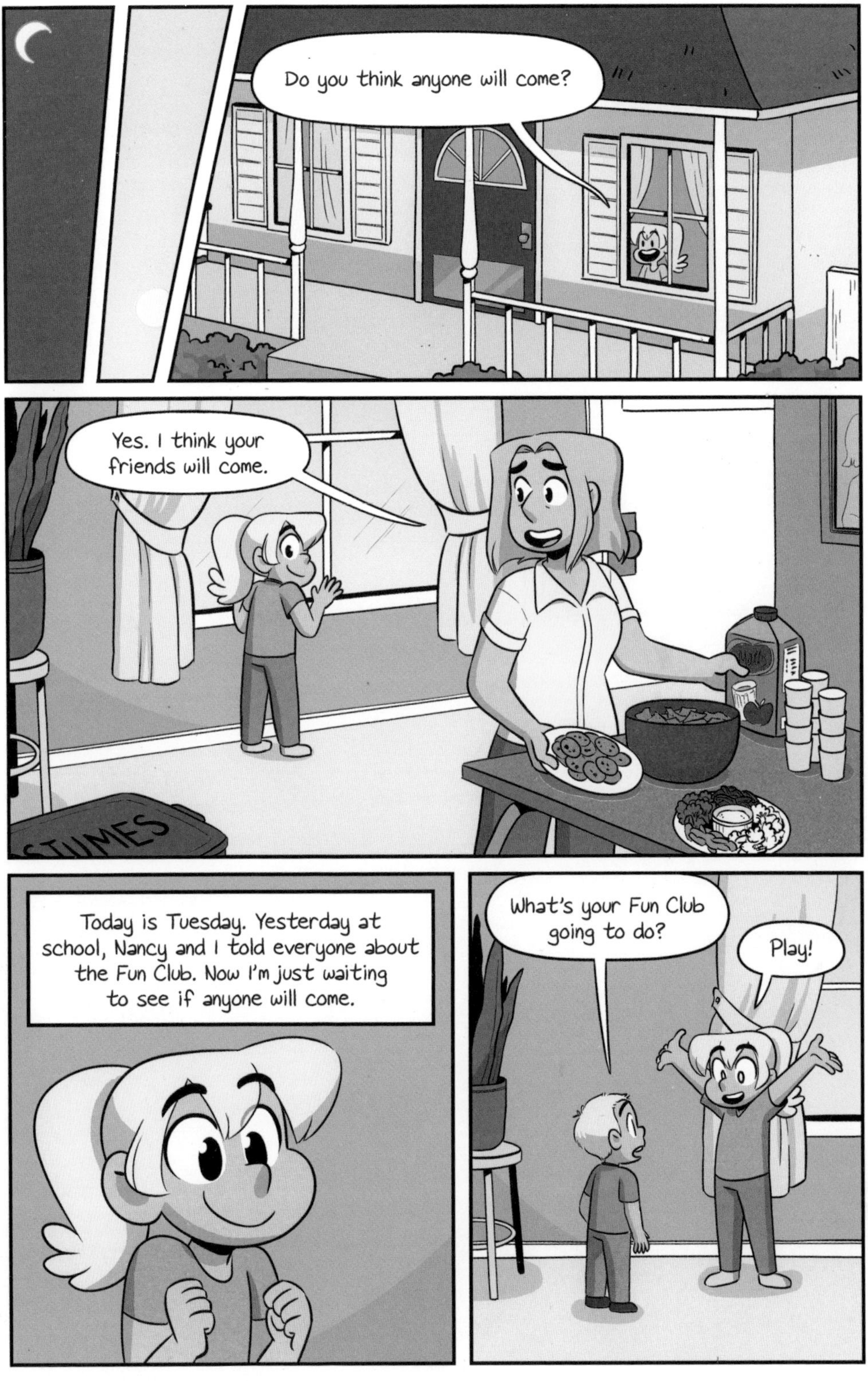
Do you think anyone will come?
Yes. I think your friends will come.
Today is Tuesday. Yesterday at school, Nancy and I told everyone about the Fun Club. Now I'm just waiting to see if anyone will come.
What's your Fun Club going to do?
Play!

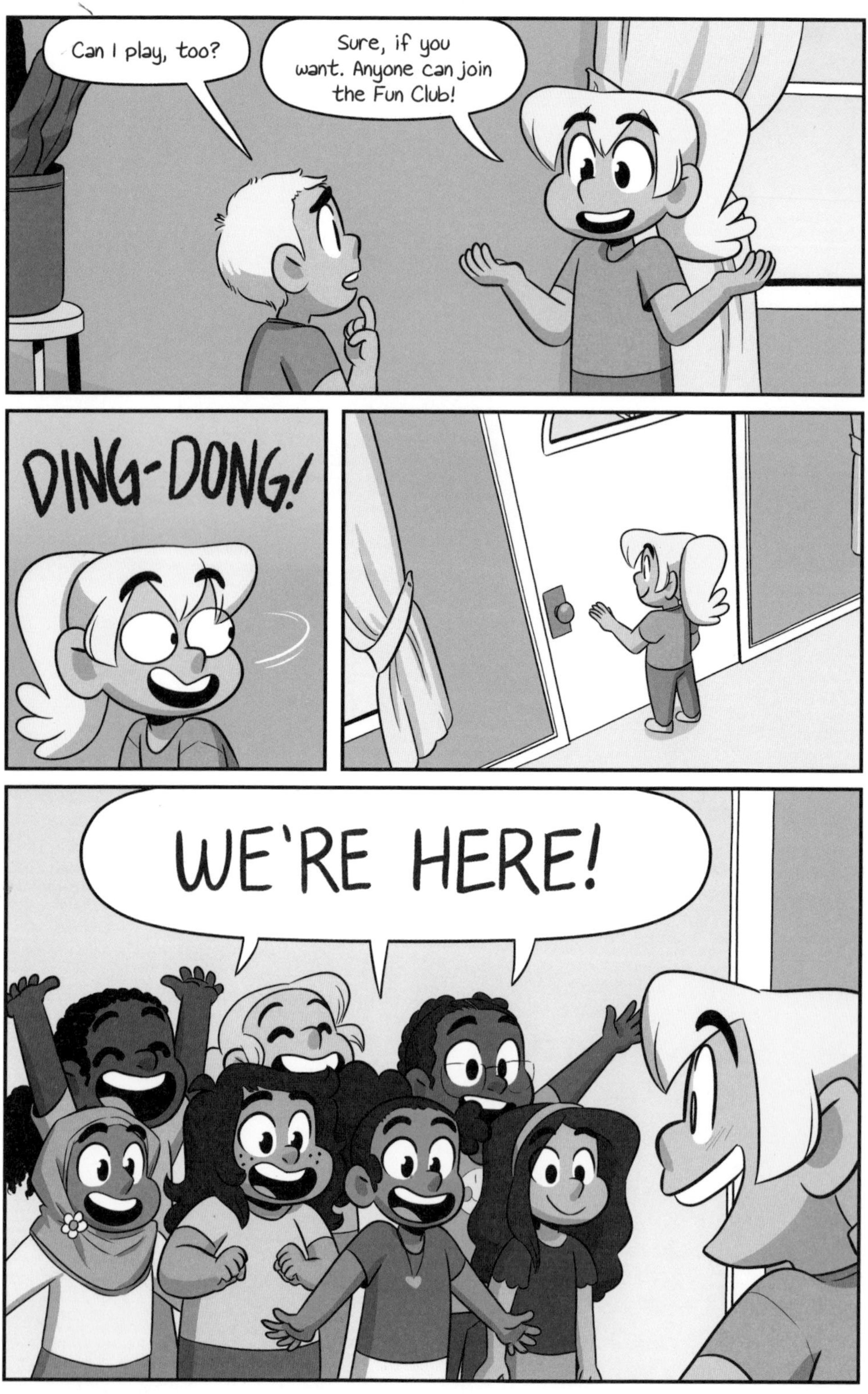
Can I play, too?
Sure, if you want. Anyone can join the Fun Club!
DING-DONG!
WE'RE HERE!

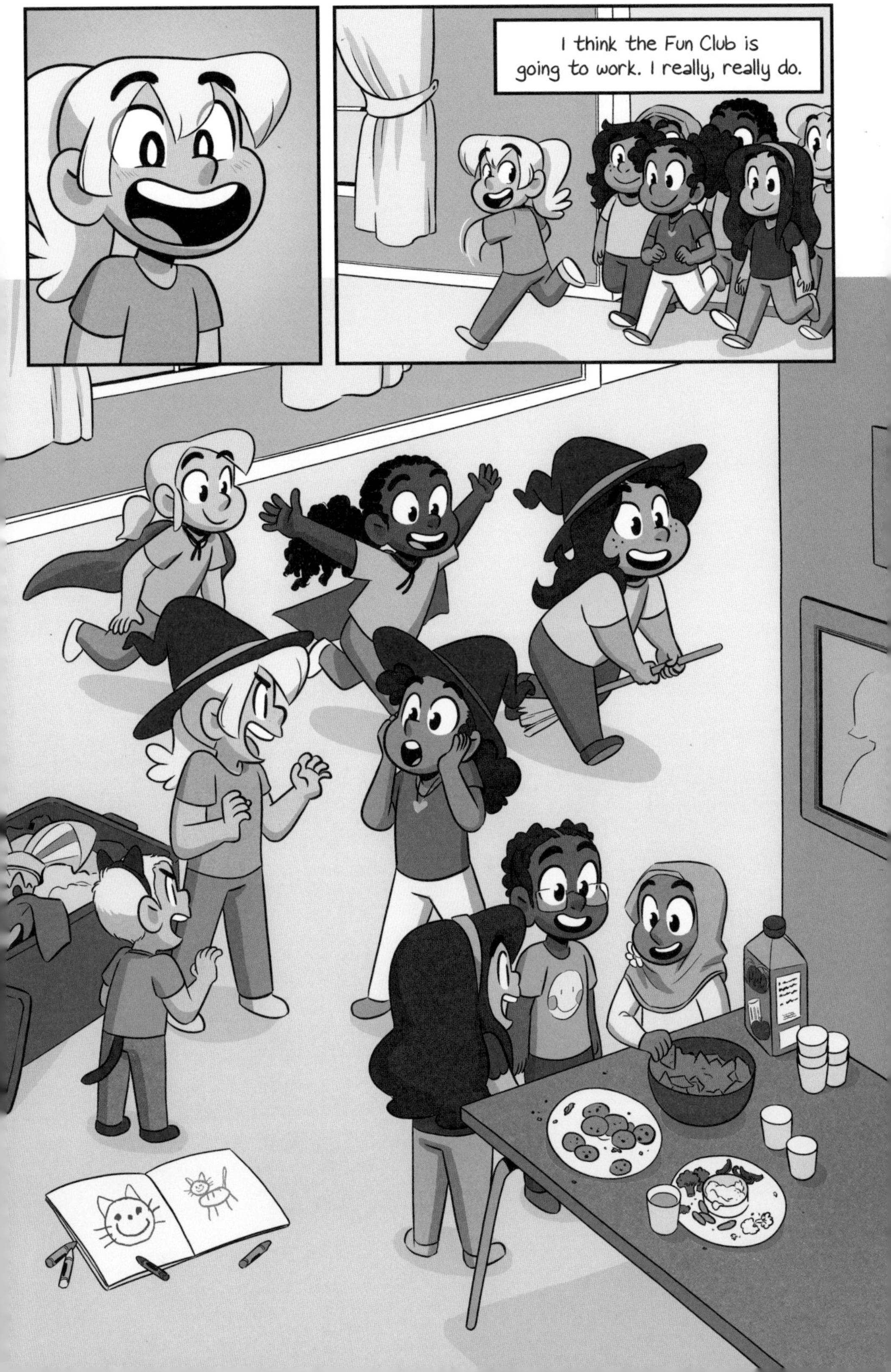
I think the Fun Club is going to work. I really, really do.

ANN M. MARTIN'S The Baby-sitters Club is one of the most popular series in the history of publishing — with more than 180 million books in print worldwide — and inspired a generation of young readers. Her novels include *Belle Teal*, *A Corner of the Universe* (a Newbery Honor book), *Here Today*, *A Dog's Life*, and *On Christmas Eve*, as well as the much-loved collaborations, *P.S. Longer Letter Later* and *Snail Mail No More*, with Paula Danziger, and *The Doll People* and *The Meanest Doll in the World*, written with Laura Godwin and illustrated by Brian Selznick. Ann lives in upstate New York.

KATY FARINA is the creator of the *New York Times* bestselling graphic novel adaptations of *Karen's Witch, Karen's Roller Skates,* and *Karen's Worst Day* by Ann M. Martin. She has painted backgrounds for *She-Ra and the Princesses of Power* at DreamWorks TV and has also done work for BOOM! Studios, Oni Press, and Z2 Comics. She lives in Los Angeles. Visit her online at katyfarina.com.

DON'T MISS THE OTHER BABY-SITTERS LITTLE SISTER GRAPHIC NOVELS!

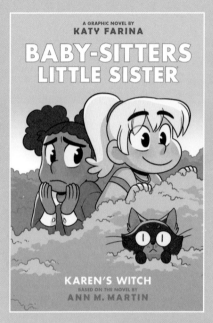

A GRAPHIC NOVEL BY
KATY FARINA

BABY-SITTERS
LITTLE SISTER

KAREN'S WITCH
BASED ON THE NOVEL BY
ANN M. MARTIN

A GRAPHIC NOVEL BY
KATY FARINA

BABY-SITTERS
LITTLE SISTER

KAREN'S ROLLER SKATES
BASED ON THE NOVEL BY
ANN M. MARTIN

A GRAPHIC NOVEL BY
KATY FARINA

BABY-SITTERS
LITTLE SISTER

KAREN'S WORST DAY
BASED ON THE NOVEL BY
ANN M. MARTIN